REVENGE PREY

ALSO BY JOHN SANDFORD

Rules of Prey
Shadow Prey
Eyes of Prey
Silent Prey
Winter Prey
Night Prey
Mind Prey
Sudden Prey
Secret Prey
Certain Prey
Easy Prey
Chosen Prey
Mortal Prey
Naked Prey
Hidden Prey
Broken Prey
Invisible Prey
Phantom Prey
Wicked Prey
Storm Prey
Buried Prey
Stolen Prey
Silken Prey
Field of Prey
Gathering Prey
Extreme Prey
Golden Prey
Twisted Prey
Neon Prey
Masked Prey
Ocean Prey
Righteous Prey
Judgment Prey
Toxic Prey
Lethal Prey

KIDD NOVELS

The Fool's Run
The Empress File
The Devil's Code
The Hanged Man's Song

VIRGIL FLOWERS NOVELS

Dark of the Moon
Heat Lightning
Rough Country
Bad Blood
Shock Wave
Mad River
Storm Front
Deadline
Escape Clause
Deep Freeze
Holy Ghost
Bloody Genius

LETTY DAVENPORT NOVELS

The Investigator
Dark Angel

STAND-ALONE NOVELS

Saturn Run (with Ctein)
The Night Crew
Dead Watch

BY JOHN SANDFORD AND MICHELE COOK

Uncaged
Outrage
Rampage

REVENGE PREY

G. P. PUTNAM'S SONS
NEW YORK

PUTNAM
— EST. 1838 —

G. P. Putnam's Sons
Publishers Since 1838
An imprint of Penguin Random House LLC
1745 Broadway, New York, NY 10019
penguinrandomhouse.com

LIBRARY OF CONGRESS CATALOGING-IN-PUBLICATION DATA
has been applied for.

ISBN 9780593852064

Printed in the United States of America
1st Printing

The authorized representative in the EU for product safety and compliance is
Penguin Random House Ireland, Morrison Chambers, 32 Nassau Street,
Dublin D02 YH68, Ireland, https://eu-contact.penguin.ie.

REVENGE PREY

1

She had long blond hair and was almost pretty, in the manner of tennis jocks and female gymnasts; too much muscle in the face and arms and butt for the smooth baby-fat look of fashion models or movie stars.

Because she wasn't one.

Despite the cold, she was lying on her parka, instead of wearing it, the better to anchor the rifle against her shoulder. She put the crosshairs on the target, took up the trigger slack, and squeezed. The recoil was sharp, but manageable.

The man lying in the dirt next to her, looking through a spotting scope, said, "Two centimeters high, a centimeter right. Once more."

She took her time and squeezed again. The spotter said, "Same hole."

She said, "I'm so fucking cold, I feel like a goddamned фруктовый лёд." In English, literally, a "fruit ice," or not so literally, a "Popsicle."

"Forget the cold," the man said. He had a hard, narrow face and black hair over black eyes. "Three rounds, fast."

The three rounds went out in less than three seconds, and he said, "All over the place, left right and high, all within six centimeters of the ten-ring."

"So it's good."

"Better than good. I've seen what it does to gelatin. If you hit the target anywhere above the waist, he's dead," the man said, rolling on his side to look at her. "These copper bullets won't defeat Level 4, but armor-piercing will. Shoots so flat . . . I want to take one home with me."

"If I could shoot as well as you do, I would find a way to do that," the woman said, handing him the rifle. "Maybe a custom barrel with handloads. The perfect weapon."

They were lying in a ditch ten miles west of the small town of Owatonna, Minnesota, an informal shooting range, located by their concierge, who was waiting nervously by the car.

"I wish it was suppressed," the woman added.

"You know the English proverb, 'If wishes were horses, beggars would ride'?"

Some wrinkles appeared in her forehead: "I'm not sure what that means . . ."

The proverb didn't quite translate, because they were speaking in Russian.

Because they were Russian.

A SNAKY BLACKTOPPED driveway led up a gentle slope to the hideout. Two other houses were fed from the same cul-de-sac, all three out of sight of one another, a carefully contrived privacy set in a suburban forest. Natural shingle siding, a gray-stone chimney, and high peaked roof gave the hideout the vibe of a Minnesota lake chalet, although the nearest big water was a mile away.

The marshals arrived in separate vehicles, Lucas Davenport pushing his Porsche Cayenne up the driveway, while Shelly White left her 4Runner in the street and walked up to meet Lucas.

"The guy gets this place for free? They just gave it to him?" White asked, peering squint-eyed at the house of her dreams, which were unlikely to be realized.

The afternoon light was draining away, a sullen, tangible gathering of gloom, as happens in Minnesota on overcast February days. "The way of the world, sweetheart. You get big enough, you get bad enough, they hand you the fat stacks."

The hideout was one of twelve houses nestled on four back-to-back cul-de-sacs. Seen from a satellite, the cul-de-sacs resembled a four-leaf clover, set down in a winter landscape of barren broad-leafed trees and evergreens that appeared black in the murky afternoon light.

SHELLY WHITE LOOKED like a semi-starved Depression-era farm wife, maybe caught on black-and-white film rattling out of Oklahoma, six snot-nosed kids in a broke-down Model T Ford. She had the knife-edge cheekbones, the pale gray eyes fixed in a thousand-yard stare, the parched lips held in a tight straight line.

White had never been in Oklahoma, wasn't starving, and she drove a Toyota SUV much too fast for the crappy suspension. She was a deputy U.S. Marshal who'd grown up in East Grand Forks, Minnesota, looking across the Red River at North Dakota. Four years as an Air Force cop and a degree in criminology got her a job with the U.S. Marshals Service.

She and Lucas, another deputy marshal, hadn't particularly liked each other when they first met, but they got along, and after a couple of years, had warmed up. Lucas had three natural children with two different women, plus an adoptive daughter; White had three children with two different men, so they had blended families to talk about. Along with guns, fugitives, and mandatory overtime.

White was on the short side, thin and tough as a razor strop. A Glock 9mm hung on her right hip. Below that hip, out of sight beneath her winter cover-ups, she had a massive scar on her thigh where she'd been shot with a fast-expanding jacketed hollow-point bullet from a deer rifle.

Just . . . life in the Marshals Service.

As they stood side-by-side, Lucas loomed over her, a substantial opposite, with expensively cut dark hair threaded with gray and crystalline blue eyes. He was tall, wide across the shoulders. A hairline scar tracked across his left eye from his forehead to his cheek, a relic of a fishing trip. Another puckered scar sat on his throat, where a teenaged girl had shot him with a piece-of-crap .22 that he hadn't seen coming. He had a nonstandard Walther 40 S&W on his left hip, in a cross-draw holster, for easier access under a suit coat.

Lucas had a tendency toward depression, exacerbated by the gloom of winter, and by the sporadic violence of the job. White shared the depressive gene, and they sometimes compared notes. When Lucas was younger, he hadn't worried about it. Now, in his later fifties, he had a tendency to think he'd been shot too often and to brood about the near-death experiences. About what he'd miss, if he were dead; about not seeing his younger children grow into adults.

White had thoughts that ran down in the same trench.

Still, they both were hunters, trackers. They liked the intensity of the work, if not always the consequences, because the intensity went some way toward offsetting the blues.

"I DON'T KNOW why they put us out here," White said, looking around like a curious cat, her nose twitching in the wind. Although she was wearing a down parka, ski gloves, and a cashmere watch cap over her streaky brown hair, she shivered. They were standing at the top of the driveway, in a grove of paper birches, the kind the Ojibwe once turned into canoes.

The ground, hard as pig iron, was covered with half an inch of crunchy snow. There'd been almost no snow over the winter months, but they'd gotten all the usual cold weather. The temperature, according to Lucas's weather app, was six degrees and falling, and a persistent breeze whipped the steam away from their mouths. "I'm not a babysitter," she added.

"This guy is no baby," Lucas said. He coughed once, covering his mouth with a gloved fist. He wasn't sick; the bitter cold set him off. He could feel his lips cracking, and he'd left his ChapStick sitting on his dresser. "He was in some kind of enforcement branch of the Russian spy agency. He's probably killed more people than the Marshals Service."

"Yeah, but why us in particular?" White asked. "Why not Remy, or that asshole Clark? They'd jump at it, hanging out with headquarters guys."

"Because I'm the smartest guy in the office, and you're a close second? They thought the job might take some brains."

"You're almost smart enough to get that almost right," White said, shivering again. She'd been a National Merit Scholar in high school and Lucas hadn't been; but then, he'd been a hockey jock, and what could you expect from somebody who'd been hit in the head with a puck, and more than once? "But really?"

"Because Witness Protection doesn't babysit, either," Lucas said. "They plug a guy into a hideout and that's it. This guy . . . The Russians would like to get at him. They need somebody with guns close by, or think they do. That's not usually Witness Protection."

"ALL RIGHT," WHITE said. She'd done time with fugitive task forces and considered her Glock to be a species of musical instrument. Lucas had a reputation as a shooter, which he didn't entirely appreciate, because it suggested he was too fast on the trigger. He felt he was barely fast enough, and he had the scars to prove it.

At the moment, White was in the Minnesota winter stance, shoulders squeezed tight, elbows to rib cage, fingers pulled out of the fingers of her gloves, hands clenched in fists. "Why aren't you cold? You're standing there in your plutonium suit and tie . . . and that coat. What's that coat made of? Pubic hair from virgins? What?"

"Wool, from goats, but highly refined, college-educated, Italian goats," Lucas said. He was a hopeless fashion plate. He leaned toward White: "Don't tell anyone, but I'm also wearing long underwear. Smartwool. Of course, if I have to pee, I'm in trouble."

"Well, that's it: you *are* smarter than me. I'm wearing cotton bikini briefs." White looked at her watch: "They're late. Jerks left us standing out here freezing our balls off."

"Not mine. They're like two chestnuts roasting on an open fire."

White: "Hey: you don't have to top me every time, okay?"

LUCAS'S CELL PHONE buzzed. He dug it out of the pocket of his coat, looked at the screen: "Now they're going to tell us why they're late."

He answered, listened for a moment, and when the person on the other side stopped talking, he said, "Okay. We'll take a look around here," and rang off.

White: "What?"

Lucas said, "They're still half an hour out. They had to find a suitcase. Knowing the Marshals Service, they probably flew last-class on Trans-New Jersey Airways."

"If we had a key . . ." White looked wistfully up at the locked and alarmed house, furnace steam puffing from a rooftop chimney. The place had what were once called "grounds." Nothing rural about it, a four-acre fenced lot heavy with white-trunked birches and brooding blue conifers and maples, a few red leaves still attached to the maples. A line of bare-naked bridal wreath bushes were strung along the driveway, while leafless lilacs waited in the dooryard for spring.

"We *could* sit in the truck, but I'd like to take a look around," Lucas said. "You know, in case we ever had to come back out here."

"Not a bad idea. We can at least see through the woods right now," White said. "Gotta be pretty dense in the summer."

"Let me change my shoes . . ."

Lucas popped the back of his truck and took out a pair of Sorel Caribous, pulled them on, tucked in the bottom of his suit pants, and carefully placed his John Lobbs on the truck's floor.

Together, they marched around the lot, past a frozen picnic table that sat next to a frozen firepit made with frozen stones with frozen logs next to it, through the maples and pines and birches and around the withered shrubs. They found a hard-frozen coiled hose that somebody had forgotten under a dwarf mugo pine, two wickets from a croquet set that somebody had forgotten to pull, and, at the back of the yard, a shovel with a rusted blade and a broken handle. Having crisscrossed the yard, they went out a gate at the back.

They discovered that the hideout was on one of four circles, which they hadn't known, with a narrow, frozen creek winding through the common area between the circles. They stumbled across whitetail deer beds tucked under balsams and racoon and coyote tracks along the iced-over creek.

There were three houses on each of the four circles. All of the houses were showing furnace exhaust, and two had older cars in the driveways, which White thought must belong to housekeepers. Nobody with common sense would park outside in this cold, if they had a heated garage.

"If the guy's a bowhunter, he could put up some venison," White said, checking out a line of deer tracks. She scuffed at one of the bigger prints and said, "Nice buck."

They were puffing out clouds of steam, and tiny icicles were forming on the tips of White's hair.

"Given his reputation, I'm pretty sure he ain't a vegetarian," Lucas said.

THEY'D JUST GOTTEN back to the house when two SUVs pulled into the driveway, both Ford Explorers, both with the tired look of rental cars. A bulky marshal, head like a half-gallon milk jug, climbed out of the first vehicle, saw them: "Davenport and White?"

"Davenport and White," Lucas answered. "Are you Derrick?"

"Yeah. You look like your pictures. You guys check out the site?"

"We did," White said. "There are four cul-de-sacs back-to-back, three houses on each circle, a common area in between them. Looks like all the lots are about the same size, three or four acres each, all fenced. Nothing but animal tracks in the snow."

"Excellent." Derrick Beard turned back toward the SUVs and waved. Seven more doors popped open, and seven more people got out. Three were marshals, all in tactical winter wear, all from Washington, as was Beard.

Another of the arrivals, an American, but not a marshal, was thinner, taller, quicker, wearing a wool knee-length camel coat with matching wool-and-leather gloves. He sported black rectangular sunglasses and a brown Borsalino hat. The clothes were well cut and subtly aristocratic. Looking at them, Lucas, the fashion plate, was stroked by the feather of jealousy. He liked browns, admired them, but given his coloring, couldn't wear them.

THE FINAL THREE to get out of the trucks were a short sixty-year-old gray-haired man with broad shoulders, a stub nose, and ruddy face, in a blue L.L.Bean parka. He was followed by a scowling forty-something woman with tight-cut blond hair, small gold earrings, and narrow shoulders; she was several inches taller than the man Lucas presumed was her husband. She was also wearing a blue Bean parka.

The third was a tall youngish man, midtwenties, whose face resembled the woman's. His dishwater-blond hair fell to his shoulders and his face was covered with dishwater blond fuzz, like a holy card Jesus. Despite the cold, the son was wearing tight fashion jeans and a hip-length black leather jacket worn open.

"Hope to God somebody has a key," Lucas said.

"We're good," Beard said. "Let's get inside. I'm already numb."

The older man said to the woman, "Look at the birches, Martha, like home. I told you." His face looked carved, rather than grown, with snarl lines starting beside his nose and extending to the corners of his mouth. The quarried look of his face was matched by that of his wife.

"Not home, Leonard," the woman grumbled. After a moment, "It's less than I hoped for. Less than they told us."

"Better than home," the son said. "I'm not fighting any fuckin' Ukrainian assholes in the middle of a fuckin' Ukrainian asshole winter."

As they walked up to the house, Beard introduced the three as Leonard Summers; his wife, Martha; and son, Bernard.

All three sounded American: in a briefing the day before, Lucas and White had been told that all three had spoken some English before they fled Russia. They'd spent the past year and a half holed up in a CIA facility near Washington. English lessons had been a daily event, including work on their accents and slang. If they added oodala-oodala-oodala vowel sounds, they might even pass as Minnesotan.

Beard opened the front door's heavy lock with a key, then handed a key ring with several keys to the older Russian. As they trooped inside, Lucas noticed that the door was three inches thick and appeared to have a quarter-inch steel plate laminated inside. Not a door you could kick, or shoot through, for that matter. Beard disarmed an alarm, and Martha said, "Small living room, Leonard." She touched the back of a beige couch in the living room. The walls were bare, awaiting a personal touch. "Where are the bedrooms?"

"I think it is comfortable," Leonard said, with a defensive note. "We should bring in the suitcases."

"Our guys will get those," Beard said. "Leonard, you and Martha should pick a bedroom—the master is here on the first floor, with one more at the back. We thought that second one would be a nice office for you, Leonard. Martha, there's a family room in back. It's three times the size of the living room and has an eighty-inch TV hanging on the wall, just like you ordered. That's where you party."

"What about the billiards table?" Leonard Summers asked.

"Yeah, there's a full-sized billiards table," Beard said. "There are two bedrooms upstairs, and a sitting room. Bernie can pick one, and Jack can take the other. All the bedrooms have attached bathrooms. Even the office."

"How long will Jack be here?" Lucas asked. Jack was a marshal with the Witness Protection Program.

"A couple weeks. We want to have one of our regular guys checking around, to make sure everything looks copacetic," Beard said. "Jack has done this fifteen times, so if there's a problem, he'll spot it. You two are the cavalry, if he screams for help."

"Where are the cars?" Bernard asked.

"They're coming, they'll be here this evening," Beard said. "We got slowed down at the DMV."

THE TEN OF them took fifteen minutes to poke around the house. A marshal told Lucas that all the furniture had come from a single home furnishings dealer in one big truckload, "so not a lot of people have been in and out of here."

Lucas reflexively checked the sight lines from the windows and noticed White doing the same thing.

"The only thing I don't like is that you could get close to the house and not be seen," White said.

"Balanced by the fact that it's hard to know what's back here. Invisibility is their friend," Lucas said. He looked out the window toward a towering cottonwood tree two hundred yards away, an easy shot for a hunting rifle. "But you have a point. Especially at night, you could sneak right up to the windows. High-rise condo might be better."

The thin man in the camel coat said, "They didn't want a condo. They wanted a dacha, like back in Russia. Isn't that right, Martha?"

"Too many apartments, all our lives," Martha said. "We wanted more space, and we wanted to hide where *nobody* could see us. But, maybe something bigger than this? Maybe with a dock to fish from?"

"If somebody came after you here, they'd have to take chances, doing reconnaissance and snooping around the neighborhood," said the camel-coated man. He spoke quietly, but with a military articulation; people stopped talking to listen. "If Leonard were sitting on a dock with a fishing pole, a sniper could hit him from six hundred yards out. From a fishing boat. In town, on the street, a killer could come from anywhere and look like anything. This house has alarms everywhere, and Leonard and Bernard both know how to use a gun."

White: "I'm assuming you're CIA?"

"Yes. John Sherwood." He shook hands with White, then with Lucas. Sherwood had what, at first glance, appeared to be delicate-looking, pale facial skin with a touch of rose on his cheekbones, as if finished with a fine French lotion. On second glance, his face looked as though it had been sanded down, like he was missing a couple layers of skin. He'd taken off the sunglasses and Lucas caught cold green eyes, which had the frigid *clink* of a fighter pilot's; eyes that might have been chipped from an old, weather-worn Coke bottle.

LEONARD WENT TO look at his potential office, while Sherwood, Lucas, White, and Martha eventually congregated in the kitchen, where a window over the kitchen sink looked across a semicircular flower garden, now a bristling clump of cut-down plants poking up through the shallow snow.

"That's a spy hat you're wearing," White said to Sherwood. "European. Viennese, like in the movies. Don't see those much in Minnesota."

Sherwood started to smile at White as Leonard wandered into the kitchen, carrying an unlit cigar. He stepped past his wife, opened his mouth to say something to Sherwood, dropped the cigar, quickly bent to pick it up . . .

WHACK/BANG!

The two sounds were not simultaneous, though nearly so, as the bullet was traveling at three thousand feet per second, and the sound of the shot itself at only eleven hundred. The high-velocity slug punched through the kitchen window glass two inches above Leonard's bowed head and hit Martha in the cheek below her right eye, splattering blood and bone around the kitchen.

"Jesus! Jesus!" somebody screamed, a gravelly masculine shriek of either alarm or fear, and Sherwood reeled away from the falling woman. Lucas, who had been looking down the hall toward the living room, jerked away and saw White, her face covered with blood, dropping toward the floor.

Sherwood snagged Leonard by his jacket and yanked him to the floor and Lucas shouted at him, "Refrigerator," and another slug punched through, lower, and missed everything, and Sherwood dragged Leonard behind the refrigerator and Lucas grabbed White, who he thought had been hit, to drag her out of the kitchen, but she slapped his hand away and said, "I'm okay, got some spatter," and crawled with him into the living room.

Lucas said, "They gotta have come in from the circle, they gotta be running . . ." and White, already fumbling for her pistol, shouted, "Go, go, go . . ."

They scrambled toward the front door, hands and knees, heard Bernie screaming, "Mama, mama . . ." and another marshal shouting at somebody, "Stay down, get in here . . . roll in here . . ." and somebody else shouted, "Watch the back door, watch the back . . ."

Lucas and White had been low-crawling across the entry space. At the front door, Lucas got to his knees and looked out through the small security window in the door, couldn't see anything but trees and parked cars.

Beard shouted, "Stay here! Stay here! Cover Leonard and Bernard, shape up, guys . . ."

He wasn't shouting at Lucas and White, but at his own men. White had gone sideways, peeked out a window that looked toward the woods where the shot had come from, and snapped at Lucas: "Nothing moving! Don't see anyone! Are they waiting to take another shot, or . . ."

Lucas: "They're running, they gotta be. They can't wait, not with the muzzle blast from the rifle. You could hear it a mile away. People will be looking at them already. They gotta know there are a bunch of guns in here."

He yanked the front door open, looked out and sideways, ran down the front steps, his Walther in his hand, watching the woods as he went, stumbling a couple of times, the heavy Sorel boots awkward at speed. White was a step behind him, gun up, peering into the woods.

A blue Jeep Wagoneer flashed by the driveway entrance as they ran past the parked SUVs. When they reached the end of the driveway, they saw it stop at the next driveway as two men burst out of the woods, both in parkas, one carrying a rifle, one carrying a spotting scope on a folded tripod.

They popped doors on opposite sides of the Wagoneer and climbed in and Lucas started firing at the truck, felt White line up next to him, as though they were on a shooting range, or a firing squad, and together they put thirty-four rounds into and around the truck, which accelerated out of the cul-de-sac and onto the main street.

Lucas reloaded, jammed the Walther back in his holster, took out his iPhone and called 9-1-1. When it was answered, he shouted, "U.S. Marshal: we've got a woman shot and the shooter is running in a blue Jeep Wagoneer north on Willow Drive in Orono toward Highway 12, it'll be full of bullet holes, shattered back window, at least three guys inside, they're armed and professionals, stop them but don't approach them, they have a rifle and probably other weapons, we need an ambulance right now, right now!"

It all came out in one long sentence, and he could hear the 9-1-1 operator shouting at someone else and he gave her the address for the ambulance and turned and saw White running toward her 4Runner, which she'd left parked in the circle so the Witness Protection people could have the driveway. She was in the truck in a minute and accelerated toward Lucas as he stepped into the street and he was repeating everything to a new voice on the 9-1-1 call and White skidded to a stop and he climbed in the passenger side and shouted, "Go," and she went.

The new 9-1-1 operator was talking to him and he repeated most of what he'd already said, but more slowly, with road directions as best he knew them, told the operator that they were in pursuit and the operator said everything was coming, but there wasn't much around, so it would be a few minutes before anything got there.

There was no traffic at all. White accelerated across strips of black ice, the tires got loose and she nearly took out a spruce tree, but she got it back and punched the truck onto Willow. Looking down the long straight road, they saw no sign of the Jeep.

There were narrow side roads coming off Willow and Lucas checked them as best he could as White said, "I don't think they'd go in there, lots of dead ends and all tangled up, can't move fast, bet they went to the highway . . ."

"Probably, but they must've scouted the area, maybe they knew a better way out . . ."

They were coming up to a cluster of buildings and a U.S. Inn motel and Lucas saw the huge blue Wagoneer in the motel's parking lot, oddly angled in a parking space and he pointed and said "Shelly! Shelly! There! There!"

White took the truck that way, bouncing across a curb past a fire hydrant and between two parked cars and a minute later they were blocking the Wagoneer and were out of the 4Runner, fresh mags in their pistols.

Lucas called, "Wait it out, wait it out," and they waited behind the 4Runner, looking for life, as a family gawked at them, trailing roller-suitcases toward the motel's front door and White screamed, "Don't go there, go back to your car. U.S. Marshals. Go back, go back, run!"

The family ran back toward their pickup, still trailing the suitcases as Lucas yelled at White, "Don't see anyone, I think they ditched it . . ."

Lucas got back on his phone, still open to the 9-1-1 operator, and said, "The Wagoneer is at the U.S. Inn off whatever the fuck it is, Willow and Highway 12. We're covering it, they're either inside the truck or they're inside the motel or they got picked up here . . ."

Nothing moved in the Jeep. The back window was mostly shot out and they could see what looked like a dozen bullet holes in the tailgate. White said, "Watch it. I'm gonna go low and peek."

"I gotcha," Lucas said.

He braced his arm on the side of the truck, pistol pointed at the Wagoneer as White scrambled toward the truck in a half-duckwalk, half-run. She sheltered behind the back right fender, got a two-handed grip on her pistol, then peeked in the back window, quickly up-and-down, hopped a couple of feet, then peeked again, more slowly, then stood up a third time for a good look from a different spot.

She turned to Lucas: "Empty . . ."

Lucas's phone rang, but he rejected it and went back to 9-1-1 and told the operator that the truck was empty and that the shooters were either inside the motel or gone.

The operator said, "One minute, two cars. We got more coming. Are you going in?"

"We gotta check the truck," Lucas said, "Then we're going inside."

"Wait for backup, Marshal! Wait for backup! It's close!" the operator said.

White had already pulled open the driver's-side door and Lucas went that way and his phone rang again: Beard, the lead marshal.

"Where are you?"

Lucas told him and told him that an ambulance was on the way to the house.

White reached out for his phone and Lucas gave it to her and she said, "Looks like there were three of them. We shot up the getaway vehicle, we've got blood in the back seat and the passenger seat, quite a bit of it, and a little blood on the windshield but none on the driver's seat. They've got at least two wounded and one, probably one, still okay, but the driver might have been hit high and that's the windshield blood. They've still got a rifle unless they threw it out the window on the way over here."

Then she listened and said, "Okay, there'll be some cops here in a minute and we're going into the motel to check it out, but I don't see any blood trails on the ground here. I think they're gone."

Lucas held out his hand for the phone and White handed it to him and he said, "I can see three video cameras in this parking lot so if they're running, we've probably got their vehicle on video. As soon as the cops get here . . ." A cop car pulled into the parking lot as he spoke. ". . . And there's one here right now. We're going in, we'll try to get the video, you've got to start talking to everybody about tracking them."

"Got it. We'll be there in a couple of minutes, me and Sherwood," Beard said.

"Martha?"

"Martha's dead," Beard said. "Half of her head is gone."

"Ah, man. We'll be inside the motel."

ONE COP GOT out of the first-arriving car, and then another pulled in, also with a lone cop. White waved them over, said one of them should cover the truck as a crime scene while the other came with her and Lucas, into the motel.

"We need a uniform," she said.

One of the cops said, "I'll come. I've been here before. More guys are on the way." He stepped back from White and added, "Uh, you've got blood all over your face. You okay?"

"I'm good. Just haven't had time to visit the spa."

THE THREE OF them went inside, guns high, where two short women clerks in beige U.S. Inn blouses were standing behind a counter, sticking up side-by-side, looking at the handguns like *Whoa*, like a couple of meerkats.

Lucas, checking the floor, said, "No blood."

"They're gone," White said. To the clerks: "Did some people . . ."

"Nobody came in here."

The cop was at the desk: "You've got recorders on your cameras. We need to see the video."

The slightly taller of the two short clerks said, "Uh. Yeah. Back here," thumb over her shoulder toward a back room. There was not a security station, as such, but a video panel divided into four sections, one for each of the three cameras focused on the parking lot and one on the front desk. The clerk dialed up the section that showed the Wagoneer bouncing into the parking lot and jamming itself halfway into a parking spot.

Seconds later, another SUV, this one cream-colored, and smaller, pulled into the lot and two people, a man and a woman, got out of the Wagoneer, one from the driver's seat and the other from the front passenger seat.

Both of them were average height or a bit taller for their sex, strong-looking. They wore dark blue wool-and-nylon ski masks, covering their hair, obscuring their faces. The man from the passenger seat was hunched, staggering, hopping on one leg, apparently wounded. The woman, the little they could see of her, showed a streak of what appeared to be blood around the rim of her eye socket.

"Window blood was from her, we scalped her," White said; the comment was technical, rather than satisfied.

The staggering man got in the back of the new SUV while the driver of that vehicle and the female driver of the Wagoneer opened the back door of the Jeep and carried the man from the back seat to the cream-colored vehicle and pushed him in beside the staggering man. As they did that, a pistol fell out of the wounded man's belt; the woman stooped and picked it up, and seconds later, thrust the sniper rifle and the spotting scope onto the floor of the back seat along with the pistol.

White said, "Subaru, I think."

The two drivers got into the small SUV, which pulled straight through the parking lot and out of sight of the video camera.

"O-M-G, that was . . ." the clerk began, and then, "There's another camera further back that'll catch them going out. Let me freeze this one and see if I can get some plates . . ."

She rolled the video back and got the plates from the second vehicle, which was a Subaru, as White had said.

Lucas went back to 9-1-1 and read the license plate numbers and a description of the two vehicles to the operator and waited. She was back in a minute: "They're from Hertz and National. We're putting out a BOLO on the Subaru and we'll get photos of the renters from car rental companies . . . Got that started."

"Call me back when you get anything. We've got a murdered woman and these guys are professional shooters, so warn everyone."

"That's already done, we've got Orono and Wayzata and everybody else swarming the highways, looking for the Subaru," the operator said. "I'll call you . . ."

THEY TURNED TOWARD the sound of people banging through the front door, loud questions, and then Beard came in, trailed by Sherwood. Beard asked, "What?"

White and Lucas filled them in and Beard said, "Got that much, anyway, at least a couple guys down." He was red-faced, frantic, trembling with energy that had nowhere to go. Sherwood stood behind him, hands in his coat pockets, icy calm. He smiled at Lucas and White and said, "Not bad, the shooting. We've got a big problem, though. I've got to make a call. Don't go anywhere."

"We've got everything available looking for the Subaru," White said. "Tell that to whoever you're calling."

"That's not my problem, that's yours," Sherwood said. "My problem is, somebody gave up the Sokolovs: identity, location, and time. We've got a leak and a bad one. That's a much more serious problem than three wounded Russian scuzzballs on the loose."

Beard looked at him for a moment, ran a hand through his hair, then asked, "A leak? My side or your side?"

"A good question," Sherwood said. He stepped away toward the hall: "Good luck with the chase. If you catch up with them, try to keep somebody alive long enough that we can have a chat. I'll go make my call."

"Hey," White called after him. "Summers or Sokolovs?"

"Used to be Summers, until fifteen minutes ago. We'll have to find a new name for them now. Sokolov is the original—Masha, Leonid, and Bernard."

"I'll keep it in mind," White said. "I need to find a restroom and wash off my face."

The desk clerk offered to show her where it was, and White followed her out. Beard turned to Lucas and said, in a stricken voice, "On the Derrick Beard one-to-five shitstorm scale, this is a Category Five. Martha, my God, her head blew up, like, like . . ."

He didn't know what it was like.

Then the family came back with their rolling suitcases. They all turned to look, and the man asked, "Can we still check in?"

2

When Lev Nikitin and Matvey Orlov burst out of the woods, they were focused on the big Jeep and getting into it. Orlov reached it first. He threw the spotting scope and its tripod on the floor of the back seat and jumped in after it, pulling the door shut behind him. Nikitin, carrying the rifle, took an extra three seconds to skid around the back of the truck to the front passenger door, popped it open and vaulted inside, putting the butt of the rifle on the floor and trapping it between his legs. Katerina Abramova was behind the wheel and was rolling before Nikitin had his door shut and she was chanting, "Fast, fast, fast . . ."

Nikitin: "What! What!"

She was looking in the rearview mirror: "In the street behind us . . ."

She was leaning on the gas pedal as the bullets started popping through the back of the truck. Orlov cried out and said, "Hit!" and then, the impacts coming like hail on a tin roof, "Hit again . . ."

Nikitin was hit next, then Abramova was hit in the rim of her left ear, blood spattering the windshield, but she ignored it and put a phone to her other ear and shouted into it, "Crash pickup, three wounded, three minutes."

The incoming bullets had all been fired in four or five seconds and they ran away from them and Nikitin turned in his seat, groaned and asked Orlov, "Matvey . . . how bad?"

Orlov groaned and Nikitin said, "Matvey . . ."

"One above my belt in my back . . . no exit. One in my butt and down my leg. Bleeding is bad. Bleeding is bad." He groaned again. He was slumped over in the back, but held up a hand, saturated with scarlet streaks of blood.

Nikitin: "Katya. How bad?"

"I have a new hole in my ear," Abramova said. "I will not bleed out. And you?"

Nikitin had pulled down the sun visor, then pushed up the cover on the mirror on the back of the visor, and was peering at his neck. "In my butt and the side of my neck. I don't think it hit the carotid, it's not pumping but it's bleeding, small hole in, bigger out, but it might have been a fragment. I think it hit the headrest first . . ."

"Two minutes or less," Abramova said.

Orlov: "I can't walk."

"We'll carry," she said.

The truck ricochetted off a pothole and Orlov screamed, groaned, said, "Don't do that . . ."

She did it again, because she couldn't slow enough to miss the potholes, and Orlov screamed each time and began farting, and he screamed with the farts and Nikitin half-groaned and half-laughed and said, "Mat, you dirty piece of shit . . ."

Abramova glanced over the seat at Orlov in the back and asked, "Mat, can you put on your mask? Can you get your mask out?"

"Yes . . ." Another groan.

Nikitin had taken a black ski mask out of his pocket and was pulling it over his head, and when it was on, reached across to Abramova and pulled a mask out of her parka pocket and dropped it in her lap. She waited until she was clear of traffic and then quickly pulled it over her face.

Three miles away, Melor Titov was sitting in a cream-colored Subaru and when the call came in—"Crash pickup"—he smothered a groan, blurted, "On the way," and put the little SUV in gear. He'd had some training in avoidance and escape driving, but much more in computer systems and language, and he wanted nothing to do with this hit team.

His job was acquiring papers, not doing crash pickups for killers. If he didn't do it, he might be next on the kill list; surely would be, if he didn't show up at the motel parking lot, and it wouldn't be a gentle death. Some display of bravery and resolution was critical, but the quicker he could get back to his regular job in Chicago, the happier he'd be.

He pulled a black ski mask over his head and took off.

ORLOV COULDN'T SEE out of the truck, but Nikitin could, and he feared that Abramova was going to kill them with speed, if the bullet wounds didn't do it first. She was cutting through traffic like a great white shark going through a pod of sea lions. Three minutes later, just as she'd said, she cut into a motel parking lot and yanked the truck to the left into a parking slot.

Abramova: "I don't see . . . Yes! He's here!"

The small SUV was right there, behind them, and Nikitin opened his door and Abramova shouted, "Lev, don't wait, get in if you can! Melor and I will take Mat!"

Nikitin nearly fell but managed to stagger and hop to the open back door of the Subaru and crawl inside, his injured leg numb with the impact of the bullet, the neck wound burning like fire. Behind him, he could see a bystander staring at them as Abramova shouted, "Move, move," and he dragged himself farther across the back seat and Abramova and the burly driver of the Subaru shoved Orlov almost on top of him.

Orlov looked at them with glassy eyes and his lips moved but nothing came out of his mouth, then a rifle, pistol, and spotting scope hit the floor at his feet and the back door slammed and then the Subaru driver and Abramova were in the front seats and the car was moving.

TITOV, THE SUBARU'S wheelman, had them out of the motel parking lot and around a corner in ten seconds, took them down the open highway at ninety miles an hour. Abramova said, conversationally, not critically, for a bleeding woman, "Don't want to attract traffic police," and Titov said, "Nobody on the road coming in."

He slowed to the speed limit as he approached a cross highway, took them onto the highway, accelerated to speed again, for half a mile, then took them into a residential neighborhood, watching the mirrors, accelerating when he safely could, and three or four minutes later, pulled into a narrow, heavily wooded lane that led back to a little-used boat-launching ramp.

Another Jeep, this one black, a Wrangler, Titov's personal car and positioned as the disaster pickup vehicle, was waiting for them. The wounded trio were in the new car in a minute, and the Jeep rolled out of the lane, through the neighborhood, and out on the highway again.

"Fifteen minutes to the house," Titov grunted. "This is fucked. This is so fucked."

"They were very fast, too fast," Abramova said. "Two shooters, a tall one and a short one."

"Sokolov?" Titov asked.

"I missed him, I might have hit his wife," Nikitin said. "It was like he knew it was coming. He ducked down just as I squeezed the trigger. I fired a second time but couldn't see what happened and then we were running."

Titov looked at Abramova: "How much damage?"

"Not much, hit in the ear," she said, brushing back her blond hair to show him the sticky blood still leaking out of the rim of her ear. She was Circassian, with the pale white complexion and long blond hair of her particular tribe, and the pallor vibrated with the crimson blood. "Lev and Mat are bleeding badly, we need to stop it."

"Thirteen minutes, maybe twelve," Titov said. He slowed as a police car, light bar flashing at them, sped past in the opposite direction, headed for the hideout.

Abramova, sitting in the passenger seat, unlocked her safety belt and got to her knees to look at the men in the back.

"Drive straight and easy," she told Titov, got her feet underneath her, and climbed over the seat into the back, between the two men.

Orlov groaned when she tumbled onto one of his legs and Nikitin asked, "What are you doing?"

"I'm going to plug Matvey, if I can find his wounds . . . and you, too."

The three members of the team had gotten Russian Army combat medical training, which was barely adequate under the best circumstances, before they'd moved on, individually, and several years apart, to GRU Unit 29155—GRU being the Russian Federation's equivalent to the CIA. Members of the Unit were not expected to encounter full-on combat. Titov had different training, as an expert in exfiltration and life as an American.

So, knowing not much, Abramova dug into a pants pocket and pulled out a five-inch switchblade, flicked out the blade. She stripped off her parka and pulled off her flannel shirt and cut it into patches. Orlov was lying on his side, with the wounds up, and Abramova pulled up his coat and Orlov groaned again. He had a pistol in a clip on his belt, and she set it aside.

Using the knife, Abramova cut away his shirt and undershirt, found a bullet wound in his back, with no exit wound. Blood was squeezing out onto his sodden clothing, and she pushed a wad of flannel into the wound, saw blood on Orlov's leg, cut his jeans away, and put another wad of flannel into the bullet hole in his butt. Again, there was no exit wound.

As Titov said, "Six minutes," she turned to Nikitin and said, "Show me."

He showed her, and she plugged the wound in his leg as best she could, although she didn't think it was very good. The neck wound was more superficial, and no longer bleeding heavily. "We need the medical kit, the bleed-stop," she said. "Lev could be okay long enough to find a plane ride, but Mat . . . Mat needs a doctor, and soon. And, I think, he might need blood."

Titov said, "One minute."

TITOV—LEON JACKSON, AS American as borscht, a sleeper agent—had spent the last two weeks in a furnished, rented house in the town of Minnetrista. He worked in Chicago as a real estate agent for a Serbian-owned agency. The agency boss knew better than to ask questions when Titov had to take days off for what the boss referred to as his "side hustle."

He'd been activated when the Russian SVR, one of the country's foreign intelligence services, learned that Orono, Minnesota, had been chosen by Sokolov and the Marshals Service as the place where Sokolov would live under the name Leonard Summers.

The house Titov rented was in an area of mixed newer, suburban-style homes and older farmhouses; it was one of the old farmhouses, on six acres of land. The landlord told him, when he rented it, if he stayed there long-term, he was welcome to revive the vegetable garden in back, and to harvest the Concord grapes off a long arbor that ran along the side of the house.

Titov had no interest in growing vegetables, or making wine, but was interested in the isolation provided by the large plot of land, and the cover created by the yard's mature bushes and trees.

He'd met only two neighbors, a man and wife, had mentioned that he was looking for a permanent place, closer to the big lake, Minnetonka, and that he hoped to be in the new place before summer.

Until then, he was scouting. He'd said he was in corporate sales with General Mills, transferring in from the Cleveland office, and when asked about a wife and family, said that he was "alone" for the time being.

The neighbors sympathized, and the husband said, "You want my best advice . . . Go Vikes."

The American football fan Leon Jackson, who laughed easily, did that, and said, "It's not that hard, giving up on the Browns." Melor Titov, the sleeper agent, was actually a Bears fanatic.

"Got that, brother. Did you see the game where the Browns were up by thirty-three, and the Vikes came all the way back and won?"

Jackson groaned: "What a disaster." They talked about that for a moment, then the neighbors waved, went on their way, and they hadn't spoken since.

Now, moving fast out of the shooting scene, Titov pulled into the long gravel driveway and Abramova said, "No bounce! No bounce, slow is better."

With no one around to see them, they first moved Orlov into the house and put him on a clean sheet on the living room carpet. They helped Nikitin in next, placed him on another sheet, on the far side of the carpet.

Abramova said, "We need to see the wounds, see what we're dealing with. Put some of the bleed-stop on them."

"I'll cut," Titov said. "You get the medical."

ABRAMOVA, NIKITIN, AND Orlov were a three-team specializing in assassinations in hostile territory. The planning was done at GRU headquarters, mostly in a long room overlooking the Institute of Cosmic Biology. Abramova was the on-site director and designated driver, with superb skills behind a steering wheel. Orlov specialized in reconnaissance, street work, and backup, while Nikitin was the designated hitter.

All three were familiar with Western personal computer systems, and were trained for work in Germany, the Netherlands, and Britain. All spoke some level of German, Dutch, and English. Nikitin spoke German at a native level, Orlov had perfect Dutch, and Abramova's English was excellent, but accented. They hadn't been trained to operate in the U.S., but the European countries were similar enough that they could manage, and they'd had a ten-day crash course in American travel, clothing, and shopping procedures.

Guns were difficult to come by in the continental countries and Britain, and to obfuscate the actual origin of their assassinations, Nikitin primarily deployed knives and clubs acquired locally and abandoned after the hit. He was also an exceptional rifle shot, and an expert with handguns. In America, with a professionally protected target, and easy access to all kinds of firearms, they expected to rely on guns.

Titov was an outsider, not yet entirely trusted by the other three; he was with the team, but not yet of it. He spoke flawless, unaccented Midwestern English, and specialized in getting Russian operatives with non-official cover, or NOCs, in and out of the country. He could provide Russian intelligence operators with money, weapons, and good IDs, including real American passports, excellent green cards, Illinois driver's licenses, and functioning credit cards. He knew doctors who would treat patients without asking questions, for good hard American dollars. He was an adequate shot with both rifles and pistols and an excellent driver.

He'd acquired all the necessary IDs and passports for the team and had drop-kicked it all to Berlin, Germany, in a Russian diplomatic bag, where it was picked up by the team. When they'd arrived in Chicago, he had provided them with a gear bag that included weapons, a medical kit, a dozen burner phones, ski masks, and an always-useful roll of black gaffer tape.

The Russian embassy had also dropped him two silenced Beretta machine pistols. He was a member of a rough-and-ready country shooting range west of Chicago. He couldn't test the machine pistols, but he had taken Nikitin to the range as a guest, to get the Russian sniper comfortable with the chosen rifle, a Sig Spear in .277 Fury, mounted with a variable-power Leupold scope.

Nikitin, after sending twenty rounds downrange at two hundred yards, had pronounced the rifle "the best thing I've ever shot."

Titov: "It should be. It cost more than four thousand dollars and the ammunition is more than a dollar and a half a round."

The three-team had begun jokingly referring to Titov as the консьерж, or concierge.

Aside from the weapons bought by Titov, the team had smuggled in a ChapStick, which was carefully isolated, swathed in cotton, in a plastic soap box. It was tucked inside a Dopp kit with shaving cream, throwaway razors, toothpaste, a toothbrush, deodorant, and a small bottle of ibuprofen.

The medical kit Titov had put together, mostly from a Walgreens drugstore, included two boxes of QuikClot, bandages soaked with a kind of clay called kaolin, over-the-counter painkillers, and a single tube of illegal opiates for bigger problems.

Abramova and Titov jammed the QuikClot bandages into the wounds suffered by Nikitin and Orlov, and the external bleeding stopped, but Abramova looked at Titov across Orlov's body, shook her head and said, "The blood stays in the body, but inside, he still bleeds. We need something better."

3

Still at the motel, Lucas and Beard watched the videos again, looking for anything they might have missed, and they made sure the desk clerks wouldn't touch the video recordings before a crime scene crew could get to them. A moment later, Sherwood came back in and said, "Made my call. Things are moving. Both with us and with the Marshals Service. And the feds—the FBI."

White came back, her face washed, and Sherwood asked, "I know you guys were a bit preoccupied when you went after them, but can you remember . . . did you hear a buzzing sound, or a flapping sound? A drone?"

Lucas looked at White and shrugged, and she said, "I didn't."

Sherwood: "You two wandered around that area where the shooter would have been, and you saw no tracks?"

"Nothing but small animals and some deer," Lucas said. "From where that shot came from, we would have crossed the tracks if they were there. They had to have come in after we went past."

Beard: "Unless they were further back, you said one guy had a rifle and another had a spotting scope. . . ."

Lucas shook his head: "Too much brush. They couldn't have been more than a hundred yards out, unless they were up in that big cottonwood, but they weren't. It would have taken them longer to get out to the street after the shots. We looped through that whole area and would have crossed their tracks. There was nothing out there."

"Nothing but deer, coons, and rabbits," White added.

"Then why bother with the spotting scope?"

"Maybe they didn't know how thick it was, or how far back they would be, until they got there," Lucas said.

"The snow's been on the ground for what, two weeks?" White said. "If it wasn't a drone, maybe they checked the spot from a satellite, even a Google satellite photo, so they knew the layout but not the specifics."

Sherwood: "We need to go back to the house and see where they shot from. I want to look at the overhead." He turned to Beard. "Unless the marshals have already located it?"

"No. My guys are clustered around Leonard and Bernie," Beard said. He scratched his forehead, rubbed his nose. "Nobody—*nobody*—is going to see them or get close to them. When we get some authorities on the scene to lock it down, we'll leave and keep moving until we have a secure spot to put them. Get them back to Washington. Minneapolis is burned to the ground. Gotta sell that house."

"If there's a drone, they could track your people as they move," Lucas said.

"Not as far and fast as we'll be moving," Beard said.

"You have to understand that the Sokolovs are a major prize for us, and a major problem for the Russians," Sherwood interjected. "It's possible that the Russians have detailed a satellite to watch over the operation, like Miz White suggested. It would be better to put the two of them in a bunker somewhere."

White: "You got bunkers?"

Sherwood nodded at her: "You know what I mean. An obscure concrete-block third-floor condo with marshals in the lobby and every hallway and on the roof with automatic weapons. Maybe a place without an outside-facing window."

"We'll find something," Beard said. "Let's get back."

The cop who'd come in with Lucas and White had been on his radio and he came over to say, "We've got six guys here and crime scene from the BCA is on the way. We'll lock everything down. Who do I talk to when we're done?"

"That'd be me," Beard said. "I'll give you a card."

ON THE WAY out of the motel, they stopped to look at the Wagoneer. Lucas and White counted eighteen bullet holes in the back hatch and side, and more had gone through the broken-out rear window. A third row of seats was lying flat, but several slugs had gotten through to the second row, where the worst-wounded man, the one who had to be carried, had been sitting. Three or four had gone through the front passenger seat. At least one had drawn body blood, and another had gone through the headrest and drawn more, probably from a shoulder or neck.

"Should have had the third-row seats up," Sherwood said. "That's a miss."

There was more blood on the windshield in front of the driver, but from what they'd seen in the video, the woman hadn't seemed seriously wounded.

"Not bad," Beard said. "Of course, it was a big target."

"But eighty, ninety yards away, and moving," Sherwood said. "I'm somewhat impressed."

"You should be," White said. "Me'n Lucas shot them full of holes."

She put up a gloved hand and Lucas slapped it.

SHERWOOD RODE WITH them in the 4Runner, back to the hideout. Lucas asked, "Why are the Russians so hot to kill this guy? Seems like it might be a little late in the day."

"Revenge," Sherwood said. "To make a point to anyone else who might think about defecting. He was one of Vladimir Putin's appointments, so it's personal."

"Can you tell us anything more about him, Leonid, or about the shooters?" White asked.

Sherwood thought for a moment, then said, "I don't see why not. Quite a bit of it has been in one magazine or Substack or another. Including some Russian newspapers."

Leonid Sokolov, he said, had been a colonel in the FSB, the Federal Security Service, focusing on counterintelligence. He was an investigator, interrogator, judge, and executioner, all rolled into one. If he found Russians working for Western intelligence services, he was brutal in his work, which sometimes, if not always, involved the torture of innocent witnesses.

"He would torture family members, friends, associates. He didn't send the work out. Most of the time, he'd do it himself, along with a couple of his buddies. He would usually do the executions himself, as we heard it. He would have the accused person restrained in a chair and would shoot him or her in the head. Not in the back of the head, but in the forehead. He wanted the accused to see the bullet coming. He wanted to be looking into their eyes when they died. He apparently took a great deal of pleasure in the whole process."

Lucas: "Christ. And we're dealing with him?"

"We are. Anyway, he probably carried out a couple of dozen executions over the years and was widely hated, but appreciated by his superiors, including Putin. He was not being considered for elimination or even demotion, as far as we know. He was comfortable there in Moscow, but a long way from rich, with retirement not too far off. As it turns out, he'd been watching all those moguls and what a mogul's lifestyle could get you. He decided he wanted that: the money. A retirement medal wasn't good enough."

"How did he actually get out with his family?" Lucas asked.

"Mmm. It's a little complicated. Before the Syrian revolution, both Russia and the U.S. had armed forces in Syria, not exactly friends, but not exactly enemies. We occasionally cooperated—what were called deconfliction channels. Usually, just phone calls or radio calls," Sherwood said. "Sometimes, when things really got messed up, we'd all go to a neutral site and try to hash things out. It was a mess over there."

"And you were . . . ?"

"An *observer* . . ." Sherwood put oral italics on the word, ". . . at a deconfliction conference. I was sent to monitor the discussion. As was Sokolov, from the Russian side. He knew who I was, and I knew who he was. When we had a moment alone, he suggested that we have a chat. I told him that I wasn't interested in moving to Mother

Russia, and he said that he didn't think I would be. But a chat could be profitable for both of us, me in my job, he in his bank account. When I realized what he was suggesting, I asked if he ever vacationed in Istanbul, and he said that he could. Later that day, I gave him a darknet address on a piece of paper the size of a postage stamp that could be easily swallowed if he had to. A couple of months later, we set up a meet in Istanbul. A week after that, he and his family were in Washington."

White: "Yowza."

"You get anything good from him?" Lucas asked.

"Yes. We got the names of four Russian spies in sensitive positions with the Pentagon. They've all been taken out, they're now in prison. We got a lot of intel stuff confirmed, things that we suspected but weren't sure about, and leads to several other Russians that he thought might be amenable to an approach. That was very interesting, because one of them was already working for us. When we found out that the Russian counter-intel people were aware that he might be vulnerable, we managed to get him out."

Lucas: "So the Russians are pissed."

"Yes. This hit team—they'll be very good, one of their best. Able to improvise, to cope with changing circumstances. Smart. Tough."

"One thing I still don't understand," Lucas said. "Why did they go after Sokolov now? I mean, this minute? Why didn't they wait a week or two, or a month or two, until things were settled down and maybe the Sokolovs would have relaxed a little? When they weren't surrounded by marshals?"

Sherwood shook his head: "Don't know. Maybe they were afraid this was a temporary stop . . . But . . . that doesn't seem right. I dunno."

"A deliberate slap in the face, was what it was," White said. "A slap in our face. The Russians want us to know, without being absolutely sure."

Sherwood nodded: "That could be it. A deniable hit. But to get away with a slap, you can't get caught. Get caught, you're risking an embarrassing show trial."

THE REST OF their conversation was jumbled, confused, bits and pieces, with a lot of silence. They'd all seen death, and Lucas and White had been shot themselves, but to see it close up, widescreen with surround sound, as they had with Masha Sokolov, left them shocked; left them with things to think about on their own. When they got back to the hideout, two local cop cars were parked in the street next to the driveway, the cops standing beside their vehicles, apparently to keep any traffic moving through.

"Let's go see where the shots came from," Sherwood said.

A Hennepin County ambulance was at the top of the drive, engine turning over, a paramedic sitting inside the open back doors, reading his phone. He glanced up and nodded as they passed and went back to his phone.

Beard had arrived a minute earlier. Inside the hideout, he'd peeled off to talk to his men, who were posted around the interior, looking out. Lucas, White, and Sherwood headed for the kitchen. They passed Bernie, who was lying on the living room couch, forearm across his eyes. He sobbed once, and then they were in the kitchen. Leonid was nowhere to be seen.

Masha was still on the blood-soaked floor, a tall woman gone small in death, curled up in a fetal position; she looked crumpled, like a paper wad. A butcher-shop odor hung in the kitchen. Sherwood stepped past her, apparently unaffected by the body and blood, looked at a cabinet hit by the slug after it went through Masha's head, and lined it up with a bullet hole in the kitchen window.

"Right in the direction of that big black tree?" he asked.

"Cottonwood, yeah." Lucas wouldn't look directly at Masha, a life gone to waste. He kept his neck bent away as he looked out the window and said, "That's about right. Let's go check it out. We saw where they came out of the woods, there's enough snow that we should be able to follow their tracks back to where they were set up. Don't think there'll be much to see."

"We gotta look," White said. "Maybe somebody dropped a matchbook from the bar they hang out at."

Sherwood frowned at her, then shrugged: "Marshals are weird," he said.

"We get that way," Lucas agreed. "Let's go."

They walked out the driveway and Lucas saw pencil-thin rims of Masha's blood coming off Sherwood's left shoe. They turned left up the street and White said to Sherwood, "You didn't seem all that upset by the shooting."

"If I'd been hit, I would have been," Sherwood said.

White persisted: "But you've seen shot-up people before."

"Oh, yeah. You know. It was a war."

"Iraq?"

"Some, earlier on. Then some in Afghanistan and Pakistan, and then later, some more time in Syria."

"I know a CIA sniper who used to go through there," Lucas said.

"What's his name?" Sherwood asked, curious.

"It's a her, though she won't admit to being with the CIA. She works with an Unspecified Agency. Barbara Cartwright."

"Wow. I know Barb, a bit." Sherwood laughed, shook his head. "She's a piece of work. She's got a legend going. How did you hook up with her?"

"Met her out in Taos, New Mexico, during that virus hassle," Lucas said.

"You're not the guy . . . There was a marshal who had a daughter . . ."

"Yeah, that's me," Lucas said. "Me and my daughter Letty."

"Didn't know that, and I should have," Sherwood said. "Wasn't in my backgrounder package. You guys did a nice job out there."

"Lucas certainly thinks so," White said. "His head was the size of a fuckin' watermelon, until he had to start doing regular marshal stuff again."

"Barb about burned down the Albuquerque airport, as I hear it," Sherwood said. "We were all pretty proud of her, the amount of damage she did."

"Two million bucks' worth of cars and trucks, up in smoke," Lucas said. "Didn't do the parking garage any good, either. I understand they've been working on the third floor ever since."

"TRACKS," WHITE SAID, pointing into a shallow roadside ditch. To Sherwood, she said, "That's not really a heavy-duty coat you got there. That's a fashion coat. Aren't you cold?"

"No."

"Why not?"

"I don't allow it." He didn't smile.

White had no response to that, and kept her mouth shut.

THE TRACKS LED back into the woods between the Sokolov house and the next one up the circle. They followed through the trees and around the brush, and Lucas pointed out White's and his own tracks where they crossed the sniper's and the spotter's.

They were close to one of the other houses, and a man shouted at them, "Hey! What are you guys doing?"

White shouted back, "U.S. Marshals. Go back inside."

"Did you shoot someone?"

"No."

"We heard a gunshot. A bunch of gunshots."

"All done now. Go back inside. Don't come out here, a crime scene crew is on its way. If you mess up a crime scene, you go to jail."

The man retreated, muttering.

THE SHOOTERS HAD been following a game trail in the thin snow, frozen leaves crisp underfoot like potato chips, and walking to one side of the trail, the three of them found the sniper's nest quickly enough.

The gunman had set up behind a fallen tree and had used a hand-sized black sandbag on the trunk to steady the rifle. The sandbag was still in place. Three holes in the snow, and elbow and knee prints, marked the spot where the spotting scope had been mounted on a tripod.

"He's a good shot," Sherwood said, looking down toward the hide-out. "Threaded that slug over and under quite a bit of brush."

"They were in and out in a hurry," White said, looking at the setup. "No snow melt where the shooter's legs were, or the spotter's knees. They came, they saw, they shot, they ran."

"Which makes me think about a drone again," Sherwood said, looking up at the sky. "Overhead's pretty thin. Maybe it'd be too high to be heard. It spots our SUVs coming in and that triggers the shooters. They were here in what, fifteen minutes? They knew where they were going and exactly how long it would take to get here, where they would go in the woods. They did all that even though they couldn't know that we'd be late arriving."

Lucas nodded and said, "Brass," and pointed. "Don't touch anything."

Sherwood and White looked at the end of a rifle shell protruding from the snow near the log. Lucas bent over it, close enough to see the stamp on the case head, stood up and said, "Huh. Says .277, never heard of it. There's another shell over there, so it's a semiauto, at least."

"That's the new Army rifle," Sherwood said. "Rare gun, at this point. I guess some of them are getting out to the public, a civilian version. If it'd been a stolen Army rifle, they could have hosed down the whole kitchen and we'd all be dead."

"The American Army, you mean, not Russian," Lucas said.

"Yeah. You can touch the shell, if you want to look at it. This won't be a basic police investigation, looking at a trial," Sherwood said. "These people are not the kind to surrender. It'll come to a bloody end, or if they manage to exfiltrate, nothing at all. We're locking down private jets, by the way. Nothing moves in or out of the local airports without a complete inspection. Wherever they are, they're going by car. They'll have to do something about their wounded."

"I'll leave the shells for the crime scene people—you can never tell what's going to happen. By the way, you also ought to lock down some U.S. Marshal cell phones," Lucas said. "If they were tipped by one of the marshals here, it would have had to be by a cell phone."

"Yes, I thought of that, and we will do that," Sherwood said. He looked through the woods to the house and said, "This was a nice op, up to the point where you two ran down the driveway and shot them up. That shouldn't have happened. The driver should have been covering them with an automatic weapon, just in case. She didn't."

"You sound disappointed," White said.

"You learn from the mistakes of the dead and wounded," Sherwood said, like a classroom professor. "Somebody didn't think this through, not quite well enough. They didn't think about the Marshal's Service and all the guns you people carry. I'd be more impressed by the hitters if you two were dead at the end of the driveway."

"Thanks," White said.

"Didn't say I'd be happy; just impressed," Sherwood said.

NOT HAPPY, JUST impressed. Lucas felt a finger of the depression ghost stroking his brain. He'd been close to two high-powered rifle slugs, hadn't been hit, but had seen the blood spraying across the hideout's kitchen, had thought for an instant that a friend had been hit—White still showed streaks of blood on her parka. If it got worse, he'd be on the meds again. He hated them, but clinical depression was a real thing, and not his friend.

It wasn't a coincidence, because White was feeling the same finger: she asked: "You okay?"

"Yeah. Sorta getting on some hate."

LUCAS'S PHONE RANG and he took it out. He recognized the 9-1-1 operator's voice when she said, "We found your Subaru, but you're not going to like it."

"Where is it?"

"I understand it's in a little lane up by Barret's Pond. Abandoned. No cameras nearby. No way to walk out of there, I'm told, so it looks like there was a third car picking them up. More blood in the Subaru."

"Gimme the address. We'll head up there." Lucas took down the address, and after a last look around, they started walking back to the house. The sky was turning darker, and the cold was getting stronger.

SHERWOOD: "BEFORE WE leave here . . . I have to ask for your phones."

White: "Aw, man, we're the ones who lit them up."

"If one of you is hard enough to be running this op, maybe that's what you would have been told to do." He held up his hands, to fend off objections: "I don't really believe that, because you guys didn't have to run out there as quick as you did. A little slower and they'd have been gone. But I have to ask for your phones as part of the routine. If I didn't, how would I explain that to everybody else? I need all the phones."

"Including yours," Lucas said. "You should call a neutral agency like the Bureau of Criminal Apprehension over in Saint Paul. They can take the phones apart as fast as you guys or the FBI and start an hour from now. Beard or one of the other marshals can help you take the phones over to Saint Paul, so they'll never be alone with one guy."

Sherwood nodded: "Let's get it done."

White asked, "What am I going to do without my phone? My life's in there. My kids might call."

"Burners," Lucas and Sherwood said together, and Sherwood continued: "We'll pay for them. Get you good ones."

"I'll need to open my contact list so I can copy down phone numbers," White said. "I don't know the phone number of a single person, except my husband's."

"We can do that," Sherwood said. "We'll all do it together. Watching each other."

"You're a suspicious sonofabitch," White said.

"My mother would agree," Sherwood said. "The woman you just referenced."

AT THE HOUSE, Beard told Sherwood that the surviving Sokolovs had been temporarily moved to the second floor, with a marshal at the top of the stairs, and others covering the doors.

Sherwood told Beard that he wanted all the phones. "I'm not giving up my phone. I need to stay in touch with my office," Beard argued. "This is a disaster, and you want—"

"I don't just want, I'm demanding. If you need the head of the Marshals Service to tell you so, he will," Sherwood said.

"You go ahead and do that, John," Beard said, moving closer to Sherwood. He was still reacting to the murder and wanted to punch somebody. Anybody.

Lucas said, "Easy there, Derrick."

Sherwood didn't back up. "I don't want to see anyone on a phone. You need to think about this, Derrick: everybody here is a suspect in a major security breach. Anyone who doesn't give up his phone voluntarily and right now will have his life stripped down to his grade-school days. Oh, and the phones will include mine. Lucas, you come with me, I want you to witness me making a call."

Lucas and Sherwood stepped aside, and Sherwood made the call: "Yes, we're still on the scene but I've got a problem . . ."

He talked for two minutes, said "yes" a couple of times.

TEN MINUTES LATER, Beard took a call, listened, and said, at the end, "I understand. I'll do it, but I'm not happy about it." He clicked off—or the person on the other end of the call did—and Beard said to Sherwood, "I didn't really think you would do that, John."

Sherwood: "Finding the leak is more important than Leonid or his kid or his dead wife. Somebody, who is very well placed, is talking to the Russians. We need to know who."

Beard waved his arm to take in the house and said, "All these men are longtime marshals. The newest one has ten years in. They're not talking to any Russians."

"Derrick, I believe you," Sherwood said. "But the possibility has to be looked at. Now. Lucas suggests that we turn the phones over to state investigators because they can start pulling calls immediately. My boss said he will arrange for the FBI office here to pick them up, and then either fly the phones to Washington, or, in consultation with Washington, turn them over to the local people who, I'm told, are competent. The government will buy you all burner phones. In the meantime, no calls. We'll get some notepaper together and you can start taking down the phone numbers of your important contacts, if you haven't memorized them . . ."

Sherwood collected phones from all the pissed-off marshals, then made them more unhappy by having the marshals pat down each other for hidden phones. No one had one, and none were found in a search of the four vehicles—the two brought by the Marshal's Service, plus those belonging to Lucas and White.

"You know what?" White said. "If one of us . . . any of us . . . made a call, it would have been done on a burner just before you guys left the airport, and that phone was ditched one minute later."

"I'll talk to the FBI about searching the area where we came in, along with all the trash cans along the way," Sherwood said. "I assume nobody saw anyone throw anything out a car window?"

Nobody had.

TWO FBI AGENTS showed up, collected the phones but said that they didn't know what would be done with them.

Sherwood: "I don't care who looks at the outgoing calls, the locals or your Washington people, but it has to be fast. As fast as possible. If you need somebody to emphasize that to your AIC, I can have somebody in Washington call him. Or her."

"Got it," one of the feds said.

When it was all sorted, Beard said, "It's unlikely that the Russians would have two separate hit teams, but I want my guys to bundle up the Sokolovs in a secure place, a different place. One that we can defend, if necessary, until we get a plane here. Then I want them back in Washington, to wherever you've had them stashed for the last year."

"That we can agree on," Sherwood said. "It won't happen as quickly as you hope. I need to make some further arrangements. I suspect the Sokolovs will be here for another day or two, at least. We have a body to deal with, for one thing. And Derrick—it won't be your guys providing the security. My boss is already talking to the FBI about a full SWAT squad. You guys protect them here, and the feds will pick them up in an armored vehicle. They'll have arranged a place to hide them."

"My guys stand around with their dicks in their hands?"

"If they find that amusing or comforting," Sherwood said. "Yes."

WHITE KNEW A nearby Best Buy store that they could hit for burner phones. Lucas, White, and Sherwood went to get them, and since Sherwood offered to pay for them, they bought the best phones and the most minutes, exchanged numbers, and started making calls before they got to the parking lot.

Lucas said to White, "We should go look at that Subaru."

"Probably nothing to look at."

"We should go anyway," Lucas said.

"Then, if anyone asks, you can say you did, and you won't have some little weasel rolling his eyes because you didn't," Sherwood said.

"You are wise in the ways of bureaucracy," White said. To Lucas: "Let's go get your car, and I'll follow you over."

Sherwood said, "Stay in touch."

"What are you gonna do?" Lucas asked.

"Probably piss off Beard some more," Sherwood said.

4

Abramova was working on Nikitin's neck wound; Nikitin sat without a sound and without flinching. He'd been hurt before, and whining and flinching didn't help anything, so he didn't.

Titov had gone back out to the Jeep to get his laptop: "I have to go online. Research."

"You won't become a doctor fast enough," Nikitin said.

"I don't need to be a doctor. I need to find the right one," Titov said. He asked, and Nikitin and Orlov said their blood types were O-positive and A-positive.

Orlov was nearly as pale as the sheet he was lying on, and said, "For me, you need this doctor soon. God damn those American shooters."

"We need some pills," Abramova said to Titov. They had ten opiate tabs. She gave Orlov three, with a bit of water; and asked Nikitin what he needed: "I'll try one. We should save them for Mat."

Abramova patted him on the shoulder: "Good man."

"Let me search for a hospital," Titov said.

TITOV WAS LOOKING for a nearby but out-of-the-way hospital with an emergency room. He found it in the small city of Bison, twenty miles to the north, explaining what he was doing as he reviewed Google photos of the emergency room exterior. He'd never done what he was about to recommend, but he'd talked through the possibility with his Russian trainers, in case one of his on-the-run clients needed help.

Abramova had cleaned the wound in her ear as best she could, washing it with alcohol and wrapping a piece of QuikClot around it. As she pulled her hair down to cover the bandage, she noticed that she actually had a kind of hole in her hair, where the slug had gone through. Four inches to the left, and she'd have been dead.

When she'd done as much as she could, she went into the bedroom to the gear bag and removed two Beretta 93R machine pistols. They were older weapons, but effective. They didn't look much like ordinary pistols—there were two thirty-round extended magazines for each pistol, with a foregrip under the muzzle. The accessories added to their apparent threat, as anyone who'd seen a John Wick movie would know.

Along with the Berettas, she picked up the roll of gaffer tape and carried it all out to the living room. Titov said, "Look at these pictures . . ."

She bent over him to look at Google satellite images of a lakeside hospital with its parking lots and entrance to the emergency room, and more images taken from the ground, and two taken from inside the room.

"I don't see cameras," she said.

"They will be there, they always are," he said. "Not as bad as London, yet, but it's getting there. They will get pictures of you, but we can't have pictures of the Jeep. Both Minneapolis and the local sheriffs use license-plate readers, both fixed and mobile, and the sheriff's department has facial recognition tech. We need to keep our faces covered."

"You are correct."

By the time they were ready, Orlov was sleeping, snoring, or perhaps was simply unconscious, and Titov said, "Good. We go thirty-two kilometers north, to a place called Bison. We should be back in an hour and a half." He was poking an address into his iPhone. "We are programmed."

"Luck," muttered a sleepy-eyed Nikitin, as he sank back on the sheet and tried to get comfortable. And, "Good speed."

THE TWO OF them walked out to the Jeep, each one with a gun, heavy in their hands; the cold wind like a slap on their faces. A dark starless bitter night. A weather app said temperatures would drop below zero, with wind to fifteen miles an hour.

"Watch for ice," Abramova said, when they'd settled into the Jeep. She pulled on a ski mask, rolled up as a watch cap. "We don't need to fall into a ditch."

"When we get there, you will walk in, look for cameras," Titov said, pulling on his own cap.

"Yes."

"And we keep the phones live, all the time that we are there," Titov said.

"Yes. Crazy American shooters. This should not have happened."

"Shit happens," Titov said. "I once had a tee-shirt that said this."

"I have to say, you have been very good, Melor. I was not certain of you," Abramova said.

"It's what I do for a living, but this shooting—not so much," Titov said. "I can pretend, but you have to be the operator at the hospital. You have to be the frightener."

"This is what *I* do for a living," she said, smiling across at him. She was a stress-seeker, and she knew it.

There weren't many house lights around—they were on a side road—and the night didn't get brighter until they got on the highway. A highway they soon left, heading north on more back roads.

The navigation system directed them through a thick, ice-fog gloom, and Titov had to be careful not to outrun his headlights. Individual houses and even small subdivisions were visible through the fog at some points, but with long stretches of stygian dark farmland between isolated lighted windows. The roads were clear, but narrow; Titov had chosen a back route because he could drive faster. He was good behind the wheel, but the fog was a problem. The navigation showed the trip as taking thirty minutes; they took thirty-five.

All along the way, they talked about the raid. This was not a specialty of the Unit, but they had enough training to have some confidence. If what Titov had read on the Internet was accurate, the hospital had only a small, limited emergency room, though it was open all night.

Ten minutes out, Abramova said, "When we do this again . . ."

Titov laughed and said, "I pray we should live so long."

Abramova didn't laugh: "When we do this again, we have local police radios in the gear bag."

"Ah. Yes. Next time."

And: "They cannot see our faces," Abramova said. "If we get a doctor, he cannot see our faces. If he does . . ."

"I don't want to do that," Titov said. He didn't want to kill the doctor.

"I don't either, but if we must. You are the concierge, I don't expect you to do the shooting."

THEY TALKED ABOUT the missed hit: "Lev said Sokolov tripped as he pulled the trigger, stumbled. He thinks he hit Masha. I don't know what to think," Abramova said.

"You might have to go back after him," Titov said "The marshals will probably evacuate them to Washington, now that Minneapolis is blown. Then, they'll be out of reach, at least for the time being."

"The marshals—they were fast. They didn't seek protection," Abramova said. "They attacked. Their reaction was excellent, as was their marksmanship. Good technique. I didn't have time to look at them carefully, but it's possible that one of them was a woman."

"You sound as though you approve."

"Well, you know . . . they are in the same business as we are." After another moment, she asked, "Is there more heat on the floor? My feet are freezing."

"Let me . . ." Titov reached over and adjusted a vent to blow heated air down to her feet.

"I would prefer to hit them again, if we can do it with a reasonable risk profile," Abramova said, resuming the discussion. "You know . . . for reasons of status."

"Not up to us," Titov said. "We can't do anything without intelligence."

"The intelligence so far has been very good. Very good. One stumble has kept us from completing the mission."

"One stumble and five bullets," Titov said. "How is the ear?"

"Bearable. Nothing, really."

THE CITY OF Bison was a satellite of the Twin Cities, fifteen or twenty thousand people in a growing suburban area. Though not large, it had a regional hospital built on the shore of Casimer Lake. The town was diffuse, built around two lakes, large lots and small jumbled together, older homes around the lakes, newer houses scattered across the rolling countryside, all of it heavily wooded.

They had to drive through a densely populated area to get to the hospital, where they followed road signs off the highway, and along side streets to the emergency room. Titov stopped on the shoulder of the closest side street, behind a clump of evergreens, and said, "Call me now."

Abramova did that, and when they were both live on the phones, Titov said, "Look for cameras. I will come as soon as you summon me."

"Don't forget the tape," Abramova said.

Titov patted his jacket pocket. "Got it. You go."

ABRAMOVA CHECKED HER Beretta, pulled the ski mask down, so nothing showed but her eyes, and climbed out of the Jeep. On the short walk up the street to the driveway that led to the emergency room entrance, she may have spent five seconds wondering what crooked path had gotten her here, in the middle of the United States, on a night as cold as Moscow, with a gun in her hand.

If she did have that five seconds of introspection, it didn't linger with her, because what had gotten her here, out of the Army and into the Unit, was the ability to focus on the critical problems.

The emergency room was located at the top of a gentle rise, which was occupied by an expansive parking lot. A cube-shaped glass entry area protruded out from the main entrance doors, with a separate ambulance entrance several meters to the left. Near the emergency entrance, two dark-glass camera housings hung from a corner of the building, looking like suspended eggplants.

She walked straight over to the cameras and fired a burst of three shots into each housing. The shots were loud, but not as loud as an unsuppressed gun. As the glass shattered, she ran over to the cubicle. No cameras. She said into the live phone, "Come now."

Two seconds later she was inside the emergency room with the gun up, scanning for signs of resistance. Three women in tan scrubs stood open-mouthed behind a counter and she said, not loud, but loud enough, "Nobody should move or call for help. If you do, I will shoot you."

Another woman came in from a back hall, didn't see Abramova at once, asked, "What was—"

Then she saw Abramova, who waved the pistol at her and said, "Come in here. If you don't, I will shoot you."

One of the women behind the desk said, "Take the drugs."

Abramova said, "You must listen to me. If you have a way to alert the police, do not do it. We will kill the police." She held up the machine pistol. "You will see that this is a machine gun, and your police will have no way to defeat it. Also, some of you will die in the shooting. We will be gone in ten or fifteen minutes and you will all be safe again."

Titov came in then, masked, gun up, and said, "Stay," and went down a hallway into the back. A moment later, he returned, herding two women and a man, all in scrubs. He flicked a finger at one of the women and said, "Doctor, I am told."

"Good," Abramova said. "Everybody but the doctor, behind the counter, and sit on the floor. Doctor, we need operating instruments, we need O-positive and A-positive blood, painkillers, anesthetics, and antiseptics, for a trauma operation. Gather them."

"I'm not a surgeon . . . and we don't have any A-positive."

"Do you have a surgeon here?"

"No, we could call one."

"No time," Titov said. "You are what we have."

Abramova pushed the doctor into the back room at gunpoint, careful not to get too close. Although she was female, the doctor appeared to be strong, and even tough, with a square chin and high blunt cheekbones. "You will be dealing with two men, both with gunshot wounds . . ."

Five minutes: three fridge packs of O-negative—universal donor blood—plus surgical instruments jumbled in a stainless operating pan, a sack full of drugs, packs of syringes and bandages and needles, a rack to hang the blood on, all scooped into an oversized plastic garbage bag.

Back out front, Titov had six people sitting on the floor. He had awkwardly bound their ankles together with the duct tape. When

Abramova and the doctor returned from the scavenger hunt, he handed the doctor the roll of tape and said, "Tape their hands behind their backs."

"Don't hurt us . . ." One of the woman on the floor began to sob.

"If we were going to hurt you, we wouldn't be taping you up," Abramova said impatiently. The doctor bound the hands of the six people on the floor, with Titov supervising. When that was done, Titov grabbed a parka that was hanging on the back of a chair and said, "Put this on. It's cold out there. Hurry. Hurry." When she had it on, he taped her hands behind her back and Abramova pulled a ski mask over her head, backwards, so she couldn't see.

"I will lead you outside," she said. "Behave and you will be safe."

WHEN THE TWO women were out the door, Titov said to the people on the floor, "Our car is coming in one minute, maybe two, maybe three. I will be in the glass shelter, watching and waiting. If I see people get up, I will shoot them in the head. Lay there for five more minutes, maybe ten, and we will be gone." He spoke with a deliberately heavy Russian accent.

A minute later, Abramova waved him out and Titov called to her, so the people inside could hear, "Tell him to hurry. We have been here too long. Tell him to drive faster . . ." He turned and called inside, "Please use patience. Our vehicle will come soon." More Russian accent, thinking about the future.

Then he slipped out the door, into the Jeep, and they were rolling silently backward, the engine off, down the sloping driveway to the street. There, he started the engine, and Abramova, looking at a map on her phone, said, "Go that way . . . and go that way . . ." Pointing with a finger, no hints for the doctor lying on the floor of the back seat.

Thirty-odd klicks back to the safe house. They passed one police car as they were passing through a small town. The patrol car was going in the opposite direction in the night; the cop saved his own life by continuing on.

5

White followed Lucas to the pond where the Subaru had been left. A police car was blocking access to the boat ramp. They pulled in, and an Orono cop lit them up with a flashlight. They got out of their cars, identified themselves, and the cop took them back into the ramp, pointing out two different sets of vehicle tracks.

"Nothing's been down this ramp probably since October. It's mostly for canoes, the water is about three feet deep," he said. "Not much in the way of fish."

"They must have been familiar with the place," White said. "How would you even know it was here if you weren't?"

"Could have scouted it with a satellite view," the cop said.

"They must have done some ground truthing, here, so they must have known where Sokolov was going, probably for days or weeks ahead of time. The leak has gotta be in D.C.," Lucas said to White. To the cop: "Is there blood in the Subaru?"

"Yeah, quite a bit on the back seat, unless somebody spilled ketchup on their home fries," the cop said. "The car that was parked here was probably empty. Doesn't seem likely there was another person waiting . . ."

Lucas: "How'd you figure that out?"

"Well, the word is, there were four people at the motel," the cop said. He pointed. "You can see the tracks from the incoming Subaru, so the other tracks are from the second vehicle, which was parked here for a while. Long enough for the motor heat to melt the snow underneath. Looking at the short wheelbase, it's not a pickup, but it has very aggressive tread. I'd say either a Jeep Wrangler or maybe a Bronco. Probably a Jeep Wrangler. Big enough for four, but not for five, not comfortably."

White: "Why a Wrangler?"

"Because it leaked oil while it was parked here," the cop said. "I figure that made it more likely a Jeep than a Bronco."

"You're a smart guy," Lucas told the cop.

"Yeah, and I'm looking for a better job," the cop said. "That was a hint, in case you didn't get it."

"We got it," White said. "I don't suppose anybody from your department is following the little oil drops to their new location?"

"Very funny," the cop said. "Anyhooo . . ."

White: "I've got some gloves in my car. We'll want to take a look inside the Subaru in case there's anything . . ."

"Your call," the cop said. "The BCA crime scene van is supposedly on the way. There are foot tracks around the Subaru, but mostly on this side, so maybe you'll want to go around to the other. Only one set of foot tracks over there, besides mine. I used my flash to look inside to see if there were any bodies. Nada."

WHITE GOT GLOVES from her truck. They opened the doors of the Subaru and, using the cop's flashlight, looked inside without touching anything. There was blood, but no rental papers. Lazy snowflakes were drifting down when they finished. They closed the door and carefully backed away.

Lucas asked the cop if he could hang around until a crime scene crew got there to process the car. "Somebody will. I'll make sure."

"Thank you."

White looked up at the starless sky and said, "Wasn't supposed to snow."

"It won't," Lucas said, with more confidence than certainty. "That's just cold flakes, the cold is squeezing out whatever water is left in the air."

"Hope you're right," White said. She was in the winter stance again, and shivering. "We're outa here, heading home?"

"I am," Lucas said. "There'll be a clusterfuck tomorrow. Get some sleep while you can."

"See you at the office," she said.

As she walked away to her truck, Lucas got a card from the cop they'd been talking to and told him that he'd give it to the U.S. Marshal for the district of Minnesota.

"You think I got a chance?" the cop asked.

"You got a chance," Lucas said.

LUCAS HAD ALREADY talked to his wife, Weather, twice, filling her in on his day. Back in his car, he called her again. "What have we got to eat?"

"We've already eaten here. Hit a drive-through on your way back. I'll be streaming *The Perfect Couple.* Sam's down the basement and wants some privacy for his study session with Ellen. Your daughter is in the middle of an end-of-days sulk because I wouldn't let her go to the mall, so . . ."

"Did Sam take a book down the basement with him?"

"I didn't notice one. He did take two Cokes," Weather said. "I'm washing enough nocturnal emissions out of his Jockey shorts that I doubt he'd have anything to spare for Ellen."

"God, women can be so vulgar," Lucas said.

"I'm sure your mother did the same for you. Go get a sandwich."

"As a much-needed alert . . . I did have enough to spare. Keep an eye out. We don't need Sam knocking up any teenagers."

"I'll wait until somebody moans."

LUCAS STOPPED AT a pizza place that might once have been a gas station, which was confirmed by the menu—he ordered a twelve-inch El Camino—and after a wait, got halfway through the pizza when the burner rang in his jacket pocket.

He found it, answered, and Sherwood said, "I apologize for the interruption in whatever you're doing . . ."

"I'm eating a pizza. What happened?"

"Our Russians hit an emergency room in the town of Bison, if you know where that is?"

"Know it like the back of my hand," Lucas said. He didn't, but he'd once had an informant who lived there, and he'd visited a few times. "Kill anyone?"

"No, but they kidnapped a doctor and took drugs, blood, and surgical equipment with them, and disappeared, to where, we don't know. If you have time . . . I'm calling from a rental car, I'm on the way there myself."

"I can be there in forty-five minutes or maybe an hour . . ."

"I wouldn't bother you, but you're local and the FBI people I've been talking to . . . they're not local."

"See you in a bit."

Lucas got a box for the remaining pizza along with a dozen napkins and called Weather to tell her what had happened. He ate the congealing slices of pizza at stoplights along the way, a napkin tucked behind his necktie.

The land around the lakes west of Minneapolis was low, marshy, with cattail swamps in the roadside ditches, narrow highways, half-seen barely lit small-town water towers floating like flying saucers in the night sky. He crossed the Crow River at a town which was called, for some reason, Rockford; shouldn't it be called Crowford? But then, maybe the riverbed was rocky? He'd been through the town a half-dozen times, and never stopped to solve the mystery, because he really wasn't that interested in it.

He was even less interested in thinking about the shooting earlier in the day, the blood spatter on White, Martha's brains on the kitchen cupboards. He thought about it anyway and experienced no revelations. He made it to the hospital in forty-five minutes.

Two black SUV cop cars, a highway patrol car, two plain vanilla sedans with micro-flashers that looked like FBI transportation, and two civilian compact SUVs were in the parking lot. A uniformed cop checked Lucas through, and he parked and walked up to the glassed-in entry cubicle.

SHERWOOD WAS STANDING inside the emergency room, talking to a couple of suits, without any apparent urgency; Lucas assumed they were feds. Sherwood saw Lucas coming and crooked a finger at him. "FBI is covering the kidnapping, but so far, we don't have anywhere to go. We thought maybe the doc had her phone with her and we could find her that way, but she didn't: her phone's laying on the floor in the back along with a pager."

"We might be looking for a Jeep Wrangler that's dripping oil," Lucas said. "That's all I got, and I'm not sure of that."

"Could confirm another sighting," Sherwood said. "A guy walking a dog saw a black Jeep Wrangler turning out onto the street, in a big hurry, about the time of the attack."

"So where are you looking?" Lucas asked.

"Everywhere, but there just aren't a lot of patrol cars out in the countryside, and there seem to be a lot of Jeeps. Every one of them we stop takes ten minutes, because we have to be so careful on the stop," one of the feds said. He had a half-empty paper cup of coffee in his hand that he was pecking at.

"The hit on the Sokolovs was what, fifteen, twenty miles south of here?" Lucas said. "When they ran, initially, when Shelly and I shot them up, they were headed further south. The Subaru was ditched even further south, on an unused trail down to a frozen-over pond, where they transferred to the Jeep. I'll bet that wherever they went, it wasn't too far from the Subaru. They'd want to get off the street as fast as they could."

The second fed said, "Good points. We alerted all the major jurisdictions around the big lake, Orono, Minnetonka, Wayzata, the county sheriffs . . . but it's a lot of territory."

"Tell him the bad news," Sherwood said.

The feds both shrugged. One of them asked, "What?"

Sherwood: "I did the numbers. The hunt got started a half hour after they left here. The people they had on the floor, the nurses, didn't get moving for maybe fifteen minutes, then it took five minutes for the first cops to arrive, and then they had to talk it over and decide what to do. They didn't even know about the shooting at the house this afternoon, so the hunt was local, right around here. By the time it got expanded toward Minneapolis, might have been an hour."

"Well, poop," Lucas said. "Let me . . ." He took out his phone, punched in a number, and ten seconds later said, "Hey, Frankie, is Virgil there? Well, go get him. He can type later. I only need him for a minute."

He waited, then said, "Virgie. Got some people running, had a thirty-minute lead. What's the circle? Yeah? Yeah. Yeah. Thanks."

Off the phone, Lucas said, "That was a friend who works down in southern Minnesota. He has lots of incidents in the countryside where people are running, but nobody knows which direction. He says with a thirty-minute head start, a runner could be anywhere in about a seven-hundred-square-mile area. Doesn't sound reasonable, but it is."

"So we're screwed," Sherwood said.

"Well, we gotta think that the hit crew is not totally familiar with the country around here, because they didn't plan on visiting this hospital. I have to believe that they'd be using a navigation app. If I were you, I'd put in a route search between here and the Orono city hall. I'd bet they'd be along there somewhere. After Orono, I dunno. They could be anywhere after that."

One of the feds said, "Hell, they could be in Des Moines."

"I don't think so. They got to the Sokolov house in fifteen minutes. They've got a safe house around there somewhere and they've got three wounded to take care of."

The feds looked at each other, and one of them said to the other, "Let's get on that," and to Lucas, "That's a good thought, sir."

"Are you going to steal credit for thinking of that?" Lucas asked.

The fed nodded: "That was my plan."

Lucas looked at Sherwood and said, "That's not something you see every day. A fed with a sense of humor."

"THAT'S ABOUT ALL we got," Sherwood said. "The people here, they got nothing. They saw eyebrows on the woman and say she's white-blond and had an accent. The guy was burly and had a bigger accent. That's it."

Lucas took a phone call on the burner. All he had was an incoming number from the 703 area code, which he knew was Arlington, Virginia, because that's where the Marshals Service was headquartered.

"Davenport," he said.

"Lucas, this is Russ." Russell Forte, his nominal boss.

"Yeah, Russ."

"Man, I don't know how you do it, but I just took a call from the Director and he told me to call you and tell you that you're full-time on this, whatever it is, shooting. I don't even know what the hell I'm talking about."

Lucas filled him in and Forte said, "Okay, that clears up some of it. The Director got called by a deputy attorney general and *he* was called by somebody so important he shares a bathroom with Jesus Christ himself. So, be good, don't piss anyone off."

"You know I try. Not to piss anyone off."

"But you *fail* so often," Forte said. "Okay, not a discouraging word. Cold out there? Of course it is. Not too bad here. I'm going to bed. Good night."

THE HIGHWAY PATROLMAN was going out the door as Forte hung up and Sherwood came over and said, "The state patrol guy says there's a small town along that route south . . . and somebody might have noticed a Jeep going by. He's headed out there to knock on doors."

"If I've steered you wrong, I apologize in advance," Lucas said.

"You're the only guy who steered me at all. The feds over there . . ." He nodded at the two FBI agents, who were listening to a call on one of their phones. "They're mostly worried about fucking something up. I don't blame them: a high-profile kidnapping and they've got nothing. Now: tell me what else I can do."

"The only thing I can think of, and the 9-1-1 center may already have it working, is the Jeep. The first two cars, the Jeep we shot up and the Subaru, were both rentals from two different agencies. If this new Jeep is a rental, most rental cars have LoJacks, or something like it. We should check and see if anyone . . ."

"That's something the FBI can do right now," Sherwood said. "That's the kind of stuff they're good at."

He hurried off to the feds, who paused the phone call, listened to him, looked at Lucas, and went back to the phone. Sherwood listened for a moment, then came back to Lucas: "Okay. They were talking to the AIC so they'll see about the Jeep."

"If it is a Jeep," Lucas said. "Let me tell you how we decided it was a Jeep."

He told the story of the oil spot on the boat ramp, and, if not for the leak, how it might be fifty-fifty a Bronco.

Sherwood shook his head and said, "Rental agencies don't rent Broncos. I spend half my days in rentals, it's something I know about. Let's go outside and look for oil spots."

The driveway to the emergency room had been scraped clean after the last snowstorm, but just about where the kidnap car might have parked, they found an oil spot that was still sticky, despite the cold. "Could be," Lucas said.

Sherwood looked at the black oil stains on his fingertips. "God bless leaky Jeeps."

THEN THEY WAITED. Talked with the feds and the locals and the nurses and the hospital director and his wife, who'd been out to a barbeque joint when the trouble started. Lucas called Shelly White, told her everything that had happened, and that he'd keep her posted.

They were standing around, not doing much, and Sherwood said, "I like your overcoat. And your shoes. Though I didn't think those brown high-top boots you were wearing this afternoon really went with the suit."

"We don't speak of such things in Minnesota," Lucas said. "What happens in winter, stays in winter."

Sherwood: "So the suit. Figueroa and Prince? N Street?"

"How'd you know?"

Sherwood opened the front of his overcoat to show Lucas the label: Figueroa and Prince, a tailor shop on N Street in Washington. "I could see Pat's AMF stitching on the lapels, keeps the edges from rolling. I like that."

Lucas reached out and rubbed the fabric on Sherwood's overcoat: "Is that vicuna? I don't think I could afford one of those."

"We've got about six guys researching you. You could afford it."

"Why are you—"

"Because of the problem. We're researching everybody who was around that house today. And you're a very odd duck."

"That was always my ambition, to be recognized as a duck," Lucas said. "How much did you pay for the coat? Couldn't have been less than ten."

"It was less, and I got a deal on top of the regular price."

"Huh. I didn't know Figgy gave deals. So . . . how important are you, anyway? Calling up people, they're jumping to do whatever you say? Giving you deals on coats?"

Sherwood shrugged and said, "I dunno. I was involved with the Sokolovs from the start, recruiting him. That was a serious win, so I had the sun shining out of my ass for a while. The deputy ops director calls me John and I call him Frank, but I throw in a 'sir' every once in a while. But you . . . you have interesting connections in Washington. Some of them, even Frank would call 'sir.'"

"Ah . . . I know some people," Lucas admitted.

THEY DRANK COFFEE, which was awful and Lucas didn't like coffee even when it was good, and they talked about menswear—they were equally interested in fashion—and Lucas enjoyed the exchange. The mayor came over to Lucas and said, "Aren't you the guy who used to hang with Bill Norton? On that drug thing?"

"Yeah. How's Bill?"

"Dunno. He moved to Oklahoma to raise horses."

"And maybe some weed?"

"Could happen," the mayor said. "He always had the quality stuff, back before it was legal."

THEN THE HIGHWAY patrolman called and said he was with a cop named Fagerberg, in the town of Delano. Fagerberg said he had seen a black Jeep Wrangler going through town at about the right time. He knew it was a Wrangler because he desperately wanted one and had researched them; and he'd noticed it because it was traveling at the speed limit, which was not that common.

Sherwood thanked the patrolman.

Lucas knew where Delano was, and they pulled up a map on the fed's laptop and Lucas touched the screen with a fingernail. "Fastest route to Orono. If you drew a ten-mile circle around the Orono city hall, I bet the Jeep would be inside it."

The fed with a sense of humor said, "I believe you. I gotta call the office."

6

The doctor's name was Carolyn Juarez.

She was short, stocky, middle-thirties with black hair and eyes. Abramova pushed her on the floor of the back seat, and then sat impatiently clicking the Beretta's safety on and off until Titov came out and got behind the wheel. He let the Jeep roll backward down the sloping driveway to the street, where he started the engine and accelerated away.

Abramova turned in the front passenger seat and began talking to Juarez: "Now listen, doctor. Try to believe. We do not want to hurt you, but we will if we have to, if you try to harm us, or lead the police to us. Earlier today we tried to kill a man, but we failed. He is a demon. Any sane person would wish him dead. My team sometimes kills, but we are soldiers, not murderers. If we were, we would have killed the women at the hospital, because we could have, and it would have given us more time to get away. Do you understand?"

Juarez: "I understand what you said."

"But you don't know if you should believe us?"

Silence from Juarez.

"I'll tell you why you should believe us," Abramova said. "Because then you come out of this alive. These drugs you will give our friends, the painkillers—you could perhaps give one of them, a . . . Овердо́з." She turned to Titov: "What do you call it?"

"Hot shot," Titov said.

"Yes." Back to Juarez. "You could give one of them or both of them a hot shot, but we will know that, of course. Then we will kill you as punishment for killing our friends. Now ask yourself, do you wish to be walking around alive tomorrow or the next day, or do you want to be dead?"

Silence.

"You don't have to answer us," Abramova said. "You should think about those options. As I say, we are soldiers, not murderers."

JUAREZ LAY UNCOMFORTABLY on the Jeep's floor between the front and back seats. She kept trying to think of what she could do to resist, but nothing occurred to her. She'd managed to look at her watch just before the hood was pulled over her eyes and tried to count the turns the Jeep made, but she quickly lost track, both of the number and direction.

She made one decision: she would believe them when they said she wouldn't be killed. She'd cooperate, but she'd try to remember every single thing she could about her captors and her environment. If she survived, she would give as much as she could to the police. An occasional glimpse of the watch could be important.

THEY WENT SOUTH in a hurry, anticipating a police search for the Jeep. There was virtually no traffic. They passed through a small city, had to jog to follow the track laid down by the iPhone's navigation system. At one point, a patrolling police car passed them going in the opposite direction but never slowed down. Out of the town, Titov jumped on the gas again. The driving conditions had improved, the fog was beginning to dissipate, and they made it back in less than half an hour.

At the farmhouse, Abramova ran up the front steps and stuck her head inside. "Okay?"

Nikitin said, "Except for the bullet holes."

She walked back to the car and she and Titov pulled Juarez out the back seat and walked her, still blind, up to the narrow porch.

"Careful, there are steps . . . Your toes are at the first step, step up now . . ."

Inside, Nikitin had moved himself to a couch, where he was lying face down, leaving behind a white sheet with a thumb-sized blood spot. He lifted his head and tried to smile at them as they came through the door with Juarez. Orlov was asleep, but not deeply.

Abramov said, "Masks."

Nikitin had his ski mask, which he pulled over his head. Abramova got Orlov's mask from his coat pocket, and as she tried to pull it over his head, he roused, and groaned, and said, in Russian, "This sucks."

When all four Russians were masked, Titov helped Juarez free her hands and get out of her parka, and said, "I'm going to pull the ski mask off."

He did that, and Juarez blinked down at the man on the floor, who was wrapped in a blanket. "He is hurt the worst," Abramova said.

Juarez knelt next to him and peeled off the blanket. Beneath it, Orlov was still partly dressed, though his clothes had been shredded around the wounds. He was more awake now, and he said, "I worry. I don't hurt enough. Maybe I die."

"Shut up, we have the doctor to help," Abramova said.

Juarez: "Help me get his clothes off, the rest of the way off."

"We have more clothes, it'd be easier to cut them loose," Abramova said, and she flicked out her switchblade, which made Juarez flinch. She cut Orlov's clothes from neckline to pants cuffs and peeled them off a piece at a time. Juarez took a moment to examine the entry wounds, then took his blood pressure, grunted, said, "Huh."

Next, she moved his leg, and found it still articulating—no broken bones, though there might be nerve damage. Orlov was too disoriented to answer questions about it. She rolled him a bit, with Abramova's help, and pressed on his abdomen with her fingers, moving her hand around, groping, then sat back on her heels.

"I can't help enough here. If we do nothing, he will die by morning, of shock and blood loss, depending on what's happening inside," she said. "If I give him blood, painkillers, and antibiotics, he might live for four or five days and then die of sepsis. If you can get him to a good surgeon, then maybe he will live a normal life span."

Titov: "Why can't you—"

"I'm not a surgeon," Juarez said. "Here's what I can do: the wounds in his buttocks aren't serious, except for the blood loss. The bullet that hit his back is very serious. Not as serious as if it hit his liver or spleen, in which case he would have already bled to death, or his spine, which could have crippled him. The problem is, it apparently hit his bowel. I believe I can feel the slug, the bullet, with my fingers—it nearly passed through him. Bowel resection is a mess. If I tried to do it, I'd kill him. He'd be dead in two hours."

Abramova: "What is our best course?"

Nikitin, an outspoken atheist, said, "We could try prayer."

Juarez ignored him. "Your best course is to take him to a surgeon."

"We obviously have a problem . . ."

Juarez: "You said you wouldn't kill me if I actually can help you."

"We will not," Abramova said.

"Then, if I were you, I would take him to a big public hospital and roll him out the car door in the emergency room parking lot and leave him there," Juarez said. She looked down at Orlov, who was looking up at her with eyes that seemed fogged over. "Big-city hospitals might have several gunshot wounds every night. Hennepin Medical Center, downtown, would work. A place like Kansas City, where I was a resident, the people who were shot would sometimes say not a word. Not a word. No ID on them, no telephone, no nothing. It's not against the law to get shot, so if a man is not talking, the police have more important things to worry about. They assume it's down to drugs or gangs and that they'll never find out what happened. The hospital does the surgery, and a week or two later, the man walks out of the hospital. The only name the hospital knows is the one they gave him. We'd name our cases after towns: John Denver. John Miami, John Nashville, just so we'd know who we were talking about when we reviewed their cases."

Titov: "What can you do now?"

"Plug the holes, put pressure on them," Juarez said. "Give him blood, for the blood he has lost. Give him a course of antibiotics. I have painkillers. If he doesn't get to a surgeon . . . four days, maybe five."

"We will think on this," Abramova said.

They took the medical gear out of the garbage sack, set up a rack, and began transfusing blood.

That underway, Juarez turned to Nikitin, looked at the wounds in his buttocks and asked, "Can you walk?"

"Yes."

"Any grinding, any catches in your walk?"

"No, but it hurts. A lot."

"Of course it does, you've been shot. Like being hit by a baseball bat, it's no joke," Juarez said. She spent a minute manipulating his legs, testing them for bone breaks, then, satisfied, said, "You've been lucky."

"This kind of luck, I should not have it every day," Nikitin said.

Juarez examined the wound on his neck, a groove that passed just under the skin above his shirt line and emerged on the other side and went nobody knew where.

"This is a fragment, maybe not even a bullet fragment," Juarez said, when she'd finished looking at the wound. "Again, not much I can do for you. Not much I *need* to do for you. I doubt you even lost much blood. I will clean the wounds, stitch up the ones on your neck. Give you antibiotics and painkillers, and you will heal. If you go to a major hospital, they would most likely not even take the bullet out. They would do what I will do: clean, stitch, give you some drugs. You should rest quietly. Watch television."

"That's good, then," Nikitin said. "I will take the drugs. Now would be very good time for that."

Juarez cleaned, applied pressure, did some stitching, applied bandages, and gave Nikitin two opiate capsules.

Abramova said, "My ear, I think it's nothing."

"Nothing until it gets infected and drives you crazy," Juarez said. "I'm here, I should take a look."

She looked at the ear—the bullet had caught just the outer rim—cleaned the wound, put on a bandage, and told her that if she survived, a plastic surgeon could fix her ear in fifteen minutes. Finally, she told the Russians that she'd done all she could. "Gonna let me go now? Or gonna kill me?"

"Right now," Abramova said, "We will put you in a closet, where you can't hear us talk. We will let you go soon enough, but we don't want you to hear our plans."

"If we were going to kill you, we wouldn't bother with the closet," Titov pointed out. "Don't try to fight us or run away."

THEY PUT JUAREZ in a closet with pillows; there was nothing else in it but the odor of naphthalene from long-gone mothballs. There was enough room for her to stretch out, or sit up, or even stand, since the closet was empty. "We will not leave you here too long," Titov said. "Just for the planning."

Juarez sat in the dark. When the door closed on her, she pulled up her coat sleeve, looked at her watch, and started doing some numbers.

With Juarez in the closet, Abramova went to her laptop, did ten minutes of research as the others waited. When she was done, she called up a map on the laptop, and said to Titov, "Milwaukee. Maybe six hours from here. St. Louis is too far. This Omaha, this Des Moines, maybe too small, too peaceful. Milwaukee has many gunshot wounds, according to AI. Lev can't move much, so I will stay here with him. You take the doctor, take this route . . ."—she traced it on the laptop screen—". . . south out of the city to this point, this Apple Valley exit. You put the doctor on the side of the road with her thumbs taped and the mask on her head, then you return to the highway going north back to the city and follow this I-94 east."

"Why the detour?" Titov asked. "North, then south?"

"Because she told us about Kansas City," Abramova said. "If you were transporting Mat to Kansas City, you would go that way. But we won't be."

"Ah."

THEY WORKED THROUGH it, all the way to Aurora St. Luke's Medical Center in Milwaukee. Titov looked at his watch: "We should go now. Prepare Matvey as well as we can, something soft in the back of the vehicle. Cushions from the couch. We will put the doctor in the front . . . thumbs taped, mask on her head."

Orlov said, "I do not like to be the one to say this, but . . ."

Titov said, "We do not injure her. If we or any of us are caught by police, we hope for mercy. In a year or two, maybe we get traded. I am sure we get traded. Especially if the only one who gets hurt is Sokolov . . ."

"Sokolov's not hurt. I don't think he's hurt," said Nikitin. "His wife was hurt, we couldn't see if the second shot hit anyone."

"They are both monsters. Nobody will mourn either one," Titov said. "But if we kill an innocent doctor . . . then there will be no mercy. No trade."

"You are correct," Abramova said. "I will put on my coat and take the couch cushions out to the car."

THEY GOT ORLOV into the back seat, and comfortable on couch cushions, wrapped in blankets, semiconscious, feeling no pain. Juarez, wearing the backwards mask again, her thumbs taped behind her back, was guided out to the front passenger seat. They shut the door, but with the window open a bare half inch.

As Abramova and Titov passed the window, walking around to the driver's side, Abramova said, "Research Medical is the easiest to get at . . ." She timed "Research Medical" to the moment they passed the partially open window, so that Juarez would hear them. Research Medical was in Kansas City.

At the other side of the vehicle, Titov said, "I have enough truckers to keep my eyes open for a week. I will see you back here tomorrow morning."

"If the truckers do not make you crazy," Abramova said. "If you start seeing two-meter rabbits, stop driving."

The trip south, to the drop-off, took forty minutes. Juarez asked, "Are you really not going to kill me?"

"Really not," Titov said, leaning on the Russian accent.

"Why do you do this?"

Titov thought up an appropriate reply: "We are patriots. Russian patriots. The man we are here to kill is a torturer and a murderer." A moment later, he added, "The money is good."

"Okay. I wondered if that came into it."

"It does, of course. We get danger pay," Titov said. "Not so much by American standards, but good by ours. Mostly, we are patriots."

They drove into the night, around the west side of the Twin Cities, then south on I-35. At an Apple Valley exit, he turned west, and a hundred feet later pulled to the side of the road. Not much traffic.

He hurried around the truck, helped Juarez out onto the shoulder of the road and said, "There is a bank. You're going down a bank. Don't try to walk from here before you turn the mask around. Free your thumbs and then the mask. You are above a pond, there's ice, I don't know how thick, but you don't want to fall. There are some cars above you. Not many, but it would be sad if you were run over now."

Juarez said, "Got it. I can't wish you good luck. You're assholes."

Made Titov smile: "You are a brave woman," he said.

He got back in the truck, made a U-turn, and Juarez began struggling to free her thumbs.

AS THE HIGHWAY patrolman at the Bison hospital set off to talk to people who might have seen a black Jeep Wrangler, Titov had already dropped Juarez on the roadside, masked and taped, had turned back north on I-35, had gotten on I-94 east. Had crossed the St. Croix River and was thirty miles deep into Wisconsin, on his way to Milwaukee, when the highway patrolman confirmed the sighting of a black Jeep, and the first BOLOs went out in Minnesota.

7

Lucas was thinking about going home.

Cops all over the Orono area were looking for and stopping black Jeep Wranglers, but there had been several of them, and none of them were full of wounded Russians. The FBI had gotten video recordings of the renters of the Jeep Cherokee and the Subaru and found that both renters were the same man being careful about cameras—he wore a long-billed fishing hat, and only flashes of his face were visible.

None of the Twin Cities agencies had rented a black Jeep Wrangler, and the FBI had begun running a nationwide net. One of the feds told Lucas that if any of the major agencies had rented the Wrangler, the LoJack should show up in the Cities. So far, nothing had.

"Don't really know where we go from here," Lucas told Sherwood, "Or what I could do."

"If I don't get to go to bed, I don't see why you should," Sherwood said.

"I'll stay for one more cup of coffee . . ."

Lucas's phone rang.

He'd left his new burner numbers with the 9-1-1 operators, and one of them was calling. He answered, listened, rang off and said to Sherwood, "The doctor, Juarez, was found alive, unhurt, down in a place called Apple Valley, south of the Cities. A few blocks off I-35. She's being taken to Fairview Ridges Hospital in Burnsville as a precaution."

"The feds can lead us to wherever that is—they've got lights on their vehicles. How far is it?"

"I don't know . . . maybe forty, fifty miles," Lucas said.

"We're outa here."

UNDER OTHER CONDITIONS, a fast run south to the hospital might have been entertaining: Lucas's Porsche was warm, comfortable, with hard-rock driving music coming through on Apple CarPlay. Lucas liked driving fast and often did. The feds, however, restricted themselves to the speed limit, and Lucas felt he had to go along with it, so the trip took nearly an hour, even with flashers. The caravan looked, Lucas thought, like the circus had come to town.

At the hospital, they all parked and went inside, talked to a couple of uniformed cops who were waiting for them. The cops led them to a room where Juarez was sitting on the bed, looking impatient.

One of the escort cops told her, as they entered the room, "They're here."

"Thank God," she said. "If it'd been any longer, I would have started smoking again."

Sherwood: "Dr. Juarez! We're very happy to see you alive."

"I'm happy to be alive," Juarez said. "It's so much nicer than the alternative."

Sherwood continued: "These two gentlemen are with the FBI, this guy is a federal marshal, and I was part of the escort for a man these Russians tried to kill . . ."

"There were four of them, three men and a woman. One man had not been injured, the other three were. I think the man who drove me was Eastern European, and I'm tempted to say Russian. The woman who was the first one in the door at the emergency room had an accent, too," Juarez said. "The man with the lesser gunshot wound had a heavy accent, the other man, who was seriously wounded, didn't talk much, so I couldn't tell. The woman was very blond, all the men had dark hair. They were all physically fit, average height or a little taller. The man with the lesser wound had several scars on his body that might have come from shrapnel or industrial accidents—they were like cuts, rather than penetrating wounds that bullets would make. Are you FBI?"

"He's CIA," Lucas said. "You got the whole federal government talking to you."

"Yeah, thanks for bringing that up," Sherwood said to Lucas. He was only mildly annoyed. "Anyway, Dr. Juarez, Carolyn, we've been looking for you . . ."

"Let me say a couple things before you start asking questions. I've got a lot of stuff in my head, numbers, and I don't want to get confused," Juarez said. "They took my phone but not my watch. I looked at my watch while we were gathering medical equipment and supplies at Bison. When we were ready to leave, they put a black ski mask over my head, backwards, so I couldn't see where I was going. Probably about 9:15 when we left the hospital, give or take a minute or two. I tried to keep track. They took me to a house in a rural area, I think. It looked and smelled like an old farmhouse, that grainy, raw-potato smell. I got another chance to check the time when we got there. When they took the mask off, so I could look at their wounded men, it was 9:56. I've been sitting here doing the math: that's forty-one minutes, more or less. There were maybe three or four minutes from the time they pulled a mask over my face and put me in their car at the hospital, and another six or seven from the time they took me out of the car into the house. So, the trip was between thirty-two and thirty-four minutes. I believe that's very close."

"That's great," Sherwood said. "We—"

"Let her talk," Lucas said.

Sherwood shut up and Juarez went on. "At the house, I treated two wounded men, one of whom urgently needs a hospital. The woman had a small wound on her ear, nothing serious, she'd already treated it herself. I told them the badly injured man would die without surgery, which I couldn't do. I told them that he urgently needed to get to a hospital, that he'd die if he didn't."

"We think—"

"Let her go," Lucas said.

She nodded at Lucas and rolled on. "After I treated their wounds, they put me in a closet while they decided what to do next. The closet had old peeling wallpaper inside, and a board floor that look crumbly. Old. Like an old house. They decided to try to take the worst-wounded man to a hospital, and that's where they were going when they dropped me off. I managed to look at my watch before they taped me and blindfolded me at the house. It was 10:40 when they did that, and another five minutes before I was in the car. When they dropped me, I managed to get the tape off my thumbs, and pull off the ski mask, and it was 11:32 when I looked at my watch. It took me several minutes to get the tape off. Maybe five. So very close to forty minutes to drive where they took me. On the way to Apple Valley, I didn't sense any effort to try to fool me about turns or directions: once we were on the highway, we stayed there. So, thirty minutes from the hospital to the farmhouse—they had to be driving south, from the hospital, because they drove thirty or thirty-five minutes to where they dropped me off, and now we're way south. From the hospital to here would be at least an hour."

"Do you think the car might have been a Jeep?" Lucas asked.

Juarez cocked her head, thought, then said, "Yes. It rode rough, like it had heavy tread. I never saw it, though."

"That's all great," Sherwood said. "We—"

"They may be on their way to Kansas City," Juarez said. "*Maybe. Maybe*. I'm not sure."

She explained why Kansas City was a possibility. One of the feds had produced a notebook and was taking down the interview in what appeared, to Lucas, to be fluent shorthand. She said that she'd suggested Kansas City as a place where a gut-shot man could be dropped and treated, and probably released, without strings attached, as long as he kept his mouth shut.

When she learned where she'd been dropped off, she realized that I-35 would take a vehicle straight south to Kansas City.

"They were so careful around me, it seems odd that they would simply adopt my suggestion," she said. "Then, when I was in the car, waiting, I heard them mention Research Medical, which is in Kansas City. That all ties together, but . . . I wondered why I overheard that."

Lucas: "You're thinking that they laid a false trail?"

"It's possible," she said.

Fed: "We need to know the details of the wounds and the treatment—"

Lucas: "Why don't we take this chronologically from the time they showed up in Bison . . . every detail you can think of. Nothing's too small. How were they dressed? Did you see their coats? Do you think you saw all of them?"

The four of them, Lucas, Sherwood, the two feds, worked her for an hour for every detail she had. The shorthand fed excused himself twice to make calls to his agent in charge, Sherwood left once to call an unspecified person, and Lucas called Weather to tell her that the doctor was safe and he'd be home in an hour or so and would need a cup of cocoa.

When Sherwood came back, he said, "The FBI will get in touch with every reasonable hospital that they might hit, including all of them here in the Twin Cities. You got hospitals up the ass. The main thing is, if you work the doc's numbers . . . they were somewhere within a ten-mile circle of Orono. You were right about that."

"Now it's a snake hunt," Lucas said. He looked at his own watch: getting late. "That's not us. We can keep the cops jacked up, but not much will be done before tomorrow daylight. You'll want somebody with authority to contact the media, get the news programs to put out word on the hunt. If Juarez was right, and they were in a farmhouse in the Orono area, somebody will have seen them."

"What authority would you suggest? To talk to the media?" Sherwood asked. "How about you?"

Lucas shook his head and said, "Not me. A friend of mine is the head of the state Department of Public Safety. I'll call her tomorrow morning and ask her to call the TV stations and push. If the FBI won't comment, I will."

"I can't, but we'd be in your debt," Sherwood said.

Lucas and Sherwood left Juarez with the two feds and headed into the night: "Maybe see you tomorrow," Sherwood said. "I would love to seriously fuck up a Russian hit team."

Thinking about that on the way home, Lucas realized that he actually liked the CIA guy, and Lucas was not somebody who liked people easily.

LUCAS'S WIFE, WEATHER Karkinnen, was a plastic surgeon. She had operations on most days, often two or three of them, starting early. She always tried to be asleep by ten o'clock at the latest, was in bed but awake when Lucas got home.

He gave her a summary of what Juarez had told them, and Weather said, "That all sounds right to me, but depending on what hit this Russian guy, the bullet might not have gotten to the bowel."

"She said she thought she could feel it, through his belly skin, but wasn't sure about that," Lucas said. "She was knowledgeable about gunshot wounds. She wasn't a medical debutante. You think she was wrong about any of it?"

"No, but given the conditions she was working under, you can't tell. If the bowel was punctured, everything she told you sounds right. I don't really know what I'm talking about. But it sounds right."

"Good," Lucas said. "Are you still planning to get up at six?"

"No, I've set my clock for seven, I've already made a call that I'll be late for my first op. I wanted to hear what happened."

"Wake me up when you get up—I've got calls to make," Lucas said. He bent forward and kissed her on the forehead. "I'm going to make myself a cup of hot chocolate, I'll sleep in after I make the calls. Tomorrow's gonna be a bureaucratic hassle."

8

Titov dropped Orlov at Aurora St. Luke's at four-thirty in the morning. Even with his iPhone navigation app calling the turns, he got lost twice, and as a Chicago resident, he naturally despised Milwaukee and everything it stood for, especially the Packers.

But he got there, and Orlov was snoring in the back seat. He had the feeling that the snoring wasn't good: he'd heard it before, a deep, rumbling snore, and the man he'd heard it from had died.

The emergency room had a wide, well-lit entrance with traffic, so he drove past the entrance down Oklahoma Avenue and dropped Orlov, wrapped in a heavy blanket, on a sidewalk just out of sight of the emergency entrance.

Orlov's eyes cracked as he laid him on the sidewalk, and Titov crouched and said, "I have to go. They will come get you in one minute. You will be okay, Matvey. This is a good hospital."

Orlov closed his eyes, snorted once, and went away again.

Titov hustled back around the Jeep, drove on down the block, stopped, and called the hospital's main number. He told the woman who answered the phone what he'd done; she didn't seem particularly surprised.

Titov was two hundred yards away when a couple of orderlies and what might have been a doctor hustled around the building with what looked like a stretcher and carefully placed Orlov on it, and a minute later carried him back to the emergency room.

Abramova, sounding alert, answered the phone when Titov called: "It's done," he said. "He's inside."

"What kind of condition are you in?" Abramova asked.

"Not sleepy, but fucked up. The drugs keep me awake, but I'm very tired. I have sand in my eyes. I'm up twenty-four hours now."

"Then find a motel. If you drive back, you will be thirty hours, and you'll be good for nothing."

TITOV DROVE EAST from the hospital, got on I-94 and then I-41 toward Chicago, drove until he was within the orbit of the larger city, in case anyone ever looked at his regular iPhone. He located a chain motel and checked in.

He felt like he couldn't sleep. He was too wired up. He lay on his bed with his eyes closed and thought about his situation. He didn't want to go back to the Twin Cities, but if he didn't, the team was probably doomed; but before doom arrived, they'd undoubtedly tell Moscow that they'd been abandoned.

He actually liked the U.S., he liked Chicago. He liked his personal possibilities, if he could ever get free from the Russian intelligence services. He'd come to view his work for Russia as ridiculous: spies sneaking around the U.S. doing what, exactly? From those he'd talked to, it seemed like they were doing little that couldn't be done by asking your favorite AI.

At some point, he thought he might have gotten some sleep that night. He wasn't sure about that, it was one of those nights when it seemed that images and ideas were constantly flashing through his mind, without pause, without rest.

His iPhone alarm went off: he groped for the phone, turned off the alarm, stumbled into the bathroom, feeling like a malfunctioning robot. He took a hot shower and hit the truckers again. When they hit, he began feeling almost human, and definitely wide awake. He got in the car and headed back to Minneapolis. The first song up on his satellite feed was "Take It Easy" by the Eagles. Almost made him laugh.

WHEN SHE'D FINISHED talking with Titov, telling him to find a motel, Abramova checked Nikitin, who was sleeping soundly, on the floor, flat on his back, his system full of painkillers. She had gotten five hours of sleep, as Titov drove to Milwaukee, felt tired but functional. She got her laptop, went online, and looked for local news shows.

She found two but learned nothing about what must be an extensive manhunt: there was not even a report on the Sokolov shooting, possibly, she thought, because the marshals and the FBI were covering it up. That would not last: they'd abandoned a shot-up, blood-soaked vehicle at a motel, and any number of people had seen them do it. They'd kidnapped a doctor and ransacked an emergency room . . .

She went back and looked at Nikitin, considered the possibilities, then gently shook him awake.

"Do you understand me?" she asked.

"Yes, but I am sleepy."

"Do you hurt?"

He had to take a moment, then said, "No."

"The situation is this. You are injured, we have no car. I have to find a car, because I believe we have to move."

Nikitin struggled to sit up, but she pushed him down. "Is Melor back already? What happed to Matvey?"

"Mel called from Milwaukee. Matvey is in the hospital. Melor will find a motel and try to sleep."

"Then . . . where will you get a car?"

"I will rent one," she said. "At the airport."

"But how will you get there?"

"I have thought about this. Now, the doctor told me that when you feel pain, you should take three of these pills . . . They will stop the pain and help you sleep some more, keep you still." She showed him three brown pills in the palm of her hand. "Can you do that?"

"I have no pain now."

"I know. But you might, before I get back. I'll leave you with the pills and a glass of water."

SHE GOT THE glass of water and they talked for another moment, and she left the pills and water on the floor within arm's reach. That done, she went into the bedroom, got the smallest of the carry-on duffel bags, put in a dress, high heels, and a dressy woolen coat that they'd packed as disguise changes, along with a crushable brimmed hat. She added a lipstick and blush.

She changed into clean jeans, a woolen sweater over a long-sleeved flannel shirt, and topped it with a jacket too light for the morning cold—the temperatures were still well below zero—but she couldn't use her blood-spangled parka, which she hadn't had time to clean. She'd put the machine pistols back in the gear bag and replaced them with her familiar PLK. When she went through the living room, Nikitin was sleeping again, and she left as quietly as she could, locking the door behind her.

She was on a side road off the main highway, a mile and a half from the Minnetrista city hall and police station, two separate buildings on the highway; they'd noted the place in their recons as the closest police station. She put the duffel bag straps over her shoulders and started jogging, a long uphill stretch to start. The cold began seeping through the clothing within minutes, but by then the body heat began to catch up: still, her face felt the frost nipping at it, like acupuncture needles.

The run to the city services area took twelve minutes, the last few hundred yards downhill. When she got there, she walked through the parking lot, got out of the wind in the shelter of a small doorway at the city hall, and called for an Uber.

She'd hoped to get one within a half hour, but she got an almost instant reply: a car would pick her up in five.

The driver, a large, heavily wrapped, incurious man, sporting a black porkpie hat like a musician might wear, said almost nothing during the forty-minute drive to Minneapolis–St. Paul International. The brightest spark from him came at the city hall, when he grunted,

"Working early, huh?" and again when she gave him a twenty-dollar cash tip at the airport, "Hey, man. Thanks."

Inside the airport, she checked an arrivals board, picked out an arriving flight from Chicago, then found a women's restroom, locked herself in a toilet booth and changed into the dress, high heels, and overcoat. She packed her running clothes in the satchel, touched her lips with the lipstick, decided she didn't need the blush; she was pink enough from the cold. A two-minute train ride took her to the parking structure that housed the car rental agencies, where a Hertz agent told her that she had no reservation for a car.

"My goddamned husband," she blurted . . .

The agent found the pretty lady a car, a huge seven-passenger Infiniti QX-60, for only $247 a day plus taxes, for a five-day rental.

"Wonderful," she gushed. "I can take my entire family to the mall in that . . ."

SHE STAYED WITHIN the speed limit back to Minnetrista. On the way, she switched the radio from satellite to local, searched the stations until she found local news, and immediately got caught with a story about an Orono-area manhunt for what was believed to be a Russian assassination team of three men and a woman.

While the news station had no details about the killing of a person in Orono, they had everything else: the cars the team had used, the wounding of three members of the team, the probable existence of a fourth member, their Russian accents, and even some information on the extent of the wounds.

The FBI had obviously interviewed the doctor, and the station had also reached two of the nurses from the Bison hospital who told of the raid, and who mentioned that the Russian woman was a blonde.

"No! Not good!"

The beautiful QX-60 might not be viable for very long, if the rental agent put together the three things he knew for sure: the vehicle had been rented by a blond woman, without a reservation, but with a foreign accent.

This thing about cars was getting serious. She had to think.

She did that on the drive back to Minnetrista. Instead of going straight back to the farmhouse, she detoured to a Walgreens drugstore. Inside, she bought an auburn hair dye, along with an eyebrow pencil, Band-Aids, Tums, a notebook, six bottles of Pepsi Cola, and a pack of cinnamon-flavored chewing gum, all the extra items bought to obscure the purchase of the hair dye and eyebrow pencil.

At the farmhouse, Nikitin was asleep. The three pills she'd left for him were gone, and the glass of water had been drunk. She had no idea of how much time she might have, but the hair was a necessity, and she let him sleep while she changed her appearance.

That took an hour; her first time as a brunette, with the eyebrow pencil matching the new hair color. While she waited for the hair dye to set, she called Titov, who was already in his Jeep. He answered, seemed disoriented for a moment, then said, "Please repeat."

Abramova told him everything she'd done. "I'm afraid they will trace the new car. We need yours as soon as we can get it."

"I'm coming as fast as I can without attracting the highway patrol."

"I think . . . I will find a motel where I can check in without the new car being seen. I will bring Lev and the equipment in from the back and leave the car somewhere. That's the best I can do, but we need a clean car, your car."

"I can't think of anything better," Titov said. "I can't think of anything right now."

"Don't go off the highway."

FEELING THE PASSING time weighing on her, Abramova took ten minutes to research motel possibilities on the west side of the Twin Cities and spotted a La Quinta Inn with two separate wings and multiple entrances. Even better, it was within jogging distance of the Mall of America.

The team had visited the mall the day after they arrived in the Twin Cities, to shop for outdoor wear. She wouldn't leave the car at the mall itself—too many cameras—but she could leave it close, and the conclusion might be that they'd dumped the car and gone to the mall to catch other transportation—Uber or a cab.

Nikitin was not easily roused, but she got him started, made him swallow an amp to wake him further, and began packing bags and equipment in the QX-60. By the time she was done, he was awake.

"Can you walk?"

"I can try." He tried and managed to hobble across the room. "I'll need more painkillers if it's more than ten meters."

"We have those. Now, we need to get you to the car."

ON THE WAY to the La Quinta, she took a call from an unknown number, but she knew the voice on the other end: a man who called himself Kuznetsov, which was a good Russian name, but one that she suspected was not his. His voice sounded like someone shoveling gravel. Titov told her that Kuznetsov had been on the front lines in Ukraine as an SVR observer. He'd breathed in flames trying to escape a house that had been attacked and set afire by Ukrainian special forces. "No more choirs for him," Titov said.

He asked for a briefing, and Abramova told him everything that had happened, from the time she dropped Nikitin and Orlov at the target house, through the wounding of Orlov, Nikitin, and herself, the subsequent flight, the kidnapping of the doctor, Titov's overnight trip to Milwaukee, and now her rental of the new car. When asked, she said she thought Nikitin should be well enough to shoot again, if they had the necessary intelligence and the opportunity.

"Leonid Sokolov is still alive, his wife, Masha, was killed," Kuznetsov said. "We understand the circumstances, and these things happen. However, we need you to be prepared to make another attempt and soon. We will get you the necessary intelligence."

"We need another car, a cold car, an older one that wouldn't be a rental car," Abramova said.

"We can arrange that, we have . . . friends in Minneapolis," Kuznetsov said.

"OPG?"

"Not so organized, not so much group, but some crime," Kuznetsov said. "An old car should not be a problem."

BY THE TIME Kuznetsov rang off, Abramova was halfway to the La Quinta. At the motel, still in the dress, heels, and overcoat, her scalp itching from the dye job, she told the desk clerk that yes, she would pay for the full day, including the previous night, because she was on business and had an extended meeting and later, a reception that she had to go to. She'd be late getting back, she said, but it was all on expenses, so . . .

The clerk was polite but not interested in her plans.

Checked in, for a full week, to a first-floor room, she hauled all the gear to the room. Nikitin was ambulatory, but wobbly, and despite the pills, in pain.

The motel was mostly empty, with the previous night's occupants checked out. They got to the room without being seen, and Abramova took fifteen minutes to help Nikitin out of his jeans, checked the bullet wound in his butt and neck, repatched the butt wound with fresh disinfectant and a tight, heavy bandage. She left him with pills and the remote for the television, changed into clothing that might credibly work with a jogger, hung a "Do Not Disturb" sign on the door, and headed back out.

Almost done.

The residential streets near the mall had no on-street parking, and she wound up leaving the QX-60 in one of the mall's satellite parking lots, judging herself far enough from any cameras that they wouldn't see her clearly enough to identify her.

She followed a looping route out of the mall—the area wasn't made for joggers—until she was on one of the residential streets and began running harder.

Two miles later, she walked back into the motel room. Nikitin was watching a news show. He turned to her and asked, "Yes? Are we good?"

"Yes. For now. Until Melor returns."

9

Lucas got up with Weather to eat breakfast and to make his phone calls to Rose Marie Roux, the head of the Department of Public Safety. After giving her the details of the previous day's shooting, she agreed to press the Twin Cities television stations to emphasize the importance of an FBI press release. Most of the time, newsrooms threw FBI news releases into the nearest wastebasket.

With that job done, Lucas went back to sleep and got another half-hour before Sherwood called: "We should talk about the meeting."

"Which meeting?"

"The one at FBI headquarters at ten o'clock, or ten-thirty, depending on when the plane gets here. An FBI counter-intel team is flying in from Washington."

"Where do you want to hook up?"

"I'm in my car, sitting in your driveway."

LUCAS INVITED SHERWOOD to wait in the den with the morning's *New York Times*, which Sherwood had already picked up from the driveway. When Lucas had cleaned up, he'd come down in suit and tie. Sherwood nodded and asked, "How many suits you got?"

"Don't know. An adequate number."

"That's a good number," Sherwood said. "This one has a nice Italian vibe."

They got breakfast at Cecil's, a diner not far from Lucas's house, corned beef hash and coffee for Sherwood, French toast and Diet Coke for Lucas.

"If the FBI is taking over, why are you still hanging around?" Lucas asked. "Reporting back to Frank?"

"That's part of it. I hate being a spectator and I figure hanging around with you might actually get me somewhere," Sherwood said. "The feds don't want me involved—I've been told that, and my side pushed back, because of my special knowledge of the Sokolovs, so I'm in, but not exactly embraced."

"What about me?"

"The Marshals Service wants you in, so you're invited to meetings, but I don't believe you'll be kept up-to-date," Sherwood said. "For one thing, this is a chance for the feds to one-up the Marshals Service and the CIA. For another, you're still not cleared of involvement. The FBI's counter-intel guys will want to talk to you. See what you think about Russians."

"Not much. My daughter killed some Russians out in California."

"What?"

He explained about Letty's investigation of Russian-involved murders and espionage, and Sherwood said, "Jesus, I heard rumors about that. I was in Syria . . . overseas . . . when it happened. Your daughter gets around."

"Check her out," Lucas said. "But yeah. She gets around."

Sherwood scooped up corned beef hash and chewed, looking around the diner at the other customers, a cross section of winter Minnesotans in sweatshirts and toques, with red noses and watery eyes; no obvious threats.

"If you had to, what would you investigate next? What would you do?" he asked. "Understand, I'm not a cop. I don't know what to do here."

Lucas said, "I had a couple ideas. Not sure that either of them would pay off. I assume the feds have the hospitals covered . . ."

"I assume that, too . . ."

"Okay. From what Juarez said last night, one of the Russians was hurt bad and needed a hospital right away. One was wounded, but she patched him up, about as well as what he would have gotten at a hospital emergency room. The third one, the woman, was barely wounded at all, and the fourth one wasn't even involved. The question is, if one of them rushed the badly wounded guy to a hospital, in the Wrangler, would the other two have another backup car? A fourth car?"

Sherwood considered the question, and then said, "No. Basically, in an op like this, you'd want two cars, at a minimum. One action car, plus a backup. A driver and a gun in each car. In this case, they had a driver and a shooter, plus a spotter in the action car, and one guy in the first backup. The third car, the Jeep, was a running-balls-to-the-wall disaster backup. I see where you're going here. They might need a fourth car now. In case the disaster backup was spotted, in case they were seen along the way, or Juarez understood what the vehicle was."

"Okay," Lucas said. He wagged his fork at Sherwood. "How would they get it? Another car?"

"They could steal one—they'll have those skills," Sherwood said. "If they're not familiar with the area, with the police culture, that'd be a serious risk. They wouldn't know when the theft might be discovered, and when the police might start looking for them, how hard they'd look, what resources would be thrown at a stolen car."

"Which, around here, would be about none," Lucas said. "I've been thinking that they might rent another one, just like they did the first Jeep and the Subaru."

"If they're out in the sticks, no car . . . Lyft? Uber? Taxi?"

"That's the kind of thing that the feds can work on. Not us, because it takes a bunch of people on phones, and we're smaller than a bunch."

Sherwood looked at his watch: "We should go. We can unload this at the meeting."

THE MINNEAPOLIS-AREA FBI was housed in a large whitish building with what looked like a black mask around a portion of it, like the Lone Ranger's mask, if the Lone Ranger had worn his mask on the side of his head.

Sherwood and Lucas drove separately and made the ten o'clock meeting with fifteen minutes to spare. They were shown to a conference room, where Beard, who'd headed the Marshals Service witness protection team, was twitching in a chair at a long conference table. A laptop computer and a projector sat at one end of the table, and a white screen hung on the wall at the other end.

Three FBI suits were in a corner, chatting, cheerful enough at the moment, because they'd been involved in the retrieval of a kidnap victim; or, at least, events could be bent to look that way.

Beard ignored Sherwood but asked Lucas, "Anything new? After the nurse?"

"No."

"Your locals, the state whatchacallit . . ."

"Bureau of Criminal Apprehension . . ."

"Yeah, those guys. They tracked all the calls by all the phones overnight, and there were exactly two, both from me, after the plane had landed. One was while the plane was taxiing, and before we knew that there'd be a delay getting to the house, and the other was to you, to tell you we'd be running late because we lost that suitcase. You didn't call anyone, and neither did White, before we got there."

"I knew that," Lucas said.

"I thought that was the likely case," Sherwood said. "I'll see about getting all the phones back, and you can keep the burners."

"I'm afraid the goddamn FBI might want them," Beard said. "The ones flying in."

"We'll see, I've never dealt with them," Sherwood said.

Shelly White was escorted into the room. She pulled out a chair next to Lucas and said, "You stayed up late."

"I did, but I didn't actually do much. Got the doctor back."

"I heard. I understand we're gonna get grilled by Washington feds," she said.

"That appears to be the case," Lucas said. He filled her in on the interview with the doctor, and the narrowing of the search area around Orono.

THE WASHINGTON FEDS arrived twenty minutes later, three men and a woman, the men in their forties, the woman a bit younger, all well-dressed, three leather and one aluminum briefcases among them.

They arrived with David St. Vincent, the FBI's agent in charge, and several more agents, all suited. The youngest one went to the projector and laptop, and after introductions, plugged a thumb drive into the computer and lit it up.

St. Vincent did a brisk PowerPoint presentation, with maps, of all the key moments in the assassination and subsequent investigation, including the interview with Juarez and the washing of phone calls by the BCA.

"We have agents and several marshals accompanying local police in a door-knocking campaign all around the Orono-Minnetonka area, concentrating on farmhouses. No results yet."

When he was done, there were questions. Sherwood outlined what Lucas and he thought might have happened with cars. There was dissension, but everyone was interested in any possible angle, so the feds would start making phone calls to the ride services and rental agencies.

With the briefing over, Sherwood and Beard were escorted to separate rooms with two of the counterintelligence team members walking with each of them. The other marshals from the Sokolov house were ushered into the conference room, and they all sat around and waited like hopefuls at a temp agency. After a half hour, Sherwood came back with the woman interrogator, and she said, "Marshal Davenport?"

The woman, middle-sized, olive-complected, and dark-haired,

with a unibrow and sharp eyes, led him down the hall to another conference room. On the way, Lucas said, "I didn't think I was important enough to go third."

"You're not," the woman said. "Mr. Sherwood wants you on the street."

"Nice guy," Lucas said.

"No, not really," she said, as if she knew; and it made Lucas wonder what she knew.

A male interviewer was waiting for them, and the interview took twenty minutes: Lucas's background, his past jobs, and how he'd gotten the Sokolov assignment.

"I didn't get it, I was told I was on it by the U.S. Marshal for Minnesota," Lucas said.

"When was that?" the woman asked. She hadn't mentioned her name.

"Two days ago. I think that's when *she* was given it, by some suit in Washington."

The male interviewer nodded: "That checks."

The woman said, "As I understand it then, you deny any involvement with any Russian intelligence service, or anyone who might be working with any Russian intelligence service . . ."

"Of course, I do," Lucas said. "I haven't . . . Oh."

The woman, who'd looked down at her notes, looked up. "Oh?"

Lucas shook his head. "I never even thought of it. Years ago, a Russian intelligence officer came here to Minnesota. We were investigating a murder case in Duluth, a Russian sailor whose father was big in the Russian oil industry. That turned out to involve an old spy ring that had been embedded there to help Russian agents get in and out of the country. Nobody on our side—you guys—cared much about the spy ring, they'd been inactive for decades. Most of them had died of old age."

He continued: "But the Russians were upset about the guy who'd been killed—his father was one of these oligarch guys, and they sent a woman here to observe our investigation. She turned out to be a member of one of their investigative services. I forget which one, it was all initials."

The man: "GRU? SVR? FSB?"

"I think it might have been the 's' one," Lucas said.

The woman said, "This is something. When was the last time she was in touch with you?"

"Like, a couple weeks after the investigation ended. She sent me and my wife a letter thanking us. When she was on her way back to Russia, we let her stay in our guest room over in Saint Paul."

The woman: "So you were close?"

"No . . . just an overnight thing, on the way to the airport."

"What was her name?"

"Nadya Kalin. Uh, Nadezhda Kalin. When I said her first name, she said it sounds like I sneezed."

Neither of them smiled, and the man asked, "When was this, exactly?"

"Let me see," Lucas said. He tipped his head back and thought about it. "Okay, my son was a baby, and Weather wasn't pregnant yet with our second kid, our daughter, so . . . mmm . . . fourteen years ago?"

"You haven't been in touch since the letter?"

"Nope. Not a word. We did bust the spy ring. Not that anyone seemed to care."

The woman said, "I'm sure somebody cared."

"The FBI was involved, probably you guys, actually, your specific office," Lucas said. "Like I said, nobody seemed to care. I was talking to a guy, let me see . . ."

"What?"

"I'm trying to remember his name . . . Andy something. Lemon? No. That's not it."

The man said, "Harmon? Andy Harmon?"

Lucas pointed a finger at him: "Yeah, that's him. Kind of a fleshy blond guy? He was all over it." The two agents looked at each other. Lucas asked, "Is he a big shot or something?"

"He's more like a middle-sized shot," the man said. "He's in our office. We'll talk to him about your involvement. And his involvement."

"That'll work," Lucas said. "Though, and don't tell him this, I thought he was a dipshit."

A smile flickered across the woman's face, and she said, "We won't tell him."

They worked him for a while longer, on the Kalin woman, and the investigation that ended with the busting of the spy ring. When that wound down, the male interrogator said, "We'll be reviewing what you told us, Marshal. We'll talk to Harmon."

"You gonna leave me on the case?"

"For the time being, anyway," the woman said. "We've looked into various connections involving the leaked information about Sokolov's location and the timing of the moves, and can't see how you were in a position to leak much. If you could help Mr. Sherwood clear this problem, the leak, we'd much appreciate it. If it turns out you are the leak, that you're lying to us, you can expect to spend many years in a federal prison."

"Thanks for that," Lucas said.

SHERWOOD WAS WAITING in the hall. "All good?"

"Not really."

"What happened?"

Lucas told him about the Russian agent he'd worked with, Nadya Kalin, and the spy ring investigation, and Sherwood said, "I gotta get this back to my boss. You're sure you're not the leak?"

"Pretty sure."

"Any more ideas?"

"I've got a question," Lucas said, as they walked down an empty, echoing corridor toward the elevators. "How many teams like this do you think the Russians have in the States?"

"I'd be surprised if they had two," Sherwood said. "An operation like this is rare, especially with all the current tension. The Europeans are cowed, so . . . there might be more of them there. But not here. These guys would be kept well away from other Russian assets. Is that important?"

"I was thinking, this team might not be done yet."

"Yeah. That's an itch I've been scratching," Sherwood said.

"Do you know where the Sokolovs are? Right now?"

"No. An FBI SWAT team took them somewhere—a private apartment, with guns pointing in six directions. We'll get them out of here and back to Washington, either tomorrow or the next day."

"Too bad," Lucas said. "If somebody tried to hit the Sokolovs again, that would tell us a lot about where the leak might be. Given the level of their intel, they might know more about the apartment than you or I do."

"Don't tell anyone I said this, but I'd be willing to lose Sokolov if

I could identify the leak," Sherwood said. "I'll talk to the AIC. Maybe we could get some agents on the street. Watchers. See if anyone's cruising the apartment."

"Might be prudent," Lucas said. "Although, I'm not sure the feds will go for it. They might think a surveillance operation would give away the actual location . . . although, hmm."

"Hmm what?"

"Maybe we need a decoy group," Lucas said. "Somebody who might look like the Sokolovs, but are actually, you know . . . not them. Put the surveillance on those guys."

"Maybe we need all of it," Sherwood said. They had gotten to the elevators and were waiting, and he said, "Let's turn around. Find St. Vincent. Talk to him about it."

THEY WENT BACK to the conference room, where most of the marshals were still waiting for their turn at interviews, and got one of the feds to call St. Vincent's office. Ten minutes later, they walked into his office, where St. Vincent was talking to two other agents, older guys in their forties or fifties, senior people.

When St. Vincent saw them, he said, "We caught a break. We got the wounded guy. Shot in the back and the buttocks, dropped at the emergency room, will not say a word to anyone. We're getting some photos we can show to Juarez."

"Sounds right," Sherwood said. "Where is he?"

"Kansas City," St. Vincent said. "Just like the nurse told us. Uh, the doctor."

10

They talked to St. Vincent about the possibility of a decoy operation. He said he'd think about it. Dismissed, Lucas and Sherwood took the elevator down to the bottom floor. Outside, Sherwood said, "I noticed a distinct lack of enthusiasm for the decoy proposal. He won't do it."

"Aw, it's not that great an idea," Lucas said.

"It's the only one we've got. No downside to trying it," Sherwood said.

"Unless the CIA decides to waterboard the Kansas City guy."

"We don't do that anymore," Sherwood said. "Doesn't work all that well, for one thing."

Lucas's phone rang, St. Vincent calling. Lucas looked up at the building, shrugged, and answered.

"Another possible break, but it's thin," St. Vincent said. "One of our phone people talked to a Hertz counter guy at the airport. He had a woman in early this morning, blond, well-dressed, said she was arriving from a Chicago flight. There was a Chicago flight about the right time, we checked that. She had no reservation for a car, but he got one for her. Illinois ID, Visa card, both good. Very fashionable, he said, long fashion coat. Said she was kinda hot. Had an accent, but he thought it might be German. We've got a lot of people around Orono, if you want to take a look at this. Like I said, it's thin . . ."

"I can run down there," Lucas said. "Do they have video?"

"Don't know."

"All right. I'll get back to you."

Lucas told Sherwood what had happened, and Sherwood said he'd follow along. He did that, threading south across town behind Lucas, and they got adjacent parking spots in one of the labyrinthine parking garages at Minneapolis–St. Paul International.

"Wonder why St. Vincent gave this up?" Sherwood asked, as they headed for the car rental area. "I got the impression this morning that you're not personally close."

"We are not. I've annoyed him in the past."

"I can see that might happen," Sherwood said.

THE COUNTER MAN was named George Loftus. He was waiting with his manager, and the manager had queued up a video of the desk during the rental process. The woman was mid-height, slender, but gave off an athletic vibration. Her hair was tucked under a floppy beige beret that fell to her neckline in back. Loftus said he'd gotten the impression of a pretty blond, and when they looked at the video, they could barely make out her eyebrows.

"That's our girl," Sherwood said, his nose two inches from the video screen. "Judging from the motel video. Body shape, size . . ."

"I think so," Lucas said. He asked the manager, "Do you know where the car's at?"

"Parked over by the Mall of America. I can tell you where it's been and how fast it was driven, but I can't tell you *when* it was anywhere. You know, the exact time. Just where it is now."

"In one of the parking garages?"

"No. It's a little north of the mall itself, but it's definitely south of 494."

He pulled up a map connected to the car's tracker. They could follow the track, which was a bit crude, from the airport rental lot to the Lake Minnetonka area, though it never quite got to the town of Orono, then back almost along the same route to the mall. For some reason, she'd done a big U-turn.

"Looks like she was thinking of bringing it back here, but then decided not to," Lucas said.

"Maybe she was planning to catch a plane out of here and suspected the car could be tracked. She parked close enough to walk here, if she wanted to," Sherwood said.

"I don't know how you could walk into the airport. Maybe you can," Lucas said.

They both looked at the Hertz employees, who shrugged. "I wouldn't want to do it," the manager said. "It's a long walk—three, four miles if it's an inch."

"I'll tell you what she was doing," Sherwood said.

"I wish you would," Lucas said.

"The uninjured guy drove the worst-hurt guy to Kansas City,"

Sherwood said. "She didn't have a car but needed to evacuate the other shot guy, because she knew there'd be a door-to-door search in the Orono area, with the information from the doctor. She came here and rented one. Then she abandoned it because she was afraid these guys here"—he nodded at the rental agents—"would be contacted by the cops and they'd remember her and the car."

"How'd she get here?" one of the rental agents asked.

Sherwood shrugged. "I don't know. How would you do it?"

Lucas and the two agents looked at each other and simultaneously said, "Uber."

"And now she's at the mall? With a shot guy?" Lucas asked.

"Dunno about that," Sherwood said. "She drove that big fast loop for a reason."

LUCAS CALLED ST. VINCENT, had to wait five minutes for the AIC to come to the phone.

When St. Vincent picked up, Lucas said, "We think the woman who rented the car was the Russian. We more or less spotted where they were in the Orono area, but it's not in Orono, it's in the town called Minnetrista . . ."

"Let me look at my map . . ." St. Vincent went away for a minute, then came back. "We're working way the hell northeast of there. Take us a while to regroup. You sure about this?"

"They track their cars, and we're looking at the track superimposed on a Google map," Lucas said, standing in front of a laptop in the back of the Hertz rental station. "We think the woman got a ride down here, maybe a cab, or Uber? I don't know. Anyway, she rented an Infiniti QX-60 SUV, white, new last year, then we think she drove it back to where they'd been hiding. The farmhouse Juarez talked about. Then she drove it back here, for some reason, and probably ditched it at the Mall of America, where it's still sitting."

"You think she's at the mall?"

"Who knows, but I doubt it. The Hertz guys tell me that the car's in a big empty area close to 494, but not that close to the mall. It looks like she was dumping it, unless she's sitting there waiting for someone to pick her up."

"Tell me about the Minnetrista site . . ."

Lucas explained that the track was somewhat crude, but: "If you look at city hall, that's the middle of town, I guess, it's on County Road 110. Now track about two miles west, there's a side road next to a hinky little bump in the highway, where the highway turns a little south . . ."

"I see it," St. Vincent said; he was looking at the same Google map image.

"There's a road going north. The car seems to have gone a few hundred yards down the road, where she apparently made the U-turn and came back to the mall. Juarez said a farmhouse and it looks like there are a couple of them back there, maybe three, it's hard to tell from the overhead view. Two are on the west side of the road, another on the east. That's all we can see on the Google satellite, and that's just an eyeball comparison to the car track from Hertz."

"Okay, I've switched over to a satellite view, and I see them. We can throw crews around all of them in an hour or two. What are you doing?"

"We can check out the car," Lucas said. "Don't think that'll amount to much. It's been sitting there for quite a while. Think she probably dumped it and got a ride out of there with somebody else."

"Okay. You get a sniff of anything, call me. Don't go tearing around like a maniac, goddamnit."

"Never."

"Yeah, right."

"Listen, David, we'll cruise it . . . Sherwood's with me . . . and if there's anything definite, we'll back off and call for help."

"Do that. I'm heading out to this Minnetrista place. Stay in touch."

THERE WAS ANOTHER QX-60 still on the lot, and Lucas and Sherwood walked out with the desk clerk to look at it. "Identical vehicles, except for the color. Hers is white," Loftus said.

"Can't miss it; big as a school bus," Sherwood said.

Sherwood followed Lucas four miles west, along I-494, then into the mall complex. North of the mall was a sprawling, mostly empty parking lot, with a couple of dozen cars scattered across it. Sherwood went one way, Lucas another, and after three or four minutes, Sherwood called and said, "I've got it. Looks empty. Can you see me?"

"Yeah. Be right over," Lucas said.

Sherwood was looking in the windows of the oversized SUV when Lucas got there. Lucas got out of the Cayenne, walked over to the big truck. Sherwood shook his head and said, "Completely and totally empty. Not even a piece of paper. Didn't even bother to lock the doors."

Lucas looked inside. The truck had a central console and he saw a key fob sitting in a cup holder.

"Hoping it'd get stolen," Lucas said. He retrieved the key fob and locked the truck. The mall was a couple of hundred yards south of them. Lucas knew the place was studded with cameras, and even if they couldn't make out the woman's features, if a camera had caught her, they might be able to see who picked her up, or which way she went.

"The Bloomington cops have a precinct here," Lucas said. "Maybe they can get us some video."

"You haven't suggested calling St. Vincent again," Sherwood said.

"It'd take him an hour to get an agent here," Lucas said. "They'd do the same thing we'd do, so why don't we go ahead and do it now? We can call him later."

"You've not only annoyed him in the past, you'll annoy him in the future."

"A burden I'll have to bear," Lucas said. "Besides, they're probably busier than hell at that farmhouse."

THE BLOOMINGTON COPS did have access to the security cameras around the building, and after some winding and rewinding, spotted the QX-60 rolling into the distant lot.

"There she is," Sherwood muttered, as the Russian woman got out of the SUV and walked briskly away. She was no longer fashionably dressed, but was wearing what looked like a sweatshirt or sweater over jeans.

"Won't be going far in that outfit," one of the Bloomington cops said. "She'd freeze her tits off."

"Maybe she's being picked up . . ." Lucas said.

But they saw no sign that she was looking for someone to pick her up. They tracked her on different cameras past several buildings, until she disappeared to the west, into a residential neighborhood. When they last saw her, she was jogging.

"Not going to the airport," Lucas said.

"No. She could have parked a lot closer, if that's where she was going," Sherwood said. "She's going the wrong direction anyway."

Lucas: "But if that *is* where she's going, she's now at thirty-five thousand feet." He touched the screen: the woman had left the SUV at 8:40. They were now at 12:26, almost four hours later.

"It's nine degrees out there, with a ten-mile-an-hour wind, according to the National Weather Service," Sherwood said, looking at his phone. "That's a windchill factor of minus five. I believe our officer friend is correct: her tits are definitely endangered."

"Let's go sit in my truck. I've got an iPad," Lucas said. "Let's see what we have in the way of motels around here, in the direction she was running."

"Think we should call St. Vincent?"

"We don't need to bother him yet," Lucas said. "We can call him when we figure out what we're doing."

THEY SAT IN the Porsche, called up Google Maps, found there was no good way to cross the interstate highway on foot, and started looking for motels south of I-494. There were thirteen, and possibly fourteen—two were not differentiated on the video map—within reasonable jogging distance. Lucas suggested that Sherwood call St. Vincent, because he had Washington cred, and Lucas tended to piss off the FBI man.

When Sherwood called, St. Vincent answered, the impatience tight in his voice: "We're moving on them now. What do you want?"

"You think they're at the farmhouse?" Sherwood asked.

"We're closing on the most likely one now, there's no car, but the car is probably in Kansas City, so . . ."

"We found the car the woman was driving this morning. She left it in a parking lot at the Mall of America. We tracked her on security cameras, and she was jogging and running west when we last saw her."

"Probably picked up," St. Vincent said.

"Maybe, but there are about a dozen motels within running distance. If getting out of the farmhouse and finding a new hideout was what all that car-driving was about, she could be holed up in one of them. Lucas and I could do a recon . . ."

St. Vincent had to think about it, then, "All right, but just a recon. You see anything at all, you call."

"Of course," Sherwood said. "Good luck at the farmhouse, David. Keep your head down."

"Thank you. Don't let Davenport shoot anyone."

Sherwood laughed and said, "I'll try to restrain him."

When Sherwood hung up, Lucas said, "I'm not saying St. Vincent is a moron . . ."

"He's probably not," Sherwood said. "He's caught in a bureaucratic morass, and that's difficult for anyone who is actually trying to get something done. The Agency is the same way, on everything above an operational level."

"All right," Lucas conceded.

"How do you want to do this? You're the cop—do we go together, or should I follow?"

"As a cop, I'll tell you that you always want to have the same number of cars as you have cops, because if you don't, somebody will get uselessly stranded. Follow me, but stay close. If we happen to stumble into them, we'd want to be together. You got a gun?"

"No."

"Okay. I've got an extra, if you want it. Revolver, point'n shoot."

"I'll pass. If I actually shot somebody in the States, I'd spend the rest of my life filling out forms and going to hearings."

11

Titov parked behind the second motel building, out of sight of both the office and the major streets on either side. Abramova met him at the door and he slipped inside. Nikitin was on the bed, apparently asleep.

"What do you think?" she asked.

"Matvey won't die, if the surgeons are good. If he can keep his mouth shut, he might even get loose," Titov said. "He's not on any police records here or with Interpol." Then he shrugged. "If the cops here have any imagination, he's probably fucked. But we've done what we could."

"These security cameras are a curse," Abramova said. "If they find this car I rented, they might be able to track me. I tell you, the cameras are everywhere."

"Then we should move again," Titov said. And, "I like your hair."

She ignored that and said, "Your Jeep might be a problem, if they find the farm. I think they will find the farm, with clues from the doctor. She would have had some idea of passing time, and style of the old house. The neighbors know your Jeep . . ."

"Maybe we should have done her."

"Last year's snow," Abramova said.

Titov nodded at Nikitin: "What about Lev?"

"He can move, with pain. The opiates kill the pain, but make him sleepy and unreliable. When I bought the hair dye, I bought more simple painkillers, not as strong, but his brain will be clear. I think we let him wake up, give him some of this acetaminophen, a lot of it, and then try to find a way to get clear. Get a new car . . ."

"I have all American identification and good driver's licenses and credit cards," Titov said. "Let's do what you did this morning: rent a new car. Call and make a reservation. It's all by computer, computers don't get suspicious, they just rent. One of my driver's licenses is from Normal, Illinois. I even have a membership with the Plus Your Points with Enterprise."

"I have nothing better," Abramova said.

"Have you had anything to eat?" Titov asked. "I stopped on the way here, I got sandwiches . . ."

"Wonderful. I could eat an ox," Abramova said. "Let's eat and wait for Lev to wake up, make an assessment. If we reserve a car now, it will be ready when you go to the airport."

NIKITIN WOKE A little after noon, had some groggy questions about Orlov and Milwaukee. He began to pull himself together after eating two sandwiches, and Abramova checked his butt wound. The blood had stopped leaking and the wound looked drier than it had, but inflamed. Nikitin swallowed more antibiotic tablets and four Tylenols, said he could move if he had to, but he'd rather not.

"I'm going to get a car," Titov said. "You'll only have to walk ten feet from the door."

"That I can do."

TITOV CHANGED INTO a suit and tie, then left in the Jeep: they all agreed there was a small risk, but he had good identification. They smuggled the couch cushions from the Jeep into the motel room, so if he was stopped, he'd look and sound like an ordinary American with a black Jeep, a common car in snow country.

And it worked smoothy enough. Titov left the car in a crowded parking garage at the airport, after wiping everything in the interior that might hold a fingerprint. DNA, he couldn't do anything about. If things worked well, he'd recover the car and drive back to his apartment in Chicago. If it didn't, he'd be in Moscow, or dead, and the car would be irrelevant. Still, the loss would sting: he liked the car. A lot. He would not get anything like it in Russia.

The deal at the Enterprise location was purely routine. Titov got a modest-looking red Ford SUV, checked the mileage and, satisfied, hurried back to the motel. When Abramova let him into the room, she'd already packed the clothes and gear bags and Nikitin was on his feet, one hand on a wall, practicing walking.

"Not bad for twenty-four hours," Titov said.

"Less than that. I would appreciate it if we could find a place to hide for a while," Nikitin said.

"We can do that, no problem," Titov said.

ABRAMOVA AND TITOV made three trips to the parking lot, hiding the rifle case, the spotting scope, and the tripod between bags. When they were ready, Titov said to Abramova, "I'll help Lev. You go ahead, make sure the hallway is clear."

Abramova nodded. Her PLK was on her belt, under her sweater, and she put her hand on it as she stepped into the hallway. She sensed—maybe heard—somebody to her left, looked down the long hallway and . . .

A woman, she thought a desk clerk, was just turning the corner, followed by a hard-looking thin man. She thought *soldier* and her hand gripped the pistol, and then a third man, tall, dark-haired, the nemesis, the man who'd been in the street, shooting at them as they were fleeing the assassination scene—he was right there, coming around the corner.

She'd seen him in the Wagoneer's big wing mirror, was for a split-second uncertain about that, but then he made a move for his pistol but Abramova already had hers in her hand and she yanked it from under the sweater and fired a blizzard of bullets down the hall, driving the three people back around a corner and she thought she'd hit at least one of them and probably two.

Then Titov was there with Nikitin, Nikitin's gun in his hand, and he shouted, "Take him," and Nikitin said, "I can go," and Nikitin stumbled toward the exit and Titov opened fire down the empty hallway, chipping away at the corner as Abramova dropped her magazine and slapped another into place and began shooting. Then Titov was gone and she backed after him through the door to the parking lot, shooting as she went, and then she was outside and into the front passenger seat, struggling to pull the door closed as Titov accelerated out of the lot, around the corner of a motel building into a side street and right away from the motel. Abramova was kneeling on the front seat, looking out the back, reloading, said, "I see nobody . . . I see nobody . . . nobody following . . ."

Titov drove hard for a block under the interstate highway, then made a right turn and slowed, went two more blocks, took a left into a side street, and then kept heading north, Abramova still kneeling on the front seat, looking for pursuit . . .

There was none.

Abramova buckled into the seat and said to Titov, "You did well, Melor. Welcome to the team, huh?"

12

Stepping back: Lucas and Sherwood spent a frustrating hour and a half checking motels along the south edge of I-494.

They'd almost finished when St. Vincent called: "We got the right house, but they're gone. Couple of bloody sheets on the floor and some medical litter. We're definitely looking for a black Jeep, and a neighbor tells us that he spoke to a man living here and he thought the guy was an American. Sounded like he came from Iowa. He only saw that one person."

Sherwood put the phone on speaker and said, "Probably a sleeper, somebody who's been living here for years, brought in to back up the team. That'll make them harder to find, with that guy fronting for them."

"Yeah. We'll get the neighbor to talk to an artist, get a facial image done, but the neighbor said he was an average-looking guy. No particularly notable facial characteristics," St. Vincent said. "What are you two doing? Still checking motels?"

"Yeah. We can't tell from the maps whether there are thirteen or fourteen motels on this strip, on this side of the highway. We've done eleven. Absolutely nothing," Lucas said. "Two more and we punt."

"Might as well finish up," St. Vincent said. "If you're interested, we'll have another briefing at three o'clock, put together everything we know."

"We should be done here in half an hour," Lucas said.

THE LA QUINTA was the twelfth motel, a sprawling place with two long wings and parking scattered around them. A diner occupied a connecting lot with even more cars. They went inside to the motel's front desk, where they were met by a tall balding man and a short chunky woman. Lucas identified himself and the man said, "Well . . . uh, we did have a woman here early this morning with an accent. Quite pretty, but she wasn't blond. She had brown hair. Reddish-brown."

"Well-dressed?"

"Nicely dressed, I guess. A businesswoman. She took the room for a week. She has family here . . ."

"See her car?"

"No, no, I didn't."

Sherwood looked at Lucas and said, "We should check. Carefully. She could have colored her hair."

"Not much time to do that," Lucas said doubtfully. "She was blond at the airport."

"Then a wig?"

"I guess we gotta check," Lucas said.

"Could you show us the room she's in?" Sherwood asked the desk clerks.

"I can," the woman clerk said. She took a minute to look up the registration, then said, "Come along."

They trailed her into one of the two wings. They turned a corner as a group, with the clerk leading, Sherwood next to her, Lucas trailing. The clerk was in the adjacent hall, Sherwood on her shoulder, turning, Lucas coming up behind them, turning . . .

BANG!BANG!BANG!BANG!BANG!

They were met with a blizzard of bullets, sprayed down the hall; Lucas lurched backward, saw the clerk get hit at least twice, blood spraying from her hip, and Sherwood yelped and fell backward, tangling in Lucas's legs, and Lucas grabbed both of them by their shirts and dragged them out of the hallway.

The bullets kept coming, spraying him with plaster, and the woman was screaming and he just didn't have time to look at her and he peeked and saw the exit door at the end of the hall swinging shut and Sherwood shouted, "Go, go get them . . ." and the woman was still screaming, a long shrill scream that sounded like the dying wail of a steam engine and Lucas ran down the long hallway with his gun in front of him and pushed the door open but took a step back in case somebody was aiming a gun at it. Nothing happened and he peeked out, carefully, into a parking lot.

In which nothing moved.

They were gone. He ran to the corner of the building and looked past it to the street: nothing moving there. He turned and ran back and down the hallway and asked Sherwood, "How bad?"

Sherwood had a phone in his hand and was shouting, "It's the one with two wings, it's right off 494, south side, La Quinta, maybe two miles west of the mall . . . Well, look on a fuckin' map . . ."

Lucas realized he was talking to a 9-1-1 operator and knelt next to the clerk who was making sobbing screams, flailing at her hip and leg with one hand as blood blossomed on her slacks, upper chest, and one arm.

He shouted at her, "I'm going to rip your pants," and she didn't reply but stared at him, her eyes sliding away until he could see almost nothing of them but the whites, as she continued to do the odd, gasping screams as if she were running out of air.

Lucas had a tiny razor-sharp knife on his car key chain and he opened it and cut away her pants where he found two wounds an inch or two away from each other, one near her hip and one on her inner thigh, and he saw the pulsing blood from her leg and said to Sherwood, "Got an artery, could be the femoral . . . Can you put pressure on it or are you . . . ?"

"I don't think I'm so bad," Sherwood said. He was on the floor, still clutching his cell phone. "Show me where to push . . ."

Lucas, on his knees, showed him where to put pressure and then cut away the woman's blouse and a bra strap and found another wound, but high on her chest and out toward her side, a small entry and another large exit that was bleeding hard, and he said to the woman, "I need to roll you up," and without waiting for her to say anything, rolled her up high enough that he could gather a wad of her blouse and push it into the exit wound.

The smell of blood was thick in the hallway, his pants soaking up blood from the floor as he worked over her, and when he'd done what he could, he asked Sherwood, "Where were you hit?"

"Left side."

Sherwood struggled to keep pressure on the woman's leg, and Lucas asked, "Ambulance coming?"

"That's what they tell me, and some cops . . ."

"Let me see where you were hit . . ." Lucas cut away Sherwood's shirt and found a narrow wound on the outer edge of his rib cage; no penetration.

The woman was still gasping and occasionally screaming and then moaning, and she reached out and grabbed Lucas's jacket and pulled at it, looking up at him. "Am I going to die? I have a daughter."

"You'll be fine," Lucas said, though he didn't know that.

There were suddenly people in the hallway shouting at each other and the balding desk clerk was running toward them and Lucas shouted, "Get outside and direct the cops and an ambulance, they're on the way."

Sherwood asked, "How bad am I?"

"I've been hurt worse playing hockey. The coach put me back in," Lucas said.

Sherwood laughed for a half second and then said, "Jesus, that hurt when I laughed."

"Maybe whacked a rib. That hurts when you laugh. Ask me how I know," Lucas said. And, "Keep the pressure on her, keep the pressure on. Where in the fuck is the ambulance?"

He didn't know it when he asked, but only four minutes had passed since the shooting started.

Sherwood didn't know that either, so Lucas got on his own phone and called the 9-1-1 operator and shouted, "U.S. Marshal, we have two down at the La Quinta . . ."

"Everything's on the way, Marshal," the operator said, in a voice that seemed almost bored. "Is there an escape vehicle, do you have a description? Are there still armed perpetrators in the motel?"

"I never saw a car, I think they're all gone, the Russians everybody is looking for, these are the Russians," Lucas said. "I can't leave where I am, we're plugging holes in one of the victims, when the cops get here tell them to look for witnesses right away, check for video . . ."

"We'll do that," the woman said. And she said, "Hold one," and after ten seconds of mostly dead air—Lucas could hear voices talking, but not make out what they were saying—she came back and said, "The ambulance is one or two minutes out, police should be there in the next minute. Hold where you're at, they're coming."

"Yeah, not like I'm going any other fuckin' place," Lucas said.

The 9-1-1 operator, who heard all kinds of language from hurt and frightened people, said, "That's good."

THEN THEY DID nothing but wait; the woman had stopped screaming, but was still moaning, still gasping, and Sherwood was putting all his weight on her leg until finally a cop came running down the hall, looking panicked.

He asked, "Are they still here?"

"I don't think so," Lucas said. "They were coming out of the second door from the end, on the right. If there are any of them left, that's probably where they'd be. But they could have another room, a bailout room, so take it easy."

Another cop came running down the hall, and there was a flurry of words and sentences that eventually took the two cops down the hall, where one stood by the door with his gun out while the other ran outside. The cop by the door shouted, "Tommy's checking the window."

"Careful, careful," Lucas shouted.

Thirty seconds later, Tommy the cop hustled back inside and said, "I couldn't see anyone. Should we kick the door?"

Lucas shouted, "No hurry. Watch the window and watch the door and wait until we get more people here . . ."

The ambulance arrived, and more cops, and the paramedics loaded up the woman and Sherwood and took them away. Lucas stood up to catch his breath, and a man in the hallway, one of the motel guests, said, "Your pants are all bloody. You're dripping blood."

Lucas said, "Ah, jeez," and leaned back against the wall, feeling the blood-wetted pants clinging to his leg hair. After a minute, trying to talk his blood pressure down, he took out his phone again and called St. Vincent.

"Well . . . we found them," he said.

ST. VINCENT WAS beyond furious. "What in the hell were you two thinking? If you had any thought at all, you'd have waited for reinforcements . . ."

"They were *leaving*, they were *running*," Lucas said. "If we'd gotten to that hallway one minute later, we never would have seen them at all."

"You don't know that. You said they just rented the room this morning, maybe they were going out for lunch and we could have ambushed them when they came back."

"But we wouldn't even have known they were there . . ."

St. Vincent was having none of that. "This is now an FBI operation and you can take your CIA guy with you. I don't want to see your ass anywhere around this. You screwed this up . . ."

"Fuck you, David. We're the only ones who've found anything . . ."

The rest of the conversation didn't go any better.

The motel room down the hall was eventually opened and found to be empty except for two couch cushions spotted with dried blood.

LUCAS HAD TO stay around and make a statement for the Bloomington cops and promise to make an even more extensive statement when needed. That done, he drove to Fairview Southdale Hospital, where the La Quinta desk clerk and Sherwood had been taken. When he arrived, he was told that the clerk was in surgery, and her condition was not known to anyone outside the surgical suite.

Sherwood, on the other hand, had his feet dangling off the side of a bed in the emergency department. He had been cleaned up, bandaged, given pain medication, and would be released as soon as his CIA insurance status was confirmed, which was taking a while.

"You never saw the car they're in," Sherwood said, when Lucas stepped inside the drape around his bed.

"Never did, and we got nothing on a camera. They're gone," Lucas said. "You good?"

"The doctors say I'm fine, I'm thinking more like mediocre," Sherwood said. "Ten years in Iraq, Syria, and Lebanon, and I heard all kinds of shooting and shit blowing up, but the worst I got it was in Beirut. I went to the American University Medical Center to get a sliver taken out of my hand. I got the sliver from a hotel railing after I had too many Long Island iced teas at the bar with an Arab dude named Lanny. I come to fuckin' Minneapolis, Minnesota, and some

Russian *durak* shoots me. In Minneapolis fuckin' Minnesota. A fuckin' Russian assassin."

After a moment, he added, "It was a big splinter. But here in fuckin' Minneapolis . . ."

He might have gone on, but Lucas said, "We like to think of ourselves as cosmopolitan." He didn't know what a *durak* was, but he recognized the tone. "St. Vincent tells me the FBI is taking over the entire case and we are no longer invited to participate."

Sherwood said, "Yeah, well, we'll see. I'm not coordinating with the FBI, I'm coordinating with the Marshals Service. If the FBI doesn't like it, they can go suck on it. Hey—where's my car?"

"Still back at the motel," Lucas said. "Listen, when they finish fixing your hangnail, or whatever it is . . ."

"Gunshot wound, suffered in the service of my country. If I play this right, I could get a month off. Maybe two."

"Like I said, a hangnail. When we get you out of here, why don't you come over to my place for dinner? I'll do us a couple of steaks, martinis, you'd like my wife. She's a doctor, she can probably slip you some extra drugs. We'll call Washington to clarify our status here."

"You had me at martinis," Sherwood said. "I gotta wait for the goddamned insurance to clear me out. You apparently need to be pre-approved for a gunshot wound."

The insurance came through, after a while. Lucas supposed that there was a conference still going on at the FBI offices, but there wasn't much that the FBI knew that he and Sherwood didn't. They went back to the motel and picked up Sherwood's car, and to Lucas's house, made phone calls, and eventually ate steaks and drank martinis.

Because that's what you do when you can't think of what else to do.

13

After fleeing the motel, Titov took the Ford west on one interstate highway, then south on another. Abramova sat backwards, watching for followers, until they were on I-35, and she turned around, buckled in, and asked, "Where are we going?"

"Iowa," Titov said.

Abramova frowned. "Iowa. That's a different state. How far is that?"

"Two hours. For now, we can do nothing, because we know nothing," Titov said. "We need to make phone calls, make consultations. Iowa is close, across a state line, which changes all of the police jurisdictions, so we're less likely to be noticed by cops. We will still be close enough to get back here in two hours if we need to."

"I like that," Nikitin said from the back seat.

Titov checked the other man in the rearview mirror, and asked, "How are you, Lev?"

"I don't hurt too much. Some."

"Have you taken pills?"

"Not in the past hour, I needed to be able to move if I had to."

"So now, we will be driving for two hours to this place, Clear Lake. In Iowa," Titov said. "I suggest, Kat, that you climb in the back and lower the back seats so you both can sleep. Also, that makes this car appear to have only a driver, not two men and a woman."

"This, I can do," Abramova said. "This has been the longest two days of my life."

ACCORDING TO GOOGLE MAPS, the run to the motel in Clear Lake, from where they were, would take two hours. Nikitin and Abramova quickly fell asleep; Titov went to a classical music station on satellite radio and played Tchaikovsky for a while, got hooked into the jazz waltzes by Shostakovich, then looked around for some classic soft rock.

Forty miles from the Iowa line, he took a phone call, listened, said, "We can do it, but we need everything you can find out about the site and where we might go. We need another car, not a rental, if one can be procured."

He listened some more, and then said, "Text me the address. Leave the keys on top of the back tire, on the street side."

They talked details for two minutes, and then he hung up. The phone call had wakened Abramova, who asked, "What was that?"

"Kuznetsov. It's as we thought. Sokolov and his son are now protected by FBI agents," Titov said. "Tomorrow, about ten o'clock, the FBI will remove them from the apartment house where they are hiding and take them to an airport in Saint Paul to fly to Washington in a government jet. His wife has already been cremated and now resides in a cardboard box that will go with them. Another car will be left for us in Saint Paul."

"What do they want of us?"

"They want us to try again. I told them they would have to create a site plan for us. It has to be something we can do with a wounded sniper who can't move fast or far. They said they are looking at all possibilities. They asked after the Berettas and the capacities of the magazines we have with us."

"Thirty rounds each, two magazines for each pistol," Abramova said. "If they're asking after the Berettas, they might not be thinking of a sniper attack, they might be thinking of an assault on the transport vehicles. Killing FBI agents."

"The man"—he was speaking of Vladimir Putin—"wants Sokolov above all. He will accept dead FBI agents."

"Sokolov above all. Above us."

"I do not think the man worries about us. If we die, there are more where we come from. If we don't die, we get medals. Medals cost nothing."

"I'd like a medal. Also, a bigger salary. I'd prefer not to die," Abramova said.

TITOV WOULD ALSO prefer not to die, and as Abramova lay back down and soon was asleep again, he thought about an assault on the FBI vehicles. If it wasn't outright suicide, it'd be the next thing to it. The cars might be armored, there'd be two or three of them, full of armed men. Even if they got Sokolov, they wouldn't walk away from the fight.

If, somehow, he managed to survive, he'd be looking at a life sentence in an American prison. There'd be no trades for the murderer of FBI agents. And he thought about the big man Abramova said was in the motel hallway, and that she believed she'd seen at the Sokolov hideout. He was almost certainly a U.S. Marshal. He, Titov, would have to think about him.

AT THE IOWA motel, as a security measure Titov and Abramova got separate rooms, Nikitin rooming with Titov. After waiting an hour to see if any alarms were generated, and to take a shower, Abramova walked down to Titov's room.

"These hotel rooms, they are . . . functional, but boring," she said. "The walls look like they were designed to be washed."

"I was once sent to a hotel in Kovrov," Nikitin said. "When I got up in the morning, I was speckled red with bug bites, like smallpox. I had six on my яичко. I prefer functional."

Titov snickered and Abramova said, "I prefer not to hear about such things."

THEY ALL OPERATED out of laptops with encrypted Proton Mail. The apartment house where Sokolov was sequestered had been spotted on satellite views of Minneapolis, and in the next three hours they got a half-dozen email deliveries: maps, angles, and propositions, generated by a planning group in Moscow.

There would be at least two vehicles picking up Sokolov, they had been told by their intelligence source, driven by FBI agents. The Marshals Service was no longer involved after the shooting that killed Masha Sokolov, and the shooting at the motel.

"That's better—from their reputations, I'd rather fight the FBI than the marshals," Abramova said. "If we have to fight. If they leave the apartment at ten, we have to be there by eight o'clock. We can't observe it too often. I prefer to snipe, if Lev can do it."

"I can do it if I can sit on my ass," Nikitin said. He was sitting on his ass as he said it, peering at his laptop. "The street view . . . the apartments are set higher than the street, and it doesn't look like they have underground parking. That means the pickup will have to be out in the open, at least for a few meters."

"They could drive the pickup vehicles on the lawn . . ." Abramova ventured.

"I don't think so. If you look closely, here and here . . ." She bent over his shoulder to look; he smelled like disinfectant. "These are steps. The building is set higher than the street. If they come out this door, and there's really no alternative, I could shoot straight down the street. That looks like . . . two hundred meters? There are some trees, but no leaves at this time of year. Mel could be down here, at the other end of the street. We park in this side street, he watches the door, and when they start to move Sokolov, you pull out into the street, my back window down, sandbag on the window sill . . ."

As they worked through the possibilities, it became clear that they would have to plan for a single sniper shot. If that became impossible, the only alternative would be a full-on assault on the FBI vehicles with the Berettas, Nikitin possibly backing them from their car with the rifle.

"An assault would be possible if they have two vehicles to move him, but three would be difficult," Abramova said. "They would have the numbers, the guns, the cars might be armored."

"We should think of ourselves as valuable assets," Titov said, who'd already worked through the obvious possibilities during the drive down to Iowa. "Even if those above . . ." He pointed at the ceiling, meaning their superiors. ". . . want to commit us, I am not interested in pointless suicide. This is not disloyal. This is practical."

Nikitin: "You're correct."

"We should think about this," Abramova said. "If we see which vehicle Sokolov is in, and which seat he is in, and we've positioned ourselves to be traveling in the opposite direction of the FBI vehicles, we could empty both Berettas into the seat and run . . ."

"And be pursued?" Titov asked.

Abramova frowned. Titov was not part of the hit team. She tried to groom him with compliments, but . . . On a scale of one to ten, she trusted the other members of the team at about a seven; Titov she trusted at about a three, although he'd done good work in the emergency pickup after the failed assassination attempt, and in getting Orlov to Milwaukee (though she had no proof he'd actually done that), and more good work in the escape from the motel after the firefight.

So a three; or perhaps a two-and-a-half. "You don't sound enthusiastic about this," she said to Titov.

Titov shrugged. "As *you* said, I'd prefer not to die. I would also like a medal. But mostly, not to die."

They talked about the possibility of an assault and concluded that they might be able to pull it off, but it would be a last resort.

"We will have to leave here at five o'clock in the morning," Abramova said. "We will have two cars that we can use for reconnaissance, but what they have sent us, this planning"—she waved at Nikitin's laptop—"is not useless, but almost so. All satellite and road maps and street views, and some of it is years old. Not good enough."

"Assuming that Lev takes the shot, we have to get away from the attack point, move to a second vehicle without being seen, and then get as far away as we can," Titov said. "This car they are leaving for us—we'll see what that is. We might want to keep this Ford, shoot from the other car. There are thousands of Fords; and red Fords."

"Complicated," Nikitin said. "We need to be early enough to rehearse shooting lanes and escape routes . . ."

"We have twelve hours before we get back on the road," Abramova said. "We should find escape routes on the maps so we're not thrashing around tomorrow morning, and we can drive the chosen routes before we shoot."

"We better not fuck this up," Titov said.

"If we do, then we're done. There will be some unpleasant music from Moscow," Abramova said.

Nikitin: "Oy."

NOT A GOOD night. Nikitin took three opiate painkillers, which put him down early, but Titov and Abramova stayed up late, tracing routes on the maps, talking about alternatives. Titov suggested that one viable alternative would be to lie about the door they were covering, claiming the agents came out of the other.

"We are not in the best of shape with the boss, because of the missed shot the first day," Abramova said. "If we run away, if we run tomorrow, from here, we could probably get away with it and spend the rest of our lives pushing brooms. Or maybe they have an observer there, and we wouldn't get away with it. Honestly, Melor, I don't want to hear this kind of talk."

"Somebody is here. Somebody left the car for us." Titov chewed on his lip for a moment, then conceded. "So, we go." He looked at his watch. "In seven hours."

THEY DIDN'T QUITE make seven hours, but they made seven and a half, rolling out of the motel at 5:30, in pitch darkness. Titov drove, matching the speed of the thin traffic on the interstate. There was a pale hint of dawn on the eastern horizon as they approached the lights of the Twin Cities. Abramova had the location of the cached car on her iPhone navigation map and called the turns as they drove into Saint Paul, where they found the car parked on a downtown street.

They were not unobserved. They were in an area of redbrick buildings, but when Abramova got out of the Ford to go to the second car, she saw a street person huddled in a doorway, shaking with cold, and staring at her. An empty wine bottle lay on its side by his feet. He was bareheaded and appeared to be barefoot, although the temperature was below zero. In Russia, she would have called for help; nothing she could do here. She looked back at the man, shook her head, and stepped away.

The key was on the driver's side back wheel, as they had asked, and she slid it off into her hand, opened the car, and got in. The car, a Chevrolet Equinox, was at least several years old, freezing cold, and the seat and mirrors were set for a large man. She took a minute to find the seat latch and move the seat up, and another to adjust the mirrors. By that time, Titov and the Ford had turned a corner, and she said into her phone, which had been on the whole time, "I'm coming."

"Did you see the man in the doorway?" Titov asked.

"Yes. I think he will die if nobody else sees him."

"Fuckin' Americans," Titov said.

She turned the corner and saw Titov rolling slowly toward the end of the block and got in behind him. "We go," he said, and accelerated toward a ramp in the crosstown freeway.

THEY WERE FIFTEEN minutes away from the target apartment house, on the northern edge of downtown Minneapolis. The highways between the two cities were growing crowded, but the gloom of the early winter morning was thick, oppressive, and the people they saw on the sidewalks were scuttling, heads down, arms tight to their bodies; half of them wore some kind of mask or face-covering scarf.

The three of them were all thoroughly familiar with the pattern of streets around the target, from the maps and satellite photos. The FBI agents would take Sokolov out the front of the building, because they had little choice—and no reason to think that there might be a threat.

Nikitin and Abramova decided that the best location for a sniper would be in the back seat of a car about two hundred meters to the north, shooting along North Second Street toward the apartment building that fronted on North Second. The shooting vehicle would be parked, nose in, on North Eighth Avenue, a stub street that led out of sight to several possible escape routes. They'd picked one escape route, but the others might confuse pursuit.

And they'd shoot from the Chevrolet. It was older than the Ford, the seats were worn and dirty, and the car stank of pizza and sausage, as if it had been used as a delivery vehicle; but the engine, transmission, and tires seemed solid. Nikitin would be shooting out the back window, off a sandbag propped on the open window ledge.

All the details, every one, were critical.

The eastern sky was growing lighter the first time they cruised the shooting location in their two vehicles. They both paused, one after the other, at the end of North Eighth Avenue. "There's a tree branch in the way," Nikitin said, from the Chevy driven by Abramova. "If we could break the tree branch, this would work."

"Small branch, we can try," Abramova said. "We should do it now, before it gets too light."

"I'll get it," Titov said; their phones were both on speaker. "I see what you're talking about. I'll go around the block."

He did that, pulled over as though parking, got out, looked around—the streets were empty. He walked across a sidewalk and grabbed the low-hanging branch, put his weight on it, and cracked it near the tree truck. He left it hanging and hurried back to the car.

Abramova took the Chevrolet past it. Nikitin: "That will work."

They couldn't stop the car on Second Street, because they were afraid they'd be spotted and checked by the FBI agents before the Sokolovs were hustled out of the apartment. Instead, Titov would wait in the Ford, parked three blocks away, near a bus shelter.

When he saw the first agents exit the apartment, he would call, and Abramova would back out of Eighth Avenue onto Second Street, just far enough that Nikitin could make the shot. Experience suggested that the FBI agents would wait until they had the transport vehicles at the doors, then send one or two agents out first, to check the surroundings, then bundle the two Sokolovs out of the apartment and into the waiting cars.

The younger man was a foot taller than his father, so they shouldn't be hard to tell apart.

With the shooting sequence worked through, they spent thirty minutes checking three separate spots where Titov could drive the Ford as soon as they saw the FBI agents leaving the apartment building; they selected the closest one, only a quarter mile to the north. After the shooting, they would dump the Chevrolet, and all three of them would take the red Ford back on the interstate, head south through the Twin Cities, and return to Iowa.

From there, if there was no obvious pursuit, they were six hours by road from Chicago, and a rapid exit via a flight to Miami, Florida, then through Madrid to Frankfurt, assuming Sokolov was dead. If there was a pursuit, a net, they'd stay away from airports, stick to the highways and back roads all the way to Mexico.

"God willing," Abramova said.

"God has no part in this," Titov said.

WITH THE SHOOTING lanes and escape lines set, they drove out in both cars to a Starbucks for coffee and scones; Nikitin and Abramova waited in the Chevrolet as Titov went inside with their orders. Titov was addicted to the scones and brought back five—he'd eat three—along with straight-up Grandes for Nikitin and Abramova, and a Venti for himself.

When he came back, Abramova asked, "What is this sign on that truck?"

She nodded at the truck parked in front of them. A bumper sticker read, "My flesh-eating bacteria are smarter than your honor student."

"It's a joke," Titov said, and spent a minute trying to explain the evolution of things that were smarter than your honor student, until Abramova waved him off. "More stupidity," she said.

They were all crowded into the Chevrolet, Nikitin lying in the back, sitting, drinking, eating, when Titov's phone rang. He checked the number, answered and said, "*Da?*" And then, to the others, "Oh, shit! We gotta go. Now!"

"What?" Abramova asked.

"The FBIs changed up the departure and are leaving at nine o'clock. Ten minutes."

"We have time. No panic, go to your place, we will go to ours," Abramova said. Titov scrambled out of the car and across the parking lot to the Ford, taking his scones and coffee, and followed Abramova and Nikitin out of the Starbucks parking lot.

Nikitin said, "The FBI timing might not be precise. Good technique to be imprecise."

"Yes, but if they're imprecise early, we have missed them. Imprecise late is better for us," Abramova said, laser-focused on her driving, running a yellow light. Titov was no longer behind them, having broken away to park the Ford near the bus stop where he'd stand watching the FBI vehicles. She added, "The intel is amazing. Minute-by-minute alerts."

"Yes. Maybe Sokolov is trying to commit suicide."

When they turned down Second Street, they saw three SUVs parked in close formation outside the apartment, and the red Ford pulling into a parking space well beyond them. They were still hooked together on their cell phones, and Titov said, "In place."

"We see you, and we were correct where they would come out. A good sign: luck is with us," Nikitin said. "They'll take him to the middle vehicle."

"How is your butt?" Abramova asked.

"Not a factor, if I don't have to run." He began humming tunelessly, a tic he'd displayed before other hits.

Abramova turned down Eighth Avenue. There was on-street parking all along the right side, but only a few cars parked along the street. She pulled into the first parking spot, left the engine running.

Nikitin had tested the electric windows, and now he sat up, rolled down the back window, and put a hand-sized sandbag on his knee, where it would be instantly accessible. The rifle sat across his knees, an ugly, ungainly weapon, with its variable-power Leupold scope.

Nine o'clock came and passed. At 9:08, Titov called: "We have movement, we have a man walking to the second car, he's opening the back door, not closing it, he's looking at the apartment door . . ."

Abramova backed up, into Second Steet, and as they looked down its length, saw a cluster of men hurry out of the apartment. They had a heavyset man in the middle of the cluster, and a taller one trailing, and then the cluster opened a notch to let the heavyset man get in the back seat of the car.

Nikitin had the sandbag on the window edge and the rifle on top of it, and he'd stopped breathing. He looked and waited and waited and waited and when the group opened that little bit, so Sokolov could turn and get into the back seat of the SUV, he squeezed off the shot.

"Go! Go! He's down," Nikitin shouted. "He went down . . ."

Abramova was looking in the rearview mirror where a blue-gray SUV had come around a corner a block away and was closing on them, in a hurry, and she said, "We have trouble, we have, maybe, a scout car, coming up behind."

She accelerated straight down Eighth Avenue, and the other vehicle came after them. She lost sight of the other car, then it fishtailed around the corner and she said, "Fuck me, we can't have it follow."

Abramova swerved to the side of the street and stepped on the brakes, hard as she could, and the right-side wheels climbed a curb and Nikitin shouted, "What are you—?"

And she was in the street, the gray SUV only sixty or seventy feet away, and coming on, and she raised the Beretta and began squeezing the trigger as fast as she could, sending rapid three-shot bursts at the other car, aiming low, at tires, and at the engine and at the windshield and back to the tires and the SUV went sideways and she emptied the Beretta at the tires and jumped back in the Chevrolet and they were gone—three minutes, which seemed like it would last forever, to Titov.

The three minutes passed, no sign of pursuit, and they were out of the Chevrolet with the rifle and sandbag and into the Ford and Titov said to Nikitin, "You hit him, he went down hard!"

"We had to stop a pursuing car," Abramova blurted. "We did that, we have no followers so far, unless there are drones, we need to get on the interstate."

"Slow down," Titov said. "Tell me about it when we are on the highway. In the meantime, reload."

14

Lucas was still asleep when Sherwood called.

"They're going to move him at nine o'clock and he'll be out of your jurisdiction," Sherwood said. "You want to go watch?"

"How do we know where they're at?" Lucas asked.

"There was some clarification done in Washington, and both the Marshals Service and the Agency want a man on the scene. That's us."

Lucas: "They don't think we're traitors anymore?"

"They don't think I am. The feds are still a little suspicious of you."

Lucas looked at the bedside clock: 7:10. "All right. Are you ready to go?"

"I will be in fifteen or twenty. Why don't I come over and pick you up?"

"I'll drive—I know the Cities," Lucas said. "Yeah, come get me. You like scrambled eggs?"

"No, but I could do some toast."

"I got toast and raisin bagels."

"Great."

"See you when you get here."

SO LUCAS ATE scrambled eggs and caraway rye toast with French butter, and Sherwood a toasted bagel with cream cheese and another with strawberry jam. The night before, at dinner, Sherwood had proven a congenial guest with a dry sense of humor that tended toward cynicism, and he and Weather had gotten along well. At the end of the evening, Weather had him take off his shirt so she could look at his gunshot wound, and when that was done, told him he'd hurt more the next day. "It didn't hit a rib, but it impacted one," she said. "You've got a bruise the size of a saucer. Like somebody hit you in the side with a big stick."

"IF I'D HAD an old lady like Weather, I might still be married," Sherwood said the next morning, as he slapped strawberry jam on a bagel. "But they weren't like Weather."

"They?"

"Yeah, there were two of them. They both still work for the Agency. Both remarried. I say hi from time to time, when I'm in-country, and see them in a hallway, and can't avoid it."

"I could talk with my daughter. See if she could set up a date with Barb, the sniper chick. She's pretty damn interesting. Physically fit, smart. Reasonably good-looking. A little younger than you. Of course, she does have that violent streak."

The jam knife paused for two seconds: "I tend to bring out the violent streak in women. Let me think about it."

AT TEN MINUTES after eight, they loaded into Lucas's Porsche and headed across town. The north side of the Minneapolis loop had once been the city's warehouse district, later invaded by condos, apartments, steakhouses and bars, ferns and potted palms, with the rare warehouse holding on.

Traffic was dense, coming to a dead stop on the I-94 bridge across the Mississippi, and they arrived at the apartment building at 8:45. They went inside the front door, where they talked to an FBI agent, who called another, higher-ranking agent. The ranking agent was friendly enough, and asked about Sherwood's wound, but also said that nobody knew that they were coming, and that they weren't really invited to take part in the move.

"Well, okay then, good luck," Lucas said. "We'll watch from a distance."

"Thank you."

Lucas and Sherwood walked back to the Porsche and Sherwood said, "Let's cruise the neighborhood. Maybe we could follow them to Saint Paul."

"We could do that," Lucas said. "Was Weather right? Did you hurt more this morning than you did last night?"

"Yeah, but I took a pill, and it's not so bad. Itches. I keep trying to scratch."

"Don't do that."

They did a slow loop around the apartment building, looking up and down streets, hoping, but not expecting, to see a black Jeep Cherokee. They crossed the Mississippi, looked toward the apartment building from the other side, couldn't see it, because another building blocked their line of sight. After the third wider loop, they decided to circle back toward the apartment to watch the FBI's caravan depart. They'd crossed back to the west side of the river, on the Plymouth Avenue bridge, and turned down Second Street, when they saw an older Chevrolet, a long block ahead, back into the street. "Hey, is that—"

"Yeah, it is." Lucas had been cruising, taking it easy, looking at everything, and now he accelerated and was only a couple hundred feet away when they saw a figure in the back seat of the Chevrolet jerk, possibly from recoil, and Lucas said, "I think they fired a shot!" and the Chevrolet pulled out of sight down the side street.

Farther down Second Street, they could see FBI agents swarming around their vehicles and looking down toward their Porsche, some of them with guns out. Lucas pushed his foot to the floor and then almost immediately braked and they fishtailed at the corner, following the Chevrolet and he was back on the gas again when they saw the Chevrolet pull up and over a curb and Sherwood said, "What are they—"

The woman jumped out in the street and bullets, a lot of them, began banging and pinging off the car and Lucas shouted, "Jesus!" and jammed on the brakes and he and Sherwood both went low, trying to get behind the engine block, but the seats were too tight to get all the way down. A burst of slugs took out the windshield, showering them with glass fragments. Lucas tried to get his phone out of his pocket, but couldn't, because he was lying on it.

The shooting stopped and they poked their heads up to see the woman getting back in the Chevrolet. As the other car began to accelerate away, Lucas hit his own gas pedal, but the car went womp-womp-womp and he said, "Got no wheels . . . got no wheels."

He jammed on the brakes and shifted into "park" in the same half second, rolled out in the street and got his pistol loose. He fired five fast shots at the side of the Chevrolet as it turned the corner down the block. It was the best part of a hundred yards away, and he thought he might have hit it once or twice, but wasn't sure about that. The Chevy was moving, swerving, and the bullet drop with his ammo was as much as fourteen inches at a hundred yards, and he wasn't certain of the range.

Sherwood had bailed out of the passenger side and was running toward the corner where the Chevrolet had disappeared. He was fast, faster than Lucas, and when he got to the corner, he stopped, arms akimbo, then bent to catch his breath. When Lucas caught up with him, he said, "Turned the next corner. They're gone, unless the feds are on them."

"I wouldn't count on it," Lucas said. "Though they must have heard the gunfire. You'd think they would have done *something*."

He fumbled his phone out and called 9-1-1 and got the Minneapolis cops looking for the old Chevrolet and the woman who was driving it. "I might have marked it: there should be at least a couple of bullet holes in the side," he told the operator.

Sherwood was jogging back toward the corner where they'd abandoned the Porsche, and Lucas followed, talking to the 9-1-1 operator as he ran.

LUCAS RAN PAST the abandoned Porsche, catching up with Sherwood, and from there they hustled around the corner into Second

Street and jogged toward the FBI cars that were still sitting behind the apartment. The agents saw them coming and two broke toward them with drawn guns and they both put their hands in the air and Lucas shouted, "Marshals Service," but the agents didn't put their guns away until they got close enough to see Lucas's badge.

Lucas and Sherwood trotted up to the cars, and the agent in charge asked, "Where'd you come from?" A half-dozen agents were gathered around Sokolov's body on the ground, while Bernie knelt next to his father, his hand pressed to the older man's heart.

Lucas: "We were cruising. Is he dead?"

"No, but he's hurt. We're waiting for an ambulance. The guy hit him right in the middle of the plate covering his heart. He might have a piece of bullet in him, and for sure has pieces of the plate. If we hadn't armored him up, he'd be as dead as Genghis Khan."

"Good move, then," Lucas said.

"Hell of a shot," Sherwood said. "How long was he exposed? One second?"

"Not long. The guy shot past two of us, threaded the needle."

"We knew he was good," Sherwood said.

AS THEY WERE talking, Abramova and Nikitin were already lying in the back of the red Ford that appeared to be driven, slowly, by an entirely unremarkable man, who said over his shoulder, "What the fuck happened back there? Did you get him?"

"Hit him in the chest," Nikitin said. "Good shot, perfect. Then some asshole came after—"

Abramova cut it: "This doesn't seem to me to be real, but I saw one of the men when he was shooting at us, when we turned the corner. He hit the Chevrolet twice, but I swear to God, it was the man who shot us at Sokolov's house, and that I saw at the motel," Abramova said. "I knocked the car out with the Beretta, but this man is everywhere. A marshal, I think."

A cop car flashed by a block away, on a major street, lights and siren, and then they were on a freeway ramp. They took I-94 to I-35, and back to Iowa, a hundred miles of barren soybean and corn fields, and were never threatened.

LUCAS TOLD THE FBI agents about how they'd happened on the shooter's car as the shot was being fired, about the short, ugly pursuit, gave the agent a quick description of the shooter's car, driven by a woman, and told him that the Minneapolis cops were already looking for it.

"I can't believe they'll be driving very far in that car, it looked like a beater," Lucas said. "They probably have another car ditched somewhere, possibly a black Jeep Cherokee."

The agent went away to speak to somebody on his own cell phone as sirens were breaking out around the neighborhood. Two or three minutes later, an ambulance arrived, with a cop car. The paramedics lifted Sokolov off the ground, the agents circled tightly around him to block a view of the body. Sokolov's face was too-white and clenched with pain, and possibly frightened, his son helping with the move. They put him on a gurney and moved him into the ambulance, his son hanging over him. "Papa, Papa, you'll be okay . . . Papa, please . . ."

The ambulance took off, with Minneapolis patrol cars and FBI vehicles front and back, lights flashing all around. The third FBI car remained at the scene. Lucas and Sherwood walked back to the

Porsche, and on the way, Lucas called 9-1-1 to tell the operator what had happened during the pursuit, and to suggest that a Minneapolis crime scene crew come pick up bullet casings from the street where the woman had stood shooting at them.

The message, he was assured, would be relayed.

At the car, they walked around it once, and then Sherwood started laughing and Lucas asked, "What's funny?"

"Gonna need new wheels, big guy. She mangled this thing. Good God, look at that. I haven't seen anything like this outside an infantry junkyard in Iraq."

He was right. The windshield and back window were entirely gone, the interior roofing was shredded, every piece of sheet metal on the front and the driver's side of the car showed irreparable bullet holes, and three of the four wheels were flat. There were many holes going into the engine compartment, and if the engine wasn't wrecked, it would be seriously compromised. "My insurance agent is gonna pass a kidney stone," Lucas said.

"It was damaged while in pursuit of the enemies of our nation," Sherwood said, in a phony portentous tone. "The U.S. government will recognize its obligations to make you whole."

"I don't think so. The Service keeps trying to get me to drive a service car, and I keep driving my own."

"Well, in that case, you're fucked," Sherwood said. "Look at this: my finger fits in the bullet hole." Then, "I'm starting to get scared."

"I started getting scared five minutes ago. They got a machine gun."

"So now what?" Sherwood asked.

"You call your boss, I call mine, then we wait for Minneapolis to show up. We make statements and . . ."

"Call an Uber?"

"We've fallen low," Lucas said.

LUCAS WALKED AROUND the Porsche, fuming; got a gym bag out of the truck and filled it with personal stuff from the car—sunglasses, iPad, parking meter coins, garage door opener, hideout Ruger .357, four hundred dollars in small bills, like that. Thought about the hit team.

Two Minneapolis detectives showed up, and Lucas and Sherwood both made brief on-the-spot statements, and promised to email complete statements later in the day. The detectives helped push the Porsche to the curb, where Lucas locked it. That done, he took a last look at the car and said to Sherwood, "We gotta try to blow these people up. The hit team."

"What do you have in mind?"

"St. Vincent doesn't like me. I've got an idea of what we could do next, but it would ramp up the hate, if he ever found out."

"I believe my reaction to that would be, fuck him," Sherwood said. "Tell me."

"Look at the possibilities. The hit team may be on the run. If they are, and if they have good IDs, they could be in Mexico by tomorrow night. Driving. I've driven from the Twin Cities to Dallas in one stretch. They'd be moving slower, so they don't attract highway patrolmen, but they could still make it to OKC without any trouble, tonight, three of them driving, and then . . ."

"OKC?"

"Oklahoma City. From there to the Mexican border is another day or so, down through Texas, Brownsville, and from there . . . Back in the USSR."

"The Beatles," Sherwood said. "Haven't thought about them in decades, but the song still plays in Russia. Okay, so if they've run, they're gone. You'd be right about that."

"If they haven't run, if they find out Sokolov isn't dead, if they set up for another shot at him, our best chance at getting to them is to make them move," Lucas said. "We need to shake them out where people can see them. If they've got a safe house here in the Cities, people would still have seen them coming and going. It's possible that the place out in Minnetrista was their only safe house, and they're ditched in another motel somewhere."

"I'll buy that. How do we shake them loose?"

"The news people know what's happened, but in a sketchy way, because the FBI is so tight-assed about releasing information that hasn't been thoroughly sterilized and is therefore uninteresting. But the media is poking around, they're looking for angles. They'll be looking for more after today."

"And . . ."

"I would suggest that I talk quietly to a friend at the BCA, which has the video taken at the motel. I get a copy of that, under the table, completely deniable on both ends, and leak it to a media friend along with some details about Sokolov's history. That'd give people an idea of what the team looks like—body styles, height, and so on."

"Interesting concept," Sherwood said. "That would also be . . . transgressive."

"But not stupid," Lucas said. "One of the things that has increasingly pissed me off about cops and the government in general is that they hide information from the public, but that everybody else knows. These Russians know what they look like. The FBI knows what they look like. Putting them on TV with an appeal for information is not going to reveal any big classified secrets."

Now Sherwood smiled. "Most intelligence work is a waste of time, and this is exactly one of the problems . . . People get information and then they hide it, for no good reason. I'm with you on this. How fast can you set it up?"

"Got to get that video . . . gonna have to talk to a guy . . . gonna have to talk to somebody in the media . . ." Lucas looked at his watch. "We need to have it organized by the four o'clock news."

THEY SPENT ANOTHER fifteen minutes talking about what Lucas should leak to the media, before the Uber arrived. They stayed quiet on the way back to Lucas's house, where Sherwood picked up his car. He'd go back to his hotel to call his CIA supervisors and to tell them what was about to happen.

"If they have a problem with it?" Lucas asked, on the way out the door.

"They won't," Sherwood said. "They'll ask, 'How does this come back to us?' The answer is, 'It won't, and it could shake the hit team loose.' They'll be fine with it, as long as nobody knows that they knew about it in advance."

"All right," Lucas said. "Stay in touch. If something comes up, and you want me to kill the release, you gotta call me in an hour or an hour and a half. After that, it'll be too late."

"Do it," Sherwood said.

WITH SHERWOOD ON his way back to his hotel, Lucas called an old friend at the Bureau of Criminal Apprehension, Jon Duncan, and said, "I need a favor. Not a big one, a medium-sized one."

"Is that fuckin' Flowers involved?" Flowers was a BCA agent and a friend of Lucas's.

"No, no," Lucas said. "I've been working this spy thing for the Marshals Service, and Virgil's typing out another book."

"I heard you've been shooting at people again."

"And they've been shooting at me," Lucas said. "You guys took video out of that motel, the shooters changing cars."

"We did. Interesting stuff."

"I need a copy of that," Lucas said. "Just so you know, I'm gonna give it to the media. It'd be best if it was the raw video, not cleaned up or anything, so it can't come back to you."

"That could have some undesirable ramifications, if anyone found out," Duncan said.

"Of course it could," Lucas said. "That's why it's a medium favor, instead of a small one."

"If I get fired, will you get me on with the Marshals Service?" Duncan asked.

"Probably not. We wouldn't want somebody who leaks stuff to the media," Lucas said.

"Thanks a lot, dipshit," Duncan said.

"Listen, I might be able to blame the release on the FBI."

A moment of contemplation. "All right. You know where I'm at, on this kind of thing. I'll email it to you. After you pass it on, burn your laptop."

"Thanks, Jon."

"You owe me big," Duncan said.

"I owe you medium."

THE VIDEO CAME in twenty minutes later, as the Uber turned into Lucas's driveway. It popped up on his iPad, anonymously, with an equally anonymous note that read "The original."

Lucas called a woman named Daisy Jones who ran a late afternoon TV show called *Jonesing for News*. When she came up, she asked, "What?"

"You sound impatient with me. That makes me sad, considering our long-term friendship," Lucas said. "Maybe I could go to Channel Three, where I have a former lover, eager to speak to me any day, any time."

"Fuck her. I'm prepping for an interview. With a guy I don't care about. So. What do you want?"

"I've got video of the Russian spies we shot up the other day," Lucas said. "When they were trading cars at that motel. Nobody else has it. I want to get it out there, so it maybe jogs the memory of somebody who's seen them. But, it can't come from me."

"Screw the guy I don't care about. When can you get it to me?" she asked.

"I could email it to you, but then there'd be a record and you'd use it to blackmail me."

"Yeah, I probably would," she said. "Put it on a thumb drive and meet me at the Starbucks across from the station."

"Thirty minutes," Lucas said.

LUCAS GOT A clean thumb drive from his home office, loaded the video on it, and took his second car, a Porsche 911, across town. Jones was waiting at a table at Starbucks with a cup of coffee and a cup of hot chocolate. She pushed the chocolate at Lucas and he handed her the thumb drive.

Jones was an attractive fortysomething woman who had been working the police beat since journalism school and knew most of the Twin Cities cops by their first names. "What can you tell me that you don't want me to say on the air, but will help me understand what I'm doing here?"

Lucas took a sip of the hot chocolate and said, "Mmm. Good." And, "We think the hit team may still be here in the Cities. We're trying to roust them, using you to do the rousting."

"Where did I get the video?" she asked.

"You won't say, but if people got the impression that it was the FBI, I would appreciate it. You could call me a source close to the FBI's investigation."

"But it didn't come from them?" she asked.

"Maybe not. I'm not sure."

"You're not sure." She rolled her eyes, thought about it, then said, "You probably got it from Jon Duncan at the BCA." She checked Lucas for a flinch.

Lucas didn't flinch. He smiled and said, "Terrific guess. Blame it on Jon. The miserable piece of shit wouldn't fix a speeding ticket for me. Highway patrol got me on I-35 down by Owatonna. He could have done it, if he wanted to."

"So where?"

"Let's just say I was alone at the motel manager's video station for a minute, after the shooting. I mean . . . you'll see, it's not BCA video, all cleaned up. It's raw. But an FBI hint would make me happy, and I am close to the investigation."

"You're fucking with St. Vincent."

"You're smarter than you have any right to be," Lucas said.

She put a finger along the side of her nose, studying him through her black-rimmed hot-librarian glasses. "About sixty percent of what you just told me are lies, but I don't know which sixty percent. I'll pretend I believe everything."

"Thank you. Daisy . . . this is a real thing. You'll be doing a service," Lucas said.

She said, "Jesus Christ, Lucas, don't get all sincere with me, okay? As for the video, I'll lead the show with it."

"You want a little more anonymous background?"

She lifted a shoulder bag off the floor next to her chair. "That's why I brought my notebook."

WHEN HE LEFT Daisy, Lucas sat in the 911 and thought about it, and especially about what Weather would have to say about the fact that he'd been in another shoot-out, and the shoot-out had ruined a car and their insurance bill would be going up again and how he was pretty goddamned cavalier about the fact, so much so that he'd actually gone out and bought another vehicle.

Then he got up some guts and drove to the Maplewood Porsche dealer.

While he was there, he got the salesman to change the TV channel to *Jonesing for News*. Daisy broke the news about Sokolov being shot, quoting, by name, two Minneapolis homicide investigators, and relaying a "no comment" from the FBI. Then she played the video twice. She said it was given her by an anonymous source close to the investigation. She said that the FBI was currently refusing to *officially* release it, which implied that it had been unofficially released by one of her FBI sources, effectively siccing all the other local stations on the feds.

Then she did something he hadn't expected: "Sources close to the investigation said that the assassin's vehicle was shot up by two well-known U.S Marshals who were at the site of the murder when it was committed, Shelly White and Lucas Davenport. White refused to comment, and we are attempting to reach Davenport."

That made him smile. Then his picture, and White's, flashed up on the screen, and he stopped smiling.

Sherwood called Lucas three minutes after the end of the segment, as Lucas was fiddling with the buttons on the inside of a new Porsche Panamera, and said, "Well done, pal. If this doesn't shake the hitters loose, they've probably left the building."

"She put my fuckin' photo up," Lucas said.

"I thought you looked nice. That was a Hermes necktie? Little white clouds?"

WHEN HE RANG off with Sherwood, the Porsche salesman said, "Look, you say you used to drive your Cayenne up to the cabin. You could do that in this Panamera, right here." He patted the gumball-colored Panamera that crouched next to Lucas's leg. "We could roll it off the floor in five minutes, take it for a run. This baby is fast, four-wheel drive, handles like your 911, and can carry all your stuff."

"And sits four inches off the ground, which wouldn't work all that well on the road to my cabin," Lucas said. "I like it, but I'm not going to buy it."

HE TOOK A call from Russell Forte at the Marshal's Service headquarters in Virginia. "You're on TV? What the heck happened, and how'd you get involved?"

Lucas explained and could imagine Forte shaking his head. "This is a mess," Forte said, when Lucas had finished. "But it's the FBI's mess. Or maybe it's the CIA's. We're only in ankle-deep, if it turns out you're not standing in quicksand."

"It's getting interesting, Russ," Lucas said. "These people are determined to kill Sokolov, and there's a serious intelligence leak somewhere. I don't think it's Sherwood, because if it was, he would have tried to steer me away from the sniper's shooting position. He was in my car when that woman damn near killed both of us with a machine gun. He's already been shot once. So there's that. And honestly, the FBI isn't real good at chasing people . . ."

Forte said, "I'm not going to forbid you from hanging around, but take it easy. Very easy."

"Have you heard anything about Sokolov's condition?"

"As far as I know, he's still in surgery," Forte said. "Apparently a piece of the slug got through his breast bone and was virtually touching his heart, and several pieces of the ceramic plate and the canvas jacket are also in there, maybe in a lung. They haven't figured out what ammo the shooter was using, but we should know by tonight."

"Gonna be one of those weird ones, a .277, like the first time."

"Yeah, well . . ."

"I'll take it easy, Russ."

DESPITE BEING TEMPTED by the Panamera, Lucas bought a new Cayenne GTS in chromite black metallic with an all-black leather interior, heated and cooled seats, heated steering wheel, Apple CarPlay and satellite radio, claimed 0–60 in 4.2 seconds, all for a low, low price that nearly stopped his heart. He was momentarily grateful that he hadn't gone for the Panamera, which would have killed him for sure. He drove the new car home, followed by the salesman in the 911, not looking forward to the reception by Weather.

He didn't spend all of his time worrying about Weather, though: "We're running behind them," he said aloud, to himself, meaning the hit team. "They've got the edge on us."

And he wondered: "Are they still with us?" No answer to that.

Back at his house, Waylon's Tow and Repo Service had dropped the wounded Porsche at the curb, and a cluster of neighbors were looking at it. He and the Porsche salesman parked the two Porsches in the garage and walked out to the curb.

One of his neighbors said, "Good lord, Lucas, this is a goddamned sin."

The Porsche salesman kept walking in circles around it, saying, "Good God. Good God."

"Appeals to a deity won't fix it," Lucas said. "I noticed that none of you hosers asked if I was okay."

Another of the neighbors said, "That's because you're not. Here comes Weather."

15

Kuznetsov called when the team was halfway back to Iowa. "We are told by our asset that Sokolov was wearing armor under his sweater. Your bullet hit him over his heart, but the armor stopped most of it. Not all of it—he has a serious chest wound and may yet die. He is in the hospital operating room, in surgery. We will know more when he emerges."

"If your asset is so close, why didn't he warn us of the armor plate?" Abramova asked.

The sigh was audible. "They put the armor on one minute before they walked out the door," Kuznetsov said.

Nikitin: "Ah! A head shot was too risky, so I shot for the heart. If I had known about the armor . . ."

"Tell me why this shot is risky, so I can explain it," Kuznetsov said.

"People move their heads all the time, and quickly, and in all directions. The chest, not so much. It is steadier and larger. We are trained for heart shots when that is possible. I could see no armor when he came out of the building. If I had known about the armor, I would have shot for the head."

"I will explain this to the people here," Kuznetsov said. "There is much disappointment."

"Call again when you know if Sokolov lives," Abramova said. "We will talk here about what to do next, if he lives."

THE RUSSIAN TEAM again took two separate rooms at the Iowa motel, and smuggled Nikitin into Titov's. When it seemed safe, they gathered in Titov's room to strategize, eat, browse the Internet, talk about possibilities, and watch television. Titov, because he could pass as American, went out to pizza parlors for food and soft drinks.

Kuznetsov called Abramova that evening. She put the phone on speaker so the others could hear, and Kuznetsov said, "Our source in Minneapolis tells us that Sokolov may yet survive. Also, you are all now famous on television."

"What?"

"You were on television this afternoon and now are streaming on the Internet on this *Jonesing for News* . . ."

"The what?"

"*Jonesing for News*. I'll spell it for you . . ."

He did, including the "*for News*" part. Nikitin, who was online, brought up a search field and typed in "*Jonesing for News*."

As he was doing that, Kuznetsov said, "This matter of the cars is perplexing. You are scattering them like potato chips. We have spoken to our friends in Minneapolis and they are finding two more cold cars for you. You will have them tomorrow morning. I will text the location and license numbers. Keys on the back tire."

"If we're to go for Sokolov again, with the rifle, we'll need them," Abramova said.

"They won't be moving him for a few days. They took some metal from his chest," Kuznetsov said.

"You have an excellent source," Abramova said.

"Yes."

"Perhaps we should deal with this person directly."

"Not possible at this time," Kuznetsov said.

"Then call us when you have the pickup arrangements for the cars. And all other arrangements."

"We're waiting for a return from our source. In the meantime, I should tell you that Orlov is on his way home."

"No! How did you manage that?" Abramova asked.

"When he was stable, we informed the hospital that his wife wanted him moved to a private clinic for recovery and physical therapy," Kuznetsov said, sounding pleased with himself. "We had him picked up by a private ambulance service and taken to a smaller Milwaukee airport and flown from there to Toronto on a Canadian passport. Two hours ago, he was in the air for Leningrad."

"This is very gratifying," Abramova said, and behind her, Titov called, "Wonderful!"

"We expect to have the new cars for you tomorrow. I remind you, and I am serious, the man is watching this operation. He asks for updates in the morning, and noon, and night."

"We will not let him down," Abramova said.

"We will tell him of your pledge."

"THIS SCARES ME," Nikitin said, when the call had ended. "The man is asking about us morning, noon, and night. I didn't need to know that."

"We could defect," Titov said. He tried to sound like he was joking. "The Americans would protect us."

"We would have to eat at McDonalds," Abramova said, with a put-on grimace. "Or this Burger King. Death would be preferable."

"You might get your death, from one side or the other, if we fuck this up," Titov said.

"We won't fuck it up, but whatever we're about to do, it will be complicated," Abramova said. "Now let's see this 'Nosing for News' that we're on."

"*Jonesing*," Nikitin said. "I don't know what that means."

"American drug slang," Titov said. "If you 'jones' for something, you want it badly."

Nikitin: "Ah. I have the video."

THEY WATCHED THEMSELVES on the computer screen, scrambling out of the oversized Jeep and into the Subaru, and then fleeing the motel. They watched it again, and again. The photos of two marshals came, up and Abramova said, "So this is the fucker who shot us."

After the third time through the video, Titov asked, "What do you think?"

Abramova: "You don't see our faces, but we are . . . a group of types. If you see the video, and then you see the three of us together, you might recognize us. One at a time, we are not distinct. We are not distinct in this motel, but if somebody walked in this room in one minute, with all three of us here . . ."

"Give me the TV clicker," Titov said. He said "clicker" in English, and Abramova and Nikitin looked at each other, and he added, "remote" in Russian. Nikitin found the remote in a couch cushion and tossed it to him.

The room television was not a particularly smart TV, but it was smart enough to bring up the TV channels from the largest nearby stations, which were the Twin Cities. It took some clicking around, but eventually they found *Jonesing for News* and again watched the replay from earlier in the afternoon.

"Even Iowa people can see us," Nikitin said, when Titov clicked off.

"Not easy to find that show. Who would watch it, anyway, if you live here?" Abramova asked.

"Almost nobody," Titov said. "But all it takes is one."

"When each of us has a car, we can check into separate motels, and then we'll be invisible again," Nikitin said.

"Tomorrow," Abramova said. "Tomorrow, in the Twin Cities. Maybe I will deliver flowers to a hospital patient in a room near Sokolov's."

"A thousand policemen there, FBI, marshals," Titov said.

"But we should have a look, somehow," Abramova said. "I wouldn't try to get close."

"We'll need some information about the hospital," Nikitin said.

"With their source, Kuznetsov should be able to help us with something as simple as that."

"Unless they've isolated Sokolov on a whole floor, or in some special security area," Titov said. "It would be better if I made the reconnaissance. I have good ID, I really can pass as American."

"Then I will leave it to you," Abramova said. "We talk about it. I have no other ideas."

NIKITIN WAS STILL in pain, though the drugs were helping, and the wound seemed to be healing. The pain was deep, and he had hand-sized bruises on his butt and leg, but they were turning yellow, which the Internet said was a good sign. Still, he wouldn't be running or even walking any distance. He felt he could drive, since he had no problem sitting upright, and had been wounded in his left leg. If they were to try sniping Sokolov again, it would have to be from a car.

"I don't believe they will give us another chance with the rifle," Nikitin said. "Not unless I can get a platform across from the hospital and hit him through a window. But they're not complete fools: if there was such a platform, they would be occupying it, and they would never open the curtains on the room."

"Maybe you should check out, see if you can get home," Titov said. "We could talk to Kuznetsov. If they could get Matvey out . . ."

Nikitin shook his head: "I can't run, but with drugs, I can walk, if I have to. Even better tomorrow. I still have eyes and a telephone. I can drive. I'm not Kat, but I'm good enough."

"That could all be useful," Titov said. "Still, we have to take care. The Americans know from the video that you were wounded: they could be looking for a man who limps."

They plucked at the possibility of entering the hospital on a reconnaissance, ate pizza and drank Dr Pepper, and at eleven o'clock,

Abramova slipped out of Titov's room and returned to her own, unseen in the night.

ABRAMOVA WAS THIRTY-SIX, unmarried, unattached, an attractive blonde who worked with two athletic, thirtyish men. Under normal circumstances, sex would raise its head, but that had been dealt with early in their relationship. She did not, and would not, sleep with either of the men on her team, nor with other operators, who, like Titov, were contracted by the Unit.

She'd had occasional sexual relationships in Moscow, mostly with men from the Russian State Agrarian University, where she was allowed to audit courses at the Institute of Horticulture and Landscape Architecture. She had nothing against sex, but didn't find it compelling. The refusal to sleep with team members was a matter of good management. They got along on that basis.

She approached the work of her team as she would a puzzle, though it was much more interesting than a common puzzle, because the pieces were always shifting shape. Time, place, methods—they constantly moved. Violent death was always the final piece, and in itself, didn't much affect her, as long as the puzzle was complete.

She didn't believe that she was either a sociopath or a psychopath, she was simply a person with muted emotional reactions to things that caused great emotion in others. Things like danger, and death.

Nikitin, on the other hand, was clever, intelligent, often amusing, often charming. He liked women and was prepared to like Abramova until she backed him off. He was also a psychopath. If what he felt in killing wasn't pleasure, it was something off in that direction—

apparently, a kind of release. It seemed to Abramova that a long period without a kill built up a psychological pressure within him, and she suspected that when the job didn't provide him with a target and a kill, he would find one on his own. A man to keep an eye on.

Orlov, however, was a self-effacing man, almost a nebbish, and brilliant in his ability to walk through the streets of even a small town without being particularly noticed or commented upon. He could follow a wary target a mile through Berlin, Amsterdam, or London without ever being seen, and could efficiently and precisely zero Nikitin to the target. He also had an instinctive sense of direction and a love of maps. He could navigate through the canyons of a major city after looking once at a satellite photo.

The team was very good at what they did, and they'd done it seventeen times, though never before in America.

BACK IN HER room after leaving Titov's, Abramova took a shower—one of the things she liked best in America, the long hot showers in even routine accommodations—then lay on the bed and thought about a new approach to the Sokolov problem.

How do you get at a man concealed somewhere in a large building, not under his own name, with hospital staff alerted to inquiries, with possible expert surveillance by non-uniformed FBI agents, and with armed and well-trained gunmen covering the target?

Could somebody go in as a patient? It would have to be Titov, since Nikitin had a strong Russian accent; she also had an accent, and either she or Nikitin would set off alarms.

It was a puzzle.

And after a long review, she decided that the puzzle had no easy solution. It did have a solution, but one that she was almost afraid to suggest.

THEY LEFT BEFORE dawn the next morning, to mitigate the possibility of being seen and identified at the motel. They checked out one at a time, five minutes apart, and once gathered in the car, Titov drove, Abramova rode in the front passenger seat, and Nikitin lay in the back, out of sight.

Two hours to the Twin Cities. As Titov settled into the flow of traffic on the interstate, Abramova said, "I have been puzzling this situation, looking for an answer. I think Lev is correct. We will not get another chance with the rifle."

Titov: "We give up and go home?"

"Not with the man watching. But, there is somebody close to Sokolov, who is on our side. Yes? I'm thinking we use this ChapStick."

Titov grunted. "Ah. Then everything is out in the open. They might learn the identity of our agent."

"Not our problem," Abramova said. "We do a dead drop with the ChapStick, and then we're out."

From the back seat, Nikitin said, "If we shoot him, it might not be an official assassination. It might be anyone, even somebody who is legal in America, but who suffered from Sokolov's actions. Revenge. If we use the ChapStick, it is a known Kremlin action. The man will be blamed."

"Does he care?"

The ChapStick had started life as an actual ChapStick, the strawberry flavor. It had been taken apart in a laboratory outside Moscow, where the waxy lip balm had been carefully removed as a tube, and cut into two portions. The top three-quarters had been set aside, and the bottom one-quarter, thrown away. That quarter was replaced with a transparent cylinder of malleable plastic, that looked much like the ChapStick. The plastic cylinder contained a bead of a waxy nerve agent known as Novichok, developed by Russian chemical warfare researchers and used in several assassinations and assassination attempts.

A thin black-glass seal with a pull tab was placed over the poisonous portion, and then the original ChapStick compound reinserted on top. An X-ray would not detect the change. In use, an assassin would turn the ChapStick dial at the bottom of the tube, pushing up the contents, until the glass appeared.

The actual ChapStick would be discarded, the glass seal carefully peeled away and flushed down a toilet. The cap would then be replaced until the actual assassination attempt. The assassin would have to get close to the target, remove the cap, and contrive to rub the Novichok compound on the victim's skin. The victim's death would resemble heart failure.

The reworked tube of ChapStick currently resided in a plastic box inside a bag of medicines that none of them used, stashed in Abramova's suitcase. They all feared it; even the smallest touch of Novichok could be a killer.

ON THE WAY north, they talked off and on about other possibilities but concluded that most were fantasies. "We have to talk with Kuznetsov," Nikitin said. "I believe the man would be consulted about the ChapStick."

"We have to ask," Abramova said. "The only other possibility I see is a direct attack on the FBI vehicles taking Sokolov to an airport. An ambush, in which FBI agents would be killed, and we might be killed as well. Sokolov might not be."

"Not that the man would suffer over our deaths," Titov said.

"Maybe a little bit," Abramova said.

Titov snorted. Then, "We must consult with Kuznetsov."

"And see what we can see at the hospital," Abramova said. "Test all possibilities."

16

The previous night, Lucas, Weather, and Sherwood again had dinner together, Weather having recovered from a mild snit about the wrecked Porsche: the snit had been partially neutralized by the fact that neither Lucas nor Sherwood had been injured. They met at an Italian restaurant on Saint Paul's Grand Avenue, where Sherwood denied leading Lucas into trouble, claiming that they'd had little idea of what they were doing when they were attacked.

Then Weather interrogated Sherwood about specific spy techniques that she'd read about in thriller novels or seen on television, and about lapses in security that had made it to national news stories.

"Most of what you read is a lot of bull. Most spies are clerks. Most of them do it for the money. There aren't very many serious secrets. The military needs to keep tactical plans secret until they're executed, but everybody understands everybody else's strategy, even in the smallest details," Sherwood told her. "You need to keep the names of your spies secret . . . but, there's not much else. Most of what we need to know we can either get from satellites or by watching Russian and Chinese and Iranian TV and reading their newspapers."

He added some stories, and between the *primi* (lobster risotto) and the *secondi* (Colorado lamb chops with black truffle demi-glace), Weather asked if he should be telling her all these things, and he said, "Everybody in Washington knows this stuff. You can keep a lot of secrets about one thing or another, but there's no keeping down a good spy story, especially when there's blatant stupidity involved."

At one point, Sherwood asked Lucas, "How much have you told Weather about what we've been doing?"

"Pretty much everything," Lucas admitted.

Weather pointed a truffle-glace-streaked fork at Sherwood and asked, "Why aren't you all over that Chevrolet? The one Lucas shot at? The Russians must have gotten it from somewhere."

The car had been found by Minneapolis police, abandoned in a narrow street not far from the shooting site. It had two bullet holes in the back fender, but no blood inside.

"BCA and the feds *are* all over it," Lucas told Weather. "There's gotta be some kind of Russian connection, but I don't know where it would come from. Not my area."

"I bet Del would know," Weather said to Lucas.

Sherwood: "Who's that?"

"Old friend, BCA guy," Lucas said. He said, "Del. Huh."

"He pretends to be the scum of the earth," Weather said.

Lucas: "Be nice. He's a good friend."

"I said *pretends*. He's a good friend, but he's convincing scum. That's why he's so useful," Weather said.

Sherwood: "Do you have Russians here? I mean, *bratva* guys? Like mafia?"

"Maybe," Lucas said. "I haven't heard much myself, but a couple of Minneapolis vice cops went on television and claimed that Russian women were turning up as high-end escorts. So there's that. That's about all I know about it."

"Where there's escorts, there's fire," Sherwood said.

Lucas leaned back in his chair, held up a finger to a passing waiter who had not yet mastered the passing waiter's skill of not seeing fingers, and when he stopped, Lucas said, "We're gonna need dessert menus."

When the waiter had gone to get them, he explained to Sherwood that Capslock's job was to hang out. In that capacity, he knew and was friendly with much of the Minnesota lowlife. "If there are Russian criminals here, he would probably know about it. He might even know them."

"The *bratva* can be an extension of the Russian intelligence services," Sherwood said. "They take the money back home, or to Eastern Europe, and they need connections to do that. They do favors. Like round up cars."

"All right," Lucas said, looking around. "Where's that waiter?"

"Could you give Del a call?" Sherwood asked. "I mean, before dessert?"

"I guess."

"Go do that. I'll get you a crème brûlée," Weather said. "Say hello to Del for me."

LUCAS CALLED DEL Capslock, who was sitting in a shithole bar called the Territorial. "Do you know anything about Russians?"

"Well, they're having a war with the Ukrainians," Capslock said.

"I mean here in the Cities."

"I heard one got shot, or shot at, or something like that. You know I don't do TV."

"I'm thinking of the guys who might be involved in running hookers, or dope, or doing extortion, that kind of thing. Crooks. Criminals. Assholes. Bratwursts."

"We don't allow extortion, but, yeah, there are some Russians involved in the escort business. We've talked to some of the escorts and they haven't been trafficked. They're here to make some money."

"You're sure about that?"

"Pretty sure, yeah. These are high-end girls. They're not locked up in whorehouses. We, I mean, you know, the Minneapolis vice guys, talked to some of the girls privately, told them that there wouldn't be any come-backs," Capslock said. "They've all got their own bank accounts and they gave up names of former escorts who left the game and moved out to LA or Miami. The vice guys checked with the California CBI, and they took a look. Said the girls were clean. Some of them had straight jobs in the industry. Fairly straight."

"If we put a pipe wrench on the neck of one of these Russians, you're saying they wouldn't have much to give up."

"Oh . . . there are some stories about loan-sharking. They might have a finger in that—banking, not street sales. You need to put some pressure?"

"Yeah. The guy who got shot at, that you didn't see on TV. He's being hunted by a Russian hit team. They've already killed a woman, and we think the local Russians have been cooperating."

"Let me get a name or two. I'll call you before you go to bed, if you're still staying up late."

"I am."

WHEN LUCAS GOT back to the table, Weather had eaten a slice of his crème brûlée and she and Sherwood were talking about Letty.

"I was telling John that Letty doesn't want to be in the CIA," Weather said. She pushed the crème brûlée dish toward him. "I ate one third of your dessert. Maybe a little more than a third. You didn't need the extra calories anyway."

Lucas asked Sherwood, "When you got your last divorce, was it because your wife ate your desserts?"

"No, no. She was sleeping with a defensive end for the Washington Redskins," Sherwood said. "Started when I was in Afghanistan. Guy was a brute. Six-seven, two-thirty. Did the forty in four-six. He could pull the arms off the Statue of Liberty."

"Eat the dessert," Weather said to Lucas. "What did Del say?"

"He was at the Territorial," Lucas said. To Sherwood: "A dive bar. He'll get me a name or two of the connected Russkis, call me tonight."

"Excellent," Sherwood said, taking the napkin off his lap and dropping it on the table. "Why don't I stop by your place in the morning, say seven-thirty?"

"How about ten-thirty? Del will probably be out until one o'clock tonight, maybe two. He won't be up before nine."

"All right. But ten's almost lunchtime back at my office . . ."

"One thing I oughta say," Weather said. "Since I work in hospitals and this Russian person is in a hospital. Big ones, like Hennepin, have hundreds of people coming and going all day and all night, and hundreds of rooms. Are you sure these Russians can't get to what's his name, Solokov, in the hospital?"

"Sokolov," Sherwood said. "Honestly, they've got FBI agents, their

SWAT guys, stacked up around him. I don't know about their competence . . ."

"They're pretty good. Their SWAT does tough stuff," Lucas said.

Weather: "But, they're not cops."

"Yeah, there's that," Lucas said.

"Why aren't they cops? They got badges," Sherwood said.

"They don't think like cops. Even the former cops, after they spend some time in the FBI, they stop thinking like cops," Lucas said. "They don't hang out. They don't notice things. They go someplace, they do something . . . and they go back to the office and sit at the computer and enter their data. I don't know if Del even has a computer. Or a necktie."

"The point being . . ."

"If somebody looked good walking around a hospital, you know, scrubs, shoe covers, I'm not sure the FBI would smell the bullshit. A street cop might," Weather said.

"How does a plastic surgeon know this?" Sherwood asked.

"Because ever since I got involved with Lucas, my house has been full of street cops. You just don't know . . ." She looked at Lucas: "You should introduce him to Jenkins and Shrake. Or Virgil."

"He's not ready for that," Lucas said.

Sherwood said, "Whatever. Maybe . . . we should take a look around the hospital?"

Lucas: "You think St. Vincent would let us?"

"Oh, probably, if I asked. I don't know what we'd get, though, if we were just there for half an hour," Sherwood said. "I don't see us staking the place out."

"Neither do I," Lucas said. "Be nice to know the territory, though."

"I'll call St. Vincent. Tell him we'll be dropping by in the morning. Let's do nine-thirty."

LUCAS ROLLED OUT of bed at nine o'clock, did a hurried clean-up, got dressed, and ate a bowl of some kind of brown flakes that claimed to be organic, and had just gone to the front door when Sherwood pulled into the driveway.

"Let's take the new Porsche," Sherwood said. "We're cleared to walk around the hospital. I got a name."

On the way to Minneapolis, Sherwood said, "My researchers say you were a jock in college. Hockey."

"I was. I still put the skates on occasionally," Lucas said. "Senior men's league."

"I ran track," Sherwood said. "Have you been reading about this NCAA name, image, and likeness? About paying jocks, football and basketball? The NIL deals? And the nonrevenue sports get screwed? The Olympic sports?"

"Of course they do," Lucas said. "The NCAA has never been about anything but money, and that's football and basketball."

"Fuckers," Sherwood said. "I get pissed reading about it, and I haven't run in twenty years."

"Were you any good?"

"Yeah, I was okay. High hurdles. Tier one recruit, never could quite cut the last quarter-second off my times."

They talked about sports for a while, and about competitiveness, and about team play versus individual sports, and how that carried into their careers.

"The CIA is different than the FBI," Sherwood said, watching the city go by. "I mean, by personality type. The FBI is all about teams, and the CIA isn't. We're about talent. The FBI is mostly Republicans, the CIA is mostly Democrats. The Marshals Service, as far as I've seen, is different than the FBI and the CIA. Haven't figured it out yet, but it seems like the brows get lower as you step down the scale."

"You're saying the Marshals Service is at the bottom?"

"It's more . . . obscure," Sherwood said. "Nobody knows exactly what you guys do, because you're all over the place. I wouldn't say you're at the bottom. You're more like sideways from all the other gun-toters."

"Thank you," Lucas said.

"You're welcome. I'm interested the way you compare street cops to FBI agents. Like they're totally different animals."

"They are."

"I had my researcher take a look at your daughter," Sherwood said. "She comes across as a hybrid of an intelligence operator and a marshal, skipping the FBI altogether. Maybe a little bloodthirsty."

"Not bloodthirsty—she doesn't back away when somebody wants to jack up the violence. She doesn't start things, but she's willing to end them," Lucas said. "She's smart, works hard, got a good education. Best female combat shooter you'd ever meet. With pistols, anyway."

"I know. She doesn't really work for Homeland Security, though, does she? She actually works for a Republican senator but pretends to work for Homeland Security. She's a shooter. You pretend to work for the Marshals Service, and sometimes you do, but you're also wound tight into the Senate. My researcher tells me you could call up almost any senator, ask a favor, and get it."

"That might be an overstatement," Lucas said. "I've worked with several senators, and, I guess, word gets around."

"My researcher says you've given significant help to seven different senators," Sherwood said. "The kind of thing that saves careers. You might even have saved the life of the lady senator from Georgia."

"There's a little more to that than your researcher knows," Lucas said.

"You mean that some people believe that you lured a right-wing nut to the senator's house so you could kill him?"

Lucas glanced at Sherwood and said, "Your researcher is picking up unsupported rumors."

"Yeah? He's a really good researcher. Really good. He's especially good at sifting out unsupported rumors."

"Is all this leading to something?" Lucas asked.

"Just wanted to let you know that I'm an excellent connection for a guy like you. You and your daughter are excellent connections for a guy like me. If you or Letty ever think you might need something I could give you, under the table, call me. I'll give you a private number."

"And you'll call us if you need something?"

"Of course. That's the way it works."

THE HENNEPIN COUNTY Medical Center was a labyrinthine complex of rooms, hallways, and elevators, decorated mostly in varieties of beige and pale gray, with splashes of blue and red; like most hospitals, it smelled of cleaning fluids. Weather wasn't on staff, so Lucas hadn't often gotten past the emergency room when he was working in Minneapolis.

Sherwood had called ahead and an FBI agent, who appeared to be fourteen, but was probably older, and was named Jason Coulter, met them in the reception area and led them through the labyrinth to a room in the birth center.

"If the Russians tried to bust in, we figure they wouldn't expect Sokolov to be in this area," Coulter said.

"Don't count on that," Sherwood said. "They have good intel."

"That's what we've been told. We don't think they'd make the effort to get him here, but in case they do, we're trying to exploit every possible edge."

"As you should," Lucas said. "These guys are good."

The ward was on the fourth level. Two more agents, dressed in scrubs and wearing hair coverings, were sitting at a nurses' station, with two more inside Sokolov's room.

"More edges," Coulter said. "Guys who look kinda like doctors, sitting with the nurses, and there's nothing in a hallway that would quickly identify a specific room. They'd have to look in each room as they run down the hallway. The hall's monitored with cameras at each end, transmitting to iPads in Sokolov's room. Even if they got in, there'd be guns waiting for them."

"Fire stairs?" Lucas asked.

"More cameras."

"Ah."

They took a quick look in Sokolov's room. Sokolov lying in bed, in a blue hospital gown, slightly propped up so he could watch television, if he was conscious and his eyes were open, which he apparently wasn't, and they weren't. The two bodyguard agents were on their feet, looking at Lucas and Sherwood, and Lucas showed them empty hands.

"We recognized you," one of them said.

"I was afraid St. Vincent told you to shoot me," Lucas said.

"He did, but we were told to let you make the first move," the agent said; he smiled as he said it, but the other one didn't.

Sherwood went to Sokolov's bed and asked, "You awake, Leonid?"

Sokolov twitched, seemed to struggle to get his eyes open, but failed. He might have tried to mutter something, but it was unintelligible.

Sherwood said, "I'm sorry about all of this, I truly am. It shouldn't have happened. We'll get you back to the Farm and figure out a new move."

No response. Sherwood patted Sokolov on the leg and said to Lucas, "Let's go look around."

One of the agents whispered, "He's been very quiet. He's only had light painkillers, but he hasn't been coming up."

Sherwood shook his head and whispered back, "Not good."

Before they left, Lucas asked for the lead agent's cell phone number, and poked it into his own phone. Ten minutes later, standing in a stairwell, he called the agent and asked, "Where am I?"

"Stairwell C4, between the third and fourth floors."

"Outstanding."

"WHAT DO YOU think?" Sherwood asked on the way out.

"The FBI has big bureaucracy problems, but their gun guys are usually okay," Lucas said. "I don't see the Russians getting on top of them. Not unless they go in with their automatic weapons and risk a massacre. Even if they did that, I don't see them getting back out. It seems to me that they're trying to stay as safe as they can and not do any more damage than they have to. Haven't killed anyone except Masha, and that looks like a mistake."

"You think Sokolov is safe?"

"In the hospital. I wouldn't guarantee he'd be safe on a ride to the airport. They've got those automatic weapons. Might be a good idea to check the plane for a bomb . . ."

"If he's safe for now, let's go see your Mr. Capslock."

17

Del Capslock lived in the Highland Park area of Saint Paul, not far from Lucas but in a smaller, early twentieth-century house that had two notable characteristics: it had been built on what amounted to a spring, so after wet weather, there was a constant flow of water from under the overhead-door of his tuck-under garage; and a serious lack of insulation in his roof that would take a major renovation to fix.

The insulation problem meant that his roof was warm when it shouldn't be, and snow melted as quickly as it fell. The eaves, however, were not warm, because they hung out over the house. That meant the melted snow water trickling over the eaves tended to refreeze, creating weighty icicles that threatened to crack the roof supports.

When Lucas and Sherwood arrived at his house, Capslock was in his yard, wrapped in a parka and ski mask, trying to knock the twenty-pound icicles off the eaves with a shovel. When he saw them pull into the driveway, he leaned the shovel against the house and walked down his lawn to meet them.

Lucas: "How in the hell did you get icicles like that, when we haven't had any snow?"

"We had enough, and I let it go," Capslock said.

"You need a flame thrower," Sherwood said.

"I need to sell the house to some other chump when the ice melts."

"That, too," Lucas said. He added, "This is John Sherwood, he's a spy who works for the CIA. If you've got a Russian, he'll come with us to chat with them."

"I've got two Russians," Capslock said, as he shook hands with Sherwood. "They stay up later than I do, so they should both be home. Until noon, anyway."

"Where are they?" Lucas asked.

"One is here in Saint Paul, the other's in Bloomington."

"Saint Paul first?"

"Let me change coats and get a different hat," Capslock said. "I'll tell you about them on the way over. I got something a little extra going on."

They followed Capslock inside, said hello to his wife, who was sitting at the kitchen table writing bills; the kitchen smelled of onions and other plants. She said, "Del tells me he's going to get you all in trouble this morning."

"Hasn't mentioned any trouble," Lucas said.

"Because he thinks it's funny. I don't think it's funny, I think Internal Affairs is going to get you all fired. I'd like to see him make it to full retirement."

"Ah, no. What's he done?"

"I'll let him explain it. I mean, he's so proud of himself."

Capslock came back dressed in jeans with a blue sport coat over a black shirt. His hair was combed and held down by something greasy. He wasn't large, but had the crooked face of a boxer, with sharp eyes and a well-bent nose. He limped, having been shot by old people who were smuggling altered, full-auto AR-15s to Mexico.

"You're all dressed up," Lucas said.

"Yeah, we're gonna go see a guy."

"What for?"

"Pick up a search warrant for the first Russian," Capslock said.

"I don't think we have enough—"

"All taken care of," Capslock said.

On the way out to the car, Lucas asked, "How did it get taken care of?" To Sherwood, he said, "We don't have any evidence for a search warrant."

Capslock said, "We're gonna go see Rob Barbier."

"I thought he was—"

"Rob Junior got over his head with some cocaine a couple of months ago, at Briscoe's. His heart got wonky and I dragged his ass over to Regions. Daddy told me to come see him if I needed something someday. I called him this morning and he said, 'Happy to do it. Those Russians sound like scum anyway.'"

Lucas said to Sherwood, "Briscoe's is a dive bar. Barbier is a district court judge. Now I see how we could get in trouble, if anyone finds out about the free search-warrant deal."

"God, I love this," Sherwood said. "I'm starting to wish I had a badge."

Capslock said, "You could probably get one. Somebody would have to break your nose, to get you looking right."

"You've both had your noses broken?"

"More than once," Capslock said. He touched his nose. "Even better, we both got our noses broken in the same fight. The guy was an orangutan."

"But you won the fight, right?"

"Only because I managed to get hold of his barbeque grill, and beat him with it until he quit," Capslock said. "Lucas was under him, holding him down."

"I was under him getting the shit beaten out of me," Lucas said. "While I was holding him down."

"Marvelous," Sherwood said. Made Lucas laugh.

LUCAS AND SHERWOOD waited outside Barbier's courtroom while Capslock picked up the warrant. The first Russian lived only ten minutes out of Saint Paul's downtown, in a mixed retail-residential strip on Grand Avenue; his name was Rick Thompson, Capslock said. Thompson lived in an older two-story house next to a children's toy store, and, Capslock had been told, in his calls the night before, had divided the place into three apartments. He lived on the bottom floor, and the two second-floor apartments were occupied by escorts.

Lucas: "Rick Thompson? We're looking for Russians."

"He is a Russian. He changed his name from something else. His friends call him Oly, which is short for something Russian," Capslock said.

"American citizen?" Sherwood asked.

"I asked, couldn't get an answer," Capslock said. "Now, the thing I've been told about the escorts is they're nothing like the ones you see on TV, those super-villain chicks with big makeup and the tight dresses. These girls look like they just drove in from Wayzata."

Lucas said to Sherwood, "Wayzata's a nice higher-end suburb for blond people."

Sherwood: "Blond, physically fit . . ."

"Shapely, well-dressed, well-groomed," Capslock said. "Your mom would be impressed, but suspicious."

"Sounds exactly like my mom," Sherwood said.

"They're not straight-up hookers," Capslock continued. "It's not like they're living in a whorehouse, taking on all comers. A downtown dress-up early-evening cocktail party might cost you a grand, with dinner afterwards. Dates for younger sons. You want more, you can get it, but it'll be another grand, or more, depending on your inclinations."

"In the meantime, you can pick up a girl outside the Target Center for a hundred bucks and a half bottle of Everclear," Lucas said. "If you have a full bottle, you might not need the hundred bucks."

"Completely different market," Capslock said. After a moment, to Sherwood, "You wouldn't drink the Everclear, you'd pour it on your dick, hoping to get a little antiseptic action after you'd parted ways."

"Sounds like certain old-timey bars in Juarez, except they use tequila," Sherwood said.

Capslock: "Really?"

Sherwood: "Really. You'd go into the bar and order a twofer. They'd have the tequila ready when you came out of the back. One shot to drink, one shot to pour on your dick."

THOMPSON'S HOUSE WAS as Capslock had been told, older, but well kept. A wide front porch spanned half the width of the house, and the steps up to the porch looked new, as did the railing around the porch. A two-person swing hung on one side of the porch, but looked unused.

Capslock led the way up the steps to the door and pushed the doorbell twice. They could hear trudging footfalls from inside, and after a minute, the front door opened, and a short, round-faced woman peered out at them. "Who are you?" she asked.

Lucas said, "U.S. Marshals Service. We need to speak to Mr. Thompson."

She frowned and said, "I'm not sure he's here. I'm the housekeeper. His bedroom door is still closed."

"He's here," Sherwood said. "We can see him on our cameras. Go knock on his door."

The woman took a half step back, said, "Wait here," and disappeared into the back of the house.

"I gotta use that cameras line," Capslock said to Sherwood. "Thank you."

"Not a problem."

They heard the housekeeper knocking, heard a man's voice, and then she came back and said, "Come sit in the front room. He is putting on his trousers."

The three of them stepped inside, into a short hall that opened onto a living room, to the left, and a set of stairs that went to the second floor, on the right. Everything looked new, and recently painted. The place smelled of root vegetables and bread.

Thompson appeared a moment later. A tall, paunchy man, sandy-haired and blue-eyed, he had a three-day beard, going white, dressed in a black V-neck tee-shirt, gray sweatpants, and pomegranate-colored slippers. He appeared to be about forty. He said to the housekeeper, "Marie, why don't you finish in the kitchen. I'll talk to these men here."

The housekeeper went trudging off; Lucas, Sherwood, and Capslock hadn't sat down, and Thompson asked, "You wanna sit down?"

The words were right, but colored with an accent.

They all sat, on a brown leather couch and two leather club chairs, and Thompson asked, "Marshals Service?"

"We're checking with local, uh, Russian nationals with connections," Capslock said. "We got your name from people familiar with your business interests."

"We're perfectly legitimate," Thompson started.

Lucas broke in: "We're not interested in your legitimacy. Or the girls you're running. We're trying to track down a Russian hit team that killed a Russian woman a couple of days ago and shot her husband. We know you guys are shipping a lot of cash back to the motherland and you couldn't do that without government contacts. We expect you've been tracking all this through the news, and we thought you might have additional information from back home. Something that could give us a lead to the hit team."

Thompson listened to it all without moving, until he began to slowly shake his head with the smallest of smiles. "I don't know what you're talking about. Running girls. I'm not running any girls; I manage a dating service. That's all there is to it. I don't ship money back to the motherland, and I don't need any contacts in the Old Country, because it's the Old Country. I'm living in the New Country."

"I didn't explain myself clearly enough," Lucas said. "We need a lead to this hit team. We know local Russians have been helping them out by supplying them with cars. We think you could probably find out who that might be. We're counting on you to do that. If—"

Thompson threw his hands up. "I don't know anybody—"

Lucas rode over him: "If you continue to say that you have no idea, then, well, we've got a search warrant for this house. We'll tear the ass off it, looking for your connections around town. You'll probably get your computers back next year. Given the guys your high-end girls are banging, I expect we'll find some interesting names and phone numbers."

"Maybe some even going back to the Old Country," Sherwood suggested.

"What the fuck? Search warrant? I haven't done nothing but run a dating service." Thompson's pale face had gone pink, and he was losing his grammar.

"Give us a break," Sherwood said. "You're running a string of whore—"

"Who the fuck are you? You look like you jumped out of a Cracker Jack's box," Thompson said to Sherwood. "You ain't a cop."

"That should worry you," Lucas said.

"Let's not everybody get all upset," Capslock said. "But I gotta tell you, Rick—can I call you Rick? Or Oly?—we will wreck this place if we don't get some help."

"If it turns out you're the guy supplying these cars, then we're talking accessory to first-degree murder," Lucas said. "So: where are we at?"

"I need to talk to my lawyer," Thompson said.

"I need to serve you the warrant," Capslock said. "I didn't want to do it . . ."

A REDHEADED WOMAN came down the stairs carrying a brown leather shoulder bag, with a hand in the purse. Capslock pushed back his sport coat and Lucas crossed his hands in his lap.

Thompson picked up on that and said, "Wait, wait, wait . . . Sally doesn't have a gun."

"Then tell her to take her hand out of her purse, without a gun in it," Capslock said. To Sherwood: "I hate shooting women. Instead of moaning, they scream. Or cry."

The woman said, "What?" and snatched an empty hand out of the purse. "Who are you? Are you with Larry?"

"They're investors, they're not with Larry," Thompson said.

"That's interesting," she said. She was nice-looking, but not crazy pretty, or sexy; she looked, as Capslock had said, like she'd just driven in from Wayzata in the BMW convertible that Daddy had given her. Low heels. Pearl earrings. Gold bracelet. Short brown-wool coat that looked expensive and subtly chimed with the bracelet.

Lucas: "Would you like to join us?"

"I have to get my hair done," she said, her voice crisp and suburban.

"Have a good time," Capslock said. "Though I gotta say, your hair looks perfect."

"Just a blow job," she said, with a smile. She crossed from the bottom of the stairs to the door in two long strides and was gone.

Sherwood said, "Wow."

THOMPSON SAID, "ABOUT that warrant . . ."

"Yeah, about that," Capslock said. "We're desperate. We admit it. We gotta have some information, one way or another."

Thompson held up a finger—wait one—and walked over to the stairs, walked up four, craning his neck, then another step, seeming to peer down a possible hallway at the top, took one more step, then turned and came back down. "The people who run my former country can be very rough. A lot of people would be happy to do them a favor as, you know, insurance, in case they decide to go back."

Sherwood: "Yes."

Thompson looked him over and said, "You're not a cop."

"No."

"Then what are you?"

"You don't want to know that," Sherwood said.

Another few seconds spent examining Sherwood, then, "Okay, I'm up to my neck in shit. I'm hoping the other lady upstairs doesn't hear us. You want to talk to Lawrence Bell, formerly Ilarion Belov, who I believe, *who I know*, is close to the people you are interested in. The people in Russia, maybe not exactly this crew you are searching for. People like . . ." He nodded at Sherwood.

"Where's he live?" Lucas asked. "Belov?"

"I don't know, exactly. Minneapolis, in general. He seems to have several places. I have his cell phone number."

"We'll take that," Lucas said.

"If you tell Belov where you got the number, I will probably part ways with my testicles, if not my entire skin," Thompson said.

"We've already forgotten your name," Lucas said, "though we have it written down on this warrant. We'll be back with it, if you're lying to us."

"I'm not. I really don't want . . . Listen, you gotta . . . If you . . ."

Like that, for ten minutes.

OUT ON THE sidewalk, after more threats and saying goodbye to Thompson, Sherwood looked back at the house and said, "You know, that place could be a little treasure chest of information. I bet there are places like it in every big city in the country."

"Probably," Capslock said. "Even some middle-sized ones. I know there's one down in Cedar Rapids."

"Local cops know that they're running sex workers out of there . . . but you don't do anything with it?"

"Nothing illegal about escorts, if all they're doing is hanging on the arms of tech bros at parties," Capslock said. "Who's gonna testify that they're providing sex for money? Even if we could prove that's happening, it would be like a two-hundred-dollar fine and harsh words for their customers. Not worth chasing after. At two thousand bucks a night, you'd be embarrassing and pissing off a lot of rich potential political donors."

"Where are you going with this?" Lucas asked Sherwood.

"Possibly simultaneous raids by FBI agents looking for information about overseas connections. Get the warrant, grab every phone and computer in the house, and then, you know, see what else we can squeeze from the women and the managers in return for nonprosecution."

"What a shitty thing to do," Capslock said. "I like it."

"Let's go see Larry," Sherwood said. "Call your phone guy at the BCA, see if he can get a billing address."

"If we get an address, we go back to the judge and ask for another warrant," Lucas said. "If he'll do it."

"He'll do it," Capslock said.

THE BCA CAME through with a billing address for Bell's cell phone, and Capslock told the judge about the possibility of Russian spies in the community, and about the hit team, and the judge came through with another warrant. He asked only that he be told of the outcome, in a narrative way, and not just through the return on the warrant. Capslock said he could do that.

The address was on the south side of Minneapolis, in a trendy neighborhood of older houses and coffee shops and people who didn't have much to do in the morning.

On the way over, with Lucas driving, Capslock riding shotgun and Sherwood in the back, Capslock asked a lot of questions about the investigation so far, and after Lucas filled him in, he turned to Sherwood and asked, "Do you know if the FBI did one of those Identi-Kit facial things with the neighbor who talked to the Russian? Out in Minnetrista?"

"Yeah, they did. It's been on TV news shows, it's on the Internet," Sherwood said.

"Do you guys, the CIA, do facial recognition stuff? Picking guys out of a crowd?"

"Sure. Not in the States, that's FBI again."

"I'm wondering what would happen . . . I mean, there are cameras all over Hennepin Medical Center . . . I wonder if facial ID could pick out the guy, based on Identi-Kit, if he shows up at the hospital? If they decide to go into the hospital, they'd have to do a recon first," Capslock said.

Sherwood said, "Hmm. I don't know. I don't know if anyone's ever tried it. I could call St. Vincent and ask."

"You're not doing anything else right now," Lucas said.

Sherwood called. St. Vincent was in a conference and couldn't be interrupted, so Sherwood left the request with an assistant, who promised to get the question to St. Vincent as soon as he was free. "I'll have him call you back. Should be within the hour." He added, in a hushed tone, "He's talking to Washington."

Sherwood rang off and Capslock said, "Talking to Washington? All of it?"

BELL'S PLACE WAS another well-kept older house, like Thompson's had been, and, as had happened at Thompson's, the door was opened by a female housekeeper. She looked at the three men on the porch and said, "I will get Mr. Bell."

She closed the door on them, but a minute later, it cracked open again and Bell peeked out. He was almost Thompson's opposite: while Thompson was tall and soft-looking, Bell was short, thick, with a face that would have fit a minor evil character in *Lord of the Rings*. He was chewing on something, possibly a cud.

Sherwood smiled and said, "Ilarion Belov, as I live and breathe. Good to see you prospering, man."

Bell swallowed and asked, with a heavy accent, "Do I know you?"

"No, you don't, but I know you. You don't know these other two people, either, but they're police officers and honestly—he switched to Russian—"You're up shit creek without a paddle."

Bell regarded him with stone eyes, and then said, in English, "I have been up this creek before, but here I am."

Capslock: "What? A creek?"

"Shit creek," Sherwood said.

Bell looked over his shoulder, as if to make sure the front room had been evacuated, and said, "You come in. Is this about Friday?"

"It might be," Lucas said, improvising. Friday? What happened on Friday? "If this keeps happening, this Friday problem . . ."

"That boy, he was spoiled and he was too rough," Bell said. "He got what he deserved and is fine this morning. I asked and his father said we are all okay. We returned the escort fee, and they will not be back, either one of them."

"That's not exactly what we heard," Capslock said.

"But that is where we are," Bell said. They followed him into a living room, and he said, "I would give you a beer, but you're working."

"That's okay," Lucas said. "Is your housekeeper a Russian?"

"Ann? No."

"I don't want to get you in trouble, in case you decide to answer some of our questions," Lucas said. "I should tell you that we have a search warrant for your house. We may not need it, if you cooperate. If you don't, I will call a BCA search crew with hammers and screwdrivers, and they will take this house apart."

"Can I see this warrant?" Bell asked.

"Sure," Capslock said. He took the folded document from his jacket pocket and passed it over.

Bell looked at it for a full two minutes, even though there wasn't two minutes' worth of information, sighed, and handed it back to Capslock. "There's nothing here, you can look," Bell said. "It might be true that you'll find things that you don't want to find. I have some very prominent clients. They hate being disturbed. This thing on Friday, it's very, very unusual."

Capslock, Sherwood and Lucas looked at each other and Lucas said, "Maybe we've pushed that as far as we can. I would kinda like to know what happened on Friday, though."

Bell said, "What?"

Sherwood: "Friday is your business. We're here for something else. There's a Russian hit crew in town. They've tried to kill a Russian defector twice. The crew needs cars, and somebody local has been getting the cars for them."

"This isn't Friday?"

"No. This is about the hit crew," Sherwood said.

"I know nothing about this thing," Bell said.

"That's too bad," Lucas said. "Because—"

"I can make some calls," Bell said.

"We need all the information we can get on what they're currently driving," Lucas said.

"All I can do is call, and talk. I make no promises."

"Then do that . . ."

"You have to leave now," Bell said. "Give me a phone number, and I will call."

"If you try to run, we'll go after you for accessory for first-degree murder," Lucas said. "So if you have to run, I'd suggest you run very far—like back to Russia. If we get our hands on you . . ."

"If I need cooperation from local police sometime in the future . . ."

"Depending on what the problem is, we can help," Capslock said.

"On the other hand, I might look into this Friday business and stick that whole thing up your ass."

"Don't do that. Just give me a number," Bell said. "I might have to talk in person. I might have to go out, play cards. I call tonight."

"Sooner is better," Lucas said. "If you think you might need a get-out-of-jail ticket someday, the sooner we hear from you, the bigger the ticket gets."

Bell nodded. "I know how this works. I have friends in Minneapolis."

Capslock: "Cops?"

Bell nodded again. "Sometimes, they want dates. I have a dating service here. I am sure you know that."

"We do," Capslock said.

Lucas: "Call me."

ON THE SIDEWALK, Sherwood looked back and said, "Mr. Belov was uncommonly cooperative."

"Not yet, he isn't," Lucas said. "Maybe Minneapolis or some other organization has him in a crack and he needs that get-out-of-jail card. On the other hand, he might decide to disappear. Without a full crew watching him, he could do that. We're five hours from the Canadian border."

"That's another thing we might be onto," Capslock said. "I wonder if the cops who want dates are getting free sex. I mean, if the BCA were to look into that . . . it would end, and right quick."

Sherwood: "I said it once, I'll say it again. I find these interactions absolutely fascinating. The good cops extort a pimp with an illegal search warrant and tell him a bunch of lies and end up possibly helping the pimp by fending off crooked cops."

"I don't find it fascinating. I find it depressing, in the nonmedical sense," Lucas said.

"Now what?" Sherwood asked.

"We have some lures in the water . . . so we wait."

St. Vincent never called back about using the Identi-Kit to look for similar faces at the hospital.

18

In Saint Paul, the Russian team found two fresh vehicles, a pickup and a minivan, parked where the Chevrolet had been. They were newer than the abandoned Chevrolet, and they appreciated the difference—they were not vehicles that would be viewed as "getaway cars." The street person they'd seen freezing in the doorway was nowhere in sight. Nikitin, still struggling with his left leg, took the pickup for its extra-wide seat, Abramova the minivan, while Titov stayed with the red Ford.

They had spotted a small city in Wisconsin, Menomonie, fifty miles from downtown Saint Paul. Straight east on I-94, the town had several motels but was less than half the distance to the Iowa motels, while still being across a state line. They would check into three separate motels.

On this morning, Titov headed to the hospital in Minneapolis while Nikitin and Abramova went to find a place where they could park and wait, maybe for a long time, without being noticed.

TITOV DROVE AROUND the Hennepin County Medical Center, scouting the layout. He'd done some research on the 'net, and once inside, was prepared to ask for the birth center, because he was a credible-looking new father, and that might be a credible destination. When he got to the hospital, he didn't have to fake anything—the place was busy with people, nobody paid any attention to him, and he never got as far as the birth center.

Instead, he got on a nearly full elevator, and when a bunch of people got off, he got off with them. He was on an internal medicine floor, and he tagged along behind an elderly couple, close enough that somebody might think he was with them. When they peeled off at one of the rooms, he kept walking, then turned back and grabbed a down elevator and got off at the first floor down and wandered some more.

He saw cameras.

A half hour after he went in, he walked out to the red Ford and called Abramova. "Call Kuznetsov. The hospital is impossible. It's a maze, and we would be trapped like rats."

ABRAMOVA WAS PARKED in a beige Toyota Sienna minivan outside the Minnesota Veterans Home on the south side of Minneapolis, near the airport. The lot was sprawling, full of cars, unlikely to attract police attention, and had good access to freeways going in all directions. Nikitin parked facing her. When nobody was crossing the parking lot nearby, he walked over and climbed in Abramova's van and lay down in the back.

"How was the drive?" she asked.

"Not good, not terrible," he said. "I can drive. This Tylenol helps."

"Good. Move over. I'm coming back."

They lay on the back seat cushions, out of sight, and killed time reading their phones, waiting for Titov to call. They didn't wait long: the hospital was impossible, and Abramova agreed to call Kuznetsov.

KUZNETSOV ANSWERED ON the third ring; he was outside, Abramova could hear traffic sounds. She explained the situation: "We almost certainly couldn't find him in the hospital, and if we could, we almost certainly couldn't get past his protection. Our two options are to attempt to spot the FBI pickup when they move him to an airport, and ambush the vehicles. We think this is a low percentage play. There are too many hospital exits for us to cover, and the teams who are moving him, the marshals or the FBI, will not make the mistakes they made the last time. I would not be surprised if they sent vehicles to all the different hospital exits, making us guess which one has Sokolov, even if we could see them all. I expect they will now use armored vehicles."

"We have time, but it's hard to tell how much," Kuznetsov said. "They have cleaned out Sokolov's wound and sewn it up. Nothing hit his heart, but there was damage to chest muscles and lung damage. He is still unconscious, but improving. They will move him in the next day or two, and I believe it will be as you say."

"We have the Novichok. We could drop it, if your asset is free to pick it up."

Silence, five seconds, ten seconds. "I will have to consult. I will call back very soon. Are you safe where you are now?"

"We are operating from the cars. We will move to another state this evening, still close by."

"Good. I will call."

He was gone, and Abramova called Titov to pass the information. Kuznetsov called back an hour and a half later.

"In this hospital, this Hennepin, there is a men's restroom on the first floor by the emergency room entrance. Our asset has used it. He says there is a paper towel dispenser on the left end of a row of sinks. If you can tape the ChapStick to the far back underside portion of the dispenser, he could get it there. He said not to tape it heavily. He needs to move fast."

"Titov can do that."

"Then if everything else you say is true . . ."

"It is . . ."

"This will be our best hope," Kuznetsov said. "This has been personally approved by the man."

"If you can, thank him for this opportunity," Abramova said.

ABRAMOVA CALLED TITOV, and filled him in. Titov said, "I need to go to a hardware store for double-sided tape. The ChapStick will be suspended under it, so it won't fall on its own, and the asset will be able to grasp it instantly."

"I wonder if the asset will survive. I can't believe that the FBI would let many people get close to the target," Abramova said.

"That is no longer our problem," Titov said. "Your problem is that you need to get the ChapStick to me. My problem is that I have to get in and out of the hospital again."

They agreed that Titov would get the supplies from a Home Depot, then drive to the Veterans Home parking lot to meet with the others. After the transfer, Abramova would drive to a parking spot close to the hospital, in case Titov needed an emergency pickup. Nikitin would remain at the Veterans Home, where he would wait until Titov had dropped the ChapStick, then trail Titov and Abramova to Wisconsin.

Titov found a Home Depot not far from the Minneapolis downtown and bought a box of thin plastic painter's gloves and a pad of double-sided stickers meant to mount small objects to walls. At the Veterans Home, he slipped into the back of the minivan with Abramova; Nikitin had moved back to his truck. The ChapStick was tightly sealed inside a small plastic box—so tightly that Abramova couldn't open it with her short fingernails and had to use her switchblade to pry it open. That done, she carefully lifted out the ChapStick, which looked ordinary enough.

"Gloves," Titov said.

They put on the gloves. Abramova picked up the small tube, and then, hesitating a few seconds, she turned it in her hands and said, "It looks like nothing."

"Made by devils," Titov said.

Abramova said, "Must be done," and she twisted off the cap. That took some effort: the cap didn't come off easily. When it was off, Titov held one of the unused plastic gloves open at the wrist, and Abramova began twisting the dial at the bottom of the tube, pushing the ChapStick out of the tube. She had ejected a little more than an inch of the waxy stuff into the open glove when the black glass separator appeared.

"We are there," Titov said, quietly. "Careful now, hold tight, I will lift the seal."

The seal had a tab sticking up from the top, not more than a half-inch long. He gripped it as tightly as he could and lifted the seal off.

Below it, in what looked like more waxy ChapStick, they could see a pink dot. "That's it," Abramova breathed.

Titov said, "Don't move, let me . . ." He carefully dropped the seal into the glove they were using for the ChapStick disposal, then tied the glove off. He set it aside and picked up the top of the ChapStick tube.

"Push up a little more," Titov said.

Abramova twisted the dial at the bottom of the tube, lifting the contents up an eighth of an inch above the rim of the tube, and Titov fitted the cap back on top. He fished another glove out of the box of gloves, dropped the tube inside, and tied the glove at the wrist.

They both sat back and exhaled. "I think we are okay," Abramova said.

"I believe so." They both looked at the two gloves sitting on the minivan seat. "You should call Kuznetsov, tell him we are ready to place the ChapStick. We need to know when his asset will be ready to pick it up."

KUZNETSOV DIDN'T HAVE a precise time, but it would be sometime after three o'clock, but before five. Titov looked at his watch: "Not much time. I've got to hurry."

"Your sticky tape?"

"Got it."

"Good luck." Abramova reached out and patted him on the hand.

AND IT WENT like the recon.

Titov walked into the hospital, found an empty booth in the men's room, put on a plastic glove, took the ChapStick out of the glove where he'd carried it, and put an inch-long piece of double-sided tape on the ChapStick tube.

Somebody had followed him into the restroom, and he could hear a man shuffling around by the urinals. Then another man came in and took the booth next to his. There was a splash of water and the sound of paper being pulled out of a towel dispenser. He waited until he heard the outer door open, and the shuffling of feet stopped.

When he was sure the other man was gone, and the man in the next booth was still occupied, he flushed the toilet, listened, then stepped out into the room, walked to the sink and, in three seconds, stuck the tube to the bottom of the paper towel dispenser. He threw the plastic gloves in the trash and felt a sudden and urgent need to pee.

He did and got out of the hospital.

ABOUT AN HOUR later, Bernie followed a bored FBI agent into the restroom. The agent looked around, saw that the room was empty, and said, "I'll be outside."

"Two minutes. I gotta pee like a Russian racehorse," Bernie said. The agent didn't laugh, but did leave. Bernie peed, for verisimilitude, washed his hands, and when he went for one of the paper towels, reached under the towel dispenser and found the ChapStick.

He looked at the door, then pulled the top off the ChapStick. The bead of poison was right there, a watery, fleshy pink. He put the cap back on, dropped the tube in his pocket, checked his hair—gave it a damp hand in back, where his hair tended to flare up—dried his hands again, and walked out.

The agent said, "Home?"

Bernie considered. "Let's go see the old man, then I won't have to go tonight. How come I don't have one of your FBI females following me around? Somebody who knows how to get it on, on the dance floor? Do you even have anyone like that?"

"We asked, and none of the women volunteered," the agent said.

Bernie said, "Don't know what they're missing." The ChapStick in his pocket pressed on his leg like a concealed carry weapon, which, he supposed, it was. "How's my hair look?"

THEY WERE ONLY at the hospital for a few minutes. Leonid Sokolov had been mostly immobile since his operation, and when Bernie entered the hospital room—his two bodyguards remained in the hall—the two agents inside the room nodded at him, and one said, "He woke up a little bit, around lunch time and again around dinner time. Couldn't eat anything. Doc said he could be more responsive tomorrow, when they start backing off the painkillers."

"I'm always surprised you're not dead from the boredom," Bernie said.

"We're okay," one of the agents said.

Bernie nodded and moved to the far side of Leonid's bed, and asked, softly, "How are you, Papa?"

Leonid Sokolov didn't respond, but did snore, a little snorting sound. The two FBI agents were in chairs oriented toward the door, both of them were looking at laptop computers, and their backs were to the Sokolovs.

Bernie slipped the ChapStick tube out of his pocket, and, watching the agents, pulled the sheet loose along the side of the bed. Leonid was wearing a hospital gown, which left his legs exposed. Bernie took the top off the tube and dragged it along the exposed flesh on Leonid's leg. The pink poison left a barely perceptible streak on Leonid's skin, which Bernie had been told would fade in minutes. He put the top back on the tube, dropped it in his pocket, tucked the sheet back in, and said in his most depressive voice, "He doesn't seem to improve."

One of the agents turned in his chair and said, "Maybe tomorrow."

Bernie bent over his father's bed, kissed him on the forehead, then whispered in his ear, which the agent thought was touching, possibly some kind of Russian prayer, because he couldn't hear Bernie say, "Suck on this, you miserable motherfucker."

19

Bell, the second Russian they'd visited earlier in the day, called Lucas at six o'clock the same evening. "I have no specific information for you, but I'm now worried for myself. This is a very sensitive subject. Nobody will talk about it."

"Do you know who specifically won't talk about it?" Lucas asked.

"I spoke to five friends. Two knew nothing, except what they saw on television and in the newspaper. The other three have heard about the, what did you call it, the group . . ."

"Hit team."

"Yes. The hit team," Bell agreed. "All they know is that somebody is helping them, rumors only, and it's best to not know who it is. Everybody is, how to say it, twitchy. I can promise you, they don't know much."

"Do they know a little?"

"They know that two more vehicles were delivered. They believe these are a pickup truck and a white van. That's all. No description or license plate."

"That doesn't help much," Lucas said, going into negotiating mode. "There are thousands of pickups and vans in the Cities . . ."

"I know. That's all I could get without the wrong people becoming curious. But you have pictures of this hit team and so if you see a group with these vehicles . . . this is something. I will continue my listening, but now you must do something for me."

"I'm not going to do much, because you didn't do much for me," Lucas said.

"You might not object," Bell said. "There are three Russians who operate dating services in the Twin Cities: me, one in Saint Paul, one in Bloomington. I need you to search all three. Including me. I will give you names and addresses."

"I see what you're thinking," Lucas said. "But that will draw some attention to you that you might not want . . ."

"I already have done that. That's why I need the police to be my enemies, and for certain people to see."

Lucas: "I would guess that you've already removed anything from your house that would be worth searching for?"

"Of course, but I have not told the other two what I am doing, so you should find their businesses . . . mmm, how do you say, intriguing? I will complain about what you took from me. I will leave laptops for you to find. If you do this, I will continue listening."

"I'll do what I can," Lucas said.

"Must be soon. Tomorrow. Whoever is doing this, helping this hit team, these are not good people."

"And you are?" Lucas asked.

"I hurt nobody. I run a clean business. No drugs."

"We'll have to disagree about that," Lucas said. "Give me the names, I'll call a guy."

WHEN THEY FINISHED talking, Lucas called Capslock, who told him that his judge was unlikely to sign a batch of search warrants. "We're both already on a tightrope." He didn't doubt that warrants could be gotten from another judge, with a proper application.

"The other guy's a Jesus and family freak. He'll sign up. I have to put together the applications, talk to some cops in Saint Paul, Minneapolis, and Bloomington, get them to back me up. I'll talk to Jon Duncan, get him to okay the raids."

"Tomorrow, if possible. Bell said we'd find the other two places intriguing."

"Talk to you in the morning. Not too early," Capslock said.

"Great. I've been getting up too early every goddamn day. I'm gonna sleep in myself."

WEATHER, FULLY DRESSED, poked him at six o'clock the next morning. "Get up, sleepyhead."

"What? What time is it?"

"Your phone says it's three minutes after six. John's been calling." She handed Lucas the cell phone. "He's called three times so far, starting at four o'clock, so leaving the phone in your bathroom drawer worked until I got up. Must be important."

"The fuckin' Russians hit the hospital," Lucas groaned. "My God, I hope it wasn't a massacre."

He took the phone, propped himself up with a pillow, and called

Sherwood. Sherwood picked up on the first ring and Lucas blurted, "Who got shot?"

"Nobody. But somebody might have gotten to Leonid."

"How? There were . . . what happened?"

"We don't know. He started convulsing during the night. None of his medication should have caused that, but you know, a blood clot to the brain could do it. One of the docs here, a woman, thinks he might have been poisoned, but the other docs are telling her to shut up. She wants to pump him full of atropine and diazepam, but . . . they're waiting for a better diagnosis."

"Sounds like what they did to that other Russian guy, the freedom fighter guy . . ."

"Alexei Navalny. Exactly. Speaking of 'exactly,' I have exactly no idea what to do. What do we do?"

Lucas didn't say anything for a moment, then: "Well, since I don't have any antidotes on me, and if it's a blood clot, I don't know much about brain surgery . . . I guess I'll go back to bed. I'll try to think something up."

"C'mon, Lucas, the FBI is running around like their asses are on fire, but nothing is getting done. Come up with something. I'll call you at nine. We'll go to breakfast."

LUCAS DID GO back to sleep, but not soundly. Sometime between seven and eight o'clock, things changed.

With a thought. Or possibly a dream.

He'd been flashing back on the three separate shootings he'd been involved in, over the space of three days. He'd been badly wounded in another gunfight a couple of years earlier, another place with hard-crusted snow and a machine gun . . . and he flashed on that night as well, something he hadn't done for a while.

He got up for a drink of water, thought about stopping to pee, but he really didn't have to. He got back in bed, lay on his back with his hands behind his head.

He ran all the attempts on Sokolov through his mind like a movie reel, stopping now and then to consider the picture in his mind's eye, then starting again.

After a while, he thought the thought. Or dreamt the dream. Whatever.

He went back to sleep and slept restlessly until his phone alarm went off at eight-thirty, and called Sherwood.

"We on for breakfast at nine?" Lucas asked.

"Yes. I'm not doing anything but standing around. The FBI guys will barely talk to me," Sherwood said.

"How's Sokolov?"

"Bad. They're working on him, but they don't like his chances."

"See you at nine."

SHERWOOD WAS PROMPT and they took his rental out to Cecil's, settled into a booth. Sherwood seemed watchful and Lucas said, "You seem watchful."

"Yeah, I'm watching you," Sherwood said. "You're onto something. Or up to something."

"I had a thought last night. Maybe this morning. I'm a little cloudy on the time."

The waitress came back with coffee and Diet Coke and took their orders, and when she was gone, Sherwood said, "You had a thought. Spit it out."

"Their intelligence is too good. Way too good. The shooter's crew."

"It's driving us nuts," Sherwood admitted. "Nobody knew about the FBI's move at the apartment house and it wasn't even on time. Now they're saying only a few people had access to Sokolov, though it turns out he might have been alone occasionally, for only a minute or two at a time . . . Okay. What?"

Lucas said, "Bernie."

SHERWOOD STARED AT Lucas for what must have been fifteen seconds, then said, "Mother of God. I'm so stupid. Or maybe I'm not cynical enough. I mean, that's an idea that would make a congressman proud."

He took his phone out of his pocket, pushed one button, and a moment later said, "Our marshal had a thought." He repeated the thought and then listened again.

"I had another thought, too," Lucas said.

"He had another thought," Sherwood said into the phone. "I'm going to put us on speaker." He put the phone on the tabletop and asked Lucas, "What was the other thought?"

"Letty, my daughter, is with Homeland Security . . ."

A tinny voice from the phone: "We know. We looked her up."

"She has a very tight connection with a woman at the NSA," Lucas said. "The NSA woman is hooked into people who do telephones. All phones. All day, every day."

Sherwood licked his bottom lip and said, "Interesting."

The phone on the tabletop burbled something unintelligible. Sherwood picked it up, said, "Say that again," listened, and then said, "We'll get back to you."

He clicked off and said, "We need to talk to Letty. The guy I just talked to? He doesn't know about it."

THEY CALLED LETTY from the diner. She picked up and said, "You get shot again?"

"No, but only because I got lucky. Listen, I'm sitting here with a guy from the Unspecified Agency. He actually knows your friend Barb. You could clear him with her, if you need to."

"You're leading up to something you want me to do . . ."

Lucas introduced Sherwood, who said, "Hi, I admire your work," and then Lucas explained in detail what had happened since the shooting at the hideout. He concluded with, "It'd help a lot if you could talk to your friend at the NSA and get her to take a peek at the phones coming out of the FBI cars and then out of the condo where the Sokolovs were stashed overnight. We can give you the phone numbers of all the cell phones involved. It probably wasn't one of them, but would help you locate them in time and space."

Letty: "Why doesn't the CIA ask? They talk to the NSA."

Sherwood leaned over the phone: "We could do that, and it'd start with me and go to my boss, and then he'd take it to his boss, and then at the NSA, it'd start the top and trickle down. We'd probably get a response in a week."

Letty made a crunching sound, said, "I'm sorry, I'm eating carrot sticks . . ." and after a couple of more crunches, said, "I'll make the call. The Marshals Service and the CIA will owe me. Owe me big."

"We can talk," Sherwood said.

They rang off and Sherwood said, "My, my. I like that girl. You *gotta* give me her number."

"She has a serious boyfriend. He's a knight. You know, a British knight."

"Yeah? Weird. Anyway, I don't want to sleep with her," Sherwood said. "I want to exploit her."

THEY LEFT THE diner and went back to Lucas's house, where he picked up the new Porsche, and they drove separately to the FBI building for the morning briefing. They learned nothing during the briefing except that St. Vincent was still pissed off at them.

St. Vincent did throw a little mystery out: "We're meeting again at five o'clock. We have a developing situation."

Sherwood: "Do you want to share?"

"No."

LETTY CALLED BACK as the PowerPoint presentation continued in endless minutiae. Lucas and Sherwood excused themselves, left the room and walked to an empty stretch of hallway to take the call.

"I could get in deep trouble for talking to you guys," Letty said. "If you tell the FBI . . ."

"We won't tell anyone," Sherwood told her.

"They went back through some dailies, that's recordings, and there was a call the night before Sokolov was shot, one minute and five seconds, and a suspicious blip the next morning at 9:07 coming out of the condo. That matched up with another suspicious blip coming out of the airport area right when Mr. Sherwood said they were leaving for Minnetonka. By a blip, I mean, somebody pushed a button and immediately hung up. Same phone, all three times, but it's a burner. It was bought at a Walmart, but it's almost impossible to pin down which Walmart because their distribution tracks quantities but not specific phones. It could have come from anywhere. My friend is a suspicious kind of person and she thinks it was probably left in a dead drop and that your leaker didn't buy it himself."

"So you got a couple of blips," Lucas said. "Do you have the phone they were coming out of?"

"Yes, getting to that. It wasn't from any of the phone numbers you have. We have a phone number, which I can give you, and my contact said she would put up a tracker for it, but it has been off the air since that nine o'clock blip. Not turned off, they pulled the battery."

"Can your contact call me directly?" Sherwood asked.

"She could call Dad, if you really need to speak to her. She didn't want to talk directly with you, Mr. Sherwood. Something about how it's illegal. It's probably illegal to talk to Dad, too, but she's worked with us before and knows we can keep our mouths shut."

"I can keep my mouth shut."

"Yeah, well . . ."

"I asked Lucas for your phone number, but he won't give it to me unless you say okay," Sherwood said. "I'd like to take you out for a walk when I get back to Washington. And call me John."

"Give it to him, Dad. Always happy to make a connection."

STANDING IN THE hallway, Lucas and Sherwood talked about what to do next: didn't argue, talked.

Sherwood said, "It's probably Bernie, but not necessarily. I've been thinking that they might have had some intelligence about where we were going from Washington, and when we were leaving. They could have had a watcher pick us up at the airport, and he signaled the shooters when we left. Figuring out a watcher would know about the condo . . . that's harder. Could have seen the handover from the Marshals Service to the feds, but . . . yeah, it's Bernie."

"If you're wondering why he'd kill his old man . . . I've started to wonder if Sokolov is really his father. Could be, but the kid looked a lot like Martha—Masha?—but not at all like his father. If he isn't, and he knows that . . ."

"Sokolov believes he's the kid's father," Sherwood said. "I've been around them or reaching out to them for most of two years. I've never had a hint of anything different."

"If it's Bernie, I wonder about motive," Lucas said. "We know he had the opportunity."

"Money. Sokolov didn't come to the States to be poor," Sherwood said. "He brought a lot of things with him, documents and photos, or Masha did, on a thumb drive that he sold us. He's got five million in the bank. His will leaves half to Martha, half to the kid, but if Martha predeceases him . . . is that right, *predeceases*?"

"Yeah, dies first."

"If Martha predeceases him, the kid gets it all. Invested, that'd be a quarter million a year, after you take out a kilo of cocaine and a Ferrari."

"All right. Motive and opportunity. Do we tell St. Vincent?" Lucas asked.

"I'd prefer to work with the Marshals Service," Sherwood said.

"We don't need an investigation and arrests, we need a location and a takedown." He added, "What we need is, we need to get Bernie to visit Sokolov, so while he's gone, we can get into his room and luggage and see about a burner."

"Search warrant or black bag?"

"Let me call home. If a black bag were needed, would there be a local resource who might provide us the necessary tools?"

"Possibly," Lucas said.

BERNIE WAS STILL at the apartment building where his father was shot. Lucas and Sherwood went back to the briefing room and made separate, careful inquiries about security arrangements around him. As it happened, Sokolov himself was being guarded at the hospital around the clock by six agents, and Bernie was being guarded by two more—and the two traveled with him.

At the end of the PowerPoint presentation, Lucas asked a casual question on Sokolov's condition, how soon he'd be able to move on to Washington, this time with better security, and whether he was able to talk. Sherwood, sitting on the other side of the room, asked if Bernie had seen his father yet.

St. Vincent said, impatiently, "He can talk, but that's not important—I mean, what's he going to say? He doesn't know as much as we do. Bernie's being annoying. He'll visit the hospital if we take him, but he seems to be more interested in hitting a couple of downtown clubs. We'll swing him by the hospital this afternoon. We're discouraging him about the clubs . . ."

"That's good," Lucas said. "Put a couple of FBI suits in most clubs and it'd clear them out in a hurry."

Another FBI man said, "We're discouraging him, but he's pretty intent. It's all he's interested in . . ."

St. Vincent was looking at Lucas, visibly fuming: "Do you have anything serious to contribute?"

"Maybe later," Lucas said.

"How about you?" St. Vincent snapped at Sherwood.

Sherwood raised both hands overhead, in a surrender. "Just watching the professionals do their stuff."

"Keep hanging out with Davenport, you might get the wrong impression."

After a moment of restrained silence, working up a burn, Lucas said, "David, you're a fuckin' cheese-eating bureaucrat. You couldn't find your own ass with both hands and a searchlight. Ah, fuck it, I'm out of here."

"You're out of here," St. Vincent shouted, and Lucas was out of there.

A HALF HOUR later, Sherwood wandered over to Lucas's Porsche, where Lucas was reading the operating manual, and knocked on the window. Lucas looked up from the manual, dropped the window, and said, "I've got a Wi-Fi hotspot. Right here in the car."

"They're taking Bernie out of the condo after lunch, for a visit and maybe a little shopping. I don't know exactly what that means, but it's not long from now. We can't actually kick the door . . ."

"Do you know which door?"

"I do," Sherwood said. "There won't be anybody watching it, because nobody thinks the Russians want to kill Bernie."

"Good. I wanted to talk to you before I left, but I have to see a friend about a tool, and you can't come. Go get a coffee or something, I won't be long."

"Meet here?" Sherwood asked.

"No. I don't want any feds to stumble over us," Lucas said. "Why don't we hook up at Bernie's condo. We can watch the door from your rental, which is the next thing to invisible."

"Unlike, say, a Porsche. Does Minneapolis have Starbucks?" Sherwood asked.

"Yeah, but I'd recommend a Caribou Coffee. Lots of them around."

LUCAS DIDN'T HAVE a friend that he wanted to see about a tool. He had a hidden drawer on the underside of a stairway in his garage; he'd designed and contracted the house himself, and the hidden drawer was part of it. He drove home, made himself a cheese-and-bologna sandwich on sourdough bread—calling St. Vincent a cheese-eater had left him peckish—went into the garage, opened the drawer and took out a cylindrical electronic lock rake about the size of an electric toothbrush. The drawer also contained two cold revolvers, a Taser, generic handcuffs, a burner phone, two hand-held walkie-talkies like hunters used—they left no cell phone trace—and five thousand dollars cash in random denominations.

He pushed the drawer back in place, finished the sandwich on the way back out to the driveway. Twenty minutes later, he'd left the Porsche and walked down the street to Sherwood's rental car.

"Got what we need?" Sherwood asked.

"Yeah."

Another five minutes and they were parked by the same bus stop where Titov had waited for Leonid Sokolov to walk out to an FBI truck.

THEY WAITED FOR more than an hour. Lucas was reading a Paul Krugman economics blog on his phone when Sherwood said, "SUV at the front door. I can see bumper flashers, but they're not flashing."

"That's them. Here's Bernie."

Bernie, escorted by a single agent, walked out of the building and they both got in the SUV.

"How far away is the hospital?" Sherwood asked.

"Hennepin General? Maybe, I dunno, a mile? Lots of traffic lights."

"Let's move."

THEY WERE AT the front door in two minutes. The door was not locked, because it led into a ten-by-ten lobby space with a call box and a wall of mailboxes. The inner door had a decent lock, but Lucas had a decent rake, and though it made a loud chattering noise, they were through in five seconds.

"Goddamn thing sounded like you dropped a spoon in a garbage disposal," Sherwood grumbled. "You need better gear."

"Hey, we're in. If you've got better gear, send it to me."

"Look for an unexpected FedEx box," Sherwood said.

THE DOOR OPENED onto a small interior lobby, with a stairwell behind a door to the right and an elevator to the left. They ran up the stairs, looked both ways down the empty hall on the second floor, and hurried to a green door that read "240" and had an empty plate that might have held the name of the apartment owner, but didn't. They hadn't yet seen a single person in the building.

Lucas knocked on the apartment door and waited, knocked again and waited, used the rake and they were in.

Sherwood walked inside as Lucas closed the door behind them, sniffed—the place smelled of nicotine and something alcoholic—and they both listened for a moment, then Sherwood took a cell phone-sized gizmo from his jacket pocket and turned it on.

"A bug detector?" Lucas asked.

"Yeah, but it'll pick up cameras and a burner if there's one hidden in the room. I'm not seeing anything yet."

"You ever bagged a place before?" Lucas asked.

"Not really. I've gone into places after the Delta guys blew the door and killed everybody inside, but we weren't all that quiet about it. I was never the first through the door."

"This is sort of like that, without Delta and the blown door and the noise, and the fact that if we're caught, we could get arrested and prosecuted and lose our jobs," Lucas said.

"Then we shouldn't stand around bullshitting, should we?"

The apartment was tidy enough, but not high-end: more designed for singles in nine-to-five clerical jobs. The carpet felt thin and cheesy underfoot, like walking across slices of pepperjack from a Subway store.

While Sherwood waited by the door with his gizmo, Lucas did a walk-through of the apartment, looking for alarms and tell-tales. He found none. There was a compact kitchen minimally equipped with dishes and silverware, along with a pot, a blender, and a microwave. Most of the cabinets were empty. Three bottles of Canadian Club whiskey sat on one countertop with a half-dozen dirty glasses.

That done, Lucas said, "Here," and handed Sherwood a pair of surgeon's gloves that he'd stolen from Weather, and pulled on a pair of his own. "You scan, however you do it, and I'll do my thing."

"Gotta make the call first," Sherwood said. Lucas waited until he'd taken out his phone and punched in the number for the burner responsible for the blips isolated by the woman at the NSA: nothing buzzed, beeped, or rang.

"Damnit all. That's not helpful," Lucas said. "On the other hand, Letty said they probably pulled the battery . . ."

THEN THEY WENT back for a closer look, beginning in the living room with its home-furniture-outlet couches, coffee tables, and chairs. A chipboard bookcase held a couple of novels and a history of World War II in the Pacific, plus some board games and a pack of Bicycle playing cards. A television was mounted on a wall facing the couch and a coffee table; there was nothing behind it but dust and wires. There were two ashtrays on the coffee table with a half-dozen butts in one of them.

They moved through to two bedrooms, one showing two packed suitcases, the other two unpacked suitcases, with clothes strewn around a double bed.

"Bernie's room," Sherwood said, moving around the room with the bug detector. He shook his head and moved into the other bedroom with the packed suitcases. "Got something here," he said.

Lucas went to look, and Sherwood dug into a heavy winter coat hung in the bedroom closet. He pulled out a long box that might once have held a pearl necklace but no longer did. Instead, it held a stack of hundred-dollar bills.

"That's not very interesting," he said, He took the stack of money out of the box, riffled it with a thumb. "Must be . . . ten grand?"

"More like ninety-four hundred," Lucas said. Sherwood glanced up at him and Lucas said, "That was a joke."

"Oh. Ha ha." Sherwood put the box back in the coat. "I'll keep looking."

LUCAS WENT BACK to the other bedroom, obviously Bernie's, saw an ashtray, picked up a couple of cigarette butts and put them in a Ziploc bag. Bernie left half of his clothes in an open suitcase and Lucas squeezed through them, found nothing of interest. The suitcase was an ordinary Samsonite, with no hidden compartments.

A twenty-liter carry-on duffel bag held sound-cancelling headphones, a deflated neck cushion for air travel, a personals sack with a toothbrush, a travel-sized toothpaste, and a bottle of Aleve—Lucas opened the bottle and the pills looked legitimate.

Sherwood was still picking through Leonid Sokolov's bedroom, and Lucas called, "See if you can find something that'd give us some DNA. Does he smoke? Cigarette butts?"

"Gotta be something in his suitcases," Sherwood said.

"Be neat," Lucas said.

The other half of Bernie's clothes were either on the floor, bed, or bedside chair, or hung haphazardly in the bedroom closet. Lucas frisked the hung clothes and found a lump in the bottom hem of a ski jacket. When he checked, he found that the bottom of the jacket pocket had been ripped out, so anything put in the pocket would slide all the way down to the bottom hem.

He fished out the lump, thinking, *drugs*, but found himself holding a small stiff metallic sack. "Got the burner, I think," Lucas called.

Sherwood came in and Lucas showed him the sack: "Faraday bag."

"Yeah. Open it."

Lucas unrolled the top of the bag, which was held by a fingernail-sized steel clasp, and pulled the phone out, with a separate battery, and handed it all to Sherwood. Sherwood popped the back, took a photo with his phone, checked the number. "We got him," he said. "Let's see who he's been talking to . . ."

He pushed some more buttons and said, "Exactly one contact." He took another photo, then handed the phone back to Lucas. "Put it back where you found it."

Lucas resealed the Faraday bag, dropped it into the bottom of the ski jacket, and asked, "You find anything in Leonard's, uh, Leonid's bag?"

"We're stealing his toothbrush."

"That'll do it," Lucas said. "So: Bernie. Let's get the hell out of here."

They did that, out the door and down the stairs.

"WE'VE GOT TO decide what to do with all this," Sherwood said as they walked out of the building and into the cold. "It's settled my primary interest: finding the leak, and it wasn't one of ours. The focus now goes to the hit team, rather than the leak."

"The hit team was *always* my primary focus," Lucas said. "I figured the leak was your problem, not mine."

"Well, you solved the leak. Maybe I can help settle the hit team question."

"I would appreciate it. The DNA stuff, I'll leave with you," Lucas said. "Ship it overnight to Washington, get your folks to compare samples. We really don't need to do it, but it would be interesting to know if Sokolov is really Bernie's father. You know, the motive thing."

"I can do that. Then we figure out how to use Bernie to pull the hit team into a trap," Sherwood said. "Another question is, how much do we tell St. Vincent? He'll want to know how we figured out that it's Bernie, and we can't tell him we bagged the condo . . ."

Lucas shrugged: "Somebody has to find the phone. Why not the FBI? You could tell them that you're really curious about the leak, and Bernie's name popped into your head. Since two FBI agents live in the apartment with him . . . they wouldn't even need a search warrant to find it. They'd ask, how did he contact them, you tell them, maybe he had a burner hidden on his body—or in his clothes."

"That'd be pretty sneaky. Basically, I don't like it. Who gets the credit? St. Vincent will jump in front of that train. I've run out of patience with him."

"So what are you going to do?"

Sherwood thought about it, then: "We don't tell St. Vincent anything, not a fuckin' word. You called him a cheese-eater. That might not do much for your career with the federal government, but you are correct. We *do* tell the counterintelligence team and warn them not to ask too many questions. Those guys . . . they'll buy that. They're like their own little piece of the FBI. They're used to working with weird situations, and they won't worry about not talking to St. Vincent."

"Will they help us trap the shooters?" Lucas asked.

They were coming up to Sherwood's car. "I'll call them, set up an off-campus meeting for this afternoon," Sherwood said. "They'll bite. There are some interesting ramifications here . . . possibilities."

"Are you going to tell your own people ahead of time?"

"I have to. They'll watch, keep their mouths shut. They'll be . . . amused."

"I don't like the sound of that," Lucas said. "I stream the *Slow Horses* TV series. You're all a bunch of treacherous motherfuckers."

Sherwood smiled and said, "Yeah, it's fun. I'll set up a meet."

"We need to emphasize that we want to pull in the hit team. I don't find them amusing at all," Lucas said. "They goddamn near killed both of us."

"You never got a scratch and goddamn near killed three of them. I'm not seeing you as the victim here."

"Killed my car."

"You got a new, better one," Sherwood said. "I'll admit killing or capturing the hit team would be a major plus. Good fodder for prisoner exchanges, if nothing else. As far as Bernie's concerned, if the counter-intel people handle him right, he could even be useful. Might be able to find out who he's hooked up to. Could lead us to more illegal Russians."

"So they'll owe us. The counter-intel guys."

"That's one way to look at it."

"Yeah, your way," Lucas said.

20

Lucas didn't ask how he managed it, but Sherwood set up a meeting in a little-used room in the basement of the main post office in Minneapolis, an old Depression-era building on the Mississippi that Lucas suspected was considered an architectural treasure. The room they were in wasn't obviously a treasure, being dusty, and possibly visited by a water leak in the not-to-distant past, leaving behind a fishy odor.

Lucas was the second to arrive, guided to the room by an intimidated postal employee who wanted nothing to do with either him or Sherwood; Sherwood was checking the room for bugs, and had found none.

"You're here," he said, when Lucas walked in. "The feds should be here in the next five minutes. No bugs. By the way, if you sit on these chairs, you'll get your suit all dirty, so just wait a minute."

There were six metal folding chairs arranged around an eight-foot-long collapsing table with a scarred chipboard top. The postal service, Lucas thought, was not doing well. "How the hell did you find this place?"

"My researcher did," Sherwood said. "I got somebody coming with paper towels . . . ah, here he is."

Another postal employee hustled in with a spray bottle and a roll of paper towels. He spent three or four minutes spraying and wiping down the chairs and table, and then hustled back out. As he left, the four counterintelligence feds filed in, looked around, and the woman asked, "What's up? Why are we in this hole?"

"We're very off the record," Sherwood said. "Very. Have a seat."

"Something smells like an old dead fish," one of the men said, as they all found chairs.

"Wouldn't be from the Mississippi," Lucas said. "That's about fifty feet lower than this place."

"Where's the Mississippi?" another of the men asked.

"About fifty yards that way," Lucas said, pointing toward the back of the building.

"Really? I'd like to see it," the man said. "I've never seen it, except from the air."

SHERWOOD, "OKAY, SO let's get into it. I will provide a short introduction to the conversation. Lucas and I found the leak."

The woman: "What!"

Lucas, representing the American Midwest, said, "Yup."

One of the men: "Who is it?"

"Bernie Sokolov," Sherwood said. "He communicates with the hit team, or maybe a telephone cutout, with a burner that I'm told he has hidden in a ski jacket. It may be inside a Faraday bag, so the feds can't see it. He used the phone to signal departure times from the airport and from the apartment building where Sokolov was shot."

The counter-intel feds all looked at each other—they didn't seem especially surprised by Sherwood's disclosure—and the woman asked, "How'd you find this out?"

"Through nonstandard investigative techniques that we are not at liberty to reveal," Sherwood said.

"So you bagged the place," the woman said.

Sherwood shook his head. "Not at all," he said piously. "I will say that the NSA has a phone record of Bernie's signals. You could talk to their phone department about how they got those. The local FBI folks have no clue."

"The NSA can be pretty tight-lipped," another of the male agents said.

"I know," Sherwood said. "But you can probably find some cheese-eating bureaucrat to talk to you about it."

All four of the agents laughed, and one said to Lucas, "You should be ashamed of yourself. I heard a woman over at headquarters referring to him as Old Cheddar."

Lucas: "Somebody had to say it. Now. Here's what John and I have been discussing. Is there a way to use the information that we uncovered to pull this hit team into another attempt on Sokolov, assuming that they're still around, that we could use to trap them?"

The woman said, "Interesting. We like the concept."

"As opposed to a concept, I'd like to have a plan," Lucas said.

"We'd have to think about it—there're lots of moving parts here and I'm sure Mr. Sherwood has probably broken a lot of laws to tell you about them," the woman said. "Which is why we're sitting in this hole."

"Just looking for a quiet, interruption-free place to talk," Sherwood said.

"How about if you guys pulled something out of your collective asses that would suggest that Bernie is the guilty one, that you could take to St. Vincent," Lucas suggested. "Say that *you* talked to the NSA, and they spotted the signals. When you looked into Bernie's background, you found he was close to, you know, whatever Russian intelligence service you might think appropriate. Tell him to search all of Bernie's clothes. They'll find the burner. They tell Bernie that he's going to disappear into the American court and prison system, and nobody will know. We'll never acknowledge having him, so he'll never get traded back to Russia."

"I like the idea, but that wouldn't happen," one of the agents said. "I don't even know *how* it could happen. He'll lawyer up . . ."

Sherwood exhaled in exasperation, and said, "Guys, you'd be *lying* to him. All you have to do is tell a couple of little fibs. Get him to feel like his back is against the wall, get him to cooperate . . . He's a Russian. He won't know anything about the American justice system."

"There *is* that," the woman said.

"If we can get St. Vincent to cooperate," another of the agents said.

Lucas: "Guys . . ."

"Yeah, we know," the woman said. "We tell St. Vincent a couple of little fibs."

"Exactly," Lucas said. "Oh, by the way, one of our contacts collected DNA samples from both Leonard—Leonid—and Bernie and they've been sent to a CIA lab to confirm that they're related. We're not sure Bernie is actually his son."

After a moment of silence, the woman said, "I wish I had your contacts."

AFTER THE MEETING broke up, Sherwood headed to his hotel room to call his bosses in Washington, to tell them that the deal with the counter-intel people had gone down as planned. Lucas walked back to his office in the federal building, where White had her nose in a computer. "I'm no longer on the case," she said, when she spotted him coming in. "I'm going up north."

"What for?"

"Guy got convicted of kidnapping his kid from his ex. He's a winger who doesn't recognize the court's authority, so he didn't turn himself in to do his time. The court, of course, does recognize *him*."

"Don't get hurt," Lucas said.

"*You* don't get hurt. You almost got your ass shot again. What is it about you?"

"I dunno. Just lucky, I guess," Lucas said.

White: "You look a little down."

"I need some sleep, is what I need."

White: "Uh-oh."

"Not that bad yet. Sherwood sort of cheers me up."

"Good for him," White said. "Though he didn't really strike me as the cheerful sort."

"He's not cheerful. He's phlegmatic. That's better than cheerful, when you don't have much to be cheerful about."

"I'll take your word for it," White said. "But . . . pills are better than into the pit. As long as they're the right kind. Stay away from the Ambien." Depression seemed endemic in the Marshals Service.

"I will," Lucas said. "In the meantime, I'll be back in my office."

"What, chokin' the chicken?"

"I'll try not to get noisy," Lucas said.

LUCAS GOT HIS drawing pad out, which gave him a broad unmarked surface to work on. He began drawing circles and squares around the individual Sokolov events, with cartoon balloon commentaries on the events. Most of the cartoons' balloons had only a word or two in them. He was still doing that, bereft of ideas, when Sherwood called.

"What are we doing?" Lucas asked.

"I dunno. I'm in a hotel downtown," Sherwood said. "You want to come over?"

"What's the hotel?"

"It's a big glassy thing . . . Four Seasons?"

"Jesus. The taxpayers put you up at the Four Seasons?"

"It's not a suite or anything. Just a room," Sherwood said. "After Masha got shot, I had to find something quick and it was the first name that came to mind. Where are you?"

"About four blocks away. There's a Whole Foods sort of kitty-corner across the street from the hotel. They've got a café. It's noisy enough that we could talk."

"When? I'm doing nothing."

"Ten minutes."

SHERWOOD HAD A café table and was eating a sesame bun when Lucas arrived. Lucas pulled out a chair and sat. "You got anything at all?"

"No. The well is dry. I was hoping we could do some plotting." Sherwood's phone rang. He looked at the screen and said, "I've got to take this."

He walked down to the end of the café area, talking on the phone, and was back in a minute.

"The Russian that was shot bad?"

Lucas: "Yeah?"

"Probably taken to Milwaukee. Came in the night you guys shot him up, perforated bowel, bullet under his stomach skin, like Doc Juarez said. They operated on him, sewed him up, fed a bunch of antiseptics and painkillers into him. The next morning he was moved to a private surgical hospital in a private ambulance, discharged with really good paperwork. The private surgical center never heard of him, and they don't have their own ambulance. They did find the ambulance, with a medical service company, and the driver says they took the injured man to a private jet."

"Man, the FBI is gonna be pissed when they find out," Lucas said.

"Oh, they know," Sherwood said. "They're just not talking about it."

"But they called you?"

"Uh, no. That was my boss. We have our sources . . ."

"In the FBI?"

"Wouldn't you? In our position?" Sherwood asked.

Lucas thought about it for one second, then said, "Of course."

"To get back to plotting. . . ."

"FIRST OFF, IS Sokolov gonna die?" Lucas asked.

"I've heard that it's a distinct possibility. He wasn't in great health to begin with, he's got type 2 diabetes. He's still recovering from being shot, even if the slug didn't make it to his heart, and that doesn't help. They're fighting it, but they're saying he's less than fifty-fifty to make it."

"If he croaks, and Bernie tells the hit team, they're gone. We gotta do something now. I think we leak the car and van descriptions coupled with everything else we have—the Identi-Kit image of the guy who rented their safe house, along with speculation that they may be staying in motels."

"If they see the leak on the cars, they'll dump them," Sherwood said.

"And have to deal with getting new ones."

"All right. Going back to your Daisy Jones friend?"

"Going everywhere. I had a child with a woman who's a big deal at Channel Three here, that's our major network station, and she's still a good friend. She'll get it on. I'll go back to Daisy . . . With those two, everybody else will pick it up. It's our best chance."

"Then we should do it," Sherwood said.

Lucas: "Any idea what the counter-intel people are doing with Bernie?"

"Not yet. Not sure they're doing anything, directly. I expect they'll have Bernie's escort search his room . . . They'll figure out some way to make it legal, being the FBI."

"Without bringing us into it, I hope," Lucas said.

"I don't think they will. There'd be no percentage in doing that, and they're familiar with percentages."

LUCAS'S PHONE RANG, and he frowned at the screen. "It appears to be St. Vincent."

"Can I listen?"

"Why not?"

Lucas answered, put the phone on speaker and they bent over it to hear a woman's voice: "Marshal Davenport?"

"Yes? You're calling from St. Vincent's phone."

"Yes, from his office phone. I've been instructed to ask you back for the five o'clock meeting."

Lucas didn't have an immediate reaction. After a few seconds, he asked, "Are you sure?"

"I am absolutely positive."

"We had a little . . . clash . . . this morning," Lucas ventured.

"I'm aware of that. Should I put you down for attending?"

"He's still a cheese-eating bureaucrat," Lucas said.

"Is that a no?" she asked.

"Uh . . . no. I'll be there."

HE RANG OFF and Sherwood said, "Just for the sake of a little discretion, hold off on the media until we know what the meeting is about."

"Yeah. That's probably a good idea."

"And maybe you can hold off on the cheese business."

21

Lucas and Sherwood got off the elevator at the FBI building and stepped toward the meeting room and a man called from behind them, "Davenport!"

Lucas turned, shook his head and said, "Butter my butt and call me a biscuit, as Virgil Flowers would say. What are you doing here, Louis?"

Louis Mallard was walking down the hall toward them; a bulky man, mid-sixties, frowning, in an FBI-blue suit and rep tie, shoes that were possibly spit-shined. He was empty-handed, but trailed by a tall fortysomething woman who was carrying a leather briefcase that looked, from the slump in her shoulder, like it might be filled with rocks, or maybe anvil irons.

Lucas said, "Hello, Jane."

"Go fuck yourself, Lucas," the woman said.

"I thought you'd be over it by now," Lucas said.

"I'll never be over it," she said.

Lucas said to Mallard, "She's such a fussbudget."

"Yes, but it works for me," Mallard said. "I spent the last hour talking with the cheese eater. I wish you hadn't run your mouth like that. It's not helpful."

"He is, and you know it."

"He's not, most of the time," Mallard said. "Sometimes, with a difficult problem, and with unfortunate results, he can come across that way, purely out of disappointment. Administratively, he's quite effective."

"He eats cheese," Lucas said.

Sherwood had been looking back and forth between Lucas, Mallard, and Chase, and now asked Lucas, "Who are these people?"

Lucas said, "Louis Mallard, deputy director of the FBI, and Jane Chase, Louis's personal fussbudget, also a lawyer and FBI agent. Guys, meet John Sherwood, a spy."

Sherwood shook hands with Mallard and Chase, and said to Chase, "I entirely agree with your apparent assessment of Marshal Davenport. He can be absolutely disgusting in his lack of regard for well-established rules of law. We could compare notes over steaks and red wine tonight, if you're free."

"I don't drink with spies, unless you want to tell me about the ones you've stuck in the Justice Department," Chase said.

"I'll never get over the cynicism of Washington insiders. It makes me sad," Sherwood said to Mallard.

Mallard smiled and went back to Lucas: "Where's this hit team?"

"We're working on that," Lucas said.

"In case you haven't been informed, there's been a major break: the FBI has identified your leak, the one feeding information to the hitters," Mallard said.

"That's terrific!" Lucas said, overenthusiastically.

Mallard didn't react to Lucas's reaction, but Chase did. She said, "Oh, shit, Louis. He's got a finger in this pie, sir. He already knows what happened. Who it is. It might even be his pie."

"David St. Vincent isn't aware of that," Mallard said, peering at Lucas. "Interesting. And how's Virgil Flowers, Lucas?"

"Working on his fifth novel," Lucas said.

"I've seen him on the *Times* bestseller list. Amazing, really. He projects a certain rural *je ne sais quoi*."

"Yeah. That's because he lives in a fuckin' haystack," Lucas said. "Let's get this meeting over with."

As they continued down the hall, Sherwood, keeping pace with Chase, asked, "What's your problem with Lucas? Am I sensing a romantic thing, or . . ."

"No. He's a killer," Chase said. "I joined the FBI to put killers in prison."

"Oh."

"What? Working with a killer doesn't bother you?" Chase asked.

"Well, once in western Iraq, I targeted a big ISIS meet-up and the Navy stuck a Tomahawk missile in their window. Killed twenty people, more or less," Sherwood said, affably enough. "We couldn't tell exactly how many. I flew in to assess the damage and see if we could salvage any hard drives. There were heads and feet everywhere. To answer your question, I guess I'd say no. It doesn't bother me."

"Bothers me. We're not in a war."

"Well. That's one opinion."

Lucas, who was walking along with Mallard, chatting about nothing, overheard the last of the conversation, turned his head to Sherwood and said, "You really are a charmer, dickweed. No steaks and wine for you."

St. Vincent, Mallard said, had gone ahead to the briefing room to make sure the PowerPoint was ready, and to make sure that everybody who needed to be there was, and anybody who didn't need to be there wasn't. "Treating this as top secret, limited access," he said.

"I'm surprised John and I were invited," Lucas said.

"I suggested that including the Marshals Service and the CIA might be politic," Mallard said.

"Ah. Being the deputy director, you get listened to."

"Yes, I suppose. I'd attributed it to my personal charm."

LUCAS AND MALLARD had worked cases going back years, to a time when Lucas was a Minneapolis homicide detective, and later, when he was with the state Bureau of Criminal Apprehension, and still later, as a marshal. Mallard was often considered the top real cop in the nation.

"Give me a minute before you come in," Mallard said. He went into the meeting room, trailed by Chase, with Sherwood and Lucas waiting in the hall for thirty seconds.

"Doesn't want to be associated with us," Lucas said. "Although, really, St. Vincent knows."

"I'd like to associate with Jane for a while," Sherwood said.

"I'd say you have a chance," Lucas said. "She likes your type."

"Yeah? You think?"

"I do," Lucas said. "Keep playing the hard-nosed outsider spy-hero. Mention Delta. She'll get curious."

"You know this, how?"

"We sort of had a little buzz between us, one time—nothing serious, nothing that might lead to anything, at least not on my part. Unfortunately, I'm in love with Weather."

"I could see that," Sherwood said quietly. "Fortunately, I'm not, and I sense a need for affection in this woman."

THEY WENT INTO the meeting room together. Mallard and Chase were already seated, and Chase was taking paper out of the overloaded briefcase. St. Vincent was at the head of the table, the four counter-intel agents sat in a line across from Mallard and Chase, and two other local agents were next to them.

Lucas muttered to Sherwood, "Go," and Sherwood led the way, sat down next to Chase and tactically ignored her.

St. Vincent: "We're all here. I want to warn *everyone* . . ." He looked at Lucas. ". . . what is said here is not to go anywhere, under very serious penalty of law."

There were glances and nods up and down the table, and St. Vincent said, "We've determined that the person who has been leaking intelligence to the Russian hit team is almost certainly his son, Bernie Sokolov."

There were no gasps or exclamations from the table, since almost everybody there carried the gene for sneakiness. St. Vincent told them about the discovery of the burner phone in Bernie's ski jacket, and confirmation by the NSA that he'd sent signals from the airport and before the apartment ambush.

"We're going to use him to trap the hit team," St. Vincent said. "There were two objectives in this investigation, after the killing of

Masha Sokolov: one, find the leak, and two, capture or kill the hit team. We've accomplished the first objective, now we work on the second."

Mallard: "How are you going to do that, David?"

St. Vincent nodded at him. "The agents acting as Bernie's bodyguards know that he's the leak, so they're not so much guarding him as sequestering him and steering him . . . although he doesn't know that. After discussions with my other senior agents"—he nodded at the two local agents—"I spoke to Frank Potts, the CIA's deputy director of operations, about John Sherwood, sitting here next to Ms. Chase."

Sherwood raised a hand.

"Potts said that John is a capable agent with good abilities of dissimulation . . ."

One of the counter-intel agents said, "You mean he lies well."

"I mean he can play roles. We're going to ask John to accidentally bump into Bernie in Leonid Sokolov's hospital room, take him aside, and grill him about where he's been and what he's been doing," St. Vincent said. "Play the role of a suspicious CIA agent. We're hoping Bernie'll panic and try to get the hit team to pull him out. The agents who've been escorting him have assessed him as a bit naïve and quite . . . stupid, is the word. He may want his father's money, but he certainly doesn't want to wind up charged with accessory to first-degree murder, espionage, and so on."

Sherwood: "I can do that. Play the role."

Mallard: "From the reports I've read . . ." He patted a stack of paper. "Bernie seemed distressed when his parents were shot."

"He was prepared to act as the shocked son," St. Vincent said. "That doesn't take a genius."

Lucas: "I believe you when you say you've identified him as the leak, David, but doesn't effective play-acting suggest he might not be entirely naïve and stupid? That he might actually be tough and clever?"

"We have the assessments of the people closest to him, including John Sherwood's associates who handled him over the past year," St. Vincent said. "They lean heavily toward the naïve and stupid."

"That was my assessment, too," Sherwood said. "I'm no longer sure about that—I could go either way, but we've got to be careful in how your people handle him. Two guards won't keep the hit team away from him . . ."

"That's the trap. That will be the obvious coverage," St. Vincent said. "We'll have a half-dozen of our most capable agents around him at all times, four of them out of sight, that Bernie won't know about."

THEY SPENT ANOTHER half hour talking about possibilities and dangers. St. Vincent said that Bernie would be moved to a different apartment in the same building, ostensibly for security reasons, but actually to take advantage of a group of vacant apartments that could house the backup agents. Bernie's new apartment would be wired for sound and video, so the watchers would see everything going on inside.

"Sounds like you've got a plan," Mallard said. He waved a finger at the line of counter-intel agents and said, "You folks should head back to Washington, and we'll leak that to Bernie."

They all nodded at once, like crows on a fence.

To Sherwood, Mallard said, "You need to script your act."

And to Lucas: "Time to step back."

SHERWOOD SAID TO Mallard, "When I brace Bernie, I want Davenport with me. Bernie knows Davenport shot up the hit team, and he's probably a little afraid of him. We'll cut him away from the FBI, gang up on him. Lucas can do that; he can play the crazy violent one, I'll play the CIA snake. If anything gets Bernie moving, that should do it."

Mallard nodded: "Okay, go that way. *Then* Lucas can step back."

Chase said to Sherwood, "But you probably ought to turn your act around. Lucas can be the snake. He's very good at that. You could be the violent one."

Mallard, "Jane . . . go easy. Lucas gets things done."

Chase said, "Fuck him."

St. Vincent: "I second the motion."

Mallard laughed, while the other agents looked like they didn't want to get involved.

ST. VINCENT SAID that Bernie slept late, and that the agents would be taking him to the hospital at noon, and that he usually only stayed for fifteen minutes or so. "He likes to go shopping. He likes a big lunch. He likes restaurants with lots of women, preferably teenagers."

"We'll show up right at noon," Sherwood said. "Make sure your agents get out of our way."

There was no milling around when the meeting broke up. Mallard and Chase went off to confer with St. Vincent and the two senior agents, the four counter-intel agents returned to their hotel to get ready to fly back to Washington, and Lucas and Sherwood went out to a Caribou Coffee to discuss the play they'd put on for Bernie.

"We want hard-nosed but not ugly, suspicious but not quite certain," Sherwood suggested over coffee and hot chocolate. "What you really need to do is loom. Let him see your gun."

"Yeah, I get it. I do this," Lucas said.

"Loom!"

THEY WERE WAITING inside the hospital's main entrance, already bathed in the soup of hospital stinks, when the agents with Bernie showed up. They watched from behind a screen of hospital visitors as Bernie and the agents turned toward an elevator, gave them five minutes, and followed.

Outside Leonid Sokolov's room, they caught a doctor coming out. Sherwood, who'd met her earlier, put up a hand to stop her and asked, "What's the prognosis now?"

The doctor, whose name was Cantor, looked back into the room as the door was swinging shut, and when it was fully closed, shook her head and said, "It's only an opinion, which is all I have at the moment, but I'd say he's in serious trouble. Whatever he has in his system is eating him up. We can't even identify the components, chemical, biological. Not radiation of any kind. He already had some physical problems, his liver, his kidneys. I'm not optimistic. We're dumping him full of medication, but . . ."

She turned her hands up, a gesture of helplessness.

They talked for another minute, Novichok was mentioned, then she headed back to her office and Lucas and Sherwood pushed through the door.

Three of Leonid Sokolov's bodyguard agents were there with him, sitting in easy chairs, each with an open laptop; Bernie and his two escort agents were standing next to Sokolov's hospital bed, talking to another doctor. Everyone stopped what they were doing to look at Lucas and Sherwood, and Sherwood asked, "How's he doing?"

Bernie said, "He's out of it. They don't know if he'll make it. How could this happen? He was supposed to be watched every minute of every day . . ."

He reached out and gripped his father's bare arm, and Lucas thought, *That's how you did it.*

Bernie simply stood there, holding his father's arm, then sighed and said to his escorts, "Let's go. He doesn't even know I'm here."

Sherwood said to one of the escort agents, "We need to talk to Bernie privately. Like, out in the hall. Away from the crowd."

One of the escorts nodded, and said, "We can give you some room, if it's really necessary. We'd want to be in the hall with you."

"That's fine."

Bernie asked, "What's going on?"

"We need to see where you're at, Bernie," Sherwood said. "I've spent a year and a half worrying about you."

"Maybe you should worry about my father . . ."

"We do that, too."

Bernie looked like he was about to blurt "Bullshit," had his lips already puffed to do that, but Lucas leaned into him and grunted, "Hallway. Now."

IN THE HALL, they stood in a doorway to a stairwell, while the two escort agents stood twenty feet away, one on either side of them, looking away. Sherwood started: "Bernie, I'm kind of worried about you. You haven't been in touch with friends in Russia, have you?"

"What? Fuck no! What are you talking about? The Russians killed my mother! I don't have any friends in Russia!"

"They killed your mother by accident," Sherwood said. "They were trying for your father. Then they tried again, and now they might have tried a third time. The only way I can think of how they could do that, three attempts, would be if somebody close to the situation was talking to them. Doing something."

Lucas, standing six inches too close: "Somebody like you, Bernard."

"You guys are crazy," Bernie said, edging away from Lucas, focusing on Sherwood. "I loved Mama. How many people are around Papa? Two dozen, three? People coming and going all the time now, doctors, nurses, so many I can't even remember them all."

"How about Papa?" Lucas asked. "You love him, too?"

"Yes! I love Papa, too! He's my papa!" Bernie protested. He was sweating, a shine on his forehead and beside his nose, and maybe tearing up. If it was an act, it was good. "He's the only one left in my family. Except for Papa, I am alone."

"Just you and Papa's money," Lucas said. "That'd keep you warm during those long Moscow winters."

"Back off, Davenport," Sherwood snapped. "I've worked with this man for a long time now. I can't imagine that he could have anything to do with what's happening . . ."

"C'mon, Sherwood. The guy's a weasel," Lucas said. "I know a weasel when I see one."

"You are the man who was supposed to protect my mother and

my father, and did you do this?" Bernie's language was beginning to fall back into Russian rhythms. "You did not do this. You failed. You are looking for somebody to blame for your failures." He turned to Sherwood: "You, too."

"I believe you're okay. We had to talk. Take it easy," Sherwood said.

"I don't think he's okay. I think he's lying through his fuckin' teeth," Lucas said. "If it turns out his father's been poisoned, who else could have gotten to him?"

"Fuck you. I don't talk anymore," Bernie said. He called to his escorts: "Come on, guys, I go back to the apartment."

AS THEY WATCHED the three of them walk toward the elevators, Sherwood asked Lucas, "What do you think?"

"He might have been about to take me on. You see him set his feet? He's had some training."

"Yeah, and I didn't know that," Sherwood said. "He's always come across as a weenie, and that's what I thought he was."

"If he gets on that phone, and does anything, even a couple little clicks, some prearranged signal, we'll know that the trap might snap. If he doesn't . . . I don't know what that would mean."

"Might not be the phone. I'll ask the FBI to get one of their tech geniuses to put a keystroke logger on his laptop, see if he's going out to anyone. We should have done it before now. All I've ever seen him do on his laptop is play games and watch videos."

"Do it," Lucas said.

"So you gonna step back? I know Mallard's got some clout, as a deputy director."

"He does, but the Marshals Service doesn't necessarily pay attention to what Louis wants," Lucas said.

"I'll go with you guys—if you can think of anything to do."

LUCAS WENT HOME and made pasta with his secret ingredient pasta sauce, which was basically regular tomato sauce with a shot of Heinz 57, and after they'd loaded the dishwasher and the kids were off to do whatever they did, which was mostly talking on her phone (Gabrielle) and studying a driver's license exam booklet (Sam), Weather cross-examined him on his status in the investigation, and why he'd been disinvited from participation.

That took a while to explain, and then she asked, "Didn't John tell us that Bernie liked to go clubbing?"

"Yeah. Being a deejay, playing video games, and clubbing, those supposedly are his things. Maybe driving fast cars, if he gets an inheritance."

"I know you don't like my commentaries on your investigations . . ." she began.

"You're wrong about that, but go ahead."

"If I were a spy, and I do read a lot of spy novels, I might have a burner phone for emergencies, but everybody knows phones can be tracked. And probably monitored. I can see him using a phone to set off an alarm when nothing better is available, like letting the assassination team know when they were leaving the airport or arriving at the hideout . . ."

"C'mon, spit it out," Lucas said.

"I can't think of a better place for serious, secret discussion than a club. Especially with people dancing and sneaking off together to snort cocaine or whatever they do now."

"How would you know that?" Lucas asked. "You've never been in a dance club in your life."

"I used to go to First Avenue . . ."

"Sure, thirty years ago . . ."

"Just like a man," Weather said. "You're not being responsive to my insight."

"I . . . Well, you're right. I gotta call Sherwood. They need to focus on the clubs. Maybe get some FBI chicks to dress up. If the FBI has chicks."

"It's at least an outside possibility," Weather said. "The chicks, I mean. Dressing up."

Lucas called Sherwood with a suggestion that the FBI heavily cover any clubs that Bernie might go to. Sherwood said, "We've already talked about that—me and the FBI troops. It's gonna be weird because it's impossible for FBI guys not to look like FBI guys. I mean, they're all carrying guns and everybody in a club knows what a guy carrying a gun looks like."

"Then you could scare off anyone trying to meet him."

"I think you could," Sherwood said. "But, they're going out tonight."

"Call me if anything happens."

"I won't be there, but I'll wait up for the feds to report back, and let you know."

Lucas got an email from Sherwood at 2 a.m., which he read the next morning. It said, "Nothing happened."

22

Sherwood was wrong about that.

The FBI agents who had searched Bernie's clothing for a burner phone, and had found it, had reseated the battery so they could look at the phone's contents and see who he'd called. When they put it back in the ripped-out pocket of the ski jacket, they forgot to pull the battery again. Which was stupid, but there it was.

That night, when Bernie went to check in with his handler, he touched the phone and instantly realized that he had been found out. He left the phone where it was, in the jacket, and lay on his bed to think about it.

If the FBI had the burner's phone number, they could easily find its connection history, but not the content of the calls.

The contact protocol was simple enough: when Bernie was alone in his room, he'd set his iPhone to wake him at four o'clock in the morning with a vibration, rather than a ring. He would get up, erase the alarm, retrieve his burner from the jacket, dial a number, let it ring once, hang up, remove the battery and go back to bed. That was the on-station, all-clear signal.

The FBI would find two extremely brief outgoing calls in daytime—two seconds at the most. They would attach those to the timing of the FBI convoy leaving the airport, on its way to the initial hideout, and the departure from the apartment house where Sokolov was shot.

The FBI would also find three outgoing phone calls, all in the afternoon, that were longer—voice contacts, to different phone numbers, all burners, used once and then never again.

If they then looked at his iPhone, they'd find three very brief incoming calls from burner phones in the Washington area—one-ring calls that vibrated rather than rang, so he'd feel it in his pocket without alerting his bodyguards. Those were call-back requests from his controller. Unless the FBI investigators were very dumb, they would connect those incoming calls on the iPhone to his outgoing calls on his burner.

So he now understood what the FBI probably knew. That's why Sherwood and Davenport had been all over him. Why hadn't he been arrested?

The hit team. They were setting a trap.

He breathed in for three seconds, held it for three seconds, gently released it over three seconds, and did it again and again. When he was sufficiently calmed, he set his alarm for four o'clock, got back in bed. Nothing more to do until then.

Couldn't sleep, not right away. Thought through all the possibilities, came to no conclusions.

Bernie had never wanted or intended to defect to the U.S. He loved his country. He liked Moscow, even in the winter. He liked the Black Sea. Hell, he even liked Tomsk, where he'd gone to Tomsk Polytechnic, despite the fact that he'd spent four winters freezing his stones off. But, the women were warm, as they had to be, given the weather.

He didn't like the Ukraine war, but he also believed in his heart that Ukraine was part of Russia, and that it must be retrieved. He didn't fully understand why the Americans were so opposed to it: they'd done the same thing to the American South, when the South tried to break away. The major difference was that Ukraine had been part of Russia for longer than the South had been part of the United States.

Still, if Putin had simply waited, had created his Greater Russia, without the Ukraine, had built stronger ties to Ukraine, integrated it into the Russian economy, provided aid, promoted friendship . . . Ukraine would have eventually been absorbed into the Greater Russia. So he didn't like the war, but Ukraine was part of Russia.

Bernie had computer skills, and the political clout of his father, which had kept him out of the Army. He also had a life in Moscow, and girlfriends, and a part-time job as an up-and-coming deejay at the dance clubs.

Too late for that.

When his father had told him that they were going to Istanbul on a shopping expedition, he'd had no objection: since the war had started, times had been hard. Couldn't get a decent, stylish, deejay-worthy Italian black leather coat anywhere but the black market, and there, the prices were absurd.

When the CIA snatch crew had showed up, and they were all shoved into a van, there was no way to get back. Once in the U.S., they'd been confined to a CIA facility in Virginia. For the first six months, he wasn't allowed out. He was essentially confined to a comfortable, intensely boring existence. For the year after that, he was allowed out once a week. He'd been pissing and moaning and whining from the beginning, and finally, understanding that the Russians had no interest in him, the CIA began letting him slide out to the clubs, Friday nights only, with an escort.

At a club one night, a not-beautiful girl had her cell phone sitting on top of her shoulder bag, while she danced; a girlfriend kept an eye on it, but with the booze and the guys all around, not a close eye. Bernie had noticed that the dancing girl would pick up the phone, check something, and put it back in her purse without entering a password. While she was dancing he'd crowded up to the girlfriend, and the purse, palmed the phone, and carried it into the restroom.

From one of the booths, he'd sent a message to a friend living in Poland, a reliable right-winger computer pal, asking that the message be passed to the SVR. He would be at Entropy, dancing, the following Friday. Back in the club, the not-beautiful girl was looking for her phone, and Bernie "found" it for her, lying on the floor, under a barstool. She was grateful, but not *that* grateful.

A week later, he was dancing at Entropy. He pushed it as far into the night as he could and was disappointed when nobody whispered in his ear. The disappointment faded when he put his hand in his jacket pocket and found a burner.

That contact had produced a series of calls and new burners. He hadn't asked for anything, only to return to Russia. But the Russians had asked. They wanted his father dead, and they wanted his help. He was happy to give it and told them so. He'd hated his father for the weekly beatings he'd taken from the time he was an infant until he was twelve years old, the last one administered with fists.

If he needed to kill his father to get back home, the only problem was how to do it.

AFTER HE FOUND the altered telephone in his ski jacket, and set the iPhone alarm for four o'clock, he slept, but restlessly; at four o'clock, the iPhone buzzed, and he got up, used the burner to call his regular contact, let the phone ring . . . twice. Maybe the NSA or the FBI could distinguish one ring from two—probably could, if anybody actually timed them—but maybe they would attribute it to an insignificant difference between that call and others made on other nights.

It wasn't insignificant.

The second ring was a disaster call: Get me out.

The Russians wanted to hear in much greater depth what he had to say about the CIA facility where he'd been held. They'd told him that in the early conversations, and he'd become a familiar figure as he wandered around the Farm's almost fourteen square miles, walking, jogging, working out. With help from Sherwood, he'd also been allowed to shoot on the huge rifle range.

As an engineer, he had a good memory for what and who he'd seen at the Farm; as an engineer, he'd become an excellent shot, because even a moron can become an excellent shot, given decent eyesight and competent training. Not a great shot, but excellent.

And he'd looked at a lot of faces.

He had that going for him: the possibility that the Russians really would get him out.

After his two-ring call, Bernie went back to bed.

23

Edie Lamb was Lucas's putative boss. She'd found Lucas with his feet on his desk, reading a C. J. Box novel, and when she asked, he said, no, he wasn't doing anything.

"Would you mind doing something? We've got things to do around here."

"Depends on what you got," Lucas said.

Lamb took a chair: "Every year, around this time, I have to kick your ass. You get down in the winter and you freeze up."

"Winter's not a happy time for me," Lucas said. "Everything closes in."

"Come see me in my office in fifteen minutes," she said, and heaved herself out of the chair.

Lucas was an independent agent, and some members of the Marshals Service were unhappy about that. Some other members weren't—and those members included the director, the deputy director, the general counsel, the associate director for operations, and so on.

Using his badge, and some peculiar circumstances, Lucas had built strong allies in the U.S. Senate, and the Senate paid the Service's bills. If a serious bureaucratic problem flared up, Lucas was happy to call his Senate contacts for a chat. Sometimes, not always, the chats paid off for the Service.

Lamb was the U.S. Marshal for the Minnesota district, and something of a friend. Fifteen minutes after she caught him with the Box novel, Lucas was in her office, where he told her about being disinvited from the FBI coverage of the Sokolovs. They were chatting about what he might do next. The hit team was somebody else's problem, although their freedom continued to nag at him.

Lamb, in her office, had produced an FBI report of a man named George DeWitt Horn Jr. "Horn is assessed by the FBI to be in the Alexandria area at a . . . hmmm . . . sixty percent confidence level," Lamb said, peering at the FBI report.

"In other words, he probably isn't," Lucas said. "The FBI always cheats on those assessment levels."

"Yeah, but if he is, and you tracked him down, that'd be a nice feather in our caps. Especially since the FBI can't find him."

Horn had murdered three young women in the Chicago area, according to DNA samples taken from their bodies and matched to Horn's DNA, a sample that had been taken after his first conviction for child molestation.

When a task force comprising FBI and local cops broke into his cubicle at a transient hotel, they found nothing but a full-color photocopy of Horn's asshole taped to one wall, and a photocopy of his right middle finger taped to another. The task force surmised that Horn had seen them coming; he was in the wind, with no known car.

He had been born and raised in Alexandria, Minnesota, a small city a hundred and thirty miles northwest of Minneapolis. He was known to have gone back several times since graduating from Alexandria Area High School, Iowa Lakes Community College with an AAS degree in wind energy and turbine technology, and from Lino Lakes Correctional Facility in Minnesota on the molestation change.

"If I went to Alexandria this week, I'd most likely freeze to death," Lucas said.

"As far as I know, this office has nothing going in Miami or Los Angeles, so it's Alexandria or nothing. I really would like to catch this asshole." She held up a photo of the asshole that Horn had left for the FBI.

"Jesus, put that back in the file. I don't want to look at it," Lucas said. "I'll make some phone calls, I know a couple of guys out there."

"I hoped you'd say that. If you go, you could take Shelly with you. She bagged that guy in Grand Marais."

"Good. Let me make my calls."

LUCAS SPENT THE day working phones, getting nowhere. He took a call from Jon Duncan at the BCA, who said that BCA agents and local cops had raided three Russian-run dating services, and returns were spotty. Lucas also checked with two marshals who worked with the Special Operations Group in Louisiana to see if they had anything really good. They didn't; but they had good gossip, which was mostly why he called them.

Sherwood called to say that the CIA lab had looked at the two Sokolovs' DNA, and had confirmed that Bernie was Leonid's son. "There's probably some kind of deep psychological trauma there, that we'll never find out about," Sherwood said.

"Not until you get Bernie to a black site."

"We don't have those anymore," Sherwood said. "Cost-cutting measures."

Lucas went home early, did a three-mile run during which he froze his face, shot one basket with a basketball that had frozen solid behind a bush in the backyard, ate dinner with Weather, watched a movie, sent the kids to bed, and then suggested that he and Weather go upstairs and fool around for a while.

"Almost too late, but not quite," Weather said, checking her watch. "Let's get up there. Time's a-wastin'."

THE NEXT MORNING, he was eating a late breakfast while reading the *Wall Street Journal* on his laptop when he took a call from a number that rang a bell, but that he didn't recognize.

"This is Lawrence Bell . . ."

"That's why your number rang a bell," Lucas said. "The guy with the whorehouse . . ."

Bell: "Not a whorehouse. Mother of God, I don't know why I make this call."

"So . . . what's up, Larry?"

"Lawrence. Your BCA and Minneapolis police raided me yesterday," Bell said.

"I heard."

"They found nothing, of course. Only me and a lonely cleaning woman."

"Good for you, Larry. Well, take it easy . . ." Lucas began.

"Wait, wait, wait. Something happened last night," Bell said. "I don't know what it is, but something happened."

"Happened?"

"With these people who interest you," Bell said. "The ones in touch with the Old Country."

"Let's start from the beginning," Lucas said. "Where were you when you heard something happened?"

"I have breakfast with . . . friends. I don't tell you who they are, because it would hurt them, and they don't know much. But they knew something happened last night. Somebody was asked to take a girl to a dance club in the northeast. Maybe this Nightshade club. These people who send the girl, they are the people who interest you. My friends say she made a delivery. We thought maybe drugs, but that seemed unusual. Drugs, you can find them laying on the street, why the big secret? My friends, they didn't know where she came from, or what she delivered."

"What girl?"

"They don't know. A girl," Bell said.

"Who sent her? Exactly?" Lucas asked.

"Nobody knows this. People talk, other people hear things. A pretty girl was taken to a dance club in the northeast. Maybe this Nightshade. That's all."

Lucas worked on him for another two minutes, but Bell had nothing but a further request: "The Minneapolis police were on the raid yesterday. One of them was . . . a friend . . . but he didn't act like a friend. He didn't want to know me. He was difficult, he wanted to tear my house apart. I'm afraid he might come back on me, trying to lay down some tracks that say he's not a friend of ours. Can you help that?"

"You could move out of Minneapolis," Lucas suggested.

"I own this house," Bell said. "I fixed it, I would not get my money back."

"This friend . . . was he slipping the old pink piccolo to your girls for free?" Lucas asked.

"What is this piccolo, what are you talking about?"

"Was he screwing your girls? And not paying?"

"He . . . Yes. Sometimes. He provided coverage for us," Bell said. "You know, if there were rumors in the police department, if there was some interest in us, we might get a warning."

"What's his name?"

"Cordell Shea. He is this big pussy hound," Bell said.

"Okay. I know a deputy chief over there," Lucas said. "I'll have a chat with her, maybe cool things off. Maybe. I'll get back to you."

"I could be a source, for a long time, for your chief, if I'm not driven out."

"I'll tell her that," Lucas said.

LUCAS CALLED SHERWOOD, who, without saying hello, went with, "I knew it. You got something that the FBI doesn't."

"Where was Bernie last night?" Lucas asked.

"Clubbing."

"Where?"

"I don't know," Sherwood said. "I spent it in my lonely hotel room, alone, since your girlfriend Jane was sincere when she said she doesn't go to dinner with spies."

"Find out if Bernie was at the Nightshade. It's a low-rent dance club and cocaine dispensary on Fourth Street. Call me back."

"Give me thirty seconds. Maybe a minute."

A MINUTE LATER, Sherwood called back: "Goddamnit, he was at the Nightshade for two hours. What happened? What have you got?"

"Our Russian friends, the ones with contacts back in Europe, supposedly sent a girl there to deliver something to somebody. A rumor, but an interesting one."

"What did they send?"

"They said not drugs, since you could probably buy them over the bar. I'm thinking . . ."

"A new burner," Sherwood said.

"Yes. He may have a new phone, which would mean that he probably knows the feds found his old burner," Lucas said. "That means he probably was talking to his handlers last night."

Sherwood: "I gotta make some calls."

"We're pretty far down the road from a rumor that something was sent to the Nightshade, to him having a phone. If he did get one, we can probably get a look at this chick on the club's videos, since they've all got them."

"Yeah, but she could be anybody. A messenger," Sherwood said. "The big question is, if he got a phone, what'd he tell the handlers? That we're onto him? Is he gonna get picked up by the hit team? If that team had gone into this club last night . . . there were two agents there that Bernie knew about, but there were four more outside. This team is gonna include a countersurveillance expert, he'd spot the extra agents in one minute. They're about as inconspicuous as a car full of refrigerators. What would they do, would they kill them? We could have wound up with six casualties."

"Is Bernie going out tonight?" Lucas asked.

"He goes out most nights. I don't know if he's going tonight, but I could find out."

"Do that. The thing is, if the hit team is going to try to pull him out, they'll have to kill at least a couple of FBI guys," Lucas said. "We've got to warn them."

Long silence, then: "I don't know, Lucas. I mean, the FBI set this trap. They're looking for the hitters. They should . . ."

"They don't have this specific information. They are apparently not good at this—you said a car full of refrigerators. We've got to tell them."

More silence. Then, "Okay, you're right. You want to call St. Vincent, or should I?"

"I'll call him. I'm also going to invite myself back in."

"And me," Sherwood said.

LUCAS CALLED ST. Vincent's office, got his secretary, who put him on hold. St. Vincent came up a minute later.

"Lucas," he said. "You and I, we gotta talk. This is fuckin' ridiculous."

"Yeah, I agree, and I'll talk. But I've got something I need to pass on, and right now."

St. Vincent knew about Lucas's and Sherwood's contacts with Russian immigrants, and the immigrant's "dating" businesses. Lucas told him about the phone call from Bell, and the rumor that something had been delivered to the Nightshade while Bernie was there.

"Sherwood and I think it might have been another burner. That Bernie may know that we've spotted him, that he may have asked for a new phone, somehow, might have gotten one, and is talking directly to his handlers. We're wondering if the hit team might try to pull him out."

"Oh, boy. You think he'd have the phone on him?"

"No idea. If he believes we found his phone, that would mean that he also knows we shook down his room. So, he could hide it someplace he's sure has already been searched . . . Or, he might have it on him," Lucas said. "The key thing is, if he's going clubbing tonight, the team could knock over your surveillance guys and Bernie's escorts like a bunch of ten pins. They're sure to do some heavy scouting before they'd try to get him."

"Or they could try to hit Bernie's ride to the club, or back from the club," St. Vincent said. "They've got those automatic weapons and if Bernie told them that the escorts are in the front seats, and Bernie's in the back . . . hit them at a stoplight."

"Your guys can figure out the possibilities. I'm not even sure Bernie got a new phone. But: I want back in, if only for this club thing. Sherwood and I want to go up to the club, pry loose some videos, see if we can actually spot a contact."

"Do it soon."

"Yeah, real soon, this morning. Before there are employees around to talk about cops looking at videos. I got a guy who probably knows the owner and can get him over to the club this morning."

"All right. Go. I'll get my people together. When this is done, we gotta talk."

LUCAS CALLED DEL Capslock, who agreed to meet at the Nightshade's front door in an hour. "Who's the owner?" Lucas asked.

"Bunch of jocks around town, couple Vikings, couple Timberwolves. It's managed by Jerry Don James, who used to run the Gamecock over on West Seventh."

"The one that burned down?"

"Yeah. Fire so hot it melted the pots and pans, in ten minutes," Capslock said. "The fire marshal says it was arson, but he can't prove it, and neither could the insurance company. They paid off two-point-one million, though I understand the bank got most of that."

"So Jerry Don James is a dirtball."

"He prefers to think of himself as an innovative businessman."

Lucas: "If Jerry Don doesn't want to cooperate, ask him how interested he'd be in a charge of multiple first-degree murder and maybe treason."

"I'll speak to him," Capslock said.

"See you in an hour."

Lucas called Sherwood, who would meet them at the Nightshade.

CAPSLOCK WAS SITTING in a rust-challenged beige Camry, reading a free paper. Lucas parked, walked down the street toward the club; Capslock saw him coming and got out. A car slowed and gave them a quick honk as it passed, and Sherwood went down the street and pulled into a parking space a half block away.

When they were all assembled outside the club's front door, Capslock leaned on a call button, and a minute later the door opened an inch and a thin, young, dark-bearded man who might have been a sixties folksinger peered out and asked, "You the cops?"

"No, we're Lady Gaga's backup band," Capslock said. "Where's Jerry Don?"

The man stepped back and opened the door. "He's waiting. He's at the bar."

The Nightshade was painted black: floor, walls, ceiling, and tables. The seating surfaces, booths and chairs, were white, and tiny, star-like LED lights sparkled from the ceiling. To one side, a raised triangular bandstand, with just enough room for a drum kit and a couple of guitars, bordered on a slightly paler shade of black that delineated a dance floor.

Jerry Don James, a pudgy man with a paper-pale face wearing an Icelandic turtleneck sweater, was sitting at the bar with a Starbucks Venti.

He asked Del, "What the fuck?"

Capslock said, "You still smell like smoke."

James laughed and he said, "You're a class act, Capslock. Remind me to put you on the banned list."

Sherwood, who had been looking around, said, "You've got a banned list? Who'd even want to come here?"

"Who the fuck are you?" James asked. "I know who Davenport is, but . . ."

"He's a fed," Lucas said. "Now the question is, how many Russians you got coming here?"

James shrugged and said, "Some, I guess. They have accents, they look like they come from that part of the world. Good dancers, they have a good time, spend money. Does this have something to do with those shootings that have been going on?"

"We're not sure," Lucas said. "We want to look at the security video from your club last night."

James was looking at Sherwood, cocked his head and asked, "You're not FBI or DEA. Are you CIA? One of those intelligence spooks?"

Sherwood said, "Let's go look at that video."

James said to the bearded man, "Jesus H. Christ, we got CIA in the shop."

Sherwood looked at Lucas: "Why does everybody know this?"

"They're criminals. They have a sixth sense."

THE CLUB HAD two cameras with wide-angle lenses that covered the main room, and no working cameras that covered a back room, which had two big TV screens on the walls, lounges in a bloodred leather, arranged in conversation pits, and a separate small bar. They followed James and the bearded man through the back room to a door that led to a stairway to the office. The office was a long, narrow space on a low second floor, a jumble of three wooden desks and a half-dozen short metal file cabinets.

The bearded man turned on one of the computers and Lucas asked, "What's your name?" and the man said, "Noah."

As they were waiting for the video to come up, Noah said, "The video is black and white because we can get better exposure that way, in the dim light. The camera in the back room doesn't work, but you can see everybody who comes in the front."

Capslock said, "The camera in the back doesn't work because that's where the jocks get blow jobs and cocaine."

James: "Why are you such a fuckin' jackass?"

"I'm not a jackass. I report obvious facts to my colleagues, so they can decide who to arrest."

"Nobody's getting blow jobs in the back room," James said.

"What about the cocaine?" Lucas asked.

"Cocaine is so 2000," James said. And, looking around, "Aren't we all adults here?"

NOAH HAD THE video up and asked, "What time?"

"Eleven o'clock to one o'clock," Sherwood said. "We don't have to watch every minute in real time; run it as fast as you can pick up the people. We're looking for a tall guy, thin, blond hair and scuzzy beard, leather jacket, open shirt collar. Arrived around eleven."

"That's probably not more than half our customers," James said.

"Just look," Sherwood said. "We want to see who he hooks up with."

BERNIE WALKED THROUGH the front door at eight minutes after eleven; he was followed, seconds later, by two guys in long coats. Capslock said, "If you closed your eyes, and imagined two FBI stiffs walking into a nightclub, undercover, that's what you'd imagine. They might as well have gunbelts strapped around their waists."

Lucas said, "Shut up and watch."

"The woman will bump him," Sherwood said.

"What if he goes in the back room?" Lucas asked.

"That's invitation only," James said. "He's not invited. Good-looking kid, though. Doesn't look like a Russian."

"Shut up and watch."

The five of them clustered around the computer screen for an hour, watching the customers come and go; Noah went down to the bar and came back with bottles of cold ginger ale. In the club, there was more drinking than dancing, but Bernie danced more than he drank and was good at it. He spent most of his time hustling young women, dancing but not touching. Just after midnight, Sherwood jerked upright and said, "There! There she is, she just dropped it."

"I didn't see it," Lucas said.

Capslock: "Neither did I."

Sherwood said to Noah, "Rewind. Slo-mo."

Noah rewound, started playing it forward in slow motion. Sherwood picked up a pen on the desk and put it on the back of a young blond woman in a dress that appeared pale in the black-and-white video. She was dancing several feet away from Bernie, with another man. She started backing toward Bernie, hands over her head most of the time, or reaching out to the unknown man she was dancing with, her head back, laughing.

Then her hands came down and she turned and seemed to randomly bump into Bernie, and she bounced away and continued dancing.

"Boy, she did it well," Sherwood said. "She's had training."

"I still didn't see it," Capslock said.

Lucas, James, and Noah didn't see it either, but Sherwood was sure. "Classic move," he said. "Right out of the book. Believe me . . . I'll tell you what. She's having a good time, dancing her little ass off, but she'll be out of there in less than five minutes."

More like three minutes. She edged off the dance floor, smiled at the man she'd been dancing with, patted him on the chest, stopped for a coat, had to wait another minute, and disappeared through the door.

James and Noah had never seen her before; if she'd been in, they didn't remember it. Sherwood said to Noah, "We need that video. Can you put it on a flash drive?"

He could.

When they had it, Sherwood said, sincerely, to James and Noah, "If you speak one word of this to anybody, ever, a man will come to your door and kill you. Look at my face. Do I look like I'm joking?"

James swallowed once, and said, "No."

Noah shook his head.

OUT ON THE street, Capslock said, "Would somebody come to their door and kill them? If they talk?"

Sherwood frowned, shook his head: "Of course not. We don't do that."

"Not ever?"

"Not ever. But it's sometimes nice that people think we do."

Lucas: "Let's show the video to Lawrence Bell. Maybe he'll know the girl."

"I'm going to ship it back to my office," Sherwood said. "By the time we get to Bell's place, we should have some enhanced stills of her. Almost like mug shots . . . Better than the video."

Capslock said, "Can I come?"

"Sure. The more the merrier."

"If that piece of junk you're driving can keep up," Lucas said.

24

They had to drive south across downtown Minneapolis, got clogged up in traffic a couple of times, and arrived at Bell's house just before noon. Sherwood brought his iPad and showed them a series of still photos of the woman, which CIA photo experts had pulled from the video, enhanced for detail and colorized. The CIA thought the woman's dress was a shimmery light green; or the CIA's AI did.

"Better than I'd hoped," Lucas said. "She pretty, but she's tough."

"Gotta get that gear for the BCA," Capslock said. He flipped through the photos, back and forward, and said, "I don't know her. She's not part of the regular club scene, I don't think."

They spent another minute looking at the photos, then walked up to Bell's door and pushed the doorbell. The same woman who answered the door on their first visit, answered on the second, and said, "Mr. Bell . . . I find him. You wait."

She shut the door and Capslock said, "Maybe I should run around back."

Lucas: "Nah. He won't run. He's in too deep with us."

Lucas was correct. Bell came to the door, looked past the three of them to the street, then said, "Come in, come in, come in, quickly." He made a brushing movement behind them, as if with a broom.

Standing just inside the door, he asked, "What is it? What happened?"

"I appreciate your phone call this morning. I might send you a certificate of commendation," Lucas said.

"You know, you think you're funny, but you're not," Bell said. "I can't have people see you with me. If you need to talk to me, call on the telephone. Now, what do you want?"

Sherwood: "Look at these pictures. Tell us who the woman is."

Bell took the iPad and expertly flicked through the photos, then said, "I don't know. I've never seen her before. She's not part of the local community, I know most of those people, or I've seen them, at least."

Capslock: "You're sure?"

"I'm positive. There's something about her . . ."

"What?"

"She doesn't look American to me. She looks, I dunno. Pinched?"

Sherwood took the iPad, contemplated the photos for a moment, then said, "You're right. She looks . . . Russian."

THEY SAID GOOD-BYE to Capslock, and back in the Porsche, Sherwood said, "I need to send these photos to a completely different unit . . . Let's sit here for a minute while I do that."

He did it, and said, "This won't take long, except the guy I need is probably at lunch."

Lucas filled the time with a story:

"Back a few years . . . well, quite a few years . . . I was trying to figure out who a serial killer was. We had some information, the kind of car he drove, the color of his hair. At a really critical moment, I was on the street with another guy, and we needed some fast information from the DMV. We didn't have cell phones, but we found a phone booth—remember those?—and it turned out neither one of us had any change to put in the phone. Didn't have a quarter," Lucas said. "A month or so before that, I'd been fishing up in Canada, and to make a call back to the States, I had to use a pay phone, but it was like five bucks, and who has five bucks in quarters? Then somebody told me I could talk to an operator, and she'd take my Amex card. So then we were in this phone booth, looking for this serial killer, no quarters to make the call, and I pulled out my credit card and made the call, which amazed the guy with me. We thought back then, it was like magic. You could use your credit card in a phone booth! Now . . . you're a thousand miles from your office, out in the woods, and you pull out your iPad and talk to the CIA. It's just . . . it freaks me out. My kids wouldn't think anything of it. I'm getting old."

Sherwood yawned.

"Fuck you," Lucas said. "I'm not that much older than you."

"There's before the year 2000, and after the year 2000," Sherwood said. "If you got your first real job after 2000, you grew up in a different world than the people who started working before that."

"That's probably true, and I'll probably even think seriously about that, someday, if I don't have anything less boring to do," Lucas said.

Sherwood's cell phone rang, and he took it out, answered, said,

"Barry," and listened, and said, "Thanks. Listen, write that up, everything I told you, and walk it up to Helsmith ASAP."

He rang off and said to Lucas, "I'm not allowed to tell you this, but given the circumstances. . . ."

"Yeah, yeah, yeah. Tell me."

"There are around two hundred and fifty Russian employees in their embassy in Washington who carry diplomatic passports. That's from the ambassador on down. The young woman we're looking at is Alina Zaitseva. We've never had any interest in her, because she does seem to be a clerk in the visa department. We know people who have gotten visas from her. There's no way the FBI can watch all of their employees, and they don't watch her. But: the way she handed that phone off to Bernie, if it was a phone . . . she's had some serious training."

"She's not just a clerk."

"No. She's a courier of some sort. We've turned over a very interesting rock, here, Lucas," Sherwood said. "We've got to talk to the FBI and not talk anymore about this woman, or about the videos from the club. She could take an FBI surveillance team to some serious Russian intelligence assets."

"Which doesn't get us any closer to the hit team."

"You know, you and I do have slightly different objectives here," Sherwood said. "I would love to get the hit team, but honestly, identifying a Russian courier is more important than finding that team. Best outcome, we capture them alive. They'd give us absolutely zilch, they'd do a couple years in prison, and we'd wind up trading them. But Alina Zaitseva, she could be the gift that keeps on giving."

"Ah, God." Lucas took his phone out, punched a number.

"Calling St. Vincent?" Sherwood asked.

"No. Louis Mallard," Lucas said.

Mallard picked up and said, "Davenport. Is your nose still in this?"

"I wasn't looking for it. It started when an informant called out of the blue, I swear to God, and gave me some information you need."

"What is it?" Mallard asked.

"Did St. Vincent tell you I called this morning and told him that Bernie took a mystery delivery at the Nightshade club last night?"

"Yes. You think it was a phone, some of the agents here think it might have been drugs. If it happened at all."

"It happened, and it was almost certainly a phone. We got video of the delivery, and Sherwood sent it off to the CIA photo department, whatever that is, and got still photos made. Then he sent those off somewhere else, and it turns out that the delivery woman is a clerk at the Russian embassy. You can get the details from the CIA or from Sherwood, but your counter-intel people need to know about the woman, and everybody has to stop talking about her. This could be a big score for the FBI, a Russian courier."

"Give me the details. What's her name?"

Lucas gave him the name—Sherwood spelled it out—and said, "We know that Bernie almost certainly has a new burner, and is talking to the hit team, or maybe to people at the embassy or in Moscow, for all we know. We don't know the phone number."

"I will pass this along," Mallard said.

"Tell me this, Louis," Lucas said. "Is the hit team still in town? As far as you guys know?"

"Until you called me just now, I'd have no idea. But think about it, Lucas: who would Bernie be calling, if they're not still in town? The burner is a serious danger to him, if we found it. He wouldn't be chatting with some guy in Moscow about the weather. It'd only be of use to talk to somebody on the hit team, or somebody who can talk to the hit team, and how they might cooperate."

"Cooperate to do what?" Lucas asked.

"I don't know. Pick him up? Make another run at Sokolov? Hire a lawyer?"

"Okay."

"Lucas, we got this," Mallard said. "Bernie's in the middle of two bodyguards and four very competent agents that he doesn't even know about . . ."

"As far as you know, he doesn't know about them," Lucas interrupted. "If the hit team doesn't have a good countersurveillance guy, who's already spotted them."

After a lingering silence, Mallard said, "Look, Lucas. If you want to hang around the edges of this, I'll clear you with St. Vincent. But don't butt in. Stay out on the edges. I'll tell St. Vincent not to mess with you."

"I'll think about it," Lucas said. "We'd need some minimal information, like where Bernie goes at night."

"Keep your phone in your pocket," Mallard said.

OFF THE PHONE, Sherwood said, "What do you mean, you'll think about it? We're in."

"Not really. Bernie knows both of us," Lucas said. "If he spots us hanging around, he'll figure something's up."

"We'll stay back. What we need is a good, well-connected surveillance guy who can talk to us in real time."

His words hung in the air for a moment, then both Lucas and Sherwood said, simultaneously, "Del."

THEY DROVE BACK to Lucas's house and found Sam, Ellen—the girlfriend candidate—and Weather in the heated garage, the Porsche 911 backed into the driveway, while the three of them practiced slapping balls into a net with hockey sticks. They left Sam and Ellen and went inside to tell Weather what they were doing. "I needed to tell you that I'll probably bag out in the guest room instead of waking you up," Lucas said. "We'll be out late. Like three o'clock. Maybe four."

"It'd bother me more if you don't come to bed than if you do," Weather said. "I'd wake up to see if there was a text from an emergency room."

Capslock pulled into the driveway, and when they told him what they wanted, he said, "Sure. I stay out late anyway, but I'm thinking it'd be nice if there was somebody to help out on the surveillance."

Lucas held up a finger, took out his phone and called Shelly White. "What are you up to, sweetie?"

"I was planning to sit slack-jawed in front of my TV and watch the fourth season of *Elementary.* You got anything better?"

"We do. It's related to Sokolov," Lucas said. "My old lady's gonna make some mac 'n' cheese for dinner and we can talk it over. Basically, we'll want you to sit in a doorway like a street person, shivering in the cold, maybe with a wine bottle between your feet. Do you have moon boots?"

"Yeah, I do, as a matter of fact. You want down-market wino?"

"That should work," Lucas said.

"I got it covered."

"See you here in an hour."

WHITE ARRIVED AT six o'clock, bundled in jeans, an enormous black parka that hung almost to her knees, and regular boots, though she had red moon boots in her car. They made an evening out of it, eating mac 'n' cheese with a decent, but not great, Italian red, talking surgery and cops and spies and surveillance and hockey. Sam went off with Ellen, who already had her driver's license, while Lucas and Weather's daughter, Gabrielle, went to practice her cello, which was Gabrielle-speak for talking endlessly on her telephone to girlfriends.

White told Weather that she still had muscle pain from the repair work done on her leg, from when she was shot two years earlier. Weather had no advice except physical therapy.

At nine o'clock, Mallard called.

"I am told," he said, "that Bernie is going out to a club called White Ducks, which is up in the northeast part of town, wherever that is. He wants to get out of the apartment by ten o'clock, and he told his bodyguards that he might bring a woman back. They're still arguing about that, but we're going to say okay, hoping that the woman is the blond shooter. We have no idea about a phone, if there is one. We'll bag his room tonight while he's gone."

"So he's already made whatever arrangements he was hoping to make, and the hit team is on its way back to Russia, or they're getting wound up for another run at old man Sokolov."

"That would be my guess," Mallard said. "One or the other."

"All right. We'll hang around the edges, except we'll have a couple of informants on the street. Tell your FBI people not to shoot anyone who looks suspicious, because it's probably my guys."

"I will tell them," Mallard said. "Good hunting, Lucas."

"WE OUGHTA GET going," Lucas said, when he was off the phone. To Sherwood: "You sure you don't want a weapon of some kind? In case the hit team shows up? I've got a cold revolver that, you know, is purely simple. Point and shoot. If you kill somebody, you could always throw it away, so you don't have to fill out reports."

"Tempting," Sherwood said. "I sometimes carried an M16 in Syria and Iraq, and a Smith six-shooter in Lebanon, so I've had some revolver work. But . . . I better not. I don't have your kind of training. We never cared if there was somebody behind the target."

"If you say so."

Sherwood scratched his nose, and said, "All right, give me a revolver."

Lucas went out to the garage, got the revolver, a five-shot .357 magnum Ruger with a two-and-a-quarter-inch barrel, along with a speed loader with five more rounds. Lucas took a minute to download the gun and speed loader with .38 Specials, carried it back to the dining room, handed it to Sherwood and said, "Extreme last resort only."

"Make sure I'm not standing behind the target," White said.

Capslock said, "Remember, this is against everybody's better judgment."

"Got it," Sherwood said. He took the gun, popped the cylinder out to the side without looking for the release, checked that it was loaded, popped it back, and said, "This is almost the exact gun I carried, but mine had a shrouded hammer. This is fine."

"Sights are a little hard to pick up," Capslock said.

"Wouldn't use them anyway," Sherwood said. "If I'm more than six feet from the guy I'd be shooting at, I'd just run away instead."

"Excellent plan," Capslock said.

Sherwood picked up his coat and dropped the revolver in a pocket.

White would follow Capslock to his house, where they'd stop for another enormous parka and a battered rolling suitcase. They'd hang in doorways close to the club, staying as warm as they could.

Lucas and Sherwood would cruise, as they did before the shooting at the apartment house, looking for cars that might also be cruising.

"If you get the car shot to pieces again, that'd be the end of our insurance for all time," Weather told Lucas.

"I'll drive," Sherwood said. "I got a Hertz."

"Good, I appreciate that," Weather said.

"Nothing's going to happen anyway," Lucas said, and they all went out the door into another brutally cold night.

25

Titov said, "This is bullshit. They're going to have him stitched up tight. They'll be waiting for us to make a move."

"The genius thing is, we won't be making the move," Abramova said. "Bernard will. If he doesn't make a move, we drive back here, pack up, and head for the Mexican border."

"If Leonid dies . . ."

"Bernard said he's dying. He wouldn't lie about that and still try to get back home."

"Ah, sweet Christ, I know this is a trap," Titov said. He turned to Nikitin, who'd disassembled his handgun and was carefully inspecting it, and asked, "What do you think, Lev?"

"I think my ass hurts less than it did yesterday. I think I might be able to run, though I'd rather not do that." He reassembled the handgun in five or six seconds, barely looking at it, slapped a magazine into the grip, jacked a shell into the chamber, dropped the magazine, yanked the slide back and caught the single nine-millimeter shell in midair after it was ejected. Like watching a magic act, Abramova thought. Nikitin added, "I don't see a trap. They can't know about the new phone."

"Unless they built a scanner into the apartment where he's staying," Titov said.

"Bernie would know about that. He's not an idiot."

"He acts like an idiot. He's twenty-six, and all he thinks about is going out to clubs. He's probably a drug addict."

Abramova shrugged.

THEY WERE IN three separate motels in Menomonie, Wisconsin, getting together only when there was nobody to see them do that. Nikitin had used his phone to make a direct call to the Sklifosovsky Institute for Emergency Medicine in Moscow for a consultation on his wound. Alerted by Kuznetsov, they'd been expecting his call, and after a twenty-minute consultation with a gunshot specialist, he rang off and told the others, "I should keep doing what I'm doing. No strenuous exercise, like running away from American cops trying to kill me."

"Sounds like good advice to me," Abramova said.

Kuznetsov had arranged a no-go signal with his Minneapolis contacts. Another woman, an employee of the people who supplied the cars, would be at the club. If the team spotted anything dangerous, she'd get a call and put on a red silk scarf with a black border. She'd make no attempt to touch Sokolov or talk to him; she'd only send the signal that the pickup was a no-go.

The day was long and boring, watching TV, browsing on their laptops, checking and rechecking maps of northeast Minneapolis.

They would be using only two vehicles, the van and the pickup. The truck, driven by Abramova, would be abandoned within a mile or less, with the team moving to Titov's van.

Assuming they got out clean, they'd return to the Wisconsin motels, and talk to Kuznetsov about exfiltration from the U.S.

At seven o'clock, they ate pizza in Titov's room, then Abramova and Nikitin went to Nikitin's room, where the pickup was parked. At eight o'clock exactly, they left their rooms and drove out to the I-95 on-ramp. They would drive five miles an hour over the speed limit, and stay a mile apart, close enough to provide support if any were needed.

None was, and at 9:30, they rendezvoused in the parking lot of the University of Minnesota's golf course in Saint Paul. The street adjacent to the parking lot gave them a straight shot into northeast Minneapolis and the White Ducks club.

And there they sat, engines running.

BERNIE SOKOLOV VISITED his father in the afternoon. The old man was unconscious, surrounded by frustrated doctors and nurses who didn't know how to help him. He'd been poisoned, but they didn't know how or when or with what, nor did they understand exactly what vehicle was used to do it.

Some thought it might have been hidden among his daily ration of pills, which was extensive—he was on blood pressure medication, a statin, a blood thinner, and, finally, on Prilosec, a treatment for gastrointestinal reflux disease. The Prilosec came in a capsule, and a capsule could be emptied and refilled with something else.

Bernie's visit was brief, because there was nothing to be done or said. Outside the hospital room, the lead doctor told him that he had to be "prepared," which Bernie correctly interpreted as meaning his father was dying.

The day before, believing that the FBI suspected he was involved with his father's impending death, he'd used the new burner phone to call for a pickup, and to arrange the details.

He'd then pulled the battery out of the phone, opened his apartment window, and dropped the phone and battery in a privet hedge directly below. He had to get out, he thought: an autopsy might show both the nature of the poison and the method of application, and that would point directly at him.

He talked his FBI escorts—he thought of them as his captors, and they thought of themselves the same way—into a trudge through the Minneapolis skyways, as a break from the relentless afternoon television at the apartment complex. They were happy enough to take him, because they'd been equally trapped. He looked at leather jackets and jeans and ate bagels and eyed the young women, who looked a lot like the young women back in Moscow.

Then it was back to the television, and late in the evening, he got dressed for his night out. Unlike other nights, he started with long underwear; covered it with Italian-made wide-leg wool slacks, a black silk shirt covered with a V-necked green cashmere sweater, which was clunky, but necessary. On other nights, he'd worn his black Italian boots, but this night he chose high-top Converse Chuck Taylor All-Star sneaks.

Checking himself in the mirror, he thought he looked seriously good, except maybe for the sweater. The sneaks would definitely work in St. Petersburg. He used his phone to check the weather: five degrees and falling.

He picked up his leather jacket and stepped into the living room, where one of his escorts was watching CNN and the other was poking at a laptop.

As he zipped up the coat, Bernie asked, "Ready to rock?"

BERNIE'S ESCORTS WERE named Dave Droll and Olaf Haskins, FBI agents with seven and eight years' experience, respectively, both married, Droll with two children, Haskins with one, neither happy to be on late-night duty with a man who they dismissed as both a simpleton and a prick, more interested in leather jackets and pants, cashmere and death metal bands than in the important things in life, like wives and children.

As they walked out to the Suburban that they'd drive to White Ducks, Droll said, "I've never seen you with that coat zipped up. You finally get cold?"

"I'm tough, but I'm not crazy," Bernie said.

Behind Bernie's back, Droll looked at Haskins and shook his head.

26

Lucas, riding shotgun with Sherwood, called Capslock and told him that Bernie was on his way to the club. Capslock, sitting in his piece-of-crap car with the heater on high, checked his weather app: two below zero, cold enough that he really didn't want to get out, but he had to. He had brought along a hunter's foam tree-stand seat that strapped around his waist and dangled below his butt, under the parka, so he had that going for him.

He climbed out of the car and stumbled down the block, the tree-stand seat banging on his butt. He found a doorway a half block from the White Ducks club and wedged himself into it. He pulled his arms out of the parka sleeves, and sank down into the parka, like a tent, so nothing froze but his face. He had his iPhone in one hand with the neck of the parka unzipped just enough that he could stick his phone up in front of his face if he needed to answer it or make a call.

He made one call, to Lucas: "I got a spot across the street from the club and down a bit, maybe twenty-five or thirty yards. Shelly should be on the back door by now."

Lucas: "She's calling me now. I'm going to take her call."

Capslock tucked his phone back in the tent; Lucas took White's call, which was the same as Capslock's, reporting that she'd found a doorway to sit in, in an alley behind the club, and she was close, no more than ten yards from the club's back door. She was warm for the time being. "I'm wearing electric socks. They must not allow weed inside the club, because there are three people outside the door passing a joint, and a couple more just went back inside."

"All right. Sherwood and I are doing stop-and-go's, we'll be moving a lot, but we won't be more than a block or two away. If you see anything, yell."

"Where are the feds? The surveillance guys?"

"I don't know," Lucas said. "Two of them are with Bernie, but the four guys in the box, I think they're parked. I haven't seen them."

"This cold, you should see some engine exhaust," White said.

"Yeah, but we haven't. I dunno, maybe they're cruising."

They all settled in to wait. Lucas and Sherwood were on a side street, and Sherwood asked Lucas, "You ever been to Moscow?"

"No."

Sherwood looked out the window: "This is what it's like in winter, except Moscow has snow."

"We usually have snow, just not this year," Lucas said.

"You got the cold, though. Like Moscow."

"Yeah, we got the cold."

BERNIE ARRIVED AT the club. It was his third visit in a week, so he was somewhat known, and known for buying drinks for friendly women, and since the drinks were not cheap, the women tended to be friendly. There was a coat check just inside the door, and he peeled off his leather jacket and handed it to the woman behind the counter and took the claim chit. His two escorts kept their coats on.

The club was large, navy blue walls covered with cartoon characters from underground comics, the paint starting to rub off on some of them. Several women wore dancing dresses, but the weather had pushed most of them into pullover turtle-necked tops and wool pants, and the men were mostly dressed the same way, so White Ducks looked more like a ski resort than a dance club. The music was loud, the love child you'd get if hyperpop knocked up disco, with lights flickering to the beat.

Bernie elbowed his way to two women dancing together and got it going with them, as his escorts went to the bar where they both ordered Pepsi, on the rocks. The bartender knew they were feds, said nothing, pushed the drinks across the bar, no charge.

Bernie was hot, circulating, buying drinks, throwing cash on the bar. He'd taken his father's stash, since his father was no longer there to object, and he had eleven thousand dollars in his pants pocket.

At five minutes to eleven o'clock, he told Droll and Haskins, "I'm gonna disappear for two minutes."

"Where to?" Droll asked.

"Gotta pee. You wanna come watch?"

"Let's face it, Bernie, you ain't got that much to watch," Droll said, one of the rare times in recorded history when an FBI agent said "ain't."

Bernie poked a finger at him: "Ha. Jealousy is always ugly."

"Go pee," Haskins said.

CAPSLOCK HAD HIS face down in his parka when he felt the car stop at the curb, and the flashers come on. He looked up as a Minneapolis cop came around and poked him with a toe and shined a flashlight on his face and asked, "You all right, partner?"

Capslock said, "I'm not only all right, I'm a BCA agent staking out the White Ducks, and you're stepping on my act. Take that fuckin' light outa my face."

The light went sideways. "You sure about that, partner?"

"Yeah, I'm sure about it," Capslock said. "Step between me and the club so they can't see you looking at my ID."

The cop stepped between Capslock and the club and Capslock fished his ID out of a shirt pocket and stuck it out the neck hole, and the cop bent to look at it with the flashlight, then backed away and said, "Better you than me."

"Go away," Capslock said, and the cop walked back around his car, turned off the flashers, and went away.

Two couples had come out of the club and had seen the cop checking Capslock, and now they walked over and a man asked, "You all right?"

Capslock: "I'm all right."

A woman said, "Give him some money, Jim."

Jim fished in his pocket and gave Capslock a one-dollar bill. Capslock said, "Why don't you keep it; you can't buy a fuckin' thing with a one. You can't even buy a fuckin' candy bar, for Christ's sakes."

The woman said, "He's right, Jim. Give him a five."

Capslock said, "A ten would be better."

The man was thumbing through his wallet and said, "All I got is tens and twenties."

"Give him a ten, the poor thing," the woman said.

The man handed Capslock a ten and the two couples went on their way.

Capslock would have laughed if he wasn't so fuckin' cold.

SHELLY WHITE WAS not quite as cold as Capslock, because she was backed up to a metal door, and though she hadn't known about it, behind the door was a collection of HVAC machinery and plumbing that kept the interior temperature in the 80s. Some of that heat warmed the metal door and seeped into her parka. Her feet would be warm as long as the sock batteries held out.

Her biggest problem was a lack of light: there was one small flickering lamp over the club's back door, but that was it.

INSIDE THE CLUB, Bernie told one of the dancers that he'd be back in a minute, don't go anywhere, and he reached out and pinched her nipples, which she didn't like, but before she could register her displeasure, Bernie was headed back toward the short hallway that led to the men's room.

Where he didn't hesitate, but kept walking. He'd done a little psychological prep on the feds when he dropped his coat with the coat-check woman, because who'd go out that night without a coat?

Bernie, wrapped in long underwear, would: he banged through the club's back door into the alley and started running. He was fast. He'd run five miles a day back at the Farm, without breathing hard.

Haskins was still holding up the bar with his Diet Pepsi, but Droll saw Bernie pass the hall to the men's room. He was across the dance floor, the other side of the pack of dancers, and he shouted at Haskins and started shoving his way through the crowd. He had an angle that let him see Bernie disappear out the back door.

When Haskins was close enough, Droll shouted, "He went out the back, he went out the back . . ."

"Why? I don't think he had any marijuana."

They went out the back door, and saw Bernie forty or fifty yards away: "He's running, he's running . . ."

Haskins had his radio handset and he shouted into it, "Mark, Mark, Bernie's running, he's running down the alley in back, we're in pursuit . . ."

A MAN AND a woman were standing outside the back door, vaping weed, which was illegal in Minnesota, but nobody paid any attention to the legalities, because the weed horse was already out of the barn.

White watched them with a little curiosity, because there was nothing else to do in her alley, until Bernie pushed past the two vapers and started running. White said, "Uh-oh" and fumbled her phone out and tapped the little star for "favorites," then Lucas's number, and Lucas came up one second later as two FBI agents pushed out the door, looked both ways, saw Bernie, and began running after him.

Lucas came up on the first ring and White sputtered, "Bernie just ran out the back door going east in the alley and the two feds are chasing him, but they're way behind. They're running like crazy."

"East? We're on the wrong side, we're going, we're going . . ."

ON THE FRONT side of the club, a Cadillac sedan suddenly burst off the curb and miniature flashers set in the grille began winking into the night, and the Cadillac, which the feds had acquired in a drug bust, roared past Capslock, who got on the phone to Lucas and said, "I think the feds in the Bernie box just blew past me . . ."

"Bernie's running," Lucas said. "Ran past Shelly with his escorts running behind, but he had a head start, she says he's moving faster than they are . . . We're trying to get into it, but we're three blocks away on the other side of the club."

"What do you want me to do?" Capslock asked.

"Hell, you can go home," Lucas said. "We're out of this."

"We're not completely out," Sherwood said. "He won't run in a straight line. He's gotta know he'd be chased, he'll go into some kind of evasion routine. This wasn't a last-minute decision: the hit team is out there to pick him up. He knows the route he's running, and it'll include some surprises."

"Then drive faster," Lucas said.

"I've got four cylinders and tires that are made out of toilet paper," Sherwood said. "I'm going as fast as the car will handle."

"C'mon . . ."

"I don't want to run over any old ladies."

"The world has plenty of old ladies," Lucas said. "One or two fewer won't make any difference."

SHERWOOD WAS CORRECT about the evasion route. Bernie ran out of the alley and down Hennepin Avenue toward the bridge over the Mississippi, but before he got to the bridge, dodged into a side street and past a Catholic church and around a curve, then right on University Avenue, across Central Avenue, dodging cars, another side street to Holmes Park, which he'd seen on a satellite map, and diagonally across it, past patches of barren trees, to Fifth Street and one more jog onto Fourth Avenue where Abramova and Nikitin were waiting in the pickup.

Bernie had gained ground on his escorts and they were seventy or eighty yards back but had the pickup in sight when they rounded the last corner onto Fourth Avenue and Droll lifted his radio to his face and shouted, "Black pickup! Black pickup!" and saw the two right-side doors of the pickup pop open and Bernie vault inside. Abramova saw all of them coming and shouted at Nikitin, "They'll shoot us, like the first time!" and Nikitin said, "No."

Nikitin popped his door and stepped out on the street, with one of the Berettas, and as Bernie leapt into the pickup, he began firing three-shot bursts down the street at the two lawmen and saw both of them go down. He jumped back inside the truck and said, "Go! Go!"

Abramova hit the accelerator, kept her foot down for a block when a sedan suddenly turned on the street behind them, flashers winking on the grill, and Abramova said, "More of them!"

"We can't let them follow us to Titov," Nikitin said. "Put me on the ground again. Gimme your gun."

He slapped another magazine into his Beretta, and Abramova handed him the second Beretta and swerved to the curb and Nikitin was out, with both guns, hosing down the oncoming Cadillac. The sedan kept coming until it was only fifty feet away then swerved across the curb and into a tree. Nikitin turned back to the truck, but one of the agents in the Cadillac rolled out of the car with the impact on the tree, and fired three shots at him, wildly, but one shot hit Nikitin between the shoulder blades, and he went to the ground.

Abramova screamed, "Up, up," but Nikitin cried, "I'm done. Go! Go!"

She went, passenger door still open as the truck lurched forward. Just as she turned onto the next street in their evasion route, she saw another car, a small SUV, turn onto the street behind them.

LUCAS YELLED, "THAT'S them, that's the surveillance team," as a Cadillac sedan flashed through an intersection a block ahead of them, flashers in the grille and on the back bumper. "They know where they're going."

Sherwood wrestled the car around the corner just in time to see the feds' car take another turn. Sherwood followed, and skidding through the next turn, they saw the federal sedan on the side of the street and a pickup disappearing around the corner a block ahead, but in the next instant registered what appeared to be two, and then three, bodies in the street.

Lucas: "We got guys down, we got guys down."

Sherwood spotted them and took the car to the opposite side of the street, pulled even with the first two bodies and stopped and Lucas popped his door and hit the ground running. The first downed man he recognized from the hospital; the man had two bullet wounds in his face and was gone. He left him and hurried to the next man, who was bleeding and who reached up and grabbed Lucas's parka and tried to say something, but failed, and Lucas shouted at Sherwood, "He's alive, we gotta get . . ."

Sherwood was already on his phone and called, "I got 9-1-1, but where do I tell them where we're at?"

"It's automatic, they can tell where we're at within fifty meters," Lucas shouted back. "Tell them to look for a black pickup running hard."

A man was staggering toward them, pistol in hand: "Who are you?"

"U.S. Marshal, you FBI?"

"I'm shot, I'm shot," the man said, and he fell down.

Sherwood ran over to him: "Where are you hit? Where?"

"Leg, leg." Sherwood looked and found the area of the bullet wound and he called to Lucas, "I'm putting pressure on this one, what are you . . ."

The agent who'd fallen screamed as Sherwood put the pressure on the wound, and Sherwood said, "I think he's got a busted bone . . ." and the man screamed again and cried, "Don't, don't."

Sherwood pressed anyway and said, "You're bleeding a lot man, I got to keep the pressure on."

The man groaned, and then said, "I shot one of the sonofabitches. He's down on the street. He had an automatic rifle or something, we didn't have a chance."

Lucas looked and saw Nikitin trying to push up onto all fours, and said, "He's still moving."

The next moment, three civilians appeared, tentatively, looking at the bodies. A woman yelled, "I called 9-1-1, they said police and ambulances are already on the way." A compact SUV, a Toyota, turned a corner and accelerated toward them, the other part of the surveillance box. The truck went sideways and two agents jumped out and ran toward them, and one of them called, "How bad, how bad?"

Lucas said, "Bad, they're running in a black pickup . . ."

Lucas had pulled open the coat of the second agent, pulled his sweater up. With one of the two late-arriving agents crouched over him, he found a bloody wound on the left side of the man's chest, another one lower, in his stomach, a third one on his thigh. He couldn't do anything about the stomach wound but gathered part of the man's coat and put pressure on the chest and leg wounds, as best he could, which wasn't very good. "We need to get some pressure on his exit wounds, we need to roll him up on his side so he doesn't drown from the chest wound . . ."

They fumbled around getting that done, heard sirens in the distance. One of the agents moved over to the first man Lucas had looked at, the dead man, and he said, "Dave is gone, Dave is gone."

The wounded agent from the Cadillac said, "So's Jerry. Jerry's dead, he's in the car. I shot that sonofabitch who killed him, he's lying on the ground the sonofabitch, the sonofabitch."

"Are you sure about Jerry?"

"His head is gone, man, his head is gone."

The agent turned toward the body at the end of the street and suddenly began running toward it. He swerved right to the Cadillac, looked in the driver's side, then went on to the body in the street. The agent who was helping Lucas said, "If that man isn't dead, he will be in one minute."

"I want him alive," Sherwood said, looking after the running agent. He shouted, "Don't do that, don't do that."

The agent got to Nikitin, prodded him with a toe. Nikitin looked up at the end of a nine-millimeter and said, "Do it," because he didn't care about anyone's life, including his own. The agent shot him in the forehead, took a minute to kick the two Berettas away from the body, then turned and jogged back to the others. When he got to Lucas and Sherwood, he looked down at the wounded agent from the Cadillac and said, "You did good. Knocked that asshole down."

Sherwood said, "You shot him."

Lucas: "The guy was trying to get to that weapon, whatever it is. The machine gun."

The agent who'd shot Nikitin looked at Lucas, nodded, and said, "That's right."

Sherwood said, "That's bullshit."

Lucas: "It is what it is. *He was going for the gun.*"

Haskins started crying and said, "Hurt, hurt. I hurt."

Lucas: "Ambulance coming, man, ambulance is coming."

THE AMBULANCES CAME and left with the two wounded men, and a cop convention began gathering in the street. Lucas got on his phone and called Mallard.

"Lucas, do you know what time it is?"

"Yeah, it's eleven forty-five, according to my phone," Lucas said. "I'm looking at three dead men, including two FBI agents. Two more agents are on their way to Hennepin General. One of them will make it, I'm not sure about the other—he was hit three times, in the chest and stomach and leg. He's bad."

"What!"

"We got one member of the hit team dead, shot by one of your guys. They're all in the street here."

"Give me the address."

Lucas gave him the address and said, "Call St. Vincent. He's probably heard already, but I'm not sure about that."

"Where's the hit team?"

"Gone."

"Stay where you are. We're coming."

27

If the truck hadn't been so heavy, it would have been on two wheels when Abramova took it around the corner. Sokolov was thrown against the back seat door. The front passenger side door was still rattling loose, and Sokolov stretched over the back seat to grab the door handle and drag it shut.

Sokolov: "Where are we going?"

"Another five hundred meters," Abramova said. Her face was twisted, but her voice was controlled, sharp. "There's nobody behind us but we have to leave this truck."

"The man we left . . ."

"Lev Nikitin. He's dead, or will be."

Sokolov shut up as Abramova took two more corners and then pushed the truck down a dimly lit lane where Titov waited in the van. Abramova pulled up behind it, and ten seconds later, she and Sokolov were in the back of the van, out of sight.

Titov: "Where's Lev?"

Abramova, her voice as tight as a guitar string: "Dead. Go. Go now."

"Dead! How . . ."

"Go now! Go!"

Titov went, pulling down the block to Eighth Street as planned, a left turn, a block later and right onto Hennepin Avenue. Then they were free in the night, merging into the traffic, no flashing lights anywhere. They passed the golf course parking lot where they'd initially staged while waiting to pick up Sokolov, driving slowly and carefully across town to I-35, then south to I-94. Twelve minutes after they got on I-94, driving east, they crossed the St. Croix River and into Wisconsin.

They hadn't spoken much as Titov drove them across town, until they got on I-94, where Titov said, "Tell me."

Abramova told him: "You were right. It was a trap. They had undercover vehicles monitoring . . ." She turned a thumb toward the man in the back, who said, "Bernard. Sokolov."

Abramova was speechless for a moment, turning in her seat to look at him, then: "Sokolov? You are the son? You are the asset?"

"Yes."

"How did this happen?"

Sokolov said, "I didn't know we were going to defect. I'm a Russian. I want to be a Russian again. Fuck this place. I thought we were on holiday in Istanbul, I was planning to buy some clothes. My mother thought the same—we were kidnapped, is what it was. They took us to Washington, to a CIA compound. A fort. I stole a phone, called the embassy and after a lot of talking, got the FSB representative. It took a while, but the CIA finally let me out on some nights to go to clubs. I stole another phone, gave my contact a club we were going to, and a date, and I got dropped a permanent phone. They call them 'burners' here in the States."

"Who is your contact there? At the embassy?"

"A man named Kuznetsov, but I don't think that's his real name," Sokolov said.

"That's what we call him," Abramova said. "How did you know how to arrange a drop . . ."

"My father arranged FSB training on Michurinsky Prospekt, the IOT."

The IOT was the Institute for Operational Training; Michurinsky Prospekt was the location of the FSB Academy in Moscow.

Titov, disbelief in his voice: "You're an operator?"

"No. I left after basic training," Sokolov said. "I thought someday I would go back. Before my mother was killed, I even thought I might stay here as an asset. Find a job, stay on."

Abramova: "You killed your father."

"He wasn't dead yet this afternoon. They are certain he will die."

"But your father."

"I've hated him since I was a child," Sokolov said. "Until I was twelve or thirteen, I thought beatings were the way life was lived. He would beat me two or three times a week. Not child whippings with a belt: he beat me with his fists. Sometimes, I couldn't walk. My mother . . . you killed my mother . . . my mother never interfered. She was bad as my father, or worse. She loved the idea that people feared her, feared what word she'd put in my father's ear."

A long silence, as they digested that, then Titov said, "Tell me about Lev."

Abramova said, "The FBI agents from the club ran faster than we thought, than Bernard thought they could, and were too close to the place we were waiting. They would have shot us to pieces, just like at the safe house. Lev dropped them but before he could get back in the truck another FBI vehicle came around the corner and Lev shot at them, but one of the FBIs shot Lev. Lev told me to go; he was dying."

"Ah, God, a disaster," Titov said. "A disaster."

"They will happen," Abramova said. "Now we are done. We go back to the motel, pack, go south tomorrow morning. We will take the van, twenty-two hours to Matamoros. Take turns driving, stop for gas and food, nothing else."

Titov said, "I don't think so. Not now. Not with dead FBI agents . . ."

"We don't know that they're dead," Abramova said.

"Lev was shooting at them. They're dead," Titov said. "That's what he did: an angel of death. They will be looking at every face trying to get across the border. Every face."

Sokolov: "What do you think? We have to get across . . ."

"I have a contact on the Canadian border, at Thunder Bay. Almost straight north from here. He can get us across a river into Canada, across the ice, pick us up. We have done that twice, in the past. There'll be less attention to the killings in Canada than here in the U.S. Canada is not as good for getting back home, because their counter-intel people are better than Mexico's, and Canada's more hostile to us. But. The embassy in Toronto has a safe house. We stay there for a week, a month, and then we go. Private flight out of a small airport."

"This sounds better," Abramova admitted. "How many hours to this Thunder Bay?"

"Maybe six or seven, depending on the road conditions and the route we take. But, one big thing: that's all on back roads. No stops at all, one full tank of gas in each vehicle, which I can get tomorrow. I will call my contact tomorrow morning, probably won't be able to cross tomorrow night. Maybe, the day after tomorrow. We'd stay out of sight in the motel for one more day."

"Call your contact when we get back," Abramova said. "We will hide Bernard in Lev's room."

She explained to Sokolov that they were spread across three motels in Menomonie, Wisconsin. Titov held the key cards for all three rooms, because if there was trouble, they didn't want a card found on a team member who was captured or killed. Titov wasn't an operator: he was the team's concierge, driving and making arrangements for travel and equipment.

"I thought there were more of you," Sokolov said.

"There were," Abramova said. "There were three members of the team, and Titov is a sleeper here, activated for this assignment. One of us was badly wounded, but we managed to get him evacuated. He should be home by now. Lev Nikitin . . . You saw Lev, down in the street."

Sokolov said, "You should never have come after me. This was a bad call by Kuznetsov. Even if I were arrested, they would have traded for me. They knew I didn't kill my mother, and they couldn't prove I attacked my father."

"You are correct, but too late," Titov said. "Now we run."

Abramova: "We have been attacked three times by one man . . ."

"Davenport, U.S. Marshal," Sokolov spat. "Look at him on the Internet. He's a killer. If he was there tonight, I wouldn't be surprised if he's the one who shot your friend. He's with a woman named Shelly

White. All I know about her was that she was once shot by a fugitive up in the northern area here. Also from the Internet. Look on Gemini, it's all there."

"I would like to meet this Davenport in an alley," Abramova said.

"I believe he would like to meet you, as well," Sokolov said. "As I said, he's a killer."

Titov: "Do you think this woman talking to you is a helpless cabbage?"

"I don't know the woman I'm talking to, but I know about Davenport," Sokolov said.

ABRAMOVA AND TITOV had known that they'd get back to the motels very late, so they'd stocked the three rooms with food and soft drinks. They agreed to stay in their rooms, in touch with their burners, the next day. Titov would go out for more food in the evening, then they'd all meet in Sokolov's room to make final plans for the trip north on the following day.

"We need discipline," Abramova warned Sokolov. "Stay inside tomorrow. If you have room service, decline it. You'll have a TV and Internet. Your face will be known, and probably on TV, so you must hide it."

"Yes, I can do that," Sokolov said. "I will."

TITOV STOPPED FIRST at his own room, where the red Ford was still parked outside. Abramova would take the van, dropping Sokolov at his motel, then go on to her own.

In his room, Titov opened the small cooler he'd bought that afternoon at a gas station and took out a Coke and a bag of beef jerky, sat on his bed, and tried to think.

Abramova had said they'd shot and probably killed two or more FBI agents. By morning, the hunt would be intense, and all over Minnesota and the surrounding states. The cops would be putting Sokolov's face on everything but milk cartons. He wasn't sure, but he thought the odds of getting across the ice to Canada were probably seventy percent. The other thirty percent, they'd be caught. And, he thought, killed. The American cops were not going to let some Russians gun down FBI agents and get away with it: if the cops spotted them, they'd be murdered.

He sat on his bed, chewing on the jerky, then got his laptop out and went online to ChatGPT. The marshal Sokolov had mentioned, Davenport, had an extensive online history, and the kid had been right: the man was a killer. He did a search for the shootings that night in Minneapolis, but nothing came up. Too soon. There were certainly cops still on the scene.

He dropped the sack of jerky on the floor, shut down the laptop, turned off the overhead lights. In the dim light coming through an open bathroom door, he fell back on a pillow, closed his eyes, and let his thoughts come to the surface.

Matvey Orlov, he hadn't really gotten to know; they'd only been together for a week before the first assassination attempt, and the team didn't talk much to him. Lev Nikitin he hadn't liked, because Nikitin was a serial murderer and that quality sat right on the surface of his personality. He'd tried to generate a couple of erotic fantasies about Abramova, but she really wasn't fantasy material. Sokolov he didn't know at all, except as a kid who'd murdered his father.

What did he owe them, that was worth getting killed for?

Lying on his pillow, he thought, *nothing*. He'd done everything they'd asked, and they'd put him in this predicament, a thirty percent chance of murder by cop.

He would not sleep well.

Davenport.

28

Lucas and Sherwood sat morosely in the rental car, looking at the cops and crime scene people pacing off distances between bodies and marking brass ejected from guns and photographing and bagging the guns themselves and Sherwood said, "So different."

"Than?"

"Anything I've ever seen," Sherwood said, "Iraq, Syria, people get killed and you pick up yours, if any of yours got dinged up, and then you'd get the fuck out. Medivac them to a hospital with trauma surgeons on call. Everybody else, fuck 'em. Let them take care of their own. None of this . . . bureaucracy. I mean, really, why are they measuring all of this? It's like surveying school. Could you really use it in court?"

"Can't tell," Lucas said. "Get in court, and if the defense attorneys can't make a deal for their clients, and don't have a decent defense, they'll attack procedure. Try to show that things were done wrong, and that their clients have somehow been cheated. Doesn't usually work, but if we don't do the procedure, they'll attack it, and sometimes, not often, they'll get away with it."

"Really."

"Then, somebody will sue us. Either the relatives of the dead and injured, or relatives of the accused, because we didn't do all the procedure. That's where we're at, now, in terms of finding justice."

"That's not good."

"Nope."

LOUIS MALLARD AND Jane Chase had been wandering around the crime scene, getting close, staring down at the bodies, while trying to stay out of the way. After a while, they started toward Sherwood's car, and Lucas said, "Here they come," and he and Sherwood got out to meet them on the street.

Mallard had tears in his eyes, and evidence that more had already trickled down his aging cheeks. "This is dreadful," he said. "This is the worst thing since Miami. If that poor Haskins dies, it'll be worse than Miami."

"Have you heard anything about him? About the guys in the hospital?" Lucas asked.

"Haskins is a mess," Chase said. "He'll be in the OR all night. The other agent has a bullet wound in his leg, torn up muscle and cracked a bone, but he should be okay, aside from any psychological trauma. Which could be extensive. Haskins, we don't know."

Sherwood asked, "But he won't die?"

"We don't know. He could," Chase said.

Mallard: "Ah. I heard just before you guys called. Leonid Sokolov died about eleven o'clock. They say that the wounds from the bullet, plus the deterioration of the poison, whatever it was, couldn't be recovered from."

"So Bernie got it done," Lucas said.

Sherwood, turning away from them: "Unbelievable."

THE AGENT WHO'D been shot in the leg confirmed what Lucas and Sherwood had seen, that the hit team had fled in a black pickup. The Minneapolis cops began scouring back streets, and a possible pickup was found in half an hour, along with a witness.

The witness, who'd left her own apartment to smoke a cigarette, said it was so cold that she stayed inside her building's outer door to smoke it, and if that was illegal, sue her. She'd seen a man and a woman get out of the pickup and get into a white van, which immediately pulled away from the curb and disappeared around a corner. The man didn't seem to be wearing a coat.

She thought that was curious, but not notably illegal, so she finished the cigarette and went back upstairs to stream a video before she went to bed. When she'd seen the flashers on the cop cars surrounding the pickup, she went back downstairs and out into the street, to ask what was going on.

The pickup wasn't quite empty: the cops found a half-empty gun magazine lying on the floor, that would match the two Berettas found at the scene of the shooting. The two guns were like nothing anyone had seen before.

That information was passed to the feds; St. Vincent had shown up, and had spoken to the agent who killed Nikitin, then put him in an FBI vehicle by himself, to be further interviewed by the FBI's own Inspection Division.

After isolating the agent, St. Vincent walked over to Mallard and Chase, and took them aside for a moment, then Mallard called to Lucas and Sherwood: "Hey, guys, Lucas, John . . ."

They went over and St. Vincent said, "Our man Tom Lawrence said you witnessed the shooting, the one where Lawrence shot the man on the ground. The Minneapolis crime scene people says it appears that the shot was fired into his forehead from a very close range, and apparently straight through his head and into the blacktop. Tom says the guy made a move for one of the Berettas and if he'd gotten it up, Tom himself might have been killed, and other people on the street. You guys were supposedly witnesses."

"That's the way I saw it," Lucas said. "We dumped our car and ran over to the two guys who were down, Haskins and the other guy . . ."

"Droll . . ." They all glanced over at the body, now covered with a black plastic sheet.

Lucas continued: "Yeah, while we were doing that, I saw the hit team guy moving. Not dead. The guy who was shot in the leg said he had an automatic weapon. After the ambulances had gone, John and I walked over to look at that Cadillac, and he was right. You can see it in the car."

"There were no guns within reach," St. Vincent said. "Those Berettas."

"That's because he made a play for one of them. Your man shot him, and then he kicked the guns away just, you know . . . like you're trained to."

"Thank you," St. Vincent said. "I appreciate it."

Mallard nodded, and then Chase asked Sherwood: "Did you see the same thing?"

"I was putting pressure on the guy's leg, the guy who got shot, and my back was half turned away. I looked when Lucas said the man on the ground was still alive, and I saw him trying to get up. I didn't actually see the shooting, but I know the man on the ground was still alive."

"Good. Somebody from our Inspection Division may want written statements from the two of you, but I'm satisfied," Mallard said.

"I think we may have to look a little more closely at this," Chase said.

Mallard turned and snapped, "I don't think so, Jane."

Mallard, Chase, and St. Vincent moved away, still talking, and Sherwood muttered to Lucas, "Jane thinks you're a lying sack of shit, you lying sack of shit."

"Fuck Jane."

"I'm trying, I'm trying," Sherwood said.

"If you get there, no pillow talk about this," Lucas said. "Besides, I did sort of see something like that."

"I didn't, and I was looking right at them."

"Stick with the half-turned-away story. They not only bought it, they desperately want to buy it."

LUCAS AND SHERWOOD stayed until all the bodies were gone, and all the FBI agents except Mallard and Chase. A crime scene crew was still looking for cartridge cases and marking frozen blood puddles. A few of the neighbors were still standing on the sidelines, but when a wrecker arrived to tow the shot-up Cadillac, they started drifting back to their homes. Then Mallard waved goodbye, and he and Chase headed for their rental car.

"THE HIT TEAM is gonna be long gone," Lucas told Sherwood. They were sitting in their own car, trying to get warm. "If they're headed for Mexico, they could already be through Des Moines. Gotta get Bernie's photo out to every border crossing, but . . . I kinda think they're gone for good. They had to have a solid plan to get out of the country."

"I'm afraid you're right. Well: I'll probably get out of here myself, tomorrow or the next day," Sherwood said. "I can't say I found Minneapolis to be overwhelmingly charming. Me being wounded and all."

"Not healed up yet?"

"I only got shot two days ago," Sherwood said.

"Yeah, but it was like being scratched by a pine needle."

"Maybe Jane could kiss it and make it better," Sherwood said.

"If that happens, I'll personally award you a hundred dollars," Lucas said. "Ask to see her bullet scar. It's on her rather attractive ass. I happened to be around when she got shot."

"Do tell."

"I do tell," Lucas said. "Listen, you won't get out of here tomorrow—too much bureaucracy to deal with. Why don't you come over tomorrow night for dinner again? We'll get Weather and go out to somewhere good. I mean, there's no chance you'll be taking Jane out, we both know that."

"I'd like to do that," Sherwood said. "What are you doing?"

"I plan to start by sleeping late." He shrugged. "After that, I suspect both of us will be up to our necks in cheese-eating bureaucrats."

LUCAS WAS RIGHT. The next day they were interviewed, jointly and separately, by FBI interrogators and Minneapolis cops, about the shooting of Nikitin, and exactly how they'd gotten involved in the chase. At night, they went out to somewhere good, for a dinner that, if not morose, was subdued.

Lucas had never been impressed by the general run of FBI agents, but had known some exceptionally good ones, including Mallard and Chase, and the killing of the two agents was a weight on them all. At their latest report, Haskins was hanging on, but his career as a street agent was over: some of his injuries would probably never fully heal.

Sherwood said he had a flight out to Washington the next day at one o'clock. Leaving the restaurant, he shook hands with Lucas and said, "Next time you're in D.C."

29

At six o'clock the next morning, Weather prodded Lucas and said, "Your phone is ringing."

Lucas, who'd been wrapped in sheets and had a foot stuck under Weather's weight blanket, groaned: "What time is it?"

"About 6:30. But it must be important. You want me to get it for you?"

Lucas had left his phone in his sock drawer, with only a thin charging cable attaching it to the outside world. "I guess," he said.

Weather was back in a minute and handed him the now silent phone. The call had come from the Marshals Service office in Minneapolis. He poked the redial and when the phone was answered, the woman on the other end said, "A man called here. Said it was critical that he talk to you, but he was going to throw his phone away in half an hour. That was . . . six minutes ago?"

"Who'd he say it was?"

"He said it was about the Russians you've been tracking. He had a Russian accent. I think it was a Russian accent."

"Give me the number."

Lucas punched in the number, which was answered on the first ring with a *"Da?"*

"This is Lucas Davenport. Who am I talking to?"

"I'm not sure I should give you my name, in case I manage to squeak out of this mess on my own," the man said. "Anyway, I'm the man whose face you've been putting on television, the sketch from my neighbors in Minnetrista."

Lucas dropped his feet to the floor, hunched over the phone as Weather sat down on the bed beside him. He pressed the speaker option so she could hear and asked, "What do you want?"

"There is an excellent possibility you will kill me later today. I don't want that to happen. I'm what you Americans call a sleeper agent. I arrange the comings and goings of Russian spies in the United States. That's all. I'm not part of the assassination squad sent here to kill Sokolov, but I'm with them . . ."

"How do I know you're not lying to me? You don't sound much like a Russian."

"I can do a Russian accent if you want me to," Titov said in a heavy Russian accent. Then back to his American voice, he added, "I'm a sleeper agent, for Christ's sake. Of course I sound like an American. I even hate the Packers."

Lucas nodded at a sentiment he recognized: "All right, so you're either from the Twin Cities or Chicago. Possibly from Dallas."

"I also hate the Cowboys," Titov said.

"Yeah, so does everybody else," Lucas said. "What do you want from me?"

"I maybe want to come in, but I don't want to get killed if I do it."

"Why should I pay any attention to what you want? Maybe I'd prefer to kill you later today," Lucas said.

"That's only a thirty percent possibility—I have calculated seventy percent we get away clean, thirty percent you catch us. If you catch us, after what happened, I think you will kill us."

"That's a good bet," Lucas said. Weather was standing next to the bed, listening, raised her eyebrows, shook her head.

"I haven't seen anything on television yet," Titov said. "The shooter, who I think you killed, was very effective. I assume you also have dead?"

"Two FBI agents dead, another one in critical condition, and another one hurt bad," Lucas said. "The FBI gunmen are seriously on the hunt."

"That's what I'm afraid of," Titov said. "I am in a position where I can give you Bernard Sokolov, who poisoned his father with Novichok and also the controller of the assassination squad, who is a woman. I'm sure you have seen her on your videos or know about her from talking to the doctor she took out of the Bison hospital."

"All you want in return is . . . what?"

"That, I would negotiate. I know how these things are done," Titov said. "No jail. That must be clear. I am going to pull the battery on my phone, so you can't track it, but sometime in the next hour, you will send me an agreement by email guaranteeing no jail, nothing like jail. Freedom in the United States. The exact conditions we can negotiate. If it takes more than one hour, I'm gone, because the squad will be here to get me. Then it will be too late."

"I'm not positive I can do that, but I think I can," Lucas said. "I am working here with a CIA agent, who I believe will be very interested in your offer."

"Good. He is exactly the man I wish to talk to. To negotiate with, because he will see the value I offer. I want his name on the email, with yours, and the highest officials you can reach. I am now by myself, but in one hour, I will be back with the squad, and unable to talk. By the way, don't bother trying to run down the location of the Gmail address I will send you. There are 1.8 billion active Gmail addresses. I have one hundred of them. I have never used the address before, and I will never use it again, after I read your guarantee. If I don't see it, I will take my thirty percent chance."

"I understand," Lucas said.

"Good. If you can arrange this, I will see you later today," Titov said.

One second later, he was gone, and Lucas looked up at Weather, who said, "My God."

SHERWOOD, TWO MINUTES later, said, "Do you realize . . . No, you probably don't, because you're a humble deputy marshal. I will send you this guarantee in five minutes and will sign it in ink and send you a PDF, you can print it, sign it, scan it, send it back to me, and I'll see if I can round up more signatures while you're doing that. We gotta get this guy! We gotta! And preferably, in a way that the Russians won't realize what's happened."

"What don't I realize? As a humble marshal?"

"This guy told you that he moves NOCs around . . ." Sherwood began.

"I don't know what a NOC is."

"A spy with no diplomatic cover. N-O-C. It stands for non-official cover. If we can keep this guy in place, as a sleeper, I mean, holy cow, Lucas, this would be a coup."

"All right, I'm willing to believe that, but I'm not sure the feds will go along."

"They will when they see the other signatures on the guarantee. I don't know who I can get out of bed, but it's after seven o'clock on the East Coast, and I bet I can get a couple of good ones."

"All right," Lucas said. "Send me the letter. As soon as I send it back to you, I'll get cleaned up and head over there to pick you up. Wherever the guy wants us to go, we'll be ready."

"I'm good with that. Listen, this is you and me and, I don't know, maybe Del and Shelly? I don't want to tell the FBI about it, because they'll go in heavy."

"Jesus, we'd really be putting our necks on the chopping block," Lucas said.

"True. That's what makes it exciting. I've already got a major hard-on," Sherwood said.

"I heard that," Weather said.

TEN MINUTES, THE letter came in to Lucas's email. Weather got it, printed it, took it to Lucas, who was shaving, had him sign it, took it back to the home office, scanned it, and sent it back to Sherwood as a PDF.

Ten minutes after that, Sherwood called back: "I got the DDO—deputy director of operations—to sign off on it. He's calling somebody at the Justice Department, but we're getting short on time."

"Get what you can," Lucas said. "You know, we could just lie, put a bunch of fake signatures on it, and grab the guy and drop him in jail."

"We could, which would just get us some spam in the can and do us no good at all. Lucas, this is large. You're going to justify your entire wretched existence with this score."

"Yours maybe, not mine," Lucas said. "I feel my neck stretched out and the axe coming down."

"Call Del. Call Shelly. Get over here," Sherwood said.

"How about St. Vincent?"

"No! Not Mallard, either, or your friend Jane! There's no way they'd want to do what we need, which is to separate this defector from the pack. If the FBI didn't flat out kill him, they'd want a show trial. We need people who don't have anything invested in revenge and can keep their mouths shut."

Lucas had to think about that. He could use a little revenge himself, but had spent enough time in Washington that he understood what Sherwood was trying to do.

He wound up calling both White and Capslock, and they agreed to meet at the federal building in Minneapolis. "I'm not sure about taking Del along, because I don't know where we're going," Lucas said. "If it's not here in the state, all he could do is stand around."

"Call Edie Lamb," White said. "Tell her to get her ass into the office."

"What for?"

"She can deputize Del. Perfectly legal, and not totally uncommon. In fact, I think you or I could deputize him, but I'm not sure about that."

"You think she could deputize Sherwood?" Lucas asked.

"I think she can deputize a ham sandwich if she wants to. Anyone she likes, including a flat-out ass-scratching sidewalk citizen."

"I'll call her."

Lucas looked at his watch: still early Saturday morning. Edie Lamb was the U.S. Marshal for the district of Minnesota. She liked to have a drink or eight on Friday nights. *All right*, he thought, *an exaggeration*. She was trying to dry out, but he wasn't sure how far that project had gotten. If it hadn't gotten far, she could be unconscious.

He called anyway. She answered the phone immediately and said, "This must be bad. I assume about the Russians?"

"Yes. There's been a development . . ."

Lucas told her about the call from the member of the hit team. "We want you to deputize Del Capslock and John Sherwood because we don't know where we'll be going. The team is on the run, and they're probably on the road somewhere."

Lamb said, "We'll be leaving here in ten minutes. I can be down in the office in thirty minutes. If you can swing by, we'll fill out some paper . . . Who else is going with you?"

"Shelly, and she's good. So just the four of us."

"I will see you in half an hour."

Sherwood was enthusiastic. "I'll walk over as soon as I'm dressed. I called my guy in Washington, told him the situation. If we can get this guy . . ."

LUCAS WAS IN his car when the hit team man called back and asked, "What are we doing?"

"You should have gotten an email."

"I did. One minute ago," the man said. "It looks okay. I was beginning to think you were going to turn me down."

"No. Tell me where you want to meet," Lucas said.

"At the Musky Hunter's bar in Hayward, Wisconsin. I'll be wearing a red ski mask with the bottom pulled up over my chin. Blue parka, blue jeans, Nike shoes."

"What time?"

"Eleven o'clock."

Lucas glanced at his watch: they had time, but with the stop at the marshals office, they'd have to move right along. "I've talked to our CIA contact about this, and he doesn't want you to, uh, I don't know how to put this . . . He doesn't want the other members of the team to know you've given them up. I don't have a tight grip on that myself, but you need to be alone at the Musky Hunter."

"I can do that. Do you know this bar? You sound like . . ."

"I have a cabin twenty miles east of Hayward," Lucas said. "So yes, I know the place. You guys, you're headed for the Canadian border?"

"Yes, but I won't say where on the Canadian border. This whole thing might still fall through."

"Don't let it," Lucas said. "C'mon. Don't let it."

"I'll see you at the bar," the man said.

CAPSLOCK WAS WAITING outside the entrance to the federal building when Lucas arrived. "I had to stick my car in a parking garage. I assume I'll be reimbursed for the charge?"

"Maybe," Lucas said. "I'm sure you'll have the sincere thanks of a grateful nation."

"I'd rather have the money," Capslock said, as he followed Lucas inside.

White and Sherwood were sitting at White's desk when Lucas and Capslock arrived, but Lamb had not yet arrived. Lucas called her and she said, "I'm just getting out of my car, I'm right outside."

While they waited, Lucas told the others about the second phone call from the hit team member, and about the eleven o'clock appointment at the Musky Hunter.

"The four of us have to talk to my boss in Washington when we get out of here," Sherwood said. "We don't need to mention that to Miz Lamb."

Lamb was in the office two minutes later, wearing wooly tights and a ski jacket. She said, "I've got to do some paper on this sooner or later, or maybe I can skip it altogether if you don't find these people and we can all pretend this didn't happen . . . But I need Mr. Sherwood to write his name on a piece of paper so I can fill it in later, and I already know Del, so . . . Anyway, I need to be able to say that I talked to you individually and you agreed to serve as temporary deputy marshals. Is that correct?"

Sherwood said, "Yes," and Capslock said, "I never aspired to anything more," and Lamb said, "I understand that perfectly, Del, but I'm afraid you're too dumb for a permanent position. Anyway, yabba-dabba-do, you're deputized." She started back toward her office. "Hang on here a minute."

"We're in a hurry," Lucas said.

"Yes. One minute." She disappeared into her office, came back in less than a minute with two badges, which she handed to Capslock and Sherwood. "In case you need them," she said. "If you don't, I want them back."

"No chance of that," Sherwood said. "I'm gonna arrest my neighbor in D.C. for using his leaf blower."

"Let's go," Lucas said. "We need to be in Hayward by eleven, and as much earlier as we can."

"You're going to Hayward?" Lamb asked.

"Yeah . . ."

"Hayward's where I'm going," Lamb said. "Today's the Birkebeiner."

Lucas looked at her, flabbergasted, and said, "Today? Today's the Birkie?"

"What's that?" Sherwood asked.

"A big goddamn cross-country ski race," Lucas said. "Fifty-five kilometers. Twelve thousand racers, probably twenty or thirty thousand spectators. The whole town has less than three thousand people in it, so it gets completely overrun."

"Maybe that's why the contact chose the place—he can get lost in the crowd if he needs to," Sherwood said.

"Maybe, but I think he would have mentioned something when he called. Maybe he doesn't even know about it," Lucas said.

"Whatever," Lamb said. "If you're gonna meet him at eleven, you better motivate. You could get clogged up going into town."

THEY LEFT THE office in a hurry, but Sherwood told White and Capslock that they needed to rendezvous in Lucas's car before they left Minneapolis. "From here, it's three hours up there on a good day, and it's coming up on seven now," Lucas said. "You're sure we gotta talk?"

"We gotta."

They crowded into Lucas's car and Sherwood made the call, put the phone on speaker. The woman on the other end said, "Yes, John."

"We're all here. Four of us," Sherwood said. He seemed to be vibrating. "We gotta go in a hurry, if we want to get this done. The meet is set at a bar in Hayward, Wisconsin, four hours from now, and it takes three hours to get there. The town is having some kind of big fuckin' ski race."

"I'll make it short, and I don't have any real authority to make this arrangement, so we appreciate any help we can get from the Marshals Service," the CIA woman said. "What we would like, the best case, the best possible outcome, is for you to kill or capture the woman in the team, but let the defector escape with Sokolov. Let them go wherever they want. Again, best case would be for the sleeper to come out of this as a hero, for the Russians, and go back to his regular job here in the U.S."

"Letting them go could create an unprecedented stink with the FBI and the Justice Department," Lucas said.

"That's not really my problem," the woman said. "My problem is how do we identify and then preserve the sleeper in his job."

Sherwood said, "Tara, we'll do the best we can. We're trying to keep the FBI out of this because they'll want to rain all over these people, and not with little water droplets."

"I understand," she said.

"Do you?"

"Yes. Their dead agents. Now you better hurry if you're going to make the meet. Talk about it on the way. You know what we want, and it will be difficult, to say the least, but it would be a great benefit if you could pull it off."

30

Abramova and Bernie Sokolov were ready to go at seven o'clock, but Titov was dragging his feet. He would be ready to leave at nine, he told them. Before then, he was doing research and trying to track down his Canadian contact who would get them across the ice.

"I talked to his wife, and he's driving back to Thunder Bay from up north, a place called Nipigon. He's been on the road for a while. She says the drive normally takes an hour and a half, but they had a dump of snow a couple days ago," Titov said. "The roads are passable, but a little slow. She says he'll be home before eight. I need to talk to him while we're both looking at the same maps, and I can't do that when I'm driving."

"How much will that slow us down?" Abramova asked.

"Not at all," Titov said. "We're about six hours from the place we usually cross, and we can't cross until it's dark. Better we stay here for a little while, than get up to an uninhabited place in Canada and stand around trying not to look suspicious. Especially with Bernard's face out there everywhere."

"You know this? His face?"

"Go online. Put Bernard Sokolov in Google," Titov said. "He's on every television station in the Twin Cities. When we go north, you have to drive, Kat. Be good if you could get Bernard to lie down in the back and maybe find something to cover him with."

"Cover him? With what?"

"Let me think about that. I'll call you when Edouard gets back to me."

EDOUARD GAGNON CALLED right at eight. He could move them that night, across the Pigeon River. "Five thousand," he said.

"We'll need a car . . ."

"Will I get it back?"

"Yes. We need to drive it to Toronto . . ."

"You could do that, but it's at least a sixteen-hour drive if we don't get any more snow. And I'd want another ten grand, you know, for the inconvenience and risk of losing the car. I could put you in an air taxi, with a guy who won't talk, for five thousand. In-country flight from a general aviation airport to another general aviation airport outside Toronto, no IDs required."

"Let's do that," Titov said. "I'll hand you the cash at the river."

"Six o'clock. Be there or be square," Gagnon said.

"I'll call you," Titov said.

TITOV WAS LYING on the motel bed as he spoke to Gagnon, watching a news program from the Twin Cities with the sound muted. A feature story came up, a rosy-cheeked woman wearing a ski hat and wearing a bright red ski jacket, and a caption at the bottom of the screen said, "The Birkebeiner, Hayward, Wisconsin."

He thought, "What?" and as soon as he signed off with Gagnon, he picked up the remote and unmuted the TV. He caught the tail-end of the young woman's cheery report and went to his laptop.

It took only a moment to confirm it: there was a huge cross-country ski race in Hayward that morning that would continue for most of the rest of the day. He thought for a moment, then went out to the 'net again, and checked for a local Walmart. He found one just across the interstate, and called up the website. The Walmart did sell cross-country skis.

He called Abramova, who said, without preamble, "Are we ready?"

"Almost. I talked to my contact, we have a crossing point." He explained about the airplane, and Abramova was good with that. "One more thing: there's a cross-country ski race in a town called Hayward, almost straight north of us, on the way to the border. There'll be thousands of people there, I'm worried somebody will spot Bernard."

"People will see him, but they won't see him," she said. "Come as soon as you can."

"There is a Walmart just across the interstate. I need to stop there for a minute. I will see you in twenty minutes," Titov said.

At nine o'clock, back from Walmart, having spent fifteen hundred dollars on the cheapest cross-country skis sets he could find, a decent-looking parka in Sokolov's size, along with a sack full of junk food,

Titov drove to now-deceased Nikitin's room, where Abramova was waiting with Sokolov.

Sokolov had been lying on the bed when Abramova let him in, and Titov gawked at the other man. "My God," he said to Abramova, "What have you done?"

"Nobody will see him," Abramova said.

"That's . . . brilliant," Titov said. And, "You're right. I think I just wasted a lot of money."

Abramova had shaved Sokolov's head, and Sokolov had shaved his previously furry face. "I look like a peeled potato," Sokolov said.

"It'll grow back," Titov said, marveling at the change. Sokolov had looked like a blond bush the night before, with the shoulder-length hair and scuzzy blond beard. His head now looked like a pale fleshy egg, with all of Sokolov's features seemingly melted into the bottom of his face.

"Then we go," Abramova said. "Why did you go to this Walmart?"

"I bought four sets of skis and poles and some boots. All junk, but it looks okay, if you don't know about brands. I thought we could push the second and third row of seats down, in the van. There'd still be enough space for Sokolov to lay on the floor between the front seats and second row. We'd throw all the skis on top of him, if you get stopped . . . you're going up to the ski race."

Sokolov: "You thought I'd lay on the floor for six hours?"

"No. Just lounge around in the back of the van. If a cop pulled you over, you'd roll into that space behind the front seat and pull a bunch of the skis over you. You'd be good. But now . . . I don't think it'll be necessary. Not with that face."

"That would work, though, if we needed to do it," Abramova said. "It is clever, and no harm to have the skis."

"I bought a parka for Bernard and some junk food so we won't have to stop to eat. I've worked out a route going up that makes it very unlikely that we'll even see a police car, much less get stopped by one."

"What if we are?" Sokolov asked.

Titov shrugged: "Listen, with that bald head . . . I wouldn't have recognized you five minutes ago if you walked past me on the street. Kat has all the ID she needs. It's good ID. She gets a ticket, you go on . . ."

"What if he does recognize me? Or Katerina? Or is suspicious, and calls for help?"

"That's why Kat has a gun. She takes the cop down, runs north, where I'll be waiting, we abandon the van and go on in the Ford."

"Complicated," Abramova said.

"Not complicated," Titov said. "Because we will not be stopped. I'll lead you along the back roads, and we won't even see many civilian cars. If I see a police car coming toward you, I'll call, and you can adjust your speed. We shouldn't drive fast, anyway. We have almost too much time."

"We should go anyway," Abramova said.

THE TRIP WENT just as Titov said it would: they followed back roads north, then east for a bit, and came into Hayward from the southeast, passing through tiny towns with no sign of a police presence, and rarely even residents. The snow was thin until the last leg into Hayward, where the world began to get whiter, the snow deeper and fresher.

On the way north, Titov considered the possibilities: he'd talked to Davenport, arranged a meeting, but he didn't have to go through with it. If he simply led the van in a loop around Hayward, he could continue north, cross into Minnesota at Duluth, take more back roads to the border, watch Abramova and Sokolov walk across the Pigeon River, and drive back to Minneapolis. He could pick up his Jeep and return to Chicago.

On the other hand, the authorities would have his DNA and probably even his fingerprints, from the cars and the original safe house. If he were ever arrested for anything, he'd be toast, as the Americans said. First-degree murder of two FBI agents; he would never be free again.

He could continue across the border with Abramova and Sokolov, and from there to Moscow, but he didn't want to go to Moscow. In Moscow he'd be, at best, a low- to middle-level bureaucrat, never quite trusted because of all his years in the U.S. He'd be looking at thirty years—if he were lucky—of boredom, followed by more-or-less gentle poverty in retirement.

The case for cooperating with the Marshals Service and the CIA was stronger. During their reconnaissance of the Sokolovs' original hideout, he'd been amazed by what the Sokolovs were getting. A dream house. If he could get the same sweet deal . . .

Yet, there was always the possibility that the Americans would betray him, put him on trial, throw his sad Russian ass in prison. He had that paper from the CIA and from the Marshals Service, but that could turn out to be faked.

He could continue to the meeting, listen to their promises, and if they weren't solid enough, walk away. If they didn't let him walk away, simply keep his mouth shut. Abramova and Sokolov would still have a reasonable shot at making it out of the country, even if he'd gone missing.

TITOV LED THE van by a mile, a little more than a minute, and coming into Hayward, encountered a detour sign with a volunteer waving traffic around a blocked road. He punched up Abramova on his phone and said, "There's a detour. Don't let Bernard wear a hat, we want the bald head to show. I'll go slow, so you'll see me when you go through the detour. They're not stopping anyone."

At the detour, Titov stopped and asked the volunteer, "Where can I get the closest, you know, to the center of town? Where the skiers are coming in?"

"Things are pretty jammed up right now, but if you go three blocks that way . . ." The volunteer pointed. ". . . to the corner with the big house with the rock chimney, take a right, and that'll get you about as close as you can get. You won't be able to go through, though."

"That's great," Titov said.

He continued down the detour, slowly, saw the van two cars behind him. He took the right, and two short blocks on, hit the traffic jam. Dozens of people in Wisconsin winter dress streamed by, happy, hurrying, jaywalking, sometimes simply walking down the middle of the street.

He got on the phone to Abramova, who'd followed behind. "Things are really blocked here. There are some spaces off the road, pull over and wait for me. I'm going to walk up and see how we can get out of here. Talk to a cop if I can find one."

Abramova: "This is a nightmare. People are looking at us . . ."

"Yeah, but you look like everybody else. Not a problem, and like I said, we have time. We might have to go back a mile, find a road around the whole town. When I was bringing people up from Chicago, to make the crossing, this was the way I went, until we got to the detour. Goddamnit, it's a pain in the ass. I'll come back and get you. I need to see what the situation is."

"Hurry, then. I don't want to get stuck here."

"If you want to get out and walk around, stretch your legs, you could," Titov said. "You really do look like everybody else. I'm seeing Swedish and Norwegian flags everywhere, I don't think a woman with an accent would raise any eyebrows. Especially since they were looking for a blonde in Minneapolis, and you aren't one now . . ."

"Maybe," Abramova said. "But you must hurry. I will be on my phone."

Titov got out of the car and headed into town. The cold they'd had in Minneapolis had eased, even though they were a hundred miles farther north—he actually felt a little too warm in his parka. He still had time to turn around, but even though there was no breeze at all, he felt like he was being pushed, by a wind, or by a hand, by something in the middle of his back. He felt as though he were *scurrying* . . . as though his feet had finally made up his mind for him.

He'd been in the bar on other trips up from Chicago, stopped for the brats, stayed for the beer. When it popped up ahead of him, an aqua-colored sign that read "Musky Hunter's Bar and Grill," he hurried toward it, as if propelled by a force outside of himself.

In the van, Abramova scanned the crowd and, grinding her teeth in frustration, said, "This is nonsense."

"Yes, but Titov is correct—nobody would pick us out of this crowd, especially if we wear our ski masks," Sokolov said. "Half the people here have them on. Maybe walk around the block, stretch ourselves."

Abramova said, "Around the block. No more. We come right back."

31

Sherwood took a half-dozen phone calls from his office as he and Lucas drove north, with White and Capslock trailing behind. He punched up the speaker phone so Lucas could understand what was going on, and after the final call, he asked, "Are you starting to get an idea of how big a deal this is?"

"Starting to," Lucas said. "I don't know how we do this, other than to talk to this guy, whoever he is, and then let Bernie and the woman escape. I'm not inclined to do that—they killed two FBI agents and Masha Sokolov, with Bernie's help. Bernie murdered his own father. You even got shot, and that poor damn motel clerk is seriously fucked up."

"You gotta think about this like a war. People get killed in a war, and you don't blame the individual soldiers," Sherwood said.

"Bullshit."

"Not bullshit. Lucas: we can work this out. We gotta work this out," Sherwood said.

"I don't know how we'll do that."

"Neither do I," Sherwood said, settling back in his seat. "But we gotta."

Lucas would never figure out how everything in the new Porsche worked, but he fiddled around with the satellite radio while he was driving and landed on the Chris Stapleton station and left it there. The trip was fundamentally boring, through a flat and low countryside, grim-looking oaks and drab pines and spruces, widely spaced small towns with nothing to recommend a stop except the need for gasoline.

Sherwood continued to vibrate, until Lucas said, "You gotta calm down."

"I'm absolutely calm," Sherwood said.

"If you don't calm down, you could screw us up. You need to calm down and think about how we do this."

"I'm thinking. I'm calm."

Three hours after leaving Minneapolis, they rolled into Hayward to the sound of "Tennessee Whiskey." The trip had taken longer than usual because of a thickening of traffic on the two-lane going into Hayward, and occasional snowpack in shady spots on the highway.

By the time they got inside Hayward, they were inching along and finally found parking spaces well out of the downtown area. As they walked the rest of the way in, Lucas told Capslock and White that they would play the part of barflies and stay well away from the conversation with Titov.

"You guys are the backup, if there's a problem. We'll talk to the manager when we go in, make sure he knows about all four of us, so we can hang out," Lucas said. "He'll probably want to keep things turning over, so two people sitting at the bar drinking one beer for forty-five minutes won't work, unless he knows what we're doing."

White asked, "Do we talk to the local cops?"

Three skiers went past on an improvised track just off the street, and then two more; they weren't racers, and fifty yards ahead, they ran into a crowd that had trampled down the track they were using; the crowd was thick and confused, individual members moving in all different directions all at once.

"Not yet," Lucas told White. "I was thinking about that on the way up. The locals wouldn't be subtle. There are too many people in town, and if we tell them what we're up to, that we're dealing with a bunch of Russian killers, they'll want to crush it as fast as they can. John wants to play it out, see what we can do here."

Sherwood explained that, and Capslock said, "All I should do is dangle my tongue in the beer, but not drink it?"

"That's about it, unless you see a fight start," Lucas said. They were winding their way through the crowd into the downtown area, and Lucas pointed at a garish aqua-colored sign and said, "There's the Musky Hunter. Let's find the manager."

THE MUSKY HUNTER'S Bar and Grill was packed to the doors and out the doors, a ton of brats going by as the four of them shouldered their way inside. The manager was behind the bar, the bald guy, a waitress told them, so Lucas rammed through to the bar, throwing a vicious hip-check into a woman who tried to push by him, and stuck his badge in front of the manager's eyes.

"Gotta talk," Lucas shouted over the noise. "One minute."

The manager, an average-looking, heavyset guy with an out-of-season tan, wearing a Green Bay Packers hat and a three-day beard, shook his head: "I can't just walk away from the bar, man, I mean, look at this place."

"One minute, down at the end," Lucas said.

At the end of the bar, Lucas pointed out Capslock and White: "Those two are going to be leaning on the bar, as soon as they can get to it. Might drink one beer in an hour. You gotta leave them be."

"They're undercover?"

"Yes."

"There's not going to be trouble?" the manager asked.

"Not here," Lucas said.

"Then, if they don't get shoved out the door by the crowd, okay with me," the manager said. "Now I gotta get back to work."

SHERWOOD LOOKED AT his watch: "Ten-forty. This is a fuckin' zoo. I'm gonna be pissed if he doesn't show. Maybe we ought to wait outside, by the door." He was chewing on a brat, with a greenish relish leaking out of the bun, along with mustard.

"Just as bad out there as it is in here," Lucas said. A man tried to push between them, but they fended him off. "We don't know what he looks like, but he knows what I look like, and we said we'd be inside. I'd hate to have him come in the back, or something, and miss us."

"All right. Well, grab a brat. These are pretty damn good. Crispy."

An elbow hit Lucas in the back, right in the spine, hard, and he lurched forward, turned, half expecting to see the Russian, but it was the woman he'd thrown the hip-check at, on her way out. She said, "Sorry," but didn't mean it.

Sherwood was gagging on the brat and Lucas said, "Shut up."

THEY WAITED, MILLING around in the sweaty crowd, eyeballing anyone who might be a candidate. A few minutes before eleven o'clock, a man walked in wearing a red hat, peering at faces as he came. Lucas said to Sherwood, "Look at this," and Sherwood turned to look at the same time as the man saw Lucas. He nodded and pushed toward them.

"You're Davenport," he said. "I saw you on television."

"You're . . ."

"Titov. I have no time. What are we doing? What are you offering?"

"We're offering to maybe not shoot you where you stand," Lucas said. He could see White and Capslock closing in on them.

Titov said, "Don't waste my time because I don't have any. Where is the CIA man?" He checked out Sherwood: "You him?"

"I am," Sherwood said. "How much time do you have to talk?"

"I can't talk ten minutes. Maybe five, then I have to run."

"What do you want?" Sherwood asked. White and Capslock closed up, boxing Titov.

"I will give you Katerina Abramova, the leader of the assassination team, and Bernard Sokolov, who you know. I want what Sokolov got: witness protection and a house in the West."

Lucas: "Where's Katerina and Bernie?"

"In a car. Before I tell you, I want to know if I get what I want."

"What if we just say 'fuck you' and put the cuffs on?" Lucas asked.

Titov shrugged: "I'm not part of the team. I have shot nobody. I don't want to shoot anybody, that's why I called you. I don't want to go back to Russia. But, if you put the cuffs on, you can do that, and you will never see Kat or Bernie again. A year from now, two years in prison, and I'll be traded back to Russia, where I'll be a hero and you'll be standing there wondering why you wasted everybody's time."

"We will give you a deal, a good deal, a great deal," Sherwood said, moving so his side and shoulder were in front of Lucas. A man pushed between Sherwood and Titov carrying two beers; he was wearing a ski cap with floppy hang-down ear coverings, like a hound's. He slopped a little beer and said, "Sorry, dude."

Sherwood stepped around him toward Titov. "I need to ask, are you really headed for the Canadian border, like you told Lucas?"

"Yes, but the Canadian border is long, lots of crossing points," Titov said. He checked his watch, and then glanced over his shoulder, scanning the crowd. "Three minutes, four minutes more, then I run, deal or no deal. They are waiting for me, Kat and Bernard, they'll be suspicious if I'm too long. If Kat suspected I was talking to you, she'd kill me without a second thought."

"Here's what we want," Sherwood said, moving to further block Lucas out. "We want you to separate this Kat from Bernie. We want you and Bernie to continue to the border, and we want you to send Bernie across, but we want you to come back and continue working as the sleeper. While we watch."

Titov hesitated, then said, "I could do that, but how do I separate them?"

"How many cars are you in?" Sherwood said. "Two, three? Are you all separate, or . . ."

"Two," Titov said. He checked his watch again, plainly nervous.

"Tell this Kat that you have seen police officers checking cars, and that it would be safer for all of you if you drove Bernie, and she went solo in your other car—because the cops are looking for a woman and a man traveling together, the woman with an accent. You can spot the car for us, and we'll grab her. You and Bernie continue on to the border. . . ."

"And I go back to Chicago to a crappy apartment and . . ."

"You'll get a stipend . . ."

"Wait!" Titov held up a finger, pulled out an iPhone, punched an app. "I'm recording this, he said. "Tell me your name, your positions, I want Davenport on it, too."

Sherwood puffed up his cheeks and blew air at the phone, then nodded. "I'm John Sherwood, I'm with the Central Intelligence Agency and I've been deputized as a temporary U.S. Marshal. I'm with Lucas Davenport of the Marshals Service. If you are successful in returning to Chicago, we will provide you with a working stipend that you can stick in a bank account that nobody knows about, and after a while, you'll get your witness protection hideout," Sherwood said.

"How big a stipend?"

"Jesus, man, I don't know? Five thousand a month?"

Titov rolled his eyes. "How about ten? I stay for . . . three years."

"Ten thousand a month for five years," Sherwood said. "Five years, and at the end you can re-up for more money, if you want it. Even if you don't, you'd have better than half a million."

"Four years, ten thousand, now I go." He held up the cell phone. "Call me, so I have your number."

"Your controller may be able to access your phone," Sherwood said.

"Not this phone. They don't know about this phone," Titov said.

Sherwood: "Give me the number."

One minute later, they'd traded phone numbers and Sherwood told Titov, "When you've gotten out of town, when you're well up north, stop for gas or something and call me. You gotta call me."

Titov nodded and they were all shoving through the crowd toward the door.

Lucas grabbed White and Capslock and said, "They've seen me. The woman and Bernie. You have to track Titov to their cars. I'll stay back. And Sherwood . . ." He tipped his head at Sherwood. ". . . He looks like he just got out of a *GQ* magazine photo shoot. He sticks out like a sore thumb, so he'll be back with me."

Capslock took Titov's arm: "What are we looking for? A white van and a black Jeep?"

"White van, yes. No black Jeep, the Jeep is burned, we dumped it." He looked anxiously at his watch. "I have to run . . . The other car you will see, it is a red Ford SUV. Kat will be in the Ford, after we trade cars. You'll see it. I have to go."

White held him for one last question: "Is she armed?"

"Of course she is," Titov said. "She has an automatic handgun. There is also an American rifle, a semiauto, like the new Army rifles, in the van. I don't think she will try to move it to the Ford. She is an excellent shot, I have seen her working with the rifle, but I don't know about the handgun. The pistol has fourteen rounds, the rifle, she has a short magazine, I don't know how many rounds. Not one of the big ones with thirty rounds. A short magazine, but it is a killer gun. If you let her get away with it, if she uses it, it could be a massacre."

"Good to know," White said. "If she shows a gun, we take her down."

Lucas said to White, "Pull your ski mask up a little more."

Titov pushed out, trailed by Capslock and White. Lucas waited until they were far enough away that he thought it unlikely that he'd be seen; Sherwood, impatient, said, "Let's go, let's go, let's go."

Lucas: "Wait, wait, wait . . . okay . . . Okay. Go."

They lost sight of Titov, but followed White and Capslock, their heads bobbing through the crowd, out toward the edge of the business district. "This is gonna work, we're gonna pull it off," Sherwood said. He was more anxious than exultant.

"We ain't there yet," Lucas said. "The crowd's getting thinner. Stay back."

"I gotta see this," Sherwood said.

"Not yet you don't. Let Shelly and Del do the job," Lucas said. "Let's not fuck it up at this point."

32

Titov thought, *Get through it.* If he could fake his way through the next five minutes, he might yet survive and prosper. If he failed, he didn't doubt that Abramova would kill him in one second, turn around, and try to go back to the original idea of crossing the Mexican border. She had a good American passport, driver's license, and credit cards. That wouldn't work for Sokolov, but he didn't doubt that working with Kuznetsov, she could find a way they could cross illegally, even if some border guardian had to die.

Get through it.

Once out of the crush of skiers and spectators around the bar, he hurried ahead, five minutes to the two parked vehicles.

He climbed into the back of the van and when Abramova said, "You were gone . . ." he interrupted with, "We have a problem."

"What's this problem?" she asked.

"I went through to see how people were leaving town, on the other side of the racecourse. There are two police cars, and they are stopping cars to take a look inside. Not search, just look."

Sokolov: "You think . . . they look for us?"

"I don't know what they're looking for. But they're looking. Could be local. We need to take a back road out."

Abramova's tongue flicked out, across her lips. "We have little choice now. We could go back . . ."

"After we failed the first time, to kill Leonid . . ." Titov glanced at Sokolov, saw no reaction. ". . . we talked about how people who saw us as a group . . . that was a problem. A woman and three men. Especially if they talked to us, and the woman didn't sound American. With Bernard and I, it's not a problem. We both sound American, I have good ID. But you . . ."

"What do we do?" Abramova asked. "You are the fixer."

"Bernard and I will take the van. Two men, American accents. You take the red Ford. One woman, she has an accent, but there are lots of Scandinavians here, men and women. We throw the skis in the back . . . if somebody asks you, you tell them you are a Swedish immigrant, your ID is good."

Abramova considered for ten seconds, then nodded. "This should work. We should never have been in this position, we should never have come here. But I think it will work."

"I didn't know about this ski race until we were committed. I still think it is better than trying to make it to Mexico. The risk is small. Keep a car or two behind us as we go out, no connection will be made."

She nodded, and a fist-like ball of tension started to unwind in Titov's gut: he could pull it off.

WHITE AND CAPSLOCK had worked through the crowd, watching Titov's head as they kept random spectators between them. When they saw Titov approaching a van and a red SUV, Capslock turned around to face White, said, "Look past my shoulder. Don't make eye contact with any of them."

"Yeah, yeah . . ."

"What are they doing?"

"Talking. Walk backwards, we need to get closer."

They fell in with a group of people moving in the right direction, and Capslock nodded at a man wearing a purple Vikings hat, as White kept an eye on the Russians. "You're taking your life in your hands with that hat, man."

"Nah, we're all friends here."

"I hope so. We're from the Cities ourselves," Capslock said. "I got a Vikings hat in the car, but I decided not to risk getting barbequed."

The man's wife had a can of beer in her hand and she said, "Puk-puk-puk chicken."

Made Capslock laugh and at his shoulder, White said, "They're trading vehicles."

Now only thirty yards away, Capslock risked a quick look, and saw Titov, Sokolov, and the woman called Kat pile out of the white van. Titov had a couple of sets of skis and poles in his hands and he looked around as he ran them back to the red Ford and threw them in the back seat. They watched as the three of them talked briefly, then Titov and Sokolov hurried back to the van, got in, did a three-point turn in the narrow street, and started south.

"Let's go now," White said.

She and Capslock started walking swiftly toward the Ford, and behind them Lucas and Sherwood saw the move and Lucas said, "Run."

They ran, Sherwood collided with a man who said "Hey," and then shut up as he saw the revolver in Sherwood's hand.

Capslock and White broke into a run as the Russian woman, in the smaller vehicle, put it into a tight U-turn and accelerated toward the corner. White said, "She's . . ." She couldn't finish the sentence because she was gasping for air.

But a car turned in front of Abramova at the corner and she stopped, glanced up to the rearview mirror out of a simple habit of awareness, and saw two people running toward her, and the woman seemed to have a gun in her hand.

"Пиздец!" She pulled around the corner and too late realized she was in a three- or four-car traffic jam. There were oncoming cars, moving slowly, so she couldn't pull around the cars in front of her.

Behind her, she saw the woman and the man coming on, running harder, and then, farther back, the tall dark-haired man, who she was seeing for the fourth time. It occurred to her, a quick flash, that Titov had betrayed them. She didn't stop to consider that: she bailed out of the car and started running along the street, around another corner, heading back into the town, and into the crowd.

She heard the woman behind her shouting something, and glanced back: she was gaining ground, the pursuers falling back. She ran as hard as she could, the crowd getting thicker around her, swerved down another side street, hoping to lose the pursuit, but sixty yards down the street, glanced back and saw that they were still with her.

Up ahead, a slow-moving Jeep-like car was approaching a stop sign. She ran to the driver's side window as the car rolled to a stop, saw the female driver was alone, pulled her gun from under her jacket and pushed the muzzle against the window glass and screamed, "Get out. Get out or I will kill you. Get out! Open the door!"

She was aware that people on the sidewalk were staring at her but she didn't have time to care. The woman at the wheel was staring at her, and she screamed again, "Get out or I'll kill you," and the woman reached down and pulled the door handle and the door popped open and Abramova grabbed the woman by her coat collar and yanked her out of the vehicle, dumping her on the ground.

As the woman tumbled out, going to her hands and knees in the street, Abramova looked back at the man and the woman chasing her, only thirty or forty yards away now and she fired two shots at them and they both went down, flat on their stomachs. A third person farther back up the slight hill also fell, and the vehicle was rolling forward on its own and Abramova jumped in and accelerated away.

Capslock and White got to their feet and Capslock asked, "You okay?"

"I'm good, but someone isn't," White said, and they turned to see people in the crowd screaming and waving their hands, some of them running after or pointing at the fleeing Bronco.

Lucas and Sherwood turned the corner in time to hear the shots and see Capslock and White go down, and Sherwood had his revolver in his hand but Lucas grabbed his arm and shouted, "Background," where dozens of people were standing.

The Bronco accelerated through the stop sign, narrowly missing a man and a woman who'd been walking across the street carrying skis, and then Capslock and White were scrambling to their feet, unhurt, looking up the slight slope toward town. Lucas said, "Somebody got hit."

"We gotta get her," Sherwood said, ignoring the crowd around the wounded person, whoever he or she was. He started running toward a man in a black Ford F-150 and the man saw the two of them coming and dropped his window and asked, "What's up?"

"The Russian spy in the Bronco, the woman, just shot somebody up the hill. We're with the U.S. Marshals Service . . . Show him your badge, Lucas . . ." Lucas and Sherwood held up their badges. ". . . and she's running and we need to keep her in sight and we need a ride."

"Well, shit-fire, get in here," the man said.

Lucas ran around and got in the front passenger seat as Sherwood got in the back and Lucas said, "See those two people?" He pointed at White and Capslock. "The woman's another marshal. Stop and roll your window down."

They pulled up to Capslock and White and Lucas shouted, "Got somebody down. She hit somebody. We're gonna chase her, you take care of whoever's down, talk to the cops."

"Del can do that," White said. "I'm coming."

She jumped in the back as Sherwood moved over, and as Capslock started running toward the wounded person, Lucas said, "Go. Go. We're losing her."

"We ain't losing her," the driver said. "I'm all over her commie ass."

They turned the corner and it seemed that he was more right than wrong: they could still see the Bronco, probably a half mile ahead of them, turning left on what Lucas recognized as the state highway going south out of town. If she got far enough ahead, there were numerous side roads off the highway, and she could get lost.

"Don't lose her," Lucas said to the truck driver, as he got on his phone. He called 9-1-1 for the Sawyer County sheriff's office, explained what was happening, and the operator told him that most of her assets were working the race, and a shooting in town, and she'd try to get a car out ahead of the Bronco if somebody could tell her where the Bronco was going, and that she'd talk to adjacent counties and ask for help.

"That'll only happen if you know where she's going, or where she is . . . call me," the operator said. "I gotta go now, I got the shooting in town."

"I'll call when we need you again." Lucas rang off, looked at the driver. "She's running away from us."

"She's really moving," the driver said. "I'm doing eighty-five, any faster I'll kill somebody."

"Don't be a pussy," White said from the back seat, and the man glanced at her in the rearview mirror and dropped the hammer and they all felt the pickup wobble in protest.

Music had been playing almost inaudibly since they got in the truck, and now the driver reached down and turned a volume knob and Queen came up with "Crazy Little Thing Called Love," and he said, "One of my favorites."

Lucas: "Just fuckin' drive, drive."

33

Abramova turned south on the highway and took off. She knew two things for sure: she couldn't outrun the American law, in the Bronco, not with seventy thousand miles on the clock and a quarter tank of gas. If she stayed with the Bronco, they would find her, and after the murders in the Twin Cities, they would kill her. So the second thing: she had to get a new set of wheels that nobody would know she had.

If she could do that, she could talk to Kuznetsov, and exit through the southern border, as previously planned. The southern border, because she suspected Titov of treachery, and that Bernard was already in an American jail.

Well ahead, she saw a side road off the highway. The Bronco wouldn't go any faster than it already was, but the side road was attractive: promised curves and driveways that would lead to another vehicle and perhaps a final escape. She blew past a tractor trailer into the face of an oncoming car, and the other car braked hard and slipped toward the shoulder and she whipped in front of the big truck and went on toward the side road.

She had to talk to Kuznetsov and groped in her pocket and found . . . no phone. The image popped up in her mind: the phone lying on the front seat of the red Ford which she'd abandoned in town, and the gear bag, with all the other burners, was in the white van. All she had with her was one pistol and the clothes on her back. "Goddamn this place," she groaned, aloud. "Goddamn this place and all its people."

She tapped her brake to make the turn on the side road. When she glanced in the rearview mirror, she saw a pickup truck coming fast, but well back, the better part of a mile, like a black beetle scrabbling along the partially snow-packed highway.

She took the turn, got straight, and accelerated.

"WE'RE GONNA LOSE her," Lucas said. "We're gonna lose her if we don't get closer."

"I'm trying," the driver grunted.

Lucas: "What's your name?"

"Doug. Penny."

"You're doing good, Doug. Don't lose her."

They saw her make the turn, and forty seconds later, made the same turn, and Penny almost lost it, but got it back. A sign that read "Rainbow Road" flashed by.

The Bronco was no longer in sight, over the top of a hill, but when they got to the top, they could still see it down a long straight section of road, as much as a mile ahead. Penny stayed on the gas, and Lucas called 9-1-1 to explain the new situation and to ask if there were any law enforcement helicopters available. There weren't.

"If you're on Rainbow, you're headed into Washburn County. I'll contact the sheriff there and see what they have available," the operator told him.

"Do that," Lucas said, and he rang off. Up ahead, the Bronco disappeared around a curve.

"Okay, we've got a problem coming up," Penny said. "I know this road pretty good, and there are a bunch of curves up ahead. One of them is a bitch, especially if there's snow on it. If she makes it through there, there's an intersection. She could go straight, or she could go right. I don't know if we'll get there in time to see her on either one . . . so what do we do if we can't see her?"

"Try to get there faster," Sherwood said. He took Lucas's revolver out of his coat pocket and flipped the cylinder out, checked, slapped it back in place and put the gun back in his pocket.

White said to him, "Remember: only in the most extreme . . ."

"Yeah, I got it," Sherwood said.

Lucas: "How do you get the nav up on this thing?"

Penny said, "Push a button." He pushed a button and the nav came up. And he added, "Hold on to your asses, we're getting to the curves, I gotta slow down or I'll kill us."

He slowed, and he was right. They went through a double curve that showed at least two sets of skid marks going into the roadside ditch, and snow-and-ice evidence of a tow truck dragging cars out of the ditch.

They went through another set of curves and could see an intersection ahead and they couldn't see the Bronco and Penny said, "This is it. Turn right or go straight?"

White was kneeling on the back seat looking at the navigation screen and she said, "Straight, straight."

Lucas: "Why straight?"

"Because if she's looking at a navigation screen, she can see that if she turns right, there's nothing ahead of her but long straight roads and if she goes straight, there's lots of turns she can hide behind . . ."

Lucas: "Go straight."

They went past a sign that read "County Road E," and Penny said, "I hope you're right."

"We gotta be," Sherwood said.

Lucas: "When she gets far enough ahead, she'll turn down a driveway, kill anyone in the house at the end of it, hide the Bronco in the garage, and take whatever vehicle they have. Then she'll drive that to another farm somewhere else, someplace that she can see is isolated, while we're looking around here, and kill those people and go on in another vehicle. She can get on her phone and maybe arrange a pickup by those Russian assholes in the Cities."

Penny glanced at him and said, "You're a real Mr. Cheerful. I mean, kill them all?"

"That's what she does for a living," Sherwood said.

ABRAMOVA WASN'T THINKING about much except to get away. As she drove, fractional pieces of plans began trickling through her brain: find a place to turn off, to hide. If she could hide for an hour, she could make it out of this freezing landscape, even if she had to walk. There was hardly any snow on the roads, and with only a sliver of moon, she should be almost invisible after nightfall.

And she dismissed that idea. Walking out was absurd. At the same time, she couldn't keep the Bronco. She needed a different car, a problem this mission had been cursed with from the start. The way to get a new car would be to pick out an inhabited house—pick one out before the alarm went out, so she had to find one soon—eliminate the people inside the house, take their car and cell phones and run for the Twin Cities.

Once she had a phone in her hand, she could call Kuznetsov and get picked up. She could see a patch of hard snow covering the road up ahead, and she slowed to take the turn, and as she did, glanced up to the rearview mirror.

The pickup was still there and seemed to be moving fast.

"Fuck these people," she muttered, and got back on the gas. She needed a road coming off the highway on a curve. She'd been poking at dashboard buttons since making it out of town and had finally brought up the navigation screen. The road she was on had plenty of curves for a couple of miles, and then the highway ran west, straight as an arrow. But just as it began the long straightaway, a narrow little road came off it. If she could stretch the distance between herself and the pickup, they would not see her leave the highway.

Had to take some risks.

She slalomed a series of turns and spotted the intersection coming up. She was breathing hard, as if she were running; and sweating. She ran fast right to the corner, slowed for the messy intersection, and once across it, accelerated up a hill, the Bronco rattling and bouncing up the loose gravel and ice. Three hundred yards up the hill, she braked into a hard turn to the left and, as she went around, looked into the mirror. There was no sign of the pickup truck behind her.

Had she lost them? Was it even chasing her? She didn't have time to worry about it. She had to find a place to hide.

LUCAS WAS ON the phone to the 9-1-1 operator. "We were on Rainbow Road but now we're on a different one, I don't what it is . . ."

"County Road E," Penny said.

"We're on County Road E, headed south right now and she's well up ahead of us, but we're afraid she's going to get off . . ."

"We've got two Washburn County sheriff's cars headed your way so keep talking to us, where you're at, the Washburn boys will know all those roads."

"How about a helicopter, we could use a chopper . . ."

"Not a chance. The state patrol has one, if you want to wait a couple hours," the operator said. They went through a series of long curves and White was kneeling on the back seat pointing at the nav screen and she said, "There's a spot she might get off, whatever it is . . ."

"If she doesn't, we should be able to see her," Doug said. "E is straight as a string past there. But there's a house right there at the turn, with a bunch of outbuildings, if you think she might jump somebody . . . She could be out of sight in fifteen seconds, behind that farmhouse."

"I dunno," Lucas said.

On the satellite radio, Foreigner came up with "I Want to Know What Love is," and Penny turned the volume a little higher. "Great song."

"Go to high school in the eighties, Doug?" White asked.

"I did."

"Drive faster," Lucas said.

They came around a turn and saw a new sharp right-hand turn up ahead. They could look across open fields to the highway going west, but couldn't see the Bronco. The side road came off the highway straight ahead, almost like an extension. There was no sign of the truck on the side road, nor could they see anything moving in any direction.

Penny: "What do you wanna do? Straight, right, look at the farm-yard? Gotta tell me, quick."

Sherwood said, "I don't think she'd go to that farm, it's too open. If she went in there, she'd be setting herself up for a standoff, which she'd lose. She's gotta keep running to a place where she might get a car, and someplace where she's broken away from us. No good if we see the new car. I think she went straight."

White: "Straight. She has to get off this highway."

Lucas: "Okay, straight."

"I hope this doesn't fuck up my truck," Penny said, as he braked to take the side road. "It's only got sixty thousand on it."

"The government will cover any damage," Lucas said. "We commandeered it. Don't run over any small children. They'd sue all our asses. But . . ."

"I know. Drive faster," Penny said. "What kind of guns does this chick have?"

"Pistol," White said. "She wasn't carrying anything when she grabbed the Bronco."

"If we get in a fight, I've got an AR in a scabbard back in the truck bed," Penny said. "Wouldn't want to get in the fight myself, I'm not a law-enforcement personnel."

"I call dibs," Sherwood said.

THEY WENT UP the side road, up a hill, saw a driveway to the left, but it was raw dirt and looked like a dead end and Lucas said, "Keep going." Farther up, another driveway, but this one had a gate with a layer of snow in front of it, with no tracks. Penny kept going.

They passed turns to the right but Penny said they were hunting trails, and there was no sign of tracked snow: "Deer season ended back months ago," he said.

They went past a closed gate to the right as the road turned sharply to the left, and the driveway showed multiple tracks in the snow, and Penny slowed and Lucas said, "I don't know."

"We can come back," Sherwood said. "The nav shows a straight road ahead, if we keep going and see her . . ."

They went ahead, rattling along the gravel road, over a couple hills and then a long straightaway, with no sign of the Bronco; but another pickup was coming straight at them and Lucas said, "Doug, block the road."

Penny turned half sideways across the road and Lucas jumped out of the truck and ran toward the oncoming pickup, waving his arms, badge in his hand. The truck slowed, stopped, and the driver dropped the window. Lucas ran up and said, "U.S. Marshal. Did a tan Bronco go past you, running fast?"

"Nope, we ain't seen nothing," the driver said. The woman sitting next to him said, "Nobody's passed us, going a mile or two back."

"Okay: listen, if a woman in a red parka tries to flag you down, don't stop. She shot somebody in Hayward, and we're trying to chase her down. If you stop, she'll kill you."

Lucas ran back to Penny's truck, got in, said, "Turn around. Take us back to the gate with the tracks."

They drove back a half mile to the gate. Penny said, "Fire Sign 928. Want me to call it in to the cops?"

"Do that," Lucas said, as he and White and Sherwood climbed out of the truck. "As you're doing that, drive back to the highway and send the cop cars in here when they show up. And send one in to that farm to look around. Tell him to be careful."

Sherwood walked around back of the pickup, dropped the tailgate, and found a leather-and-plastic scabbard fastened to the side of the truck. He pulled out an AR-15 and took a thirty-shot magazine from a side pocket, slapped it home and yanked the charging handle and let it go, loading the rifle. He shut the tailgate and said, "Get it on."

He and Lucas pushed back the gate and Sherwood said, "Lucas, stay way over to the left side of the driveway, and lead us in. I'll be back five yards on the right, Shelly, trail us by twenty yards. If she's in here, we don't want her to shoot us all at once. We need to stay spread out. We need to shut up and be as quiet as we can, so she can't pinpoint us, if she's in here."

"Got it," White said, and Lucas nodded, and they started down the driveway, guns in hand, well separated. The driveway ran downhill through a forest of small barren aspen trees, probably three- or four-year-old regrowth covering a clear-cut.

ABRAMOVA HAD KNOWN that she'd have to get off the road as soon as she could, especially if the pickup was still trailing her. When she saw the closed, rusty steel gate, standing open a foot or so—not locked—she pulled up, dragged the gate open, drove through, dragged the gate fully closed, hurriedly got back in the Bronco and drove it down the hill. At the bottom, she found a two-story darkwood cabin on a small pothole lake with a garage to one side.

There was no smoke coming from the two chimneys she could

see, no vehicles in sight: the place appeared to be closed for the winter, although there'd been car tracks in the snow. The snow was crusty, probably three or four days old. She pulled the Bronco into the yard, but behind the garage where it couldn't be seen from the driveway.

Nothing was moving. She walked around to the front stoop, which had been cleared of snow, but the snow piled off to the side appeared to have crusted over, so it hadn't been cleared that day and probably not the previous day. She was tempted to kick the door, but after a moment's consideration, decided that it might be alarmed, and turned away.

Back at the Bronco, she went through it quickly, found a pair of cross-country skis, poles, a boot bag, and a sack of Cheetos, partly eaten. She had no use for the skis, but opened the Cheetos and gobbled the rest of them, then walked around to a deck that looked over the lake, planning to look in the lakeside windows for an alarm.

As she did that, she heard a truck go by on the road above the cabin; she couldn't see it, but it sounded as though it was moving fast. She still had pursuers.

From the deck, peering through the windows, she saw nothing on the walls near the doors that might be an alarm pad. She hesitated, then went to the door and kicked it. Inside, the cabin was as cold as it was outside.

Moving fast, she checked closets on both floors, looking for weapons, preferably a scoped deer rifle; she found nothing useful. The only food in the cupboards was sealed in cannisters or unopened bags. The refrigerator was empty, except for five cans of PBR.

She did find heavy ski gloves, and she took them. Back outside, on the deck, she looked over the lake, and far away, on the western horizon, she saw a trace of smoke above the trees. The smoke seemed to dissipate, then came back. There was another house out there.

She walked off the deck, saw trails through the woods both left and right, took the one on the left and started jogging.

LUCAS, SHERWOOD, AND White moved carefully toward the house, then Sherwood waved them farther off, until White was fifty yards to his right, and Lucas twenty-five. As they closed in, Sherwood said, quietly, "Guns up, guns up."

Sherwood spotted the car, and pointed, and said, "The car," and then, "She's here, you two, hold where you are. Get behind some cover."

He moved slowly up to the Bronco, then looked at the side of the house, and eased around to the deck, before backing away. "She's gone, on foot. She kicked in the door on the deck, and it appears that she's running up a trail, there are fresh footprints in the snow."

Lucas and White came to look, one at a time, then White and Lucas cleared the house, came back out, and found Sherwood fifty feet up the left-hand trail.

"She's headed toward that smoke. She hopes to get a car," Sherwood said, pointing at the wisp of smoke beyond the trees above the lake. "Lucas, you stay back a bit, but on the trail, following the footprints. Yell if they swerve off. Shelly, you work your way along the lakeside, look for other prints. I'm going farther up to the left . . . She may expect us to be back here somewhere, so if you need to shout, do it."

"I'm good with that," Lucas said.

"But stay back. You'll be more in the open than Shelly and me, so . . . we'll probably see her first."

THEY BEGAN MOVING along the trail, more widely separated than they had been, and sometimes, for a minute or more at a time, lost sight of one another in the oaks and aspens.

Sherwood got out fifty yards, then seventy, and when he topped a ridge running in the same direction as the trail below him, where Lucas was, he moved slightly off the far side of the ridgetop, so Lucas couldn't see him, and began running through the snow, brambles and small saplings tearing at his coat.

He was wearing leather oxfords, to go with his woolen pants and coat, but he ran hard for five minutes, leaving the other two behind. About the time he began worrying that they might be on a wild-goose chase, he saw Abramova.

And Abramova saw him.

ABRAMOVA SAW THE man closing on her. He was oddly dressed for the wilderness, in what appeared to be a camel-colored dress coat that dropped to his knees. She'd been walking as quickly as she could, but now broke into a run. She needed to get to the house putting out the chimney smoke: if they had cars there, she could disable all but one, and run in that one, until she found another target.

She still couldn't see the house, and after two or three minutes, running with the heavy coat, through the crusty snow, she was breathing hard, snot running down her face and across her lips and chin, until she wiped it off with the ski glove.

She slowed to look back: the man was measurably closer, and still running hard, despite the long coat flapping around his legs. She came to a three-wire barbed-wire fence, climbed through it, and kept running, but the man was only seventy or eighty yards away, coming up to the fence. The house was down a gentle slope, but across an open field. She ran as hard as she could for a hundred yards, looked back, dropped the heavy ski gloves and pulled her pistol. There was nobody behind the man, backing him up.

SHERWOOD STOPPED AT the fence, looking down the hill at the woman who'd turned on him. She had a pistol in her hand, and she was a trained professional shooter, so he had no time: he braced the rifle on the fence post, but had no idea where the gun might be sighted-in at—it had the simple original iron sights.

She fired at him: a bullet flicked past his head, but he ignored it, and the one that followed.

He'd always been good with an AR-16, and this was essentially the same thing. He put the sights on the middle of her chest, pulled the trigger three times, letting the light recoil make his aim adjustments for him.

His second shot hit her, knocked her down, the third shot, he thought, missed. He crossed the fence, turned around and shouted, "She's here, she's here." She was down, but was she silenced?

He ran through the snow, coming up on Abramova as she struggled to sit up. She must have had a gun in her hand when she was hit, because it was lying in the snow two feet away from her. She looked up at Sherwood and said, "I am done. I'm . . ."

She didn't get to finish, because after a quick look around, Sherwood shot her in the heart.

Then she was silenced, as she needed to be.

SHERWOOD SCRATCHED HIS nose and again looked back up the hill. Still couldn't see Lucas or White, so he shouted: "Got her! Got her!" Then he stepped over to the pistol in the snow, picked it up, scuffed over the mark it had made, and shoved the pistol under the cuff of her coat, at the end of an outflung arm.

It was a full two minutes more before Lucas ran up to the fence, and another minute before White showed up. They could see the red coat on the ground, unmoving, and they walked down the slope toward Sherwood and the body. Abramova was twisted on one side, a dimple in her coat where the last rifle shot went through, but no sign of blood.

White said, "Jesus."

Lucas asked Sherwood, "You okay?"

"I am, but it was damn close," Sherwood said. "She shot at me twice, I knocked her down, but when I came up, she pulled her gun again. I don't know what she was thinking, I was right there."

"You sure about that?" White asked.

"Absolutely," Sherwood said.

Lucas looked from the body, to White, to Sherwood, then said to Sherwood, "Shelly's saying you're a lying sack of shit, you lying sack of shit."

"Yeah, well." Sherwood said. "Prove it."

White shrugged: "I wouldn't want to go that far. Just sayin'."

"We can't screw around here," Sherwood said. "We've got to get a press release out, we gotta talk to the local law. We're almost done, but we have to figure out a way to explain why you guys were here. *We've got to erase you.*"

34

White took a step back. "Erase us?"

Sherwood handed her the rifle and said, "Not literally, you dunce. Your presence here needs to be minimized. We should leave the body and walk down to that farmhouse and get all the local cops we can find up here. We need to talk to the sheriff and . . . what do you call it when you marshals work with other law enforcement agencies?"

"Task force," Lucas said.

"Yes. We need to create an after-the-fact task force and give as much credit as we can to the locals," Sherwood said. "I mean, how do we explain your being here, except that somebody gave her up? And who gave her up? Titov. The only possibility. Can't have that."

"Won't work," White said. "The locals will leak like crazy. I think we claim that the Menomonie cops caught the van's plate on a license plate reader, called us, and we responded. A motel clerk saw them headed north out of town."

Sherwood: "That could work. But: motel clerk heard them talking about Hayward."

"She gave herself away when she, for some reason, shot somebody in Hayward."

"The motel clerk's name isn't being released for her own safety," Lucas said.

Sherwood: "That's all good—we need to fuzz up the circumstances as much as we can. We should walk down to the farmhouse, find out what the address is, and call the sheriff, get a bunch of cops out here. The more the better."

On the way down the hill, Lucas said, "I have a spy-like suggestion."

"That would be?" Sherwood asked.

"The first couple Russians that Titov handles, you ignore. Let them go. No surveillance at all. You're gonna have him for four or five years, so back off the first few Russians. As far as you know, they might set up surveillance on Titov, just to make sure he's not turned on them."

"We'll talk about that. I mean, we the CIA. And the FBI. There's gonna be some nasty deal-making."

"Keep us out of it," White said.

"I can promise you, we'll do that," Sherwood said.

SEVENTY-FIVE MILES FARTHER north, Titov and Sokolov went through Duluth, Minnesota, three hours after they left Hayward.

They'd stopped at a roadside rest, to wait for Abramova. They waited for an hour and a half. She never showed up.

"What happened to her?" Sokolov wondered.

"I don't know, but it can't be good," Titov said grimly. "We need to go on. Keep trying to call her. There's more burners in the gear bag, get another one, she'll know it's you."

They went on for half an hour, and Sokolov called every ten minutes, and on the third call, got an answer. A baritone voice, rather than Abramova's soprano, said, "Hello?"

Titov, quietly, urgently, "Hang up. Hang up."

Sokolov hung up, and Titov told him to pull the SIM card. Sokolov did that, and the battery as well, and he threw the parts out the window, one at a time, hundreds of yards apart.

"Who do you think that was?" Sokolov asked.

"Sure as hell wasn't Kat. Something happened to her," Titov said.

ONCE THROUGH DULUTH, they took Highway 61 north along Lake Superior, stopping at Two Harbors for gas.

"I thought we had enough," Sokolov said.

"We probably do, but if it turns out we don't, I'd be stuck in about ten thousand square miles of frozen wilderness," Titov said. "I'd rather not do that. You want anything to eat or drink? Last chance."

Inside the station, Titov called Sherwood.

"Where are you?" Sherwood asked.

"Gas station, way north, I don't know this town," Titov lied. "How is our plan?"

Sherwood was blunt: "The woman is dead. Our plan is working."

"Ah, well. I hope she gave a good account of herself," Titov said.

"She shot an innocent woman," Sherwood said. "Other than that, she didn't do much."

"But our plan is working."

"Yes, it is, from this end. How about your end?"

"My end is good. I will return to Minneapolis after I deliver Bernard, and I will call you."

"I need to know . . ." Sherwood began, but Titov had hung up. When Sherwood called him back, Titov's phone was dead.

In Two Harbors, Titov handed Sokolov a sack of jerky and two Cokes. "Try not to fart. It's too cold to open a window."

From Two Harbors, they went north along the lake until they turned off on Old Highway 61, which they took all the way to the border, and from there, they turned a quarter mile east on Joe's Road. No traffic, and they were moving slowly. "It's right around here somewhere," Titov said, peering into the roadside ditches.

Sokolov: "Somewhere? I thought you knew where the fuck you were going . . ."

"I do. It's right around here . . . There!" A light flashed in the ditch on the north side of the road. When they got there, they found a two-up snowmobile in the ditch. They stopped, Titov got out, and introduced Sokolov to Edouard Gagnon. Gagnon was a tall, bearded man, thin as a rope, wearing a snowmobile suit, boots, and a helmet. He handed another helmet to Sokolov and said, "You might get a little cool dressed like that. We're half an hour from the car."

"Cool, or frozen?" Sokolov asked.

"Nah, just cool," Gagnon said. To Titov: "You said something about money?"

Titov nodded, went to the gear bag and came back with ten thousand dollars. "Try not to ditch Bernard and run off with the money.

The Russians would find you and kill you and all your family and probably anybody who knows you."

"I will be careful about that," Gagnon said, with a smile. They'd done business twice before, and he'd now heard the warning for the third time.

Sokolov turned to Titov and said, "You will find out what happened to Kat?"

"Might be on her way to Mexico," Titov said.

"Or she might be dead," Sokolov said. "Let us know."

Titov said, "You can count on it. Hey, it just occurred to me, Bernard . . . You're skinnier than I am. Let me get . . ."

He went to the van and opened up a suitcase, took out a pair of jeans and said, "Put these on over your pants. You'll be less cool."

Sokolov did that. Edouard said, "We should go," and Titov and Sokolov shook hands and Sokolov said, "I will see you at home, I hope."

"I will find you when I get there," Titov said. And he thought, *Когда рак на горесвистнет,* which literally meant, "when a crawfish whistles on a mountain" or, not so literally, "in a pig's eye."

A minute later, the sled had disappeared into the trees, headed for the frozen-over Pigeon River, and Canada.

Titov was looking at a long drive. He sat in the van, looking out in the now empty darkness, then sighed, and turned it around.

35

Sherwood hadn't quite become intolerable, though he was getting close. Pacing, muttering to himself, speculating that Titov had made fools of them, was probably on his way to Moscow . . .

Lucas tried to reassure him: "Shut the fuck up."

Sherwood had managed to frighten three sheriffs and two police chiefs to the point that they would have done anything he asked. What he'd asked was that the sheriffs and police chiefs take credit for spotting and tracking the Russians out of Menomonie to Hayward, where they'd isolated, and with help from the Marshals Service, killed Abramova. The northern Wisconsin law enforcement community was happy to fall on that sword.

The Sawyer County sheriff gave an ill-attended and somewhat confusing press conference to that effect, and Abramova's death was a one-day, one-night sensation, falling off by the second day.

That said, they hadn't heard from Titov, and the FBI had gotten on Sherwood's case about shooting Abramova. Not that they objected, but they were unhappy that they hadn't been notified, in triplicate. Mallard had spoken directly to the director of the CIA, and told Lucas, "I think that asshole was yawning while was I talking."

"That's possible, Louis, since you people have been walking around with sticks up your butts," Lucas said. He was sitting at the kitchen table with Weather and Sherwood, and with the phone on speaker. "The CIA is trying to do something important, while the FBI tries to take credit for something they didn't do. Get over it."

Mallard said, "Let me give the phone to Jane for a minute."

Chase came on and said, "Fuck you, Lucas," and hung up.

Made Lucas, Weather, and Sherwood laugh, and Lucas told Sherwood, "I don't think you need to worry. If Titov comes through, you'll hand the connection off to the FBI anyway, the counter-intel group. When it all comes out in the end, they'll be there to get the credit."

"Everyone who counts will know what happened. I don't need to have it in the newspapers," Sherwood said. "But where in the hell is Titov? Did he ditch us?"

"I don't think so," Lucas said. "He wants the American dollars, and that house out west. He'll show."

"I swear to God, if he doesn't come through, I'll find him and go to his front door and shoot him myself."

"You don't do that, remember?" Lucas said. "You've been pissing and moaning for two days now. Stop. Relax. If it doesn't work out . . ."

"If it doesn't work out, what?" Sherwood asked.

"I'm just a humble marshal, so, I'll be okay," Lucas said. "You, on the other hand, after the promises you've made, will probably be screwed. Looking at an assignment in . . . Canada. Or maybe Iceland."

"I didn't make any promises . . ."

"Some were certainly implied," Lucas said, sticking the fork in. "For Christ's sake, where is he?"

TITOV HAD DRIVEN most of the way back to the Twin Cities and then had pulled in to a motel, and spent a day talking with Kuznetsov, searching the Internet, and watching TV for reports on Abramova, trying to figure out exactly how secure he might be.

By the second day, he decided he was good.

Oddly, the near collapse of the American mainstream media was a help. No newspaper or television reporters had gone to Hayward to question the cops and poke holes in the stories, because there weren't enough reporters to go around.

Sherwood stopped whining the next morning when Titov called Lucas and arranged to meet that afternoon at a Cinnabon store at Mall of America. Asked why the mall, he said it was one of the few places in the Twin Cities that he knew about, and besides, he liked cinnamon rolls. "If the CIA decides to kill me, I'd like to go with a cinnamon roll in my mouth."

Lucas called Sherwood, told him about the appointment with Titov, and asked whether Mallard or St. Vincent should be notified. Sherwood had to think about it, then said, "I guess. When we told them what happened in Hayward, they turned a couple of those counter-intel people around and brought them back from Washington. They've been sitting on their asses not believing me."

Lucas called St. Vincent and told him about Titov. "You'll want to send your counter-intel people along with us."

"I haven't heard anything about this from Louis," St. Vincent said.

"That's because I haven't told him. I thought I'd leave it to you," Lucas said.

Pregnant pause, then: "Thank you, Lucas. I'll tell him."

It was a step, anyway.

THE AFTERNOON MEETING was an anticlimax: at three o'clock Lucas, Sherwood, and two counter-intel agents were sitting on benches across from the Cinnabon store when Titov ambled up, lifted a hand to them, and got a regular Cinnabon and a soft drink. He was wearing a Chicago Bears sweatshirt, jeans, and running shoes, took a moment to chat with one of the server women.

The counter-intel agents shook hands with him, identified themselves as being with the FBI, and suggested that they find a quiet place to talk.

"I need to be back in Chicago this evening," Titov said. "I told my contact that I want to pick up my Jeep and return the van to whoever gave it to us. I have my Jeep here at the mall, and I can identify the van if you want to put a watch on it, see who picks it up. It's over in the airport parking ramp. But I gotta be in Chicago tonight."

"We won't need you for long," the agent told him. "We need to pound out the deal. We want you back in Chicago as much as you do."

"Can I eat my bun?"

The agent looked around at the mall shoppers walking by, and asked, "Can you eat while you're walking? We'd like to get you out of sight. There are too many cameras in here."

That was about it with Titov: he shook hands with Sherwood and Lucas, said nothing at all about the killing of Abramova.

"I would have thought he'd show a little regret, a little worry, a little *something*, you know, about Abramova," Lucas said, after the agents and Titov had gone, and he and Sherwood were walking out to the Porsche.

"Ah, he's probably a sociopath," Sherwood said. "Not that there's anything wrong with that."

THE NEXT DAY, Sherwood flew back to Washington, where a few days later, he went for a walk with Letty Davenport, and they came to a mutually beneficial arrangement. Lucas later found out that there were several walks, and they seemed likely to continue. "He tells me things that I might find interesting, and I do," Letty said. "He's not wasting my time. I tell him things and try not to waste his time. We get along."

SIX DAYS AFTER the shooting in Hayward, Bernard Sokolov flew commercial out of Toronto to Paris, on an Irish passport, and on from Paris to Budapest, and from there to Moscow. Neither Lucas nor Sherwood expected to hear any more about him, but weeks later, Sherwood called and said, "I got a back-channel note from the FBI. Titov has gotten a commendation for getting Sokolov out of the country. He's quite pleased with himself."

"Are you quite pleased with him?"

"I'm on to other stuff, but I understand the FBI is pleased: quite pleased."

NOBODY KNEW EXACTLY what to do with the cremation ashes of Leonid and Masha Sokolov—the Russian embassy denied knowing who they were, when asked—and the FBI eventually took charge of the ashes. What happened from there, Lucas never found out.

ABRAMOVA WAS BURIED in a small cemetery in Hayward, with only the barest of plaques on the grave. The Russians said they'd never heard of her, but a few months after the funeral, a mystery man, with a gravelly voice and a heavy Eastern European accent, paid for a modest marble stone that read "Katerina Abramova—A Faithful Warrior."

HASKINS, THE AGENT severely wounded in the street fight with the Russians, retired from the FBI with a disability pension. The other wounded agent recovered and continued in his career. The agent who shot Nikitin was cleared of any wrongdoing, and eventually got a commendation for preventing Nikitin from recovering a machine pistol and continuing to shoot at the other agents at the scene.

A HAYWARD SKIER was hit in the lower leg by a bullet fired by Abramova, but recovered without a problem. A Hayward lawyer urged her to sue somebody, but she declined.

LUCAS'S DAMAGED PORSCHE, after some nimble paperwork by Edie Lamb, was paid for by the Marshals Service, somewhat to everybody's surprise.

A FINAL NOTE on the story that began with the murder of Masha Sokolov came almost six months later, when Lucas took an early-morning call from Sherwood, who asked, "Did I wake you?"

"Yeah, you did. What's up?"

"I thought you might like to know how things are working out. I'm in London, and I don't want to put too many names or other stuff on the airwaves, so be careful about what you say."

"Isn't that a little paranoid?"

"No."

"Okay . . ."

"I heard from my boss that some amazing information has come out of what we did. I don't want to brag, but we are unacknowledged heroes. Actually, I'm an acknowledged hero with the right people in, mmm, *my business*, but you remain obscure. At least, you're obscure unless you've been bragging around the office about what really happened."

"Shelly and I skated around the precise circumstances. Edie knows, of course, she helped fix the written reports. She can keep her mouth shut. And I've always aspired to be an unacknowledged hero," Lucas said.

"I thought you aspired to be an odd duck."

"I'll take both," Lucas said. "Listen, when . . ."

His phone produced a whining sound, and Sherwood was gone.

ABOUT THE AUTHOR

John Sandford is the pseudonym for the Pulitzer Prize–winning journalist John Camp. He is the author of thirty-four Prey novels; two Letty Davenport novels; four Kidd novels; twelve Virgil Flowers novels; three YA novels coauthored with his wife, Michele Cook; and three other books.